# Death in Venice and Other Stories

Thomas Mann was born in 1875 in the ancient Hanseatic town of Lübeck, of a line of prosperous and influential merchants. His father, head of the ancestral firm, and also had been a senator and twice mayor of the free city; his mother was of Germanic-Creole heritage. Brought up in the company of five brothers and sisters, Mann completed his education under the discipline of North German schoolmasters and entered an insurance office in Munich at the age of nineteen. During this time he secretly wrote his first tale, *Fallen*, and shortly afterwards left the insurance office to study art and literature at the University in Munich. Then, after spending a year in Rome, he devoted himself exclusively to writing.

He was only twenty-five when *Buddenbrooks*, his first major novel, was published. Before it was banned and burned by Hitler, it had sold over a million copies in Germany alone. His second great novel, *The Magic Mountain*, was published in 1924 after twelve years of labour. In 1926 the chance request of a Munich artist for an introduction to a portfolio of Joseph drawings was the genesis of the tetralogy *Joseph and his Brothers*, the first volume of which was published in 1933. He was awarded the Nobel Prize for literature in 1929.

In 1933 Thomas Mann left Germany to live for a time in Switzerland. Then, after several previous visits, in 1938 he settled in the United States, living first in Princeton, New Jersey, and later in California, where he wrote *Doctor Faustus* and *The Holy Sinner*. Among the honours he received in the U.S.A. was his appointment as a Fellow of the Library of Congress. He revisited his native country in 1949 and returned to Switzerland in 1952, where *The Black Swan* and *Confessions of Felix Krull* were written, and where he died in 1955.

The Works of Thomas Mann

# Death in Venice
## and Other Stories

THOMAS MANN

*Translated and with an Introduction by*
DAVID LUKE

Minerva

**A Minerva Paperback**
DEATH IN VENICE AND OTHER STORIES

First published in Great Britain in two volumes 1990
by Martin Secker & Warburg Limited
This Minerva edition published 1996
by Mandarin Paperbacks
an imprint of Reed International Books Limited
Michelin House, 81 Fulham Road, London SW3 6RB
and Auckland, Melbourne, Singapore and Toronto

Original German publication 1897, 1898, 1900, 1902, 1903, 1912,
Original German book editions published in 1898, 1898, 1903,
1903, 1903, 1903 by S. Fischer Verlag
*Death in Venice* in 1912 by Hyperionverlag Hans von Weber
Copyright © 1898, 1898, 1903, 1903, 1903, 1903 by S. Fischer Verlag
*Death in Venice* Copyright © 1912 by Hyperionverlag Hans von Weber

These translations of *Little Herr Friedemann, The Joker,*
*The Road to the Churchyard, Gladius Dei, Tristan* and *Toniö Kroger*
originally published in the United States in 1970 by Bantam Books,
a division of Bantam Doubleday Dell Publishing Group, Inc.,
as *Toniö Kroger and Other Stories;* this edition including *Death in Venice*
originally published in the United States in 1988 by Bantam Books.
Copyright © 1988 by David Luke

A CIP catalogue record for this title
is available from the British Library
ISBN 0 7493 8623 1

Printed and bound in Great Britain by
BPC Paperbacks Ltd
a member of The British Printing Company Ltd

# Contents

# Contents

# Introduction

The present selection of Thomas Mann's stories represents a period in his work of about fifteen years, from his first maturity until just before the First World War. This period contains at its end his greatest story, *Death in Venice* (1912, first book edition 1913), and also, near its beginning, his first and (as many would still say) greatest novel, *The Buddenbrooks*\* (1901). The other stories here selected all belong to the turn of the century, when Mann (born in 1875) was in his twenties; two were published a few years before *The Buddenbrooks*, the rest shortly after it. Mann is generally thought of as a novelist rather than as a writer of short stories (or *Novellen*, as they are usually called in German), and his total output of about thirty stories is quantitatively only a small fraction of his output of major novels. Mann himself, however, was not convinced that the major fictional form was really more suited to his characteristic talent than the short story. Late in his life, when working on *Doctor Faustus* (1947), he wondered, rather over-despondently, whether he would ever be able to write a better novel than his first, which had almost at once established his national fame and twenty-eight years later won him the Nobel prize. He always felt more confident, however, about the value of his short stories, stating more than once that this more succinct form, which he had learned from Maupassant and Chekhov and Turgenev, was his 'own genre'; and some at least of them bear out this judgement. *Death in Venice* in particular is

\*The traditional translation of this title, simply *Buddenbrooks*, is not a translation at all: the normal German way of referring to a family is without the article, but it would not be English to say 'Smiths' when we mean 'the Smiths'.

vii

an acknowledged masterpiece of European short fiction, and possibly the most artistically perfect of all Mann's works. The short story was a form to which he kept returning between ambitious novel plans, not all of which were realized; and it is significant as well as surprising that all his major novels, from *The Buddenbrooks* to *Doctor Faustus* (as well as the long picaresque fragment *Felix Krull*, begun in 1910 and finally reaching the end of only its first volume in 1953), were originally conceived as short or 'long-short' stories.

Mann was a prolific critic, essayist and letter-writer, and among his many comments on himself and his own work is one, also made in later life, that applies particularly clearly to these pre-war stories, though it is true of *The Buddenbrooks* and most of the other novels as well. In his autobiographical essay *A Sketch of My Life*, looking back in 1930 at what was by then the greater part of his literary output, he remarked that each of a writer's works is a kind of exteriorization,

> a realization, fragmentary to be sure but self-contained, of our own nature, and by so realizing it we make discoveries about it; it is a laborious way, but our only way of doing so.

And he added: 'No wonder these discoveries sometimes surprise us.' This has been recognized as an unmistakable echo of Goethe's much-quoted observation (also made in middle life) that all his works were 'fragments of a great confession'; and although Mann's is a modern, more complicated, psychologically coloured version of the point, it remains an irresistible invitation to us to see his works, like Goethe's, as among many other things a series of exercises in more or less latent autobiography. The fact that so many critics have insisted on this view of them, apparently with authorial blessing and often to the point of tedium, does not mean that we can or should wholly eschew the biographical or psychographical approach, which at one level is a necessary part of the commonplace of general information about both Goethe and Mann. Mann transmuted his personal substance into art with a great deal more self-conscious irony than did Goethe (and irony is another word which, despite its endless reiteration, is impossible to avoid when discussing him); but he was not engaged merely in an introspective or literary game. It was more like a serious process of self-discovery and practical self-analysis, of fictional experimentation with actual or potential selves and actual or potential intellectual attitudes. Despite the cynical mask he often wore, especially in his early years, it was ultimately a quest, a search for some kind of balance and wholeness, for human values that would (by reason of that very balance) be personally sustaining as well as intellectually satisfying and positively related to the culture of his times. In most, perhaps all, of the stories here presented we can observe, deeply disguised though it may be, this process of self-educative experimentation.

Something like it is certainly happening in *The Buddenbrooks*, which stands as a monumental and dominating feature in the background of the first six of these early stories. At one level it was a vast mirror in which Mann's German public recognized itself, an ironic yet not hostile study of North German middle-class life; but it is far more than a 'social' novel. It is autobiographical in the sense that Mann was here exploring his own origins, the roots of his personality and talent as they were to be found in his family and immediate forebears. Artistically the novel is a masterpiece, but as its subtitle, 'Decline of a Family', might suggest, the exploration yielded a bleak message. The two characters most closely identifiable with aspects of Mann himself, Thomas Buddenbrook and his son Hanno, who represent the last two Buddenbrook generations, both die (one in his forties, one in adolescence) for no other very good reason than that they have lost their will to live. The positive and humane values embodied in the traditions of this great Hanseatic trading family seem in the end to be negated. Thomas loses faith in them, and his life becomes a mere exhausting keeping-up of appearances; the inward-looking, sensitive Hanno never had any faith in them anyway, and solves his existential problem by succumbing to typhus when he is about fourteen. In the closing pages the surviving womenfolk sit round like a naturalistic Greek chorus, trying not to doubt the Christian message of a reunion in the hereafter. Despite the great zest and comic verve with which the detailed substance of the story is presented, *The Buddenbrooks* in the general tendency of its thought may be described (using another here unavoidable word) as an exercise in nihilism.

Thomas Mann himself clung to no kind of Christian faith. His intellectual mentors were Schopenhauer and Nietzsche, particularly the latter, whom he read avidly from an early age; the former he did not encounter at first hand until he was well on the way to completing *The Buddenbrooks*, but from Nietzsche's writings he could have absorbed much of the Schopenhauerian message. Schopenhauer, the supreme exponent and stylist of philosophic pessimism, had published his masterpiece *The World as Will and Idea* as far back as 1818; unrecognized at the time, it had become increasingly influential in the later nineteenth century. It offered an atheistic but metaphysical system, beautifully elaborated into a symphony of concepts, founded on a deep and imaginative appreciation of the arts (and of music above all, the art Mann most deeply loved), but first and foremost on a rage of compassion for the suffering of the human and animal world. Schopenhauer regarded any kind of 'optimistic' philosophy as not merely stupid but actually wicked, an insult to the immeasurable pain of all sentient creatures. In his own later essay on him (1938) Mann remarked on the strangely satisfying rather than depressing character of this great protest of the human spirit: 'for when a critical intellect and great writer speaks of the general suffering of the world, he speaks of yours and mine as well, and with a sense almost of triumph we all feel ourselves avenged by his splendid words'. The young Thomas Mann, especially, seems to have agreed with Flaubert (and with his own Tonio Kröger) that to write was to avenge oneself on life. Art was redemptive and, so to speak, punitive. That at least was Mann's theoretical and deeply temperamental starting-point: a vision, as he was to put it in *Tonio Kröger*, of 'absurdity and wretchedness'. It is part of the essential theme of *The Buddenbrooks* that in proportion as the family loses its nerve its later members become more intellectually sensitized and inward-looking, they participate more deeply in this negative vision. The two processes, culminating in Hanno, are aspects of one and the same 'decline'.

Nietzsche's influence on Mann was more complex and far-reaching even than that of Schopenhauer. From both of them Mann would learn a high mastery of German prose and, more especially from Nietzsche, a kind of polemical, sceptical and ironic attitude of mind that was perhaps even more important to him than many of the particular conclusions of Nietzsche's thought. Nietzsche, whose own intellectual life had begun under Schopenhauer's spell and who spent much of it trying to turn his master upside-down without ever quite succeeding, had been the supreme protester not only against life and against God but against any kind of complacently rationalistic, secular ideology, to which he felt even Christian belief to be preferable. Writing between the early 1870s and his mental breakdown in 1889, he was a thinker of such radical scepticism that his thinking was inevitably fraught with paradoxes. (As a French contemporary had remarked, '*il ne faut croire à rien, pas même à ses doutes*'.) As a young man, at the same age as the Thomas Mann of *The Buddenbrooks*, Nietzsche had adopted the atheistic metaphysic of Schopenhauer's universal life-drive, or 'will to live', the 'will' that must be negated if life is to be redeemed into nothingness. But a contrary instinct in him seemed, or tried at least, to reject this nihilism. What avenue of escape from it was open?

Nietzsche utterly despised literary Naturalism but was no poet, hard and embarrassingly as he sometimes tried to be. In his youthful, incalculably influential work *The Birth of Tragedy* (1872), he had hailed the masterpieces of Aeschylus and Sophocles as the redemptive aesthetic visions of a deeply pessimistic culture and had saluted Richard Wagner as the genius in whose dramatic music the spirit of classical Greek tragedy was now to be reborn. But he turned away both from Wagner (who for Mann was to remain the supreme and representative musical genius) and from metaphysics, and set about exploring the possibilities of a modern, total scepticism, fortified by acute psychological insights of a kind that in some ways anticipated Freud. In the aphoristic writings of what is usually called his second, 'positivistic' period (though the label puts him in company he disliked, and 'second period' is also doubtful, since it never really ended), Nietzsche set out to unmask and undermine all the traditional values and preconceptions of European philosophical, ethical and religious thought. In the first Nietzsche, the devotee of Schopenhauer and Wagner, the young Thomas Mann could embrace a kindred spirit; the 'second' Nietzsche taught him that nothing was sacred and everything suspect, that an attitude of guarded self-conscious irony was constantly required and single-mindedness difficult or impossible. The Nietzschean irony was not simply a cautious pose or a literary method: it reflected the contradictions in his thought and temperament, which later became those in Mann's thought and temperament. Nietzsche's persistent polemic against traditional Christian theism as he understood it (its collapse as a respectable option for modern intellectuals was what he called the 'death of God') had shrunk from no conclusions or corollaries. The full implications of the disappearance of God must be faced, all consequential losses ruthlessly cut: good and evil, humility and self-denial, charity and mercy and compassion (although, and because, Nietzsche was himself a deeply compassionate man), must be buried with their divine inventor and sponsor. But what of the puritanical lust for objective scientific truth, for relentless fact, which Nietzsche came to see as a last disguise of God even for atheists, a last secular 'absolute' value in which 'the Absolute' had taken refuge? Must it not also be discarded, is it not in any case dangerous to know too much, unhygienic to believe too little? What positive vision can be constructed in this emptiness?

The 'third' Nietzsche, of *Zarathustra* and the 'Eternal Recurrence of the Identical' and the Superman, tried to meet this challenge. The response must be adequately sophisticated, heroic, noble and grandiose, imaginative and creative. The earth from now on must not be made merely comfortable but invested with inherited glory; man must not be made merely happy like a sheep, or multitudinous and long-lived like a flea, but develop into a 'Dionysian' higher being, dancing on the grave of transcendent divinity. Seeking an antidote or at least a palliative for the destructiveness of his own thought, Nietzsche devised an aristocratic humanism centred on the idea of human self-transcendence, a pantheistic monism affirming above all else the divine self-sufficiency and 'innocence' of the eternally repeated evolutionary cycle of history. He offered a philosophy which might be called 'vitalism' which in the sense that its supreme positive value was now Life and Life's enhancement, its supreme negative value biological decadence, and its most far-reaching corollary a critique of intellectual consciousness as such. 'Life' itself thus became a quasi-religious absolute value, relativizing the value of Truth. In so far as the critical and morally conscious intellect stands, as it stood for Schopenhauer, over and against the mindless brutality of the life-drive, judging and condemning it on grounds of compassion, that intellect (*Geist*) must itself be held suspect: it is revealed as the chief form of 'decadence', the handmaid of nihilism, an anti-vital poison. By making Life (*das Leben*) the central touchstone in relation to which everything – art, morality, science and even truth – was to be evaluated and rethought, Nietzsche was offering the epoch that followed him its dominant idea and watchword: Life would now be something like what Reason had been to the Enlightenment or Nature to the age of Goethe. But Nietzsche cannot be defined in terms of one idea, only in terms of dialectical conflict. His failure to integrate the Truth-Life polarity meant that his influence too was ambiguous, indeed paradoxical. Mann and others could find in him both scepticism and the desire to escape from scepticism, both nihilism and the struggle to overcome nihilism, both 'decadence' as a reaction against naïve complacency and the quest for 'the higher health' as a reaction against decadence. These dilemmas, in various forms, show themselves in the early stories by Mann that we are here considering.

Mann's first collection of stories in book form appeared in Berlin in 1898. Samuel Fischer, the head of the great publishing firm then still in its infancy, had an eye for 'modern' literature and for Mann's talent, and Fischer-Verlag was now to become the exclusive publisher of Mann's entire work. The firm also owned the important literary periodical *Neue Deutsche Rundschau*, in which most of these stories also first appeared before publication in book form. The first collection took the title of one of the stories, *Little Herr Friedemann*, which the *Rundschau* had brought out in the previous year; Mann had finished it in 1896. He himself regarded it as the first of his important stories, telling a friend that in writing it he had discovered the 'discreet forms and masks' under which he could communicate his intimate experiences and problems as published fiction. The story is his first fully developed treatment of the theme of the isolated outsider-type, who recurs in variants in many of Mann's works including all these early stories. In this case, the central character has grown up a hunchback as the result of a childhood accident and has attempted to contract out of 'life' by forgoing all sexual attachments; he devotes himself to aesthetic and intellectual pleasures (*Geist*), only to find them all unavailing against the sudden irruption of long-frustrated libidinal forces. We can only guess at the autobiographical basis for this tale, written at the age of twenty-one or less. What is obvious however is the parallel with *Death in Venice*: in both cases the central character's carefully structured way of life is suddenly and unexpectedly destroyed by an overwhelming sexual passion. This motif of erotic 'visitation' (*Heimsuchung*) seems, as he himself observed, to have been of some importance to Mann, in whose later work it continues to recur (examples are Potiphar's wife in *Joseph in Egypt*, Ines Rodde in *Doctor Faustus*, the heroine in his last story *The Delusion*). The point is one to which we must return in the context of *Death in Venice*.

*Little Herr Friedemann* may fairly be classified as a 'Naturalist' story in the specific sense that it reflects the methods of the contemporary school of literature which adopted that label, and to which Mann always acknowledged his indebtedness; a few of his first *Novellen* were, indeed, published in Naturalist periodicals such as *Die Gesellschaft* and *Die Zukunft*. The movement's chief German practitioner, Gerhard Hauptmann, also used the theme of sexual infatuation or enslavement in his stories (*Bahnwärter Thiel*, 1892) and plays (*Fuhrmann Henschel*, 1898): it was a telling way of emphasizing man's dependence on his physical nature, in accordance with the doctrinaire deterministic positivism that underlay Naturalist theory. To advance beyond Naturalism, as indeed Hauptmann himself did, was one of the young Thomas Mann's main concerns, and we may trace a 'post-naturalist' element in the opening paragraph of *Little Herr Friedemann*, which deliberately parodies the movement's other favourite programmatic theme of alcoholism. The story belongs to a further literary context as well, as an interesting creative variant by Mann of a peripheral situation in Theodor Fontane's recently published and much admired novel of North German life, *Effi Briest* (1895). In Fontane's story the little hunchbacked apothecary, Gieshübler, a modest connoisseur of the arts and a drawing-room musician, is emotionally drawn to the heroine (the beautiful young wife of the new district administrator) but succeeds with tact and good humour in preserving his peaceable existence, based as it is on renunciation. In Mann's more *fin de siècle* version of this, the sad little Herr Friedemann (his name, meaning literally 'peace man', is not accidental) is exposed to the disturbing influence of Wagner's music as well as to the attractions of a woman very different from the innocent Effi. There is already a certain Nietzschean colouring in the motif of the physically inferior type fascinated by ruthless physical vitality, though Frau von Rinnlingen is also conceived as an inwardly sick, problematic nature who recognizes in her deformed admirer a companion in suffering but at the last moment (rather like Ibsen's Hedda Gabler) is too proud to admit their affinity and cruelly spurns him.

*Little Herr Friedemann*, though to a lesser degree than some of the other early stories such as *Tobias Mindernickel* (1898) or *Little Lucy* (1900), may be said to reflect a Naturalist predilection for 'unpleasant' themes, but in Mann this was far more than a doctrinaire matter. Looking back on his pre-war period, he described himself in one essay as

> a chronicler and analyst of decadence, a lover of the pathological, a lover of death, an aesthete with a proclivity towards the abyss.

And it was also because he was a born storyteller that the later Mann, too, never quite lost his taste for the horrible. Another constant feature of his mature narrative writing also first shows itself in *Friedemann*, where in the already mentioned parodistic opening he uses sophisticated detachment and understatement to make the pitiable event of the baby's accident at the hands of the drunken nurse seem tragicomic. It has been said that the novel, by its realism, is essentially a comic form, whatever tragedies it may contain; and Mann's method certainly bears this out. Parallel examples occur in deathbed scenes in *The Buddenbrooks* (the clinical symptomatology of typhoid as Hanno dies) and *The Magic Mountain* (the onlooker's reflections on the chemical composition of his tears) or in the final scene of *Doctor Faustus*, where, as the hero makes his shocking public confessions before collapsing into madness, his landlady worries about sandwiches and his audience about how to get back to Munich. The effect in all these cases is of course not to destroy pathos but to heighten it, by inverse countersuggestion and an increased illusion of reality.

*The Joker*, another of the stories in Mann's first book, was finished in April 1897 and first appeared later that year in the *Rundschau*. The German title, *Der Bajazzo*, means literally 'the clown', being formed from the Italian word used in the title of Leoncavallo's opera *I Pagliacci* (1892), which Mann would have known; I have translated it as 'the joker' because this word also suggests the oddity in the pack, the outsider. *The Joker* strongly develops this theme and is also the most clearly autobiographical of the stories before *Tonio Kröger*. Mann, of course, used real material from his own life and family background not only in *The Buddenbrooks* but to a greater or lesser extent in most of his important early fiction. Either Lübeck, his native town, or Munich, his city of adoption, is the at least implicit location in nearly all cases; other recurring motifs are the old patrician family house and its garden, and the central character's parents with their contrasting influences on him. *The Joker* combines all these features and others. In real life, Mann's maternal grandfather, a Lübeck citizen who had settled as a planter in Brazil and married a Portuguese Creole, had returned to Lübeck as a widower with his young daughter, Julia da Silva Bruhns; she, at the age of eighteen an exotic Latin beauty with considerable musical talent, had married Thomas's father, Consul (later Senator) Heinrich Mann. As a child Thomas had felt very close to her; she would play Chopin to him (as in *The Joker*) as well as singing him *Lieder* and reading him fairy-tales. As in *The Joker*, too, the young Thomas Mann used to spend long hours producing his own operas on a toy puppet theatre. His father had inherited the old-established corn business, but it had done badly during the 1880s and Senator Mann had lost heart. He died in early middle age, when Thomas was sixteen, and the firm went into immediate liquidation (*The Joker*, *Tonio Kröger*). His widow settled in Munich, and Thomas joined her there a little later, in 1893; Munich now became his permanent residence until his emigration in the Nazi period.

The most important autobiographical feature in *The Joker*, however, is its reflection of the young Thomas Mann's state of mind in the years before writing *The Buddenbrooks*, and in this respect it differs interestingly from *Tonio Kröger*, which came after the novel. In both stories the central figure leads a free-floating, unattached existence, as Mann himself was enabled to do by his modest share of the family inheritance, even before his writing began to earn him any income; between 1893 and 1898 his experience of regular employment was limited to six months in an insurance office (a formality scarcely more serious than the Joker's brief apprenticeship to the timber firm) though from November 1898 he worked for nearly two years as reader or junior editor with the satirical weekly *Simplicissimus*. In the late 1890s Mann could not be sure that he was a major creative artist and that he would successfully establish this as his social role: *The Buddenbrooks* had not yet been written. Was he really more than a talented dilettante, lacking the skill and training for any serious occupation?

*The Joker*, written during his third year in Munich, reflects these uncomfortable doubts, extrapolating them into an experimental *alter ego*, a figure embodying the possibilities of unattached dilettantism. The narrator in this story (the use of the first-person convention is unusual in Mann) resembles in some ways the 'superfluous man' of Russian literary tradition; he is in fact just as much a marked man, a doomed outsider, as the hunchbacked Friedemann, though in a subtler and less obvious way that takes him some time to discover. He begins by thinking himself one of a socially privileged élite and ends by recognizing that he is a decadent failure – not *vornehm* (noble) but *schlechtweggekommen* (inferior), as Nietzsche would have said – with no real identity or place in society at all. Like Friedemann, he discovers that aesthetic epicureanism cannot in the end compensate for human isolation. The unwitting intervention in his life by Anna Rainer, superficially resembling that of Gerda von Rinnlingen in Friedemann's, is however not so much an erotic irruption as a critical revelation of his social nullity, reducing him to self-contempt and despair. Only genuine creative talent will redeem the 'decadent' outsider and at least to some extent integrate him with society. But Mann, in the next three years, proved his status as the creator of a major and successful masterpiece. With *The Buddenbrooks* written, the more confident 'mask' of Tonio Kröger could be adopted.

Mann sent the manuscript of *The Buddenbrooks* to Fischer in July 1900, and a few weeks later wrote *The Road to the Churchyard* as a kind of light-hearted afterthought; it appeared in *Simplicissimus* in September. This short piece parodies not only Naturalism (by reverting for instance to the alcoholism motif) but also Mann's own sub-Nietzschean theme. The boy on the bicycle is referred to merely as 'Life': *das Leben* is personified as a commonplace young cyclist brutally pushing aside the melancholic drunkard who tries to regulate his heedless progress. Mann has here deliberately trivialized Nietzsche's notorious vitalistic myth of the 'blond beast', the heroic aristocratic embodiment of ruthless energy; a similar sentimentalizing reduction will give us the innocuous blond innocents in *Tonio Kröger*. At the same time the grotesque Lobgott Piepsam represents, in the comic vein, a kind of rudimentary intellectual or religious protest against ignorant, unreflecting vitality. This protest is a recurrent one in Mann and was clearly something close to his own feelings. It also obviously contained an element of envy, plain enough in several stories including *The Road to the Churchyard*, the contemporaneous *Tobias Mindernickel* (a psychological study in which the Piepsam-like outsider kills his small dog in a rage at its animal high spirits), *The Joker* and *Gladius Dei*.

Both this last story and *The Road to the Churchyard* were included in Mann's second collection of six *Novellen*, which Fischer brought out early in 1903; it also contained *Little Lucy*, *The Wardrobe*, *Tonio Kröger* and *Tristan*, which gave the volume its title. *Gladius Dei* and *Tristan* are linked in a number of ways, as well as both having been written at about the same time (though we know more about the earlier prehistory of *Gladius Dei* from a jotting of 1899 which notes the germ of the story, the motif of a young religious fanatic in an art shop). *Tristan*, possibly also conceived a year or two earlier, was probably finished shortly before Mann's journey to Florence in the spring of 1901, and *Gladius Dei* shortly after his return. Mann gave a public reading of both stories in November of that year, and *Gladius Dei* was first printed in a Vienna periodical in July 1902, whereas *Tristan* did not appear until the 1903 *Novelle* volume. Mann had visited Florence for reasons connected with both *Gladius Dei* and a longer work with which this story had been associated from the beginning, namely the three-act historical drama *Fiorenza* (1905). *Fiorenza* has no great merit as a play and was never successfully produced; but both it and *Gladius Dei*, a brilliant story which Mann himself underrated, are highly significant expressions of a conflict which Mann took over from Nietzsche and which was also deeply rooted in his own temperament.

It may again be abstractly defined as a form of the *Geist-Leben* dilemma: a conflict between his puritanical, morally critical intellect on the one hand, and on the other the experience of visible sensuous beauty, especially as represented in the visual arts and more particularly the art of the Italian Renaissance. The hero in *Gladius Dei* rejects 'art' in this sense for the same reason as he rejects 'life': namely, that both are expressions of unreflecting sensuous vitality. He claims to represent art of a different kind: something more inward, an intellectual literary art that criticizes life in the name of moral values and religious feeling. These complex relationships and antitheses were to be further explored in a major aesthetic essay under the title *Intellect and Art* (*Geist und Kunst*), for which Mann wrote copious notes in the two years immediately preceding *Death in Venice*, but which not surprisingly he never finished. There seems to have been considerable ambivalence in Mann's attitude to the visual arts. His spokesman in *Gladius Dei* objects to them puritanically as products and elaborations of the sexual drive, and therefore as allied to 'life', which is itself a product and elaboration of the sexual drive. (Mann had first learned this from Schopenhauer, who had called the genitals the 'focal point of the life-will', and had even suggested that we are ashamed of them because of our unacknowledged moral awareness that life is an intolerable evil which should be ascetically renounced, or aesthetically redeemed, instead of merely reproduced.)

Mann's ambivalence also embraced Munich, where *Gladius Dei* literally takes place, and Italy, where it symbolically takes place. Of Italy, which he repeatedly revisited, he was to say in Tonio Kröger's words:

> All that *bellezza* gets on my nerves. And I can't stand all that dreadful southern vivacity, all those people with their black animal eyes. They've no conscience in their eyes.

As for Munich, which became his home and that of so many of his fictional characters, it was after all a metropolis of the arts, more especially of the visual arts, and never was this more the case than in the later nineteenth century and in Thomas Mann's time. There was around 1900 what amounted to a German cult of the Italian Renaissance, with Munich as its centre. Since the reign of Ludwig I, the main royal architect of modern Munich, it had been fashionable for Bavarian architects and sculptors and painters to use Italian and especially Florentine models. In the 1840s, for instance, the King had had the Ludwigstrasse built, with the Odeonsplatz at its southern end and on the Odeonsplatz the Feldherrnhalle, an imposing military monument deliberately copied from the Loggia de' Lanzi on the Piazza della Signoria in Florence. Mann refers to the Feldherrnhalle in the story as 'the loggia', and an association, indeed symbolic identification, of Munich with Renaissance Florence at the time of the Medici is central to his concept. But his tribute at the opening of *Gladius Dei* to Munich, this 'resplendent' latter-day city of art, is of course ironical. The negative side of the ambivalence, the unintegrated puritanical part-self, is projected into the dark figure of the fanatical monkish Hieronymus: and he in his turn is to be symbolically identified with the Dominican prior Girolamo Savonarola (1452–98), the fanatical ascetic reformer who rose in protest against the luxuriant neo-pagan cult of sensuous beauty in Lorenzo de' Medici's Florence, won a popular following and political success for a time but was finally condemned and executed as a heretic. Mann had read Villari's biography of Savonarola, and a reproduction of Fra Bartolommeo's portrait of him, on which the description of Hieronymus is based, stood permanently on his desk. 'Hieronymus' and 'Girolamo' are of course the same name, and indeed the whole story might be said to be an ironic elaboration of the fact that the name of the Bavarian capital is derived from the Latin word for a monk.

These latent, almost explicit identifications reach their climax at the end of the story, where Hieronymus, ejected humiliatingly from the art shop, conjures up in his mind's eye a vengeful vision of the 'burning of the worldly vanities' (the notorious incident that took place on the Piazza della Signoria at Savonarola's behest) and himself quotes the imprecation from the Dominican's own *Compendium Revelationum*: 'May the sword of God come down upon this earth, swiftly and soon!' Mann's visit to Florence in 1901 had of course been for the purpose of further researching his historical hero, whom he was to celebrate more explicitly in *Fiorenza*. The core of this drama is the intellectual confrontation between Savonarola and the dying Lorenzo, seen by Mann as the supreme representative of Renaissance neo-paganism and aestheticism. Hieronymus-Girolamo's protest is against an unspiritual philosophy, an 'amoral' cult of form and beautiful physical externalities, against the kind of art that is not an analysis or criticism of life but a mindless glorification of it. But does the creation of beauty not depend upon sensuous inspiration? How, on the basis merely of the protesting (and indeed Protestant) critical intellect, is it possible to achieve a creativity that will be genuinely poetic (*dichterisch*) as distinct from merely literary (*schriftstellerisch*)? For years this problem preoccupied Mann – as a Nietzschean humanist, as a Naturalistic and would-be post-Naturalistic writer. The preoccupation continued in *Intellect and Art* and then in *Death in Venice*, to the hero of which the authorship of the unfinished aesthetic essay was appropriately transferred.

Nietzsche's destructive psychological theories about the basis of critical intellectuality and morality loom large behind *Gladius Dei* and *Fiorenza*. Savonarola's zeal is seen, in Nietzschean terms, as a disguised will to power; both he and Hieronymus represent the psychology of the 'ascetic priest', which Nietzsche analyses in *The Genealogy of Morals*. But the Schopenhauerian ingredient is also plainly detectable in Mann's conception. In both *Gladius Dei* and *Fiorenza* he gives, through the mouths of his protagonists, a definition of *genuine* (literary) art – a definition scarcely intelligible except in the light of Schopenhauer's metaphysics, and which amounts, oddly enough, to a kind of Schopenhauerian aesthetic of literary Naturalism. 'Art', declares Hieronymus at the peroration of his futile sermon in the art shop,

> is not a cynical deception, a seductive stimulus to confirm and strengthen the lusts of the flesh! Art is the sacred torch that must *shed its merciful light into all life's terrible depths, into every shameful and sorrowful abyss*; art is the divine flame that must set fire to the world, until *the world with all its infamy and anguish burns and melts away in redeeming compassion*

(italics mine). The visual arts are being attacked here because they are the wrong sort of art – because they are allied to immediate life, naïve vitality, unreflecting sensuality; and literature ('these luxurious volumes of love poetry') comes under the same condemnation in so far as it, too, is content to be a mere 'seductive stimulus', an 'insolent idolatry of the glistering surface of things'. Such art asserts and celebrates life at the merely empirical level, its subject-matter is no more than what Schopenhauer called 'the world as *Vorstellung*': his word has been rather misleadingly translated as 'idea' and as 'representation' but means something more like 'illusory show', that which is 'put in front' of one, the merely phenomenal ('shown') world which appears to the senses as the manifestation of the universal underlying life-will. For Schopenhauer the portrayal of this 'show' was of course primarily the function of the representational visual arts: music, by contrast, was something profounder, as an expression of pure emotion, the 'will itself'. (It then became possible to assign, as the young Nietzsche did in *The Birth of Tragedy*, an interesting intermediate position to literature.) But Schopenhauer had conceded that in all aesthetic experience, including that inspired by beautiful phenomena, there was that 'will-less' (passionless) contemplative element, by virtue of which the artist could be credited with some degree of asceticism, even described as being half-way between the ordinary man and the saint. When Mann puts into Hieronymus's mouth his rather improbably sophisticated speech on the nature of 'true' art, he seems intent on emphasizing this ascetic, as opposed to sensuous, element in the artist's vision and creative process. He also makes interesting use of Schopenhauer's central ethical concept of compassion –against which, since it entailed 'negation of the life-will', Nietzsche had chiefly polemicized. An apologia of 'compassion' is appropriate in the mouth of Hieronymus, as the representative of a mentality Nietzsche had attacked; but it is also not foreign to Mann, who tended to distance himself from Nietzsche's more ruthless theoretical positions. Hieronymus, in fact, is really talking about Mann's own art, the narrative fiction especially of his early period, in so far as Mann's fiction does indeed explore and illuminate the 'shameful and sorrowful abysses of life', and does so with the basic compassion of the realistic writer. Seen in this light, and in the light of his rather more Schopenhauerian than Christian peroration, Hieronymus's imaginary holocaust of books and pictures is not simply the prescient fantasy of a barbarous act but a vision – almost paralleling the close of Wagner's *Götterdämmerung* – of the redemption of sensuality, and thus of the world, in the 'fire of compassion' that must burn it away.

In *Tristan* Mann uses the same complex procedure as in *Gladius Dei*: its central figure, like Hieronymus, is presented in a parodistic, ironic light during most of the story, but has towards the end, like Hieronymus, a 'peroration' (in this case a letter) in which he comes into his own and reveals himself to be speaking with Mann's voice. In both stories an experimental *alter ego* is caricatured, explored as an extreme case of what he represents (religious fanaticism in the one case, *fin de siècle* aestheticism in the other). Of the writer Detlev Spinell, Mann later explained, in an essay published in 1906, that his intention had been to use this figure satirically, as a judgement on

an undesirable element *in myself*, that lifeless preciosity of the aesthete which I consider supremely dangerous. I gave this character the mask of a literary gentleman I knew, a man whose talent was exquisite but remote from life . . . For the rest, I made my writer an intellectual and a weakling, a fanatical devotee of beauty and a humanly impoverished person. I elevated him to a type, to a walking symbol, and made him suffer a miserable defeat in his confrontation with the comically healthy brutality of a Hanseatic businessman – the husband of the lady in the sanatorium with whom my author has been conducting a high-minded flirtation. It must not be overlooked that *in this character I was castigating myself*

(italics mine). The literary gentleman in question has not been identified with certainty, and Mann may have fictionally combined characteristics of more than one person. In any case, since he twice in this passage acknowledges that Spinell is an aspect of himself, the presentation of him in the story cannot be regarded as wholly negative.

It is interesting to note, as a technique of this carefully ambiguous presentation, Mann's use in *Tristan* of a shadowy narrator-figure with a viewpoint recognizably distinct from his own. This interposed narrator conducts the reader round the sanatorium which is the scene of the story, addressing him in reassuringly humorous tones and, so to speak, mediating between Mann's identification with the aesthete-protagonist and his identification with the normal world of common sense ('there is even a writer here, idling away his time – an eccentric fellow with a name reminiscent of some sort of mineral or precious stone'; '. . . it must be admitted that Herr Spinell's letter did give the impression of smooth spontaneity and vigour, notwithstanding its odd and dubious and often scarcely intelligible content'). Masquerading in the role of this narrator and commentator, Mann ironically affects to share the 'philistine' values of the other patients in the sanatorium and (by implication) of the reader; the comic protagonist thus appears to be further distanced from the author than he in fact is. A similar narrator-device was used in *The Road to the Churchyard* ('It is hard to explain these matters to happy people like yourselves . . . a ruinous liquid which we shall take the precaution of not identifying . . . We are reluctant to acquaint our readers with such matters . . .') though it is a less noticeable feature of *Gladius Dei* and is for good reasons absent from *Tonio Kröger* and *Death in Venice*. It remains, however, one of Mann's characteristic comic or ironic techniques and gains prominence in his increasingly self-conscious later novels.

*Tristan* is remarkable for its blend of rich farcical comedy with serious and touching elements. Writing to his brother Heinrich in 1901 about his early work on the story, he announced it as 'a burlesque' and commented on the piquancy of writing 'a burlesque with the title *Tristan*'. And although it contains two of Mann's most brilliantly realized comic characters and the great comic scene (comparable to anything in *The Buddenbrooks* or *Felix Krull*) of their final encounter, we should overlook neither the poignancy of their innocent victim, Gabriele (there is no comparable figure in *Gladius Dei* or the other stories), nor the basically serious element of identity between Spinell's values and Mann's. Spinell represents not only the snobbish and absurd affectations of the *l'art pour l'art* cult but also a pessimistic, sceptical, psychologically sophisticated intellectuality entirely characteristic of the young Thomas Mann, and which Mann in his description of this 'figure of satire' barely mentions. Spinell reveals this aspect of himself occasionally in his conversations with Gabriele (in the passage about his early rising for example) but chiefly in his letter to Klöterjahn – a letter which we must take seriously despite the ironic disclaimers deliberately put into the mouth of the narrator. Spinell here declares it to be his 'mission' to uncover uncomfortable truths and 'use intellect and the power of words' to destroy naïvety and disturb complacency. If this is Spinell's view of the function of literature, it may not seem to be borne out by his own novel (to judge by the way the narrator describes it); nevertheless, it is not essentially different from the view expounded by Hieronymus, and both are recognizable as an important aspect of Mann's own literary programme. Spinell and Hieronymus also resemble each other, and Mann, in their basic protest: that of Hieronymus against the vulgar commercialism of near-pornographic *bellezza*, that of Spinell (as of Hanno Buddenbrook before him) against the vulgar materialism of Wilhelmine Germany; that of both, against the mindless grossness of 'nature'.

Spinell sees 'life' as what Klöterjahn stands for and declares himself its mortal enemy – enviously no doubt, but with passionate conviction and in the name of a 'higher principle', as Mann himself later explained in a letter to a young reader. Spinell, he added, is meant to be a comic character but not totally contemptible. The same, of course, can be said of Klöterjahn, and the story brilliantly develops the complex contrast between these two polarized figures. Even their names are symbolic: Klöterjahn's is derived from a Low German dialect word meaning testicles (in High German it might be *Hodenhans*, in English Bollockjohn), whereas 'Spinell' suggests the inorganic sterility of 'some sort of mineral or precious stone' (and according to one perspicacious medical critic, he is in the sanatorium to be treated for impotence resulting from *dystrophia adiposogenitalis*). For Klöterjahn life is business success, buxom women and savoury meals; for Spinell, as for Villiers de l'Isle Adam, it is something that should be left to the servants. The beautiful, consumptive Gabriele is for him not 'Herr Klöterjahn's wife' but a sylph-like creature not of this world; accordingly, comic character or not, he plays the slightly sinister role of deliberately accelerating her death. But her health had been broken in the first place by her marriage to Klöterjahn and by bearing his gross child. In a sense they are both responsible for her death but also for the enhancement and fulfilment of her existence: Klöterjahn on the 'natural' level by making her a wife and mother, Spinell by enlarging her intellectual horizons and taking her, in a ceremony of Beauty and Death, into Tristan's 'magic kingdom of the night'.

Nowhere is the secret identification of Mann with Spinell more evident than in the scene in which this extraordinary Wagnerian seduction is carried out. The composer's name is nowhere mentioned, any more than Lübeck is named in *The Buddenbrooks* or *Tonio Kröger*, or Nietzsche in *Doctor Faustus*. To understand the central role of the *Tristan*-music in the story, we do not need to read this scene as a pastiche of Act 2 of the opera, or a satire on the Wagner cult, or even to know that Mann could have recently read D'Annunzio's *Il Trionfo della Morte* in the *Neue Rundschau*. The 'love duet' scene is an emotional climax to the story, a scene during which Mann's usual irony is almost completely suspended. Even the bored departure of Frau Spatz and the eerie intrusion of Pastorin Höhlenrauch are merely technical devices necessary to punctuate the transitions from the Prelude to the love duet and from the latter's interruption to the *Liebestod*. Mann's evocations of the music follow closely, even verbatim at times, his descriptions of the adolescent Hanno Buddenbrook's solitary pseudo-Wagnerian improvisations at his piano; in both cases he further underlines the erotic implications already evident in the sublime near-pornophony of

Wagner's score. Gabriele Klöterjahn, persuaded that 'the beauty that might come to life under her fingers' is more important than her mere survival, performs this canon of the high mass of nineteenth-century suicidal romanticism; Mann sees no need, moreover, to trivialize with further explanation or comment the mystery into which she is being initiated:

> . . . 'I am not always sure what it means, Herr Spinell . . . What is: *then – I myself am the world?* . . . He explained it to her, softly and briefly. . . . 'Yes, I see . . .'

It has been pointed out that *Tristan* is also linked to the *Jugendstil* or *art nouveau* taste of the period and has a pictorial as well as a musical centrepiece. A turning-point of Gabriele's life has been her first meeting with Klöterjahn on an occasion when she and several of her friends were sitting round a fountain in the garden of her father's house. She mentions this recollection in her first slightly more personal conversation with Spinell, so that in a sense it becomes his first 'meeting' with her too. He at once stylizes the scene in his imagination: with a little golden crown in her hair, the young queen and her six maidens sat round a fountain singing. This is pure *Jugendstil*, and Mann may even have had a particular drawing or painting in mind. In reality, according to Klöterjahn, they were not singing but knitting and discussing a potato recipe. Both versions are equally absurd, and each is true on another level. The garden scene is thus a focal point representing the contrasting aspects of Gabriele herself as the two men see her. The fountain itself seems to symbolize her destiny: its rising and falling jets are the waxing and waning of human life, the assertion and surrender of individuality. Lives perish, the flow of life continues, the great cycle of life and death is unbroken. *Tristan* is thus a story rich in symbolic implications, and this is one of the ways in which it may be said to anticipate *Death in Venice*, both technically and thematically.

Although *Tonio Kröger* was not finished until late in 1902, the germ of its conception goes back to September 1899, when Mann left Munich for a short holiday in Denmark, spending about a week at the little seaside resort of Aalsgaard on the Øresund. On the way there he had revisited his native Lübeck for the first time since leaving it five years earlier, and spent a few days there incognito. It was then, at the Hotel Stadt Hamburg, that the bizarre incident occurred in which, like Tonio Kröger, he was nearly arrested by mistake as some kind of adventurer from foreign parts. The story evidently first took shape in his mind during this journey, though it did not reach its final form until more than three years later. It was intended for inclusion in the *Tristan* volume, but even after the publication date of this had been deferred until March 1903, *Tonio Kröger* was still unfinished when the proofs of the other five stories in the volume were already to hand. In the event, it appeared in this second collection, as well as in the February issue of the *Neue Rundschau*.

*Tonio Kröger* had essentially been born of two interacting themes, one intellectual and one deeply personal (in this respect it resembles *Death in Venice*). The intellectual material was Mann's continuing argument with himself about the psychological origins and effects of literary talent: particularly, at this time, the question of whether an intellectually sophisticated kind of literary creativity, involving irony and detachment, did not dehumanize the artist, diminishing his capacity for compassion, driving him into a kind of emotional limbo, depriving him increasingly of his ability to feel. This was compounded by the already familiar Nietzschean problem of philosophical dyspepsia: knowledge and insight (*Erkenntnis*) that seemed inevitably to entail disillusionment, pessimism and ethical nihilism, to the point at which one rebels against it in what Tonio Kröger was to call *Erkenntnisekel*, the nausea of knowledge. The intellectual artist's necessary constant struggle against naïvety and cliché, both of style and thought, thus appears as a chilling and humanly alienating process. In this dilemma Mann was not helped by the reaction of many critics to his early stories, which were widely judged to be unpleasant and morbid in their themes and to betoken cynicism and heartlessness in their author. Mann continued to be particularly sensitive to the accusation that he lacked human warmth. Writing in August 1904 to his future wife, Katia Pringsheim, he complains of 'that old whining about my coldness of heart' and adds:

> Only four or five people in Germany know what irony is, and that it is not necessarily the product of a withered mind. One tries to write pointedly and to husband one's resources, and thereby proves that one

is a soulless conjuror. I am always surprised they have not declared Wagner to be an ice-cold *faiseur* because he puts the *Liebestod* at the end of the act.

The accusation cannot, however, have entirely surprised him, and it is clear that his main purpose, as he came to complete *Tonio Kröger*, was to perform with it a public recantation of his alleged cynicism, nihilism and inhumanity.

Privately, the young Thomas Mann was anything but unemotional. The other indispensable element in the story's genesis, which enabled him to use the 'Tonio Kröger' theme for the intended personal manifesto, was the complex of emotional experiences associated with his nostalgic journey of September 1899. The way this journey is elaborated in the closing chapters of the *Novelle* makes it clear that it is no mere episode but an inner event which the whole of the rest of the story prepares. The opening chapters, laying the foundations that make this closing sequence meaningful, describe the northern land of lost content to which Tonio Kröger will make his dreamlike, haunted return. As in *The Joker* and *The Buddenbrooks*, Mann here draws heavily on facts and memories of his early life. He had in fact disliked his Lübeck school as much as all three of these works suggest; he had despised the masters, earned bad reports, been happiest during the family's summer holidays by the sea at the old Kurhaus in Travemünde. But, as *A Sketch of My Life* also tells us, there had been an original of 'Hans Hansen': a 'beloved friend', Armin Martens, to whom he had written poems. The boy, in adult life, took to drink and came to a sad end in Africa. Later, there had been a 'dark girl with pigtails' whom he met at private dancing lessons conducted by a Herr Knoll from Hamburg; she became the 'blonde Ingeborg' of the story. A factor that Mann does not mention, however, was evidently more immediate and important for the story than either of these memories, namely his intensely emotional attachment to the young painter Paul Ehrenberg, one of two brothers with whom he became friendly in December 1899. Ehrenberg was three years younger than Mann, had some physical resemblance to Armin Martens, and must have taken over the latter's role, as well as perhaps that of Willri Timpe, another beloved schoolmate. The gestation period of *Tonio Kröger* largely coincided with the most intense phase of this friendship.

Mann married Katia Pringsheim in 1905, and the marriage, of which there were six children, was so far as we know happy enough. His posthumous private diaries however, published since only recently, confirm that he retained a homosexual orientation of feeling: in later life he could still, if only fleetingly, fall romantically in love with young men. Entries of 1935 and 1942, for instance, refer nostalgically to his passion for the seventeen-year-old Klaus Heuser whom he had met in 1927:

> . . . the last variation of a love that will probably never be kindled again. How strange: happy and requited at fifty – and there's an end to it. Goethe stayed the erotic course till he was over seventy-nine – 'always girls'. But in my case I suppose the inhibitions are stronger and one tires earlier, even apart from differences in vitality

(14 September 1935). In 1942 he records poring over 'old diaries' (which a few years later he destroyed):

> from the Klaus Heuser period, when I was a happy lover . . . Well, there it is – I have 'lived and loved'. Dark eyes that shed tears for me, beloved lips that I kissed – it all happened, to me too it was given, I shall be able to tell myself this as I die

(20 February 1942). Mann kept such diaries all his life but allowed no one to see them. In 1945 he burned them all except some written between 1918 and 1921 and those written after the beginning of his involuntary exile in 1933; those not destroyed were to be kept unpublished until twenty years after his death. The diaries of the Paul Ehrenberg period have therefore also disappeared.

Curiously, however, another contemporary document indirectly expresses the intensity of Mann's feelings in that case: namely, the still extant work notes for a novel about Munich society which he was planning in 1902 but later abandoned. It was to have been called *The Loved Ones* (*Die Geliebten*) and was apparently to have been largely about the relationship between a charming and rather flirtatious young violinist called Rudolf and a woman, Adelaide, who is infatuated with him over a period of years. She eventually murders him by shooting him in a tramcar after a concert (this incident was to be based on an exactly similar murder that had taken place in Dresden, probably in 1901). The biographical significance of the copious notes for this work, dating chiefly from 1902, lies in the way Mann refers to them in a diary of 1934, unpublished until 1977. In 1934 he was working on *Joseph in Egypt*, and in particular on the story of Potiphar's wife Mut-em-enet's fatal passion for the beautiful young Joseph. The entry (6 May) reads in part:

> I was looking through old notebooks for some verses of Elizabeth Barrett Browning and became engrossed in notes which I made at that time about my relations with P. E. in the context of the projected novel *The Loved Ones*. The passion and melancholy psychologizing emotion of those far-off days came through to me with a familiar ring of the sadness of life . . . I had already been quietly searching for my notations of passion from that period, as material for Mut-em-enet's infatuation, and I shall be able to make partial use of them in depicting her helpless stricken state.

Mann appears here to be referring to the work notes rather than to his personal diaries; we can only speculate on what further 'passionate' material for use in the Joseph story he may or might have found in the latter, but it is clear enough that the line between them and the work notes for *The Loved Ones* cannot be rigidly drawn, and that both must have recorded emotions which Mann was then himself experiencing. About ten years after the surviving 1934 diary entry. Mann finally made a more direct use of the Paul Ehrenberg material by incorporating it in *Doctor Faustus*: 'Rudolf' appears as the young violinist Rudi Schwertfeger who is shot in the tram by his infatuated former mistress, after having also formed a homosexual relationship with the composer-hero, who regards himself as secretly responsible for Rudolf's murder. The crisscrossing identifications here are material for further speculation on Mann's emotional life and working methods. In the same diary entry of 6 May 1934 Mann remarks of the Ehrenberg relationship that so 'overwhelming' and 'intoxicating' an experience had 'only happened – and quite rightly – once in my lifetime'. He adds that the earlier attachments to 'A. M. and W. T.' were childlike by comparison and refers to the 'youthful intensity of feeling, the careless rapture and deep shock of that central experience of my heart when I was twenty-five'.

Nevertheless, the memory of Armin and of the 'passion of innocence' he felt for him was also (according to a letter written to another old schoolfriend in the last year of his life) nostalgically cherished to the end 'like a treasure' (19 March 1955, to Hermann Lange).

The fact that in later life Mann so often declared *Tonio Kröger* to be his favourite among his works and even (which is not quite the same thing) his best work is partly to be explained by the story's close association with these youthful loves. The 'experiment' of the story was to give 'Tonio Kröger' the problem he himself had experienced, namely the dilemma of how to be human without losing the ability to write well, and to make his *alter ego* solve this problem by recovering his ability to feel, in the course of a nostalgic return to the scenes of his youth. The effect of nostalgia is chiefly brought about by Mann's use of leitmotivistic repetition, a technique which he did not invent but notably developed in various ways, especially in *Tristan, Tonio Kröger* and *Death in Venice*. The story is unified by a 'musical' nexus (as Mann liked to call it) of recurring phrases, descriptions, and even characters and situations. Thus as Tonio revisits Lübeck in Chapter 6, Hans Hansen is never mentioned by name but poignantly recalled by the exact repetition of words associated with him in Chapter 1; and in Aalsgaard the scene of the dancing class 'repeats itself' exactly, culminating in the 'recurrence', as it seems, of Hans and Inge themselves. The text makes it clear, on closer inspection, that they are not the 'real' Hans and Inge but representatives of the Nordic type which for Tonio Kröger has acquired symbolic value (it may also be that Mann intended a private allusion to the 'recurrence' of Armin Martens in Paul Ehrenberg). They represent innocence, immediacy, the unproblematic norm, 'life in its seductive banality', the very un-Nietzschean kind of Life that Tonio Kröger has declared himself able to love. The leitmotif closest to the story's central theme is the recurring statement about the hero that 'his heart was alive then' (in Lübeck) and its contrary 'his heart was dead' (in Munich); and the essence of the 'positive' ending is that in this case the experimental self is not repudiated, divided off from the author as what 'but for the grace of God' he might have been, but accepted into the more complex substance of the experimenter, welcomed so to speak into the joy of his creator. Tonio Kröger's function is to represent a conciliatory solution which Mann would have liked to find for the Intellect-Life problem: he is to reverse Spinell's declaration of hatred, repudiate aristocratic aestheticism and disclaim nihilism. Art and Intellect are to be no longer at open war with ordinary existence but sentimentally, unhappily of course and with 'just a touch of contempt', in love with it. Mann and Kröger are thus identified in the new position of still distanced but reconciled outsider. Their identity is signalized at the end by the repetition, as the last sentence of the story, of the statement made about the hero in the last sentence of Chapter 1: there it was made of him by the author, now he says it of himself.

So optimistic and programmatic a conclusion represents a considerable personal investment by Mann, and it is not surprising that *Tonio Kröger* was a work he came to value so highly. This is partly also to be explained by its immediate and continuing success with the critics. The recantation had worked, and it became a critical tradition simply to endorse Mann's judgement of the story. More recent commentators have been less sure, and even Mann seems to have had doubts at first, writing to a friend that *Tonio Kröger* contains 'a declaration of love for life which is almost inartistic in its clarity and directness. Is this declaration incredible? Is it mere rhetoric??' (to Kurt Martens, 28 March 1906). On his own showing (in Kröger's aesthetic theory as expounded to Lisaveta in Chapter 4), it could have been expected that a piece of writing so full of the author's own heart and hopes would not wholly avoid the pitfall of sentimentality. Many readers today, perhaps, will prefer the harder cutting edge of *Tristan* or *Gladius Dei*, both of which may also, after all, be read as repudiations of decadence. In addition, *Tristan* and *Gladius Dei* both point forward in interesting ways to *Death in Venice*: if *Tonio Kröger* did so, it was chiefly in a sobering negative sense. The Devil, notoriously, has most of the good tunes, and the new 'positive' *Tonio Kröger* position could not last: *Death in Venice* was to represent a reversion to the tragic view of the artist, while at the same time advancing into a new dimension of art.

During the eight years or so between the completion of *Tonio Kröger* and the writing of *Death in Venice* – a period which also included the first six years of his marriage – Mann produced no major work. *Fiorenza* is generally accounted a failure, and the short novel *Royal Highness* (1909), though it has interest and charm, cannot begin to compare in significance with *The Buddenbrooks* or *The Magic Mountain*, any more than the few *Novellen* written during those years can stand comparison with those of the breakthrough period at the turn of the century, 1897–1902, which must count as Mann's first mature creative phase. On the other hand, these relatively unproductive intermediate years saw a number of important beginnings and reorientations. Mann's reflections were now being influenced by his own increasing fame and by new ideas about art current in the generation that was following him. What were the special problems and vulnerabilities of being the kind of writer he was, in the years of maturity that lay ahead? Could he perhaps become a different kind of writer? Could not some intoxicating impulse be found, some *Rausch*, even if it were of diabolic origin, that would give his flagging creativity a new direction? It is no accident that in 1904 one of Mann's notebooks briefly records for future use the motif of an artist of genius who bargains with the Devil for special inspiration by deliberately contracting syphilis. It is the germ of *Doctor Faustus*, to be used forty years later; and one of the at first inconspicuous links between *Doctor Faustus* and *Death in Venice* is that the latter opens with Aschenbach, a mature but tired writer, unconsciously desiring just such a new and mysterious stimulus.

At the *Tonio Kröger* stage, the problem of *Geist*, of the critical intellect, had been that it combined with artistic creativity to threaten the writer with personal dehumanization. But *Geist* is now threatening his creativity itself, by binding it to a mode now outmoded. The coming generation seemed tired of analysis and introspection, of pathological themes, of naturalism and psychology. The appeal was increasingly to the other pole of the Nietzschean dialectic: *Leben*, regeneration, vitality, irrationalism, the Renaissance cult. The world of passion and beauty was now again intellectually fashionable. But Mann, although he had already taken sides with Savonarola against Lorenzo, had not yet resolved the personal Lorenzo-Savonarola conflict in himself, the conflict between passion and puritanism. It seems also to underlie his continuing interest in the Friedemann motif, that of the erotic visitation, the emotional invasion that changes a whole existence. He perceived the same conflict in Nietzsche and was fascinated by a perhaps apocryphal anecdote which he had read in the memoirs of one of Nietzsche's friends: the young Nietzsche, it reported, had as a shy and austere student unwittingly strayed into a brothel, fled from it in embarrassment, but returned later to seek out the beautiful prostitute he had encountered. Mann was to transfer this story to the Nietzsche-like hero of *Doctor Faustus*, combining it with the 1904 germ idea for his Devil's-bargain novel. It was a variant of the Friedemann theme, and a variant also of the theme of the creative artist's tragedy. A further modulation of the latter also appears in a 1905 notebook, as the tragedy of an *older* writer who destroys himself by ambitiously pursuing achievements that exceed his capacities. This version (also eventually reflected in the Aschenbach story) clearly had dramatic possibilities if combined with the Friedemann motif as well.

At some stage in these pre-*Death in Venice* years (we do not know the exact chronology) Mann came to consider a specific historical instance of an elderly and renowned writer who loses his dignity by falling in love: that of the seventy-four-year-old Goethe and his infatuation, while on holiday in Marienbad in 1823, with the seventeen-year-old Ulrike von Levetzow. (Goethe, in fact, came quickly to his senses, though not before going so far, almost incredibly, as to initiate a proposal of marriage with the girl.) It seems from Mann's own account that his plan to write a story on this subject which might be called *Goethe in Marienbad* dated from before 1911; in any case, it was not dropped until some years after the publication of *Death in Venice*, to which the proposed Goethe-*Novelle* would have been a tragi-comic parallel piece. The story in both cases was that of a highly disciplined but emotionally isolated and perhaps instinctually deprived man of mature years whose 'Olympian' existence is invaded by the dark inner forces of disorder. The *Novelle* Mann actually wrote, as we know, was this story with a difference. It was still a story about an artist's *loss of dignity* (*Entwürdigung*), and Mann afterwards frequently insisted that the essential theme was this, the capacity of 'passion' as such – any infatuation or obsessive love – to destroy dignity. In Mann's personal variant the passion becomes a homosexual one, although by his account this was not of the essence of the original conception. The reason for the change, we are not surprised to learn, was the final precipitating personal factor in the genesis of *Death in Venice*: a journey involving an emotional experience. The same had happened in the genesis of *Tonio Kröger*, but with the journey taking place at the beginning of the work's incubation period: in 1911 it came at the end.

In May of that year Mann travelled to the Adriatic for a short holiday with his wife and his brother Heinrich; they stayed first on the island of Brioni near Pola, where they read in the Austrian papers the news of the death of Gustav Mahler (whom Mann had recently met and whom he deeply admired). After about a week they crossed to Venice. Mann tells us in A *Sketch of My Life* that on this journey everything played into his hands, as indeed it had done in *Tonio Kröger*:

> Nothing is invented: the wanderer at the Northern Cemetery in Munich, the gloomy ship from Pola, the foppish old man, the suspect gondolier, Tadzio and his family, the departure prevented by a muddle with the luggage, the cholera, the honest clerk at the travel agency, the sinister singer . . .

He did in fact modify certain details (the cholera outbreak was in Palermo, not in Venice, the lost luggage was Heinrich's, etc.), but the essential point which he of course does not underline in the autobiographical essay, the inner event round which the rest of the story crystallized, was the 'passion' itself, his sudden intense, if brief, infatuation with the real 'Tadzio'. The Polish boy was identified in 1964 as Wladyslaw, the future Baron Moes, born on 17 November 1900, who was on holiday at the Lido in May 1911 with his mother and three sisters. Mann heard this attractive child addressed by diminutives of his name such as 'Wladzio' or 'Adzio' and, after taking advice, decided to stylize this as Tadzio (from Tadeusz). Baroness Moes's friend Mme Fudakowska was also there with her own son, Jan, the Jasio (vocative 'Jasiu') of the story who fights with Tadzio. Wladystaw Moes learned twelve years later that a story had been written 'about him' and read it, but never identified himself to Mann; only some years after the latter's death did he give Mann's Polish translator an impeccable account, supported by photographs, of the details of that particular Venetian holiday (including 'an old man' looking at him on the beach and his quarrel with Fudakowski). Curiously, too, while Luchino Visconti was making his film of *Death in Venice* in the late 1960s, Jan Fudakowski also turned up, bearing a photograph of himself and Wladyslaw taken on the Lido in May 1911.

Mann no doubt somewhat dramatizes his feelings about this preadolescent boy, whose age he amended from ten and a half to fourteen.

Katia in her later recollections confirmed that her husband was 'fascinated' by him, though no to the point of following him all over Venice. But in this extrapolated self 'Aschenbach' (his age too is fictionalized to fifty-three, seventeen years older than Mann was in 1911) the experiment is clearly, on the personal level, an exploration of the possibilities of homosexual emotion, while on the intellectual and creative level it tries out in earnest those of a certain kind of post-naturalistic, post-decadent aesthetic theory and practice. Mann was here specifically influenced by the short-lived 'Neo-classical' reaction against naturalism, a movement represented by some of his minor contemporaries (Paul Ernst, Samuel Lublinski) to which for a time he felt drawn. We have to distinguish here (though the distinction is very fine) between what Aschenbach is represented as doing in writing his own works and what Mann himself does in writing *Death in Venice*. In the former, the emphasis falls strongly on the creation and exaltation of beauty, though this is not the neo-romantic, musical and decadent, introverted and life-negating aesthetic cult represented by Spinell (which Aschenbach has 'overcome') but a 'neo-classical' principle, with a strongly ethical, educative and humanistic colouring; Aschenbach stresses the 'moral' value of disciplined artistic form, as well as resolutely repudiating all introspective *Erkenntnisekel* and cynicism. Mann, too, in telling the story of Aschenbach, seeks to create and evoke a kind of visible, concrete, external but symbolic beauty, such as he has not aimed at before in his fiction; the basis, nevertheless, is still one of 'naturalism' in the sense of literary realism, and there is a continuing 'naturalistic' implication of compassionate psychological understanding. He thus seems both to encapsulate the contemporary neo-classical tendency and to distance himself from it. The *Death in Venice* 'experiment' with the noble aesthetic moralist Aschenbach ends unsuccessfully, that is to say tragically, in Aschenbach's destruction; nevertheless, the story itself, transcending the traditional and prosaic modes in what was probably Mann's most important technical breakthrough, creates a noble stylistic synthesis worthy of its regretfully repudiated hero.

In achieving this striking fusion of realism and concrete symbolism, Mann was decisively assisted by the nature of the subject-matter and by the strange complex of real-life experiences on his Venetian journey,

this uncanny coming-together of seemingly significant and intercon-
nected events as if by some unwitting and magical authorial command.
A nexus of coincidences and chance impressions, none inexplicable but
many indefinably disturbing, is heightened in its meaningfulness by the
use of leitmotif: recurring phrases hint at the identity of recurring
figures, noticeable to the reader but apparently never to Aschenbach,
who thus moves ironically to his doom like a Greek hero only half aware
of what is happening. Strangers he 'happens' to meet or observe are on
another level messengers of death, incarnations of the wild god
Dionysus to whom his excessive Apolline discipline betrays him.
Lingering too long in the breakfast-room at the behest of his still half-
conscious passion (and one of the most remarkable features of the story is
the subtlety with which it portrays the *process* of falling in love), he
himself unwittingly causes the 'fateful' loss of his luggage. Sinister,
half-apprehended forces intrude into the naturalist-realist world as
externalizations of half-understood psychological developments.
Aschenbach's 'case' could have been presented merely as a medical-
psychological study (reaction against libidinal over-deprivation, a
'climacteric' episode at the age of fifty-three, as Mann himself pointed
out): instead, it is given a mythological dimension as well, as the drama
of a foredoomed initiate and the revenge of an insulted god. Venice,
too, as a setting both shabbily real and mythically mysterious, lent itself
to this double purpose. Even the cholera epidemic, invading Europe
from India, is on its other level the irruption of Dionysus, whose cult
swept into Greece from the east.

But the chief visible yet enigmatic, real yet symbolic element is of
course Tadzio himself. He is the meeting-point of the Apolline cult of
disciplined sculptured beauty and the dark destructive longing of Eros-
Dionysus. He is presented with extraordinary subtlety, mysteriously yet
very realistically poised somewhere between innocence and a certain
half-conscious sensuous coquetry. The remarkable descriptions of him
in the last three chapters rise above Mann's normal ironic tone to an
ecstatic seriousness, lyrically exalted yet saturated with sensuality and
emotion, in which the narrating author and the fictional contemplative
lover are unmistakably identified. Tadzio's 'sublime background', the
sun and the sea, are evoked in similar celebratory language, which
breaks from time to time into the rhythm of Homer's hexameters. These

central 'hymnic' passages (as Mann was to call them) resemble in some ways the unironic evocations of Wagner's music in the central scene of *Tristan*, but with a decisive difference. Ten years after *Tristan*, Mann is seeking to break both the Wagnerian spell and the naturalistic counterspell. His post-*Tonio Kröger* aesthetic programme has been a struggle to move from *Geist* to *Kunst*, from moralizing or demoralizing analysis to a more resolute and extroverted cult of beautiful form. But he now seems more clearly than before to be engaged in a corresponding personal struggle to achieve the kind of neo-pagan sensibility in which his sensuous impulses could be affirmed. The model for such a break-through was evidently the culture of ancient Greece, as Mann came to understand it at the time of writing *Death in Venice*.

The classical Greek element in the story is essential and central, and one of the ways in which Visconti seriously damaged his film version was by totally omitting it, preferring to identify his Aschenbach with the post-Wagnerian, neo-romantic atmosphere of Mahler's music (although, in fact, Mahler has virtually nothing to do with *Death in Venice* except that Mann had been moved by the news of his death and decided to give Aschenbach the composer's first name and physical appearance). But in treating a homosexual theme, it was natural that Mann should seek to associate it strongly with a pre-Christian world which looked upon homosexuality as normal; and his notebooks attest that while working on *Death in Venice* he not only refreshed his memories of Homer but, above all, immersed himself in the study of the Platonic theory of love. He read especially the *Symposium* and the *Phaedrus* and Plutarch's *Erotikos* – all of which he interestingly and perhaps knowingly misquotes in the text of the story. His understanding of the theory (for purposes of the Aschenbach project and as transmitted through Aschenbach) has a strongly monistic and paganizing, aesthetic and sensuous tendency; in fact it has been shown that Mann's use of the material seems to aim at a synthesis of Platonic doctrine with pagan mythological elements. He evidently understood Plato's perception of the profound continuity between 'Eros' and the 'higher' intellectual or spiritual faculties – a perception which of course amounts to a transfiguration of sexual love rather than a devaluation of it. Mann was familiar with Nietzsche's observation that human sexuality (*Geschlechtlichkeit*) branches upwards into the highest reaches of our intellectuality (*Geistigkeit*); and this observation may be said to reach back to Plato as well as forwards to Freud, if we understand Freud as integrative rather than reductive, and Plato as integrative rather than 'puritanical'. Mann's excerpts from Plato and Plutarch in his *Death in Venice* work notes, as well as the Platonizing passages in the story itself, suggest that he was aware of this. The Platonic Eros theory, with its 'positive' aspects thus emphasized, offered him the most appropriate cultural framework for an experience of love which was both sexual and visionary: it could become the classical philosophic endorsement for Aschenbach's passionate vision of Tadzio. Why then, we may ask, is Mann's view of this passion polarized rather than integrated? In other words, why does *Death in Venice* end tragically, rather than as a story of inner liberation? The answer seems to lie both in Mann's psychology and in his artistry, his instinct as a dramatic storyteller.

In Mann's presentation of Aschenbach's experience, the reader is constantly invited to take two opposite views simultaneously: one of them positive (because aesthetic, neo-pagan, imaginative and mytho-logizing) and the other negative (because naturalistic-moralistic). This *ambiguity* in the best sense of the word is of course an artistic enrichment, but it also seems to reflect a profound *ambivalence* (in the sense of emotional conflict) in Mann himself, such as we have already noticed in other contexts. *Death in Venice* is even plainer evidence than *Friedemann* or *Gladius Dei* that Mann's 'puritan' temperament conflicted at a deep psychological level with the passionate and sensuous elements in his nature, whether homosexual or otherwise. The inner drama of the story is sustained by this struggle, this schizoid cerebral dread of instinctual disorder, which we encounter again and again in Mann's works. In Aschenbach's case we have a man committed to order, who in his maturity has turned even beautiful form into moral affirmation and art itself into discipline and service, into respectability and dignity. But the compromise solution cannot hold, the element of sensuality in the vision of beauty cannot be accepted and integrated. Instead, it is rejected (in a quite un-Platonic way), and the opposites thus remain dramatically polarized. Mann projects into Aschenbach not only his homosexuality but also his puritan repudiation of it: Aschenbach's declaration of love to the absent Tadzio at the end of Chapter 4 is described as 'impossible, absurd, depraved and ludicrous' as well as 'sacred nevertheless, still worthy of honour', and in his last interior monologue of Chapter 5 he condemns it as 'horrifying criminal emotion (*grauenhafter Gefühlsfrevel*)'. The absurdity of imagining such strictures in the mouth of Plato or even of Socrates at once reveals their modern, quite un-Greek and indeed idiosyncratic character.

Mann's own most far-reaching and interesting published statement about *Death in Venice* is his letter of 4 July 1902 to Carl Maria Weber. Weber was a young poet who had understandably formed the impression that the story was an exercise in anti-homosexual propaganda (that the opposite impression was formed by some of its other indignant readers is also understandable). He wrote anxiously to Mann for clarification. Mann replies diplomatically that he respects homosexual feeling, that it is far from alien to his own experience, and that he had no intention of negating or repudiating it in the story. He goes on to analyse the conflicting underlying tendencies of *Death in Venice* as he sees them:

> The *artistic* reason [for the misunderstanding] lies in the difference between the Dionysian spirit of lyric poetry as it individualistically and irresponsibly pours itself out, and the Apolline spirit of epic narrative with its objective commitment and its moral responsibilities to society. What I was trying to achieve was an equilibrium of sensuality and morality, such as I found ideally realized in [Goethe's novel] *The Elective Affinities*, which, if I remember rightly, I read five times while I was writing *Death in Venice*. But you cannot have failed to notice that the story in its innermost nucleus has a hymnic character, indeed that it is hymnic in origin. The painful process of objectivization which the necessities of my nature obliged me to carry out is described in the prologue to my otherwise quite unsuccessful poem *The Lay of the Little Child*:
>
> > 'Do you remember? A higher intoxication, amazing
> > Passionate feelings once visited you as well, and they cast you
> > Down, your brow in your hands. To hymnic impulse your spirit
> > Rose, amid tears your struggling mind pressed urgently upwards
> > Into song. But unhappily things stayed just as they had been:
> > For there began a process of sobering, cooling, and mastering –
> > See, what came of your *drunken song*? An *ethical fable*!'*

But the artistic occasion for misunderstanding is in fact only one among others, the purely intellectual reasons are even more important: for example, the *naturalistic* attitude of my generation, which is so alien to you younger writers: it forced me to see the 'case' as *also* pathological and to allow this motif (climacteric) to interweave iridescently with the symbolic theme (Tadzio as Hermes Psychopompos). An additional factor was something even more intellectual, because more personal: a fundamentally *not at all 'Greek'* but Protestant and puritanical ('bourgeois') nature, my own nature as well as that of the hero who undergoes the experience; in other words our *fundamentally mistrustful, fundamentally pessimistic view of passion as such and in general* . . . [italics here mine]. Passion that drives to distraction and destroys dignity – that was really the subject-matter of my tale.

Mann goes on to explain that he had not originally intended a homosexual theme but that of Goethe and Ulrike, and that what had changed his mind was 'a personal lyrical travel-experience which moved me to make it all still more pointed by introducing the motif of "forbidden love" '. The letter then continues at some length, but these extracts contain the essential points. Mann was evidently aware that neither he nor 'Aschenbach' had been 'Greek' enough for a real breakthrough into an integrated neo-pagan sensibility, much as he perhaps desired to achieve this. Nor, indeed, were they moralists enough either; certainly no whole-hearted moralist speaks in the letter to Weber, in one passage of which Mann also remarks that 'the moralist's standpoint [is] *of course one that can only be adopted ironically*' (italics mine). In *Death in Venice*, it seems, he had been nearly successful in achieving an affirmative view of the 'Aschenbach' experience, only to be defeated by the old self-punitive puritan tendency which comes so strongly to the fore in the last chapter of the story. How, under its pressure, was he to devise a more positive, balanced ending?

We should bear in mind that this whole last chapter belongs to the purely fictional stage of the 'experiment', when Aschenbach has been acting as Mann himself never did in reality. It is here that Aschenbach embarks on his final self-destructive course and (to use Mann's terms)

*Translation (which I have slightly altered) by T. J. Reed, in *Thomas Mann: The Uses of Tradition* (1974), p. 152. As Mr Reed points out, these lines taken in conjunction with Mann's remarks to Weber may mean that his original impulse was to write about the Venice experience in verse, probably in hexameters, rather than to turn it into a *Novelle*.

'loses his dignity', both in a quite ordinary sense (by following Tadzio about, resorting to cosmetics, letting his passion become noticeable to the boy's family) and more importantly in the deeper sense of losing that rational freedom of the will which moralists in the Kantian tradition would call the specific dignity (*Würde*) of man. Aschenbach becomes unable to do the rational, self-preservative and 'decent' thing, which is to warn the Polish family of the epidemic and leave Venice himself immediately. This failure (and not of course the homosexual infatuation as such) is his real 'fall', his *Entwürdigung* as Mann calls it — meaning 'degradation' in the strict sense of demotion from a higher rank to a lower, from dignity to indignity. In terms of Mann's psychology, we may interpret this self-damaging, 'degraded' behaviour of the experimental ego as a fictional development or extrapolation which Mann's own self-disapproval needed in order to corroborate and rationalize itself. There are, however, artistic as well as psychological reasons why the last chapter of *Death in Venice* should take this negative turn. Whatever may have been the degree of Mann's or Aschenbach's intolerance or tolerance of the emotional and behavioural extravagance portrayed by the story, *Death in Venice* was clearly intended as a *dramatization* of the Venice events in *Novelle* form, a dramatic *Novelle* which required a dramatic conclusion. It is structurally necessary that 'Ashenbach's' experience should be brought full cycle; rather as Goethe remarked of the tragic ending of his *Elective Affinities* that it was needed to restore the balance after 'sensuality' had triumphed. Mann knew that tragic implications were inherent from the start in such a love, as in any serious realistic treatment of an erotic theme, and they demanded to be represented in the story's structure.

This temperamentally and artistically necessary combination of contrasting elements in *Death in Venice* was seen by Mann himself, in the letter to Weber, not as a discrepancy or inconsistency but as an 'iridescent interweaving' (*changieren*; I have slightly expanded the translation of this word to bring out the clearly implied metaphor of *changierende Seide*, i.e. alternating or 'shot' silk, in which threads of contrasting colour are interwoven). This striking image is in fact the key to the structure of *Death in Venice*. It is not really necessary to postulate (as T. J. Reed did in the book already referred to and in his earlier annotated edition of the story\*) any radical change of plan by Mann in the course of writing it, if by this is meant a simple linear development from an originally celebratory conception of the homosexual theme (possibly in verse) to a later more prosaic, critical and, at least ostensibly, moralizing treatment. It is more likely that a complexity of conflicting elements was fully present from the beginning. There may have been some shift of emphasis (as seems to be suggested by the last two lines of the passage from *The Lay of the Little Child* that Mann quotes to Weber), but we know too little about the process of the story's composition to be able to reconstruct it with certainty. The finished version is the only one extant and the only one we need. To detect an author's exact attitude to his fictional hero is always problematic, not least with an author of so ironic a disposition as Mann. The remarkable thing is that, notwithstanding any complexity of conception or underlying dramatic conflict in his sensibility, Mann has achieved in *Death in Venice* (as Mr Reed also points out) so near-perfect an artistic synthesis. The finished *Novelle* is, in fact, remarkably lucid and formally integrated; its *opposita* are paradoxically and realistically embraced in a convincing organic whole. Mann himself, after its completion, remarked that for once he seemed to have written something 'completely successful', something entirely self-consistent ('*es stimmt einmal alles*'), which he compared to a many-faceted and 'pure' crystal (letter to Philip Witkop, 12 March 1913). In his letters to his friends during the year it took him to write the story there are, not surprisingly, occasional complaints that he is finding it a difficult task, but the correspondence also, no less naturally, contains expressions of confidence in the progress of his work. Indeed the *Sketch of My Life*, looking back, recalls how the happy coincidences of the 'given' material filled him during the process of composition with a sense of being 'borne up with sovereign ease'. If he felt some indecision about how to end the story (as a letter of April 1912 to his brother suggests), we may guess that this may have been due to a sense that if Aschenbach's drama was to be brought to a not wholly negative, aesthetically satisfying (because balanced) full close, he would have to reach an accommodation with his past and take a step back from Homer and Plato towards naturalism –

*Thomas Mann, *Der Tod in Venedig* (with introduction and notes), Oxford University Press, 1971 (Clarendon German Series).

and perhaps also towards the kind of consummation he had celebrated ten years earlier in *Tristan*.

He did both these things in the two climaxes of the last chapter: the scene of Aschenbach's concluding reflections by the fountain in the depths of Venice, and the closing scene of his death on the beach. In the inner monologue by the fountain, both Mann and Aschenbach finally spell out their negative, disillusioned view not only of Aschenbach but of artistic creativity and 'classical' beauty in general, as well as of the neo-pagan, integrative interpretation of the Eros theory that Mann had tried and failed to embrace. Yet, even at this point, as the defeated and degraded hero collapses despairingly in the shabby, haunted little square, his dramatically necessary 'tragic fall' is mitigated for the sake of a more complex truth. His bitter recital of the ironies of his own situation ('There he sat, the master . . .') itself ironically recalls the 'forthright' moralism of his earlier stance, and this too-much-protesting moralism is thereby implicitly relativized. And Aschenbach's speech of final self-*Erkenntnis* has a sad, paradoxical dignity, the dignity of man's awareness and acceptance of his own destruction ('And now I shall go, Phaedrus . . .'). Contemplating the failure of his *alter ego* to achieve regeneration, Mann must himself revert to the psychological method of his own unregenerate days and to the all-embracing principle that 'understanding is forgiving'. Aschenbach, refusing unlike Mann to mix irony with morality, had repudiated this principle, which now is his only absolution. The 'moral' of Mann's unintended 'ethical fable' seems to be his sobering insight into the difficulty of radically changing, by sheer 'resolution', the kind of person and the kind of artist one is; his conclusion that a writer born into a 'decadent' generation is and remains a vulnerable type, since even the 'overcoming' of decadence may reveal itself as decadence in yet another form.

In the last short section of Chapter 5 that follows, the naturalistic and symbolic threads are again 'iridescently interwoven', and a double view is demanded. Aschenbach sits on the beach watching Tadzio for the last time as he wanders out to sea. Prosaically and factually, Aschenbach is now dying of cholera (in its milder form of rapid collapse into coma) and is in a state of 'menopausal' infatuation verging on delusion. Mythically and poetically, Tadzio's allurement has now become that of the death-god Hermes Psychopompos, the 'guide of souls' to the underworld. And whether or not Aschenbach merely imagines the boy's final gesture as it beckons him out to sea into 'an immensity rich with unutterable expectation', this last pursuit of his vision – of the finite god silhouetted against infinity – raises him paradoxically into a mysterious apotheosis, into that region of indefinable reconciliation in which true tragedy has always ended. In Plato's *Symposium*, the 'wise woman' Diotima explains to Socrates how the initiate of Eros, in the end, 'turns to the open sea of Beauty'; and it may be significant that Mann copied and underlined these words (in Kassner's rather neo-romantically elaborated translation) in his *Death in Venice* notebook. Equally it may be relevant here to notice the subject-matter of Mann's short essay written in May 1911 on the paper of the Hotel des Bains, which became the 'page and a half of exquisite prose' written by Aschenbach, at an earlier and central scene of the story, on the beach in Tadzio's presence. Mann's essay, in reality, was about Wagner; but we are not told that this was Aschenbach's topic, merely that he had been asked in a circular letter to contribute his views on 'a certain important cultural problem, a burning question of taste'. Transmuting the biographical reality, the text seems here to hint ('the theme was familiar to him, it was close to his experience') that the topic proposed to Aschenbach was the role of homosexuality in literature and the arts. In reality, again, Mann in this essay (originally published in 1911 as *A critical view of Richard Wagner*) was anti-Wagnerian as so often, calling for a post-Wagnerian 'neo-classical' culture. But there was perhaps a further transmutation when, about a year later, he wrote the carefully balanced scene of Aschenbach's death, the scene that has been called the '*Liebestod* ending' to this classical and classic tale of romantic passion. The city in which Aschenbach dies was profoundly associated with Wagner, the arch-romantic, who had composed much of *Tristan and Isolde* there and had died there; Aschenbach himself seemed to allude to him in his thoughts as he drifted along the canals in pursuit of Tadzio ('Venice . . . where composers have been inspired to lulling tones of somniferous eroticism'). If in the fictional death-scene's nexus of associations Diotima's words implicitly accompany the hero's last journey, so too perhaps does the final climax of what to Mann, even in 1912, was still music's ultimate statement: the mystic trance of Isolde as she contemplates the dead Tristan and breathes the murmur of waves, listens and drowns as the odour of music, 'the world-soul's vast breath', engulfs her consciousness.

So movingly retrogressive a 'full close' is of course immediately followed by the few lines prosaically narrating Aschenbach's physical collapse and death, rather as Goethe's *Werther* ends with chilling details of what happens after the hero has in final ecstasy shot himself. They are the necessary naturalistic postscript, by which the preceding passage is not so much contradicted as completed.

A double view also suggests itself when we consider the prose style of the story and Mann's comments on this aspect of it. In the lecture *On Myself* delivered in Princeton in 1940, he described *Death in Venice* as

> a strange sort of moral self-castigation by means of a book which itself, with intentional irony, displays in its manner and style that very stance of dignity and mastery which is denounced in it as spurious and foolish.

And quite soon after the story's publication, irritated by critics who read into the elevated prose a pompously implied authorial claim to magisterial status, he insisted that it was not his own style but Aschenbach's, that it was parody and mimicry, yet another way of exposing Aschenbach's pretensions (10 September 1915, to Paul Amann; 6 June 1919, to Joseph Ponten). But this self-interpretation, like some of Mann's remarks on Spinell, is again too one-sidedly negative: if it were the whole truth, the language of the story, as a deliberate *reductio ad absurdum*, would carry a faint aura of ridicule throughout. Instead, it remains a serious, heightened and noble language, 'parodistic' only if parody can also be filled with sadness, the sadness of leave-taking from a noble impossibility.

*Death in Venice* was written between July 1911 and July 1912, much of it in Mann's recently built summer villa in Bad Tölz, Upper Bavaria. It was published in two parts in the October and November numbers of the *Neue Rundschau* in 1912, then in Fischer's book edition in February 1913 (a special luxury edition of a hundred copies had also appeared in 1912 with another publisher). Fischer's first printing of eight thousand was sold out at once, sales of eighteen thousand were reached at the end of the year, thirty-three thousand by the end of the First World War, eighty thousand by 1930. During Mann's lifetime,

*Death in Venice* appeared in twenty countries and thirty-seven editions, being translated more than once into some of the languages. The first English translation was by Kenneth Burke (Knopf, 1925); in 1928 Secker and Warburg published the version by Helen Lowe-Porter, who remained for many decades, on both sides of the Atlantic, the exclusively copyrighted translator of nearly all the works of Thomas Mann. It is now increasingly recognized that Mrs Lowe-Porter's grasp of German was rather less than adequate and that a fresh attempt to translate Mann into English is overdue; the present volume is conceived as a step in that direction. It is embarrassing but necessary at this point to put on record some examples of the shortcomings of the hitherto accepted sole mediator of Mann's *oeuvre* to the English-reading public. They can be representatively illustrated even from a few of the stories, indeed from *Death in Venice* alone. The following brief catalogue of errors confines itself in the first instance to unwitting factual mis-representations of the meaning, due to obvious incomprehension of the German vocabulary or syntax; I am not here concerned with the kind of acceptable conscious inexactitudes which are within a translator's limited but legitimate area of freedom. The main list also excludes the more imponderable defects of style and taste which are matters less of fact than of judgement, though I refer later to a few of these; the reader may perhaps fairly infer their prevalence from that of the more palpable failures. The page-references below are to *Stories of Three Decades* (Secker and Warburg, 1936; I quote from the 1946 reprint). The English words in parentheses immediately following the quoted German material are correct translations or explanatory paraphrases; the English in quotation marks is Mrs Lowe-Porter's. In most cases I have then added a summary indication of the nature of the mistake.

From *Tonio Kröger*:

'quadratischer Liniennetz' (the squared-off network of LINES on the painter's canvas): 'a square LINEN mesh' (p. 100). (Confusion of *Linien* with *Leinen*.)

'ungeWÜRZT' (savourless): 'without ROOTS' (p. 103). (Confusion of *Würze* with *Wurzel*.)

'mich vor dem Frühling meines Künstlertums ein wenig zu schämen' (feel a little ashamed of my art when confronted with the spring): 'feel a little ashamed of the SPRINGTIME OF MY ART' (p. 103). (Misconstruction of the syntax.)

'heiligend' (sanctifying): 'healing' (p. 106). (Confusion with *heilend*.)

### From *Tristan*:

'(ich kann) das *Empire* einfach NICHT ENTBEHREN' (cannot bear NOT to be surrounded by *Empire* furnishings): 'I cannot ENDURE *Empire*' (p. 141).

'(eine) unsäglich EMPÖRENDE Geschichte' (an unspeakably REVOLTING story): 'unspeakably TOUCHING story' (p. 158).

### From *Death in Venice*:

'innigere Geistigkeit' (the more INWARD SPIRITUALITY of a clergyman among Aschenbach's ancestors): 'a LIVELIER MENTALITY' (p. 382).

'sinnlicheres Blut' (the more SENSUOUS blood of Aschenbach's mother): 'more PERCEPTIVE blood' (p. 382).

'Wertzeichen' (the foreign stamps on Aschenbach's mail): 'tributes' from abroad (p. 383).

'Er hatte dem Geiste gefrönt, mit der Erkenntnis Raubbau getrieben, Saatfrucht vermahlen, Geheimnisse preisgegeben, das Talent verdächtigt, die Kunst verraten' (he had BEEN ENSLAVED TO intellect, had exhausted the soil by excessive analysis, had ground up the seed-corn of growth, GIVEN AWAY SECRETS, made talent seem suspect, betrayed the truth about art): 'he had DONE HOMAGE to intellect . . . had TURNED HIS BACK ON THE "MYSTERIES" ' (p. 385).

'sich ein Schicksal erschleicht' (cheats his way into a destiny of sorts): 'manages to lead fate by the nose' (p. 386).

'Nichtswürdigkeiten begehen' (behave with contemptible baseness): 'trifle away the rest of his life' (p. 386).

'UNBEFANGENHEIT' (naïvety, single-mindedness): 'detachment' (p. 386, p. 435). (Thought and context misunderstood.)

'eine Vereinfachung, eine sittliche VEREINFÄLTIGUNG der Welt und der Seele' (a simplification, a morally simplistic and naïve view of the world and of human psychology): 'a dangerous simplification, a TENDENCY TO EQUATE the world and the human soul' (p. 386). (A wild guess that makes no sense.)

'WÜRDE' (dignity). In *Death in Venice* the theme of 'dignity' and its loss is central, and the word recurs in the story as a kind of technical term and continuing leitmotif. In defiance of this and of the contexts in which the word appears, Mrs Lowe-Porter translates it variously as 'HONOUR' (p. 385), 'UTILITY' (p. 386), 'WORTH' (pp. 387, 434), etc.

'die WÜRDE des Geistes ausdrucksvoll WAHRZUNEHMEN' (to be an expressive representative of the dignity of the intellect): 'RECOGNIZES his own WORTH' (p. 387). (*Wahrnehmen* here has the less common sense of *vertreten*.)

'von schon gestalteter Empfindung mühelos bewegt' (effortlessly moved by a passion already shaped into language): 'easily susceptible to a PRESCIENCE already shaped within him' (p. 391). (The allusion to August von Platen's sonnet has been missed, but the resulting version in any case makes no sense.)

'QUER über die Insel' (the avenue running straight across the elongated Isola del Lido from the steamship pier to the Hotel des Bains): 'across the island DIAGONALLY' (p. 395); cf. 'QUERstehende Hütten' (bathing huts at right angles to the main row): 'DIAGONAL row of cabins' (p. 401). (The correct sense in these two cases could have been ascertained from a map or by personal inspection.)

'Schönheit schaffende Ungerechtigkeit' (the injustice that creates beauty): 'THE BEAUTY THAT BREAKS HEARTS' (p. 397). (Syntax misconstrued.)

'seine BILDUNG geriet ins Wallen, sein Gedächtnis warf uralte, seiner Jugend überlieferte . . . Gedanken auf' (his mind's store of culture was in ferment, his memory threw up thoughts from ancient tradition which he had been taught as a boy): 'his whole MENTAL BACKGROUND [was] in a state of flux. Memory flung up in him the PRIMITIVE thoughts which are youth's inheritance' (p. 412). (Missing the specific and clearly implied theme of school or college education in the Greek classics.)

'als sei DER Eros, der sich seiner bemeistert, einem solchen Leben auf irgendeine Weise besonders gemäß und geneigt. Hatte er nicht bei den tapfersten Völkern vorzüglich in Ansehen gestanden' etc. (it seemed to him that THE KIND OF love that had taken possession of him [i.e. homosexual love] did, in a certain way, suit and befit such a life. Had it not been highly honoured by the most valiant of peoples, etc.): '[he wondered] if such a life might not be somehow specially PLEASING IN THE EYES OF THE GOD who had him in his power. For EROS had received most countenance among the most valiant nations' etc. (p. 422). This glosses over (for reasons of prudery perhaps) the specific point about Greek homosexuality as such.

'(der Flötenton lockte ihn) schamlos BEHARRLICH zum Feste' (the flute music was enticing him with shameless INSISTENCE to the feast): 'beguiling too it was to him who struggled [etc.] . . . shamelessly AWAITING the coming feast' (p. 431). (Vocabulary and syntax misunderstood.)

Some of these errors are of no great consequence, merely contributing to a cumulative effect of minor irritation; most are relatively serious distortions of the intended meaning of Thomas Mann's text. In addition, Mrs Lowe-Porter was in the habit (and this applies to her translations generally) of unnecessarily and often damagingly excising words, phrases, even whole sentences. I will mention here only two cases of such omission, the second very much more important than the first, from *Death in Venice*. In Chapter 3 Aschenbach is hurrying to catch his train and leave Venice, very much against his own secret wishes:

> Es ist sehr spät, er hat keinen Augenblick zu verlieren, wenn er den Zug erreichen will. Er will es und will es nicht. Aber die Zeit drängt . . .

In Mrs Lowe-Porter's version (p. 407) the reference to the train and the significant words 'er will es und will es nicht' (he both wants and does not want to catch it) have simply vanished without trace: she writes merely 'It was very late, he had not a moment to lose. Time pressed . . .' The more crucial and almost incredible case comes at the very end of the story, in the passage describing Aschenbach's final vision and death, to which I have referred earlier. Tadzio turns round to glance

l

at the dying Aschenbach at the moment of his collapse into unconsciousness, and we read:

> Ihm war aber, als ob der bleiche und liebliche Psychagog dort draußen
> ihm lächle, ihm winke; als ob er, die Hand aus der Hüfte lösend,
> hinausdeute, voranschwebe ins Verheißungsvoll-Ungeheure. UND
> WIE SO OFT, MACHTE ER SICH AUF, IHM ZU FOLGEN.

Mrs Lowe-Porter's version of this (p. 437) is so far as it goes
unexceptionable – indeed, her phrase 'an immensity of richest
expectation' is even a felicitous rendering of 'das Verheißungsvoll-
Ungeheure'; unaccountably, however, ending her whole paragraph at
'expectation', she omits altogether the final, dramatically indispensable
sentence 'And as so often, he set out to follow him.'

No one is incapable of oversight, and Mrs Lowe-Porter was clearly
working under great pressure of time to complete her immense task of
translating the many long volumes of Mann's work as each appeared;
more vigilant copy-editing might have improved the result. Regrettably,
none of the errors was corrected in later reprintings.

In my own versions, as well as trying to be more accurate, I have tried
to reflect, so far as is possible in English, the complexity of Mann's prose
generally and especially the enhanced, ceremonious prose which he
uses, for reasons already discussed, in *Death in Venice*. It is well known
that Mann's sentences tend to be long and elaborate (he himself parodies
this in the opening paragraph of *Doctor Faustus*). They are however
never ill-balanced or obscure, at least not in his best works of fiction.
Because of the inherent differences between the languages, a translator's
equivalent English sentences should not try to follow the structure of
Mann's German sentences too closely, or they will cease to be
equivalent; but they should be as complex as is consistent with what
sounds natural for a single sentence by English standards. Mrs Lowe-
Porter ignores this point; the most flagrant example is her cavalier
treatment of the deliberately complex opening sentence of Chapter 2 in
*Death in Venice*, where Mann inserts a catalogue of Aschenbach's most
important works into his bare statement of the place of his birth. Mrs
Lowe-Porter quite unnecessarily breaks this sentence up, shifting most
of it to a later point after four intervening sentences, so that the
paragraph's whole structure is rearranged and destroyed (in addition to

the already mentioned garbling of some of its details). Her version of *Death in Venice* in general also ignores the characteristic style of this story: its solemnity and just detectable preciosity, its preference for the unusual, elevated (*gehoben*), 'literary' word. She also ignores the passages in which Mann's prose, 'hymnically' celebrating Tadzio and his Homeric-Platonic background, breaks into hexameters, once or twice quoting actual lines from Homer; the most notable case of this occurs at the opening of Chapter 4, where dactylic rhythms are woven into the first paragraph, and Aschenbach's delight at being no longer in the gloomy Bavarian Alps is expressed in a clear sequence of almost three complete hexameter lines (Mann's adaptation of Erwin Rohde's translation of *The Odyssey* iv, 536ff): '. . . als sei er entrückt ins elysische Land, an die Grenzen der Erde, wo leichtestes Leben den Menschen beschert ist, wo nicht Schnee ist und Winter, noch Sturm und strömender Regen'. I have attempted to devise prosodic equivalents in this and the other cases.

I have preferred not to overburden this introductory essay with references and footnotes, but must gratefully acknowledge much indebtedness to my colleagues H. R. Vaget (specifically his *Kommentar* to the complete stories, Winkler-Verlag, 1984) and T. J. Reed (especially his valuable new edition, with much interpretative and auxiliary material, of *Death in Venice*, Hanser-Verlag, 1983); my debt to Proffesor Reed is not diminished by my disagreement with him in certain respects. Miscellaneous particular points are also attributable to other Thomas Mann scholars such as Erich Heller, the late Peter de Mendelssohn and the late Wolfdietrich Rasch. I am grateful to Professor Hans Wysling and Mr Gilbert Adair for additional information on Wladyslaw Moes.

My versions of the first six stories in this selection were published as *Tonio Kröger and Other Stories* by Bantam Books (New York) in 1970, by which date the originals had come into the public domain under the current United States copyright law. This did not happen in the case of *Death in Venice* until 1987, when it became possible to re-issue the volume with a new translation of that story added (*Death in Venice and Other Stories*, Bantam Books, 1988; the earlier translations were here slightly revised and the introduction rewritten). For the present British edition further slight revisions have been made.

D. L.

# Little Herr Friedemann

*Der kleine Herr Friedemann*

1897[*]

[*]The dates are those of first publication.

# Little Herr Friedemann

## 1

It was the nurse's fault. In vain Frau Consul Friedemann, when the matter was first suspected, had solemnly urged her to relinquish so heinous a vice; in vain she had dispensed to her daily a glass of red wine in addition to her nourishing stout. It suddenly came to light that the girl had actually sunk so low as to drink the methylated spirits intended for the coffee-machine; and before a replacement for her had arrived, before she could be sent away, the accident had happened. One day, when little Johannes was about a month old, his mother and three adolescent sisters returned from a walk to find that he had fallen from the swaddling table and was lying on the floor making a horribly faint whimpering noise, with the nurse standing by looking stupidly down at him.

The doctor's face, as he carefully but firmly probed the limbs of the crooked, twitching little creature, wore an exceedingly serious expression; the three girls stood in a corner sobbing, and Frau Friedemann prayed aloud in her mortal anguish.

Even before the baby was born it had been the poor woman's lot to see her husband, the consul for the Netherlands, reft from her by an illness both sudden and acute, and she was still too broken in spirit to be even capable of hoping that the life of her little Johannes might be spared. Two days later, however, the doctor squeezed her hand encouragingly and pronounced that there was now absolutely no question of any immediate danger; above all, the slight concussion of the brain had completely cleared up. This, he explained, was obvious if one looked at the child's eyes; there had been a vacant stare in them at first which had now quite disappeared . . . 'Of course,' he added, 'we must wait and see how things go on – and we must hope for the best, you know, hope for the best . . .'

## 2

The grey gabled house in which Johannes Friedemann grew up was near the north gate of the old, scarcely middle-sized merchant city. Its front door opened on to a spacious stone-paved hall, from which a stair with white wooden banisters led to the upper floors. On the first was the living-room with its walls papered in a faded landscape pattern, and its heavy mahogany table draped in crimson plush, with high-backed chairs and settees standing stiffly round it.

Here, as a child, he would often sit by the window, where there was always a fine display of flowers; he would sit on a little stool at his mother's feet, listening perhaps as she told him some wonderful story, gazing at her smooth grey hair and her kind gentle face, and breathing in the slight fragrance of scent that always hung about her. Or perhaps he would get her to show him the portrait of his father, an amiable gentleman with grey side-whiskers. He was (said his mother) now living in heaven, waiting for them all to join him there.

Behind the house was a little garden, and during the summer they would spend a good deal of time in it, notwithstanding the almost perpetual sickly-sweet exhalations from a nearby sugar refinery. In the garden stood an old gnarled walnut tree, and in its shade little Johannes would often sit on a low wooden stool cracking nuts, while Frau Friedemann and her three daughters, now grown-up, sat together in a grey canvas tent. But Frau Friedemann would often raise her eyes from her needlework and glance tenderly and sadly across at her son.

Little Johannes was no beauty, with his pigeon chest, his steeply humped back and his disproportionately long skinny arms, and as he squatted there on his stool, nimbly and eagerly cracking his nuts, he was certainly a strange sight. But his hands and feet were small and neatly shaped, and he had great liquid brown eyes, a sensitive mouth and soft light brown hair. In fact, although his face sat so pitifully low down between his shoulders, it could nevertheless almost have been called beautiful.

4

## 3

When he was seven he was sent to school, and now the years passed uniformly and rapidly. Every day, walking past the gabled houses and shops with the quaintly solemn gait that deformed people often have, he made his way to the old schoolhouse with its Gothic vaulting; and at home, when he had done his homework, he would perhaps read some of his beautiful books with their brightly coloured illustrations, or potter about in the garden, while his sisters kept house for their ailing mother. The girls also went to parties, for the Friedemanns moved in the best local society; but unfortunately none of the three had yet married, for their family fortune was by no means large and they were distinctly plain.

Johannes, too, occasionally got an invitation from one or another of his contemporaries, but it was no great pleasure for him to associate with them. He was unable to join in their games, and since they always treated him with embarrassed reserve, it was impossible for any real companionship to develop.

Later there came a time when he would often hear them discuss certain matters in the school yard; wide-eyed and attentive, he would listen in silence as they talked of their passions for this little girl or that. Such experiences, he decided, obviously engrossing though they were for the others, belonged like gymnastics and ball games to the category of things for which he was not suited. This was at times a rather saddening thought; but after all, he had long been accustomed to going his own way and not sharing the interests of other people. .

It nevertheless came to pass – he was sixteen years old at the time – that he found himself suddenly enamoured of a girl of his own age. She was the sister of one of his classmates, a blonde, exuberant creature whom he had met at her brother's house. He felt a strange uneasiness in her company, and the studied self-conscious cordiality with which she too treated him saddened him profoundly.

One summer afternoon when he was taking a solitary walk along the promenade outside the old city wall, he heard whispered words being exchanged behind a jasmine bush. He cautiously peeped through the branches, and there on a seat sat this girl and a tall red-haired boy whom he knew very well by sight; the boy's arm was round her and he was pressing a kiss on her lips, which with much giggling she reciprocated. When Johannes had seen this he turned on his heel and walked softly away.

His head had sunk lower than ever between his shoulders, his hands were trembling and a sharp, biting pain rose from his chest and seemed to choke him. But he swallowed it down, and resolutely drew himself up as straight as he could. 'Very well,' he said to himself, 'that is over. I will never again concern myself with such things. To the others they mean joy and happiness, but to me they can only bring grief and suffering. I am done with it all. It is finished for me. Never again.'

The decision was a relief to him. He had made a renunciation, a renunciation for ever. He went home and took up a book or played the violin, which he had learned to do despite his deformity.

## 4

At seventeen he left school to go into business, like everyone else of his social standing, and became an apprentice in Herr Schlievogt's big timber firm down by the river. They treated him with special consideration, he for his part was amiable and cooperative, and the years passed by in a peaceful and well ordered manner. But in his twenty-first year his mother died after a long illness.

This was a great sorrow for Johannes Friedemann, and one that he long cherished. He savoured this sorrow, he surrendered himself to it as one surrenders oneself to a great happiness, he nourished it with innumerable memories from his childhood and made the most of it, as his first major experience.

Is not life in itself a thing of goodness, irrespective of whether the course it takes for us can be called a 'happy' one? Johannes Friedemann felt that this was so, and he loved life. He had renounced the greatest happiness it has to offer, but who shall say with what passionate care he cultivated those pleasures that were accessible to him? A walk in springtime through the parks outside the town, the scent of a flower, the song of a bird – surely these were things to be thankful for?

He also well understood that a capacity for the enjoyment of life presupposes education, indeed that education always adds at once to that capacity, and he took pains to educate himself. He loved music and attended any concerts that were given in the town. And although it was uncommonly odd to watch him play, he did himself become not a bad violinist and took pleasure in every beautiful and tender note he was able to draw from his instrument. And by dint of much reading he had in the course of time acquired a degree of literary taste which in that town was probably unique. He was versed in all the latest publications both in Germany and abroad, he knew how to savour the exquisite rhythms of a poem, he could appreciate the subtle atmosphere of a finely written short story . . . One might indeed almost say that he was an epicurean.

He came to see that there is nothing that cannot be enjoyed and that it is almost absurd to distinguish between happy and unhappy experiences. He accepted all his sensations and moods as they came to him, he welcomed and cultivated them, whether they were sad or glad: even his unfulfilled wishes, even his heart's longing. It was precious to him for its own sake, and he would tell himself that if it ever came to fulfilment the best part of the pleasure would be over. Is not the sweet pain of vague desires and hopes on a still spring evening richer in delight than any fulfilment the summer could bring? Ah yes, little Herr Friedemann was an epicurean and no mistake.

This was something of which the people who passed him in the street, greeting him with that mixture of cordiality and pity to which he had so long been accustomed, were doubtless unaware. They did not know that this unfortunate cripple, strutting so quaintly and solemnly along in his light grey overcoat and his shiny top hat (for oddly enough he was a little vain of his appearance) was a man to whom life was very sweet, this life of his that flowed so gently by, unmarked by any strong emotions but filled with a quiet and delicate happiness of which he had taught himself the secret.

5

But Herr Friedemann's chief and most absorbing passion was for the theatre. He had an uncommonly strong sense of drama and at moments of high theatrical effect or tragic catastrophe the whole of his little body would quiver with emotion. At the principal theatre of the town he had a seat permanently reserved for him in the front row, and he would go there regularly, sometimes accompanied by his three sisters. Since their mother's death they had lived on in the big house which they and their brother jointly owned, and did all the housekeeping for themselves and him.

They were, alas, still unmarried; but they had long reached an age at which one sets aside all such expectations, for the eldest of them, Friederike, was seventeen years older than Herr Friedemann. She and her sister Henriette were rather too tall and thin, whereas Pfiffi, the youngest, was regrettably short and plump. This youngest girl moreover had an odd habit of wriggling and wetting the corners of her mouth whenever she spoke.

Little Herr Friedemann did not pay much attention to the three girls, but they stuck loyally together and were always of the same opinion. In particular, whenever any engagement between persons of their acquaintance was announced, they would unanimously declare that this was *very* gratifying news.

Their brother went on living with them even after he had left Herr Schlievogt's timber firm and set up on his own by taking over some small business, some sort of agency which did not demand much exertion. He lived in a couple of rooms on the ground floor of the house, in order not to have to climb the stairs except at mealtimes, for he occasionally suffered from asthma.

On his thirtieth birthday, a fine warm June day, he was sitting after lunch in the grey tent in the garden, leaning against a new soft neck-rest which Henriette had made for him, with a good cigar in his mouth and a good book in his hand. Now and then he would put the book aside, listen to the contented twittering of the sparrows in the old walnut tree and look at the neat gravel drive that led up to the house and at the lawn with its bright flower-beds.

Little Herr Friedemann was clean-shaven, and his face had scarcely changed at all except for a slight sharpening of his features. He wore his soft light brown hair smoothly parted on one side.

Once, lowering the book right into his lap, he gazed up at the clear blue sky and said to himself: 'Well, that's thirty years gone. And now I suppose there will be another ten or perhaps another twenty, God knows. They will come upon me silently and pass by without any commotion, as the others have done, and I look forward to them with peace of mind.'

# 6

It was in July of that year that the new military commandant for the district was appointed, a change of office that caused a considerable stir. The stout and jovial gentleman who had held the post for many years had been a great favourite with local society, and his departure was regretted. And now, for God knows what reason, it must needs be Herr von Rinnlingen who was sent from the capital to replace him.

It seemed, in fact, to be not a bad exchange, for the new lieutenant-colonel, who was married but had no children, rented a very spacious villa in the southern suburbs, from which it was concluded that he intended to keep house in some style. At all events the rumour that he was quite exceptionally rich found further confirmation in the fact that he brought with him four servants, five riding and carriage horses, a landau and a light hunting brake.

Shortly after their arrival he and his wife had been to pay calls on all the best families, and everyone was talking about them; the chief object of interest however was definitely not Herr von Rinnlingen himself, but his wife. The men were dumbfounded by her and did not at first know what to think; but the ladies most decidedly did not approve of Gerda von Rinnlingen's character and ways.

'Of course, one can tell at once that she comes from the capital,' observed Frau Hagenström, the lawyer's wife, in the course of conversation with Henriette Friedemann. 'One doesn't mind that, one doesn't mind her smoking and riding – naturally not! But her behaviour isn't merely free and easy, it's unrefined, and even that isn't quite the right word . . . She's by no means ugly, you know, some might even think her pretty – and yet she totally lacks feminine charm, her eyes and her laugh and her movements are simply not at all calculated to appeal to men. She is no flirt, and far be it from me to find fault with her for that, goodness knows – but can it be right for so young a woman, a woman of twenty-four, to show absolutely no sign of . . . a certain natural grace and attractiveness? My dear, I am not very good at expressing myself, but I know what I mean. The men still seem to be quite stunned, poor dears; mark my words, they will all be sick to death of her in a few weeks' time.'

'Well,' said Fräulein Friedemann, 'she has made a very good marriage, anyway.'

'Oh, as to her husband!' exclaimed Frau Hagenström. 'You should see how she treats him! You will see it soon enough! I am the last person to deny that up to a point a married woman should act towards the opposite sex with a certain reserve. But how does she behave to her own husband? She has a way of freezing him with her eyes and calling him *"mon cher ami"* in pitying tones, which I find quite outrageous! You have only to look at *him* – a fine upstanding first-class officer and gentleman of forty, well behaved and well mannered and very well preserved! They've been married for four years . . . My dear . . .'

7

The scene of little Herr Friedemann's first encounter with Frau von Rinnlingen was the main street of the town, a street lined almost entirely with shops and offices. He was vouchsafed this first sight of her at midday, just after leaving the Stock Exchange, where he had been making his modest contribution to the morning's business.

He was trudging along, a tiny and solemn figure, beside Herr Stephens, the wholesale merchant, who was an unusually large and solid man with round-trimmed side-whiskers and formidably bushy eyebrows. They were both wearing top hats, and had opened their overcoats as it was a very hot day. They were discussing politics, and their walking-sticks tapped the pavement in regular rhythm. But when they were about half-way down the street Herr Stephens suddenly remarked: 'Devil take me, here comes that Rinnlingen woman driving towards us.'

'Well, that's a lucky coincidence,' replied Herr Friedemann in his high-pitched, rather strident voice, and peered expectantly ahead. 'I've never yet set eyes on her, you know. Ah, so that is the yellow brake.'

And so indeed it was: Frau von Rinnlingen was using the light yellow hunting brake today, and she herself was driving the pair of thoroughbreds; the groom sat behind her with his arms folded. She wore a loose-fitting, very light-coloured coat, and her skirt was of a light colour as well. From under her little round straw hat with its brown leather band came her luxuriant auburn hair, well curled at the sides and thickly tressed at the back where it fell almost to her shoulders. The complexion of her oval face was pale, and there were blue shadows in the corners of her unusually close-set eyes. Across her short but finely shaped nose ran a very becoming little ridge of freckles; the beauty or otherwise of her mouth, however, was hard to judge, for she kept protruding and withdrawing her lower lip, chafing it continually against the other.

Herr Stephens greeted Frau von Rinnlingen with an exceedingly respectful salutation as her carriage drew abreast of them, and little Herr Friedemann also raised his hat and stared at her very attentively. She lowered her whip, inclined her head slightly and drove slowly past, glancing at the houses and shop-windows on either side.

A few paces further on Herr Stephens remarked: 'She's been out for a drive and now she's on her way home.'

Little Herr Friedemann made no reply but gazed down at the pavement in front of him. Then he suddenly looked up at Stephens and asked: 'What did you say?'

And Herr Stephens, the wholesale merchant, repeated his perspicacious observation.

8

Three days later, at noon, Johannes Friedemann returned home from his regular morning walk. Luncheon was served at half-past twelve, so there would be time for him to spend another half-hour in his 'office', which was just to the right of the front door. But as he was about to enter it the maid came up to him in the hall and said:

'There are visitors, Herr Friedemann.'

'In my room?' he asked.

'No, upstairs with the ladies, sir.'

'But who are they?'

'Lieutenant-Colonel and Frau von Rinnlingen.'

'Oh,' said Herr Friedemann, 'then of course I'll . . .'

And he climbed the stairs to the first floor and walked across the lobby towards the room with the landscape wallpaper. But with the handle of the tall white door already in his hand, he suddenly stopped, drew back a pace, turned and went slowly down again the way he had come. And although he was completely alone he said out loud to himself:

'No. Better not.'

He went into his 'office', sat down at his desk and took up a newspaper. But presently he let it drop again, and sat with his head turned to one side, looking out of the window. Thus he remained till the maid came and announced that luncheon was served: then he went upstairs to the dining-room where his sisters were already waiting for him, and seated himself on his chair on top of three volumes of music.

Henriette, ladling out the soup, said:

'Who do you think has been here, Johannes?'

'Well?' he asked.

'The new lieutenant-colonel with his wife.'

'Indeed? That is very kind of them.'

'Yes,' said Pfiffi, dribbling at the corners of her mouth, 'I think they are both very agreeable people.'

'Anyway,' said Friederike, 'we must return the call without delay. I suggest we go on Sunday, the day after tomorrow.'

'On Sunday,' said Henriette and Pfiffi.

'You'll come with us of course, Johannes?' asked Friederike.

'Naturally!' said Pfiffi, wriggling. Herr Friedemann had completely ignored the question and was swallowing his soup, silently and apprehensively. He seemed somehow to be listening, listening to some uncanny noise from nowhere.

# 9

The following evening there was a performance of *Lohengrin* at the city theatre, and all well-educated people were present. The small auditorium was packed from top to bottom and filled with the hum of voices, the smell of gas and a medley of scent. But every eyeglass, in the stalls and in the circles, was trained on box number thirteen, just to the right of the stage; for there, this evening, Herr and Frau von Rinnlingen had appeared for the first time, and now was the chance to give them a thorough inspection.

When little Herr Friedemann, in faultless evening dress with a glistening white pigeon-breasted shirt-front, entered his box – box thirteen – he stopped dead on the threshold: his hand rose to his brow and for a moment his nostrils dilated convulsively. But then he took his seat, the seat immediately to the left of Frau von Rinnlingen.

As he sat down she contemplated him attentively, protruding her lower lip; she then turned and exchanged a few words with her husband, who was standing behind her. He was a tall well-built man with upturned moustaches and a tanned, good-humoured face.

When the prelude began and Frau von Rinnlingen leaned forward over the balustrade, Herr Friedemann gave her a quick, furtive, sideways look. She was wearing a light-coloured evening gown and was even slightly *décolletée*, unlike any other woman present. Her sleeves were wide and ample and her white evening gloves came up to her elbows. Tonight there was something voluptuous about her figure which had not been noticeable the other day under her loose coat; her bosom rose and fell slowly and firmly, and her heavy auburn tresses hung low down behind her head.

Herr Friedemann was pale, much paler than usual, and below his smoothly parted brown hair little drops of sweat stood out on his forehead. Frau von Rinnlingen had removed her left glove and was resting her bare arm on the red plush balustrade: a round, pale arm, with pale blue veins running through it and through her hand, on which she wore no rings. This arm lay constantly just where he could see it; there was no help for that.

The violins sang, the trombones blared, Telramund was struck down, the orchestra sounded a general triumph and little Herr Friedemann sat motionless, pale and silent, with his head drooping right down between his shoulders, one forefinger propped against his mouth and the other hand thrust under his lapel.

As the curtain fell, Frau von Rinnlingen rose to leave the box with her husband. Herr Friedemann, without looking at them, saw them go; he drew his handkerchief across his brow, stood up suddenly, got as far as the door that led into the corridor, then turned back again, resumed his seat, and sat on without stirring in the same posture as before.

When the bell rang and his neighbours came back into the box, he sensed that Frau von Rinnlingen was looking at him, and involuntarily he raised his head and returned her gaze. When their eyes met, so far from turning hers away, she went on scrutinizing him without a trace of embarrassment until he himself felt humiliated and compelled to look down. His pallor increased, and a strange, bitter-sweet rage welled up inside him . . . The music began.

Towards the end of that act Frau von Rinnlingen happened to drop her fan and it fell to the ground beside Herr Friedemann. Both of them stooped simultaneously, but she reached it first and said with a mocking smile:

'Thank you.'

His head had been close to hers, and for a moment, unavoidably, he had caught the warm fragrance of her breast. His face was contorted, his whole body was convulsed and his heart throbbed with such appalling violence that he could not breathe. He sat for half a minute longer, then pushed back his chair, got up quietly and quietly left the box.

## 10

The clamour of the orchestra followed him as he crossed the corridor, reclaimed his top hat and light grey overcoat and stick from the cloakroom and went downstairs and out into the street.

It was a warm, still evening. In the gaslight the grey gabled houses stood silent against the sky, and the stars gleamed and glistened softly. Only a few people passed Herr Friedemann in the street, their steps re-echoing along the pavement. Someone greeted him but he did not notice; his head was bowed low and his misshapen chest shuddered as he gasped for breath. Now and then, scarcely audibly, he exclaimed to himself:

'Oh my God! my God!'

He examined his feelings with horrified apprehension, realizing that his so carefully cherished, prudently cultivated sensibility had now been uprooted, upchurned, stirred into wild upheaval. And suddenly, quite overcome by emotion, drunk with vertiginous desire, he leaned against a lamp-post and whispered in trembling anguish:

'Gerda!'

There was complete silence. Far and wide there was not a soul to be seen. Little Herr Friedemann pulled himself together and trudged on. He had reached the top of the street in which the theatre stood and which ran quite steeply down to the river, and now he was walking northwards along the main street towards his house . . .

How she had looked at him! Was it possible? She had forced him to look away! She had humbled him with her gaze! Was she not a woman and he a man? And had not her strange brown eyes positively quivered with pleasure as she had done so?

Again he felt that impotent, voluptuous hatred welling up inside him, but then he thought of the moment when her head had touched his, when he had breathed her fragrance – and once more he stopped, half straightened his deformed back, and again murmured helplessly, desperately, distractedly:

'Oh my God! my God!'

Then mechanically he resumed his slow advance along the empty, echoing streets, through the sultry evening air, and walked on till he reached his house. He paused for a moment in the hall to sniff its cool, dank atmosphere, then went into his 'office'.

He sat down at his desk beside the open window and stared straight in front of him at a big yellow rose which someone had put there for him in a glass of water. He took it and inhaled its fragrance with closed eyes; but then, with a sad, weary gesture, he put it aside. No, no! All that was over. What was that sweet smell to him now? What were any of them now, those things that had hitherto constituted his 'happiness'? . . .

He turned and looked out into the silent street. Now and then the sound of passing footsteps approached and faded. The stars glittered in the sky. How dead tired he was growing, how weak he felt! The thoughts seemed to drain from his head, and his despair began to dissolve into a great soft sadness. A few lines of poetry floated through his mind, he seemed to hear the music of *Lohengrin* again, to see again Frau von Rinnlingen sitting beside him, her white arm resting on the red plush. Then he fell into a heavy, feverish sleep.

## 11

Often he was on the point of waking up, yet dreaded to do so and sank back every time into unconsciousness. But when it was broad daylight he opened his eyes and gazed sorrowfully round. All that had happened was still vividly present to him; it was as if sleep had not interrupted his suffering at all.

His head was heavy and his eyes hot, but when he had washed and dabbed his forehead with eau-de-cologne he felt better, and quietly resumed his seat by the window, which was still open. It was still very early, about five o'clock in the morning. Occasionally a baker's boy passed, but there was no one else to be seen. In the house opposite all the blinds were still down. But the birds were twittering, and the sky was blue and radiant. It was an absolutely beautiful Sunday morning.

A feeling of well-being and confidence came over little Herr Friedemann. What was there to be afraid of? Had anything changed? Last night, admittedly, he had suffered a bad attack; very well, but that must be the last of it! It was still not too late, it was still possible to avert disaster! He would have to avoid everything that might occasion a renewal of the attack; he felt strong enough to do so. He felt strong enough to overcome this thing, to nip it completely in the bud . . .

When half-past seven struck, Friederike brought in his coffee and set it down on the round table in front of the leather sofa by the far wall.

'Good morning, Johannes,' she said, 'here is your breakfast.'

'Thank you,' said Herr Friedemann. Then he added: 'Friederike dear, I am sorry, but I am afraid you will have to pay that call without me. I don't feel well enough to come with you. I haven't slept well, I have a headache – in short, I must ask you to excuse me . . .'

Friederike replied:

'What a pity. I think you should certainly call on them another time. But it's true that you're not looking well. Shall I lend you my migraine pencil?'

'No, thank you,' said Herr Friedemann. 'It will pass.' And Friederike left the room.

Standing at the table, he slowly drank his coffee and ate a crescent-shaped roll. He was pleased with himself and proud of his strong-mindedness. When he had finished he took a cigar and sat down again at the window. Breakfast had done him good and he felt happy and hopeful. He took up a book, read, smoked and looked out from time to time into the dazzling sunlight.

The street had grown lively now; through his window he could hear the clatter of carriages, the sound of voices and the bells from the horse tramway. But the birds twittered through it all, and a soft warm breeze stirred in the shining blue sky.

At ten o'clock he heard his sisters crossing the hall and the front door creaking open, and presently he saw the three ladies walk past his window, but thought nothing much of it. An hour passed; he felt happier and happier.

A kind of elation began to fill him. How balmy the air was, and how the birds sang! Why should he not go for a short walk? And then suddenly, spontaneously, the sweet and terrifying thought simply surged up inside him: Why not call on her? Warning apprehensions followed the impulse, but with an almost muscular effort he suppressed them and added with exultant resolve: I will call on her!

And he put on his black Sunday suit, took his hat and stick and hurried, breathing rapidly, right across the town to the southern suburb. His head rose and fell busily with every step, but he saw no one, and remained absorbed in his exalted mood until he had reached the chestnut-lined avenue and the red villa that bore at its entrance the name 'Lieutenant-Colonel von Rinnlingen'.

## · 12

At this point he began to tremble and his heart pounded convulsively against his ribs. But he crossed the outer hall and rang the doorbell. The die was cast now and there was no going back. Let it take its course, he thought. In him there was a sudden deathly stillness.

The door was thrown open, the manservant came across the hall towards him, received his card and carried it smartly up the red-carpeted stairs. Herr Friedemann stared motionlessly at the red carpet till the servant came back and declared that his mistress would be glad if Herr Friedemann would kindly come up.

On the first floor he placed his walking-stick outside the door of the drawing-room, and glanced at himself in the mirror. He was very pale, his eyes were red and above them the hair clung to his forehead; the hand in which he held his top hat was trembling uncontrollably.

The manservant opened the door and he went in. It was a fairly large, half-darkened room; the curtains were drawn. On the right stood a grand piano, and armchairs upholstered in brown silk were grouped about the round table in the centre. A landscape in a massive gilt frame hung on the wall to the left above the sofa. The wallpaper was also dark. Palm trees stood in the bay window at the far end.

A minute passed before Frau von Rinnlingen emerged from the curtained doorway on the right and advanced noiselessly towards him across the deep-pile brown carpet. She was wearing a quite simply cut dress with a red and black check pattern. From the bay window a shaft of light, full of dancing motes of dust, fell straight on to her heavy red hair, so that for a moment it flashed like gold. She was looking straight at him, studying him with her strange eyes, and protruding her lower lip as usual.

'Frau Commandant,' began Herr Friedemann, looking up at her, for his head reached only to her chest, 'my sisters have already paid you their respects and I should like to do so myself as well. When you honoured them with a call I was unfortunately not at home . . . to my great regret . . .'

He could think of absolutely no more to say, but she stood gazing implacably at him as if she meant to force him to continue speaking. The blood suddenly rushed to his head. 'She wants to torment me and mock me!' he thought, 'and she has guessed my feelings! Her eyes are simply quivering. . . !' Finally she said in a quite high, clear voice:

'It is very kind of you to have come. I was sorry, too, to miss you the other day. Won't you please take a seat?'

She sat down quite close to him and leaned back in her chair, laying her arms on the armrests. He sat leaning forward, holding his hat between his knees. She said:

'Do you know that your sisters were here only a quarter of an hour ago? They told me you were ill.'

'That is true,' replied Herr Friedemann. 'I did not feel well this morning. I thought I should not be able to go out. I must ask you to excuse my late arrival.'

'You still do not look quite well,' she remarked calmly, with her eyes fixed steadily on him. 'You are pale, and your eyes are inflamed. Perhaps your health is usually not very good?'

'Oh . . .' stammered Herr Friedemann, 'in general I cannot complain . . .'

'I am often ill too,' she went on, still not averting her gaze, 'but no one ever notices it. My nerves are bad and I have very odd moods sometimes.'

She paused, lowered her chin to her breast and looked up at him expectantly. But he made no answer. He sat on in silence looking at her, wide-eyed and thoughtful. How strangely she talked, and what an extraordinary effect her clear, cynical voice had on him! His heart was beating more quietly now; he felt as if he were dreaming. Frau von Rinnlingen spoke again:

'If I am not mistaken, you left the theatre last night before the end of the opera?'

'Yes, Frau Commandant.'

'I was sorry you did. You were a very appreciative neighbour, although it was not a good performance, or only a relatively good one. I suppose you are fond of music? Do you play the piano?'

'I play the violin a little,' said Herr Friedemann. 'That is to say – really hardly at all . . .'

'You play the violin?' she asked. Then she gazed past him for a moment and seemed to reflect.

'But then we could play together now and then,' she said suddenly. 'I can accompany a little. I should be glad to have found someone here who . . . Will you come?'

'I shall be delighted to place myself at your disposal,' he replied. He still had the feeling that he was in a dream. There was a pause. Then suddenly her face changed. He saw it twist into a scarcely perceptible expression of cruel mockery, and saw again, for the third time, that uncanny tremor in her eyes as they unswervingly scrutinized him. He blushed scarlet, and not knowing where to look, helpless, distraught, he let his head droop right down between his shoulders and stared in utter dismay at the carpet. But again, for a moment, that impotent, sweet, agonizing fury shuddered and trickled through him . . .

When with a desperate effort he raised his eyes again she was no longer looking at him, but gazing calmly over his head towards the door. He forced himself to utter a few words:

'And are you tolerably satisfied so far with your stay in our town, Frau Commandant?'

'Oh, yes,' said Frau von Rinnlingen indifferently, 'yes indeed. Why should I not be satisfied? Of course, I do feel somewhat constrained and conspicuous, but . . . By the way,' she added at once, 'before I forget: we are thinking of inviting some people round in a few days' time. Just a small informal party. We might play a little music and talk about this and that . . . Also we have rather a pretty garden behind the house; it goes right down to the river. In short, you and your ladies will of course be sent an invitation, but I should like to ask you here and now if we may have the pleasure of your company: shall we?'

Herr Friedemann had scarcely expressed his thanks and signified his acceptance when the door handle was pressed smartly down and the lieutenant-colonel entered. They both rose, and as Frau von Rinnlingen introduced the men to each other her husband bowed to her and to Herr Friedemann with equal courtesy. His tanned face was glistening in the heat.

As he removed his gloves he said something or other in his loud energetic voice to Herr Friedemann, who stared up at him with wide, vacant eyes, fully expecting to be slapped benevolently on the shoulder. Meanwhile the commandant turned to his wife. Standing with heels together and slightly bowing to her from the waist, he said in a noticeably softer voice:

'I hope you have asked Herr Friedemann if he will come to our little gathering, my dear? If you agree, I think we should arrange for it to take place a week today. I hope this weather will last and that we shall be able to use the garden as well.'

'As you think best,' replied Frau von Rinnlingen, gazing past him.

Two minutes later Herr Friedemann took his leave. As he bowed again at the door his eyes met hers, which were expressionlessly fixed on him.

## 13

He went on his way, not returning into town but involuntarily taking a side-road that led off the avenue towards the old fortified wall by the river, where there was a well-kept park with shady paths and seats.

He walked hurriedly, aimlessly, without raising his eyes. He was flushed with an unbearable heat, he could feel it licking up in him and subsiding like flames, and his weary head throbbed relentlessly . . .

Were those not her eyes still gazing into his? Not empty of expression as they had been when he left her, but with that earlier gaze, that quivering cruelty which had filled them the very moment after she had spoken to him so strangely and softly. Did she take delight in his helplessness, in driving him to distraction? And oh, if she did read his feelings, could she not at least feel some pity? . . .

Down by the river he had walked along the bank, beside the old city wall overgrown with green, and he sat down on a seat half encircled by jasmine bushes. The sweetish fragrance hung heavily in the air all round him. In front of him the sun brooded over the tremulous water.

How weary and worn-out he felt, and yet what an agonizing turmoil filled him! Surely the best thing to do would be to take one more look round him and then walk straight down into the silent water, where he would suffer for a 'few moments and then be free and rescued from existence and at peace! Oh, all he wanted was peace, peace! Yet not peace in an empty, unheeding nothingness, but a quiet place in gentle sunlight, where he might sit and think good, quiet thoughts.

At that instant all his deep love for life came back to him, piercing his heart with poignant nostalgia for his lost happiness. But then he looked about him, he looked at the mute, infinite tranquillity and indifference of nature, he saw the river wending its way in the sun, saw the grass waving and the flowers standing each in its place, just where it had bloomed, waiting to wither and be blown away: he saw all these things, all bowing in dumb submission to their existence – and suddenly he was overcome by that feeling of goodwill, of acceptance of necessity, which can in a certain sense lift us above all the adversities of fate.

He remembered that afternoon of his thirtieth birthday, when he had been happy in the possession of a quiet mind and had told himself that he could look forward, without fear or hope, to the remainder of his life. He had seen ahead of him neither brightness nor shadow, but a future bathed in gentle twilight, stretching away to a point where it merged almost imperceptibly into the dark; and with a calm and confident smile he had surveyed the years that were yet to come. How long ago had that day been?

Then this woman had come, she had had to come, it was his fate, she herself was his fate, she alone! Had he not sensed this from the very first moment? She had come, and he had tried to defend his peace of mind – but for her there had to be this rebellion within him of everything he had suppressed since his youth, because he had known instinctively that for him it meant misery and destruction. It had seized him with terrible, irresistible violence and it was destroying him!

It was destroying him, that he knew. But why go on with the vain agonizing struggle? Let it all take its course! Let him continue on his way, with his eyes closed to the gaping abyss beyond, obedient to fate, obedient to the invincible, sweetly tormenting power from which there is no escape.

The water gleamed, the jasmine breathed out its heavy pungent scent, the birds twittered in the branches all round him, and between the trees shone a dense velvet blue sky. But little hunchbacked Herr Friedemann did not stir from his seat. He sat on and on, leaning forward with his head bowed down into his hands.

## 14

Everyone agreed that the Rinnlingen party was a vast success. About thirty people sat round the long, tastefully decorated table which ran the length of the large dining-room; the butler and two hired waiters were already hurrying round serving ices, the room was filled with the clink and clatter of glasses and tableware and the warm aroma of food mingled with scent. The guests included a genial assemblage of men of business with their wives and daughters, almost the entire corps of officers from the garrison, an elderly doctor whom everyone liked, a few lawyers and other representatives of the best local society. Also present was a student of mathematics, a nephew of the commandant's who was here visiting his relatives; he was engaged in profound conversation with Fräulein Hagenström, who sat opposite Herr Friedemann.

The latter had been placed at the far end of the table, on a fine velvet cushion, next to the rather plain wife of the headmaster of the classical grammar school. He was not far from Frau von Rinnlingen, who had been escorted in to table by Consul Stephens. It was astonishing what a change had come over little Herr Friedemann in the last week. Perhaps it was partly the white gaslight in the dining-room that made his face look so alarmingly pale; but his cheeks were sunken, his eyes reddened, dark rings surrounded them, they shone with an unspeakable sadness; and he seemed more stunted and crippled than ever. He drank a lot of wine, and occasionally addressed a remark to his neighbour.

Frau von Rinnlingen had so far spoken not a word to Herr Friedemann at table; now she leaned forward a little and called across to him:

'I've been waiting in vain these last few days for you to pay me a visit with your fiddle.'

He gazed at her vacantly for a moment before answering. She was wearing a pale-coloured, light evening gown that left her white neck showing, and in her gleaming hair she had fastened a Maréchal Niel rose in full bloom. Her cheeks were slightly flushed this evening, but there were blue shadows, as always, in the corners of her eyes.

Herr Friedemann looked down at his place and stammered out some kind of reply; whereupon he also had to answer the headmaster's wife, who inquired whether he was fond of Beethoven. At this point however

Lieutenant-Colonel von Rinnlingen, at the head of the table, exchanged glances with his wife, tapped his glass and said:

'Ladies and gentlemen, I suggest we take our coffee in the other rooms. And it must be rather pleasant in the garden too, on an evening like this; if anyone cares to take a spot of air out there, I'll be very glad to do the same.'

Lieutenant von Deidesheim tactfully cracked a joke to break the silence which followed, and everyone rose from table amid peals of laughter. Herr Friedemann was one of the last to leave the dining-room with his partner; he escorted her, through the room decorated in medieval style in which the guests were already beginning to smoke, into the dimly lit luxurious drawing-room, and there took leave of her.

He was most carefully attired, in faultless evening dress with a dazzlingly white shirt and with patent leather shoes on his slender, neatly shaped feet. From time to time it could be observed that he was wearing red silk socks.

He looked out into the corridor and saw that quite large numbers of people were already going downstairs into the garden. But he sat down with his cigar and his coffee near the door of the medieval smoking-room, in which a few of the gentlemen were standing around talking, and from here he looked into the drawing-room.

At a table immediately to the right of the door a small circle had formed around the student, who was discoursing volubly. He had asserted that more than one parallel to a given straight line could be drawn through one and the same point; Dr Hagenström's wife had exclaimed, 'But that's impossible!' and he was now proving his proposition so cogently that everyone was pretending to have understood it.

But at the back of the room, on the divan, by the low lamp with the red shade, sat Gerda von Rinnlingen, in conversation with young Fräulein Stephens. She sat half reclined against the yellow silk cushion, with her legs crossed, and was smoking a cigarette in a leisurely manner, blowing the smoke out through her nose and protruding her lower lip. Fräulein Stephens sat facing her bolt-upright like a statue, answering her with a nervous smile.

No one noticed little Herr Friedemann, and no one noticed that his large eyes were fixed incessantly on Frau von Rinnlingen. He sat limply and gazed at her. There was no passion in his gaze, scarcely even any pain; only a dull, dead expression of senseless, powerless, will-less surrender.

About ten minutes passed in this manner; then Frau von Rinnlingen suddenly got up, and without looking at him, as if she had been secretly observing him all this time, she walked over and stopped in front of him. He rose to his feet, looked up at her and heard her say:

'Would you like to come into the garden with me, Herr Friedemann?'

He answered:

'With pleasure, Frau Commandant.'

## 15

'So you haven't yet seen our garden?' she asked him as they went downstairs. 'It's quite big. I hope there won't be too many people there already; I should like to get away from them all for a little. I got a headache during dinner; perhaps that red wine was too strong for me . . . This is our way out, through this door.' It was a glass door leading from the hall into a small cool passage, from which they went down a few steps into the open air.

It was a wonderfully warm clear starlit night, and all the flower-beds were pouring out their fragrance. The full moon was shining down on the garden, and along the gleaming white gravel paths the guests were strolling about, talking and smoking. One group had gathered round the fountain, where the elderly doctor whom everyone liked was causing general merriment by sailing paper boats.

Frau von Rinnlingen walked past them with a slight inclination of the head, and pointed into the distance where the elegant flower garden darkened into a park.

'Let's go down the centre avenue,' she said. At the head of it stood two short thick obelisks.

At the far end of the dead-straight chestnut-lined avenue they could see the greenish glint of the moonlit river. All round them it was dark and cool. Here and there a side-path branched off; these probably all curved down to the river as well. For a long time not a sound could be heard.

'There's a pretty place beside the water,' she said, 'where I've often been. We could sit there and talk for a few minutes. Look, now and then one can see a star glittering between the leaves.'

He made no answer, and stared at the green glimmering surface of the water as they approached it. The far bank was visible, where the public gardens were and the old city wall. At the end of the avenue, as they emerged on to the open grass that sloped down to the river, Frau von Rinnlingen said:

'Here is our spot, a little to the right; look, there's no one else there.'

The seat they sat down on had its back to the park, a few yards to one side of the avenue. It was warmer here than among the great trees. The crickets chirped in the grass, which at the very edge of the water ended in a thin line of reeds. The river gleamed palely in the moonlight.

They both sat in silence for a while, looking at the water. Then he listened with a sudden shock of emotion, for she was speaking again in that soft, gentle, pensive voice he had heard a week ago.

'How long have you had your disability, Herr Friedemann?' she asked. 'Were you born with it?'

He swallowed, for his throat felt constricted as if he were choking. Then he answered gently and politely:

'No, Frau Commandant. When I was a baby I was dropped on the floor, and that caused it.'

'How old are you now?' she went on.

'Thirty, Frau Commandant.'

'Thirty,' she repeated. 'So you have not been happy during these thirty years?'

Herr Friedemann shook his head, and his lips trembled. 'No,' he said. 'It was a lie and an illusion.'

'So you believed you were happy?' she asked.

'I tried to,' he said, and she replied:

'That was brave of you.'

A minute passed. Only the crickets chirped, and the tree behind them rustled softly.

Then she said: 'I have had some experience of unhappiness. These summer nights by the water are the best remedy for it.'

He made no reply to this, but gestured weakly, pointing across to the opposite bank, where all was peaceful and dark.

'I sat there the other day,' he said.

'Just after you had been to see me?' she asked.

He merely nodded.

Then suddenly, shuddering all over, he started to his feet, uttering a sobbing noise, a moan of sorrow which was somehow at the same time a cry of relief, and slowly sank to the ground in front of her. He had put his hand on hers, which had lain beside him on the seat; he clutched it now and seized the other as well; and as this little, totally deformed creature knelt there before her, quivering convulsively and burying his face in her lap, he stammered out in a hardly human, strangled voice:

'But you know! You know I . . . Let me . . . I can't go on . . . Oh my God . . . my God . . .'

She did not push him away, nor did she lower her head towards him. She sat erect, leaning back slightly, and her small close-set eyes, which seemed to mirror the liquid glint of the water, stared intently straight ahead, beyond him, into the distance.

And then, with a sudden violent movement, with a short, proud, scornful laugh, she had snatched her hands from his burning fingers, seized him by the arm, flung him sideways right on to the ground, leapt to her feet and vanished into the avenue.

He lay there with his face in the grass, stunned and desperate, with his body shuddering and twitching. He picked himself up, took two steps and collapsed again on to the grass. He was lying by the water's edge.

What was really his state of mind, his motive in what followed? Perhaps it was that same voluptuous hatred he had felt when she humbled him with her eyes; and now that he was lying here on the ground like a dog she had kicked, did this hatred perhaps degenerate into an insane fury which had to be translated into action, even if it was only action against himself – did it become an access of self-disgust, a craving to annihilate himself, to tear himself to pieces, to blot himself out . . .?

He dragged himself on his stomach further down the slope, lifted the upper part of his body and let it drop into the water. He did not raise his head again; even his legs on the bank lay still.

The splash had silenced the crickets for a moment. Now they began their chirping as before, the park rustled softly and down the long avenue came the muted sound of laughter.

# The Joker

*Der Bajazzo*

1897

# The Joker

The end of it all, the upshot of life – of my life – is the disgust with which it fills me. A worthy ending indeed! Disgust with it all, disgust with the whole thing, this disgust that chokes me, goads me to frenzy and casts me down again into despair – sooner or later, no doubt, it will give me the necessary impetus to cut short the whole ridiculous, contemptible business and clear out for good. True enough, I may well hold out for a month or two yet; maybe for another three or six months I shall carry on eating, sleeping and passing the time – in the same mechanical, calm and well ordered fashion in which my life has outwardly gone by all this winter, contrasting so hideously with the vile process of my inner disintegration. One might almost suppose that a man's inner experiences become all the more violent and disturbing the more undisturbed and uncommitted and detached from the world his outward life is. There is no help for it: life has to be lived – and if one refuses to be a man of action and retires into the quiet of a hermit's solitude, even then the vicissitudes of existence will assault one inwardly, they will still be there to test one's character and to prove one a hero or a half-wit.

I have equipped myself with this neat notebook in order to write down my so-called 'story'. Why, I wonder? Perhaps just in order to have something to do? As an interesting psychological study perhaps, and to relish the thought that it was all in accordance with necessity? Necessity is so consoling! And perhaps even in order to enjoy an occasional sense of superiority over myself, an occasional moment of something like indifference? For I realize that indifference would be happiness of a kind.

# 1

It seems so far away and long ago, the little old town with its narrow angular streets and gabled houses, its Gothic churches and fountains, its industrious, respectable and simple inhabitants and the stately old grey patrician house in which I grew up.

The house stood in the centre of the town, and had outlasted four generations of rich and respected merchants. 'Ora et labora' was the motto over the front door. The great stone-paved entrance hall had a white wooden gallery running round it, and a wide stairway leading up to another spacious landing, after which one still had to walk along a dark little pillared lobby before passing through one of the tall white doors into the drawing-room where my mother sat playing the piano.

She sat in a dim light, for heavy dark red curtains hung across the windows; and the white gods and goddesses on the wallpaper seemed to stand out like real rounded figures from their blue background, and to be listening to the deep heavy opening notes of that Chopin nocturne, the piece she especially loved and always played very slowly as if to savour to the utmost the sadness of every chord. The grand piano was old and not as resonant as it had once been, but with the help of the soft pedal, which veiled the high notes so that they sounded like dull silver, the most unusual effects could be produced on it.

I would sit on the massive, straight-backed, damask sofa, listening to my mother and watching her. She was small and delicately built and usually wore a dress of soft, pale grey material. Her slender face was not beautiful, but under her parted, slightly wavy, unobtrusively blond hair it was like a peaceful, delicate, dreamy child's face, and as she sat at the piano with her head slightly to one side she resembled those small touching angelic figures often seen on old pictures, at the feet of the Madonna, playing on guitars.

When I was little she would often, in her gentle discreet voice, tell me tales of wonder such as no one else knew; or she would simply lay her hands on my head where it rested on her lap, and sit without speaking or stirring. I think those were the happiest and most contented hours of my life. Her hair did not turn grey, and she never seemed to me to grow any older; her figure merely became more and more fragile and her face slenderer, dreamier and more peaceful.

But my father was a tall stout gentleman in an elegant black coat and a white waistcoat, on which his gold pince-nez dangled. Between his short iron-grey side-whiskers his chin, clean-shaven like his upper lip, stood out roundly and firmly, and between his eyebrows there were always two deep vertical furrows. He was a man of considerable power and influence in public affairs; I have seen some men leave his presence with quickened breath and eyes aglow, others apparently broken and in utter despair. For it sometimes happened that I, and occasionally my mother and two elder sisters as well, were present at such scenes; perhaps because my father wanted to stimulate in me an ambition to rise as high in the world as he had done; or perhaps, as I suspect, because he needed an audience. Even as a child I was led to surmise this by the way he had of leaning back against his chair, with one hand thrust into his lapel, to watch the departure of his elated or discomfited visitor.

I would sit in a corner and observe my father and mother, rather as if I were choosing between the two of them and considering whether it was better to lead a life of dreamy meditation or one of action and power. And in the end it was on my mother's peaceful face that my eyes lingered.

2

One could not say that I resembled her in my outward behaviour, for the greater part of my occupations were by no means quiet and noiseless. I remember one to which I was passionately devoted: I preferred it to any association with companions of my own age and the kind of games they liked, and even now, when I am nearly thirty, the thought of it amuses and delights me.

What I am referring to was a large and well equipped puppet theatre: with this I would shut myself up all alone in my room and on its stage I would produce very remarkable music dramas. My room was on the second floor and contained gloomy portraits of two of our ancestors with pointed seventeenth-century beards. I would draw the curtains and stand a lamp near the theatre, for I considered that artificial lighting was necessary to heighten the effect. I seated myself immediately in front of the stage, for I was also the conductor, and I placed my left hand on a large round cardboard box which was the only visible orchestral instrument.

The performers now also arrived: I had drawn them myself with pen and ink, cut them out and fastened them to strips of wood so that they could stand. The men wore overcoats and top hats, and the women were very beautiful.

'Good evening, ladies and gentlemen!' I would say. 'I trust you are all in good health? I have arrived already, as there were still a few preparations to be made. But I think it is now time to proceed to the dressing-rooms.'

They proceeded to the dressing-rooms at the back of the stage, and presently returned completely transfigured into colourful theatrical characters. I had cut a peep-hole in the curtain through which they could look to see if the house was well filled; and so indeed it was. I rang the bell to warn myself that the performance was about to begin, then raised my baton and paused to savour the profound silence which this gesture imposed. But immediately, upon my next motion, the overture began with a deep premonitory roll of drums, executed by my left hand on the lid of the cardboard box; this was joined by the trumpets, clarinets and flutes, the timbre of which my mouth reproduced with incomparable fidelity; and thus the music continued until, at a mighty crescendo, the curtain swept up and revealed the dark forest or resplendent hall in which the opening scene of the drama was to take place.

The action had been roughly thought out in advance, but the details had to be improvised. The vocal strains, accompanied by the warbling of the clarinets and the drone of my cardboard drum, were sweet and passionate, and the text was strange and sonorous: verses full of bold and grandiose words, which occasionally rhymed but seldom made sense. The opera nevertheless took its course: with my left hand I drummed, with my mouth I sang and played, and with my right hand I conducted not only the performers on the stage but everyone else, with such diligent care that as each act ended enthusiastic applause broke out, the curtain had to rise again and again and the conductor was often obliged to turn round on his rostrum and express his thanks with a dignified but gratified bow to the auditorium.

And indeed, as I packed up my theatre after such a performance, flushed by my exertions, I would feel both exhausted and happy, as a great artist must feel at the triumphant completion of a work in which he has given of his best. This game remained my favourite occupation until I was thirteen or fourteen years old.

## 3

How in fact did they pass, my childhood and boyhood, in that great house with its ground-floor rooms where my father conducted his business, while my mother sat upstairs dreaming in an armchair or softly and pensively playing the piano, and my two sisters, who were two and three years older than me, busied themselves in the kitchen or with the household linen? I can remember so little about it all.

What is certain is that I was a prodigiously lively boy, and that I succeeded in making myself respected and liked by my schoolmates on account of my privileged background, my exemplary imitations of the masters, a large variety of histrionic feats and a rather superior manner of expressing myself. But in class I did badly, for I was far too preoccupied with studying the comic possibilities of the masters' movements and gestures to pay attention to anything else, and at home my head was so full of operatic plots, verses and a medley of other nonsense that any serious attempt to work was out of the question.

'Disgraceful!' my father would say, with the furrows deepening between his brows, when I had brought my school report into the drawing-room after luncheon and he had read it through, standing there with one hand in his lapel. 'You're a disappointment to me, I must say. Will you have the goodness to tell me what is to become of you? I can't see you ever making your way in life . . .'

That was depressing; but it did not prevent me from reading aloud to my parents and sisters, after dinner on that same day, a poem I had composed during the afternoon. My father laughed as I read, making his pince-nez bounce about all over his white waistcoat. 'What a pack of nonsense!' he kept exclaiming. But my mother drew me close to her, stroked my hair back from my forehead and said: 'It's not at all bad, my dear. I think there are one or two quite nice passages in it.'

Later, when I was a little older, I taught myself on my own initiative to play the piano after a fashion. I began by striking F-sharp major chords because I found the black notes particularly attractive; from this point I explored modulations into other keys and gradually, by dint of long hours at the instrument, acquired a certain facility in the art of harmonic variation and could produce a mystic wash of sound which had neither rhythm nor melody but was as expressive as I could make it.

My mother said: 'He has a very tasteful touch.' And she arranged for me to have piano lessons, which were kept up for six months; I really had no aptitude for learning the correct fingering and rhythm.

Well, the years went by and I grew up, enjoying myself enormously despite my troubles at school. I circulated among my acquaintances and relations, happy and popular, and I behaved adroitly and charmingly to them because I liked playing the charmer, though instinctively I was beginning to despise all these prosaic, unimaginative people.

## 4

One afternoon when I was about eighteen and on the point of entering the top classes at school, I overheard a short conversation between my parents, who were sitting together in the drawing-room at the round sofa table and did not know that I was next door in the dining-room, lying idly in the window-seat and contemplating the pale sky above the gabled roofs. When I heard my name mentioned I tiptoed to the white double door, which was standing ajar.

My father was leaning back in his chair with his legs crossed holding the Stock Exchange journal with one hand on his knee and slowly stroking his chin between his mutton-chop whiskers with the other. My mother was sitting on the sofa with her peaceful face bowed over some embroidery. The lamp stood between them.

My father said: 'In my view it's about time he was removed from school and entered for training with some large, well established firm.'

'Oh!' exclaimed my mother, looking up in dismay. 'Such a talented boy!'

My father was silent for a moment and carefully blew a speck of dust from his coat. Then he hunched his shoulders and spread out his arms, turning the palms of his hands towards my mother, and said:

'If you suppose, my dear, that to do well in business requires no talent, then let me tell you that you are mistaken. In any case I regret to say that it is becoming increasingly clear to me that the boy is getting absolutely nowhere at school. His talent, as you call it, is the talent of a kind of mimicking buffoon or joker – though let me hasten to add that I do not by any means underestimate such gifts. He can be charming when he wants to be, he knows how to handle people, how to amuse and flatter them; he has a need to please them and to be a success with them. Many a man with that sort of disposition has made his fortune by it; and in view of his indifference to everything else I would say that his qualifications for a fairly successful business career are relatively good.'

Having thus delivered himself my father leaned back with a satisfied air, took a cigarette from his cigarette-case and lit it with deliberation.

'I dare say you are right,' said my mother, and her eyes wandered unhappily round the room. 'It's just that I have often thought, and in a way hoped, that one day he might become an artist . . . It's true I suppose that his musical gifts have remained undeveloped and that we can't expect anything to come of them; but have you noticed that since he went to the little art exhibition recently he has been doing some drawing? And he draws not at all badly, I think.'

My father blew a puff of smoke, adjusted himself in his chair and said curtly:

'That's all clowning and hocus-pocus. Anyway we can, of course, as is only right, consult the boy's own wishes.'

My own wishes! And what might they be? But I found the prospect of a change in my outward circumstances distinctly cheering. I declared with a solemn face that I was willing to leave school and become a businessman; and I was duly apprenticed to Herr Schlievogt's big timber firm down by the river.

# 5

Needless to say, the change was purely external. My interest in Herr Schlievogt's big timber business was extremely slight, and I sat on my revolving stool under the gaslight in that dark narrow office feeling as much a stranger and as absent in spirit as I had felt in the schoolroom. I had fewer worries now; that was the only difference.

Herr Schlievogt, a corpulent, red-faced man with a stiff grey nautical beard, paid little attention to me, since he spent most of his time in the sawmill which was some distance from the timber yard and offices. His employees treated me with respect. I entertained friendly relations with only one of them, a gifted and self-satisfied young man of good family whose acquaintance I had already made at school and whose name was Schilling. Like myself he made fun of everyone and everything, but he none the less took a very lively interest in the timber trade and never let a day pass without declaring it to be his definite purpose to become, somehow or other, a rich man.

I for my part mechanically carried out my necessary duties and devoted the rest of the day to sauntering about the yard among the workmen and the stacks of timber, gazing through the high wooden fence at the river, where a freight train occasionally lumbered by, and as I sauntered and gazed I would be thinking about some theatrical performance or concert I had attended, or some book I had read.

I read a great deal, in fact I read everything I could lay my hands on, and I was exceedingly impressionable. I had an intuitive understanding of the personalities of authors, I seemed to see in each of them a reflection of myself, and I would go on thinking and feeling in the style of a particular book until a new one had influenced me in its turn. In my room, the room where I had once set up my puppet theatre, I now sat with a book on my knees, looking up at the portraits of my two ancestors, savouring the inflections of the writer to whom I had surrendered myself, and with an unproductive chaos of half-formed thoughts and fanciful images filling my mind . . .

My sisters had got married in quick succession, and when I was not at the office I often went down to the drawing-room, where my mother would now usually be sitting quite alone. She was slightly ailing and her face was growing more and more placid and childlike. When she had played me some Chopin and I had showed her some newly discovered trick of harmonic modulation, she would sometimes ask me whether I was contented in my work and happy . . . There was no doubt that I was happy.

I was not much more than twenty, my situation was a merely provisional one, and I not infrequently reflected that I was by no means obliged to spend my life working for Herr Schlievogt or for any other timber business, however prosperous. I told myself that I should one day be able to kick over the traces, leave this town and its gabled houses behind me and live somewhere or other doing exactly as I pleased: reading good, elegantly written novels, going to the theatre, playing the piano a little . . . Happy? But after all I ate extremely well, I wore the best clothes, and even when I was younger and still at school I had noticed how my poorer and shabbily dressed contemporaries habitually deferred to me and to others like me, treating us with a kind of flattering diffidence which indicated their willing acceptance of us as lords and leaders of fashion: and this had made me happily conscious of the fact that I belonged to the élite, to that class of rich and envied persons whose birthright it is to look down on the poor, the unlucky and the envious with benevolent contempt. Had I not every reason to be happy? I was content to let things take their course. For the time being it was very gratifying to live as a rather alien, effortlessly superior figure among these acquaintances and relations of mine whose limited outlook I found so amusing but to whom, because I liked to be liked, I behaved with adroit charm. I basked complacently in the respect which they all showed me; but it remained a puzzled respect, for they obscurely sensed something antagonistic and extravagant in my nature and character.

# 6

A change was beginning to come over my father. Every day when he joined us for dinner at four o'clock the furrows between his brows seemed to have grown deeper, and he no longer thrust his hand into his lapel with an imposing gesture, but looked depressed, nervous and diffident. One day he said to me:

'You are old enough by now to share with me the anxieties which are undermining my health. It is in any case my duty to acquaint you with them, in case you should be entertaining any false expectations with regard to your future position in life. As you know, the marriages of your sisters entailed considerable sacrifices. And recently the firm has suffered losses which have reduced the capital quite severely. I am an old man, I have lost heart, and I think it is too late now to expect any appreciable improvement in the situation. I must ask you to take note that you will be cast upon your own resources . . .'

He said this about two months before his death. One day he was found slumped in the armchair in his private office, pallid, paralysed and mumbling inarticulately. A week later the whole town attended his funeral.

My mother sat quietly on the sofa by the round table in the drawing-room; she looked frail and her eyes were nearly always closed. When my sisters and I attended to her needs, she would perhaps nod and smile, but then she would sit on in silence, motionless, with her hands folded on her lap and her strange sad wide-eyed gaze fixed on one of the gods in the wallpaper pattern. When the gentlemen in frock coats came to report on the liquidation of the firm, she would nod in the same way and close her eyes again.

She no longer played Chopin, and when now and then she gently stroked her hair, her pale, frail, tired hand would tremble. Hardly six months after my father's death she took to her bed and died without a murmur, letting her life go without a struggle . . .

So now all that was over. What was there to keep me in the place? The business had been wound up, for better or for worse, and it turned out that my inheritance was about a hundred thousand marks. That was enough to make me independent – completely independent, particularly as I had, for some reason or other which is of no consequence, been declared unfit for military service.

There were no longer any ties between me and these people among whom I had grown up, who looked at me now with an air of increasing estrangement and bewilderment, and whose outlook on life was far too narrow for me to have any wish to conform to it. True, they recognized me for what I was – an absolutely useless individual. Even I recognized this. But I was sufficiently sceptical and fatalistic to take a light-hearted view of what my father had called my 'talent of a buffoon or joker'. I was cheerfully determined to enjoy life in my own way, and thoroughly satisfied with myself.

I took possession of my small fortune and left my native town, almost without saying goodbye. I intended in the first instance to travel.

# 7

The three years that now followed, those years in which I surrendered myself with eager appetite to a host of new, changing, enriching impressions, have remained in my memory like an enchanting, faraway dream. How long is it since I spent that night with the monks up on the Simplon Pass, celebrating New Year's Eve amid ice and snow? How long since I strolled across the Piazza Erbe in Verona? since I stepped out for the first time from the Borgo Santo Spirito into the colonnade at Saint Peter's and let my eyes wander awestruck over that enormous square? since I stood on the Corso Vittorio Emmanuele looking down over the gleaming white buildings of Naples and saw the graceful silhouette of Capri far out to sea, just visible in the blue haze? . . . In actual fact it was all scarcely more than six years ago.

Oh, to be sure, I lived very prudently and in a manner befitting my situation: in simple private rooms, in cheap boarding-houses – but what with moving from place to place, and because I found it hard at first to do without the upper-middle-class comforts to which I was accustomed, I nevertheless could not help spending considerable sums of money. I had set aside fifteen thousand marks from my capital for my period of travelling; this sum, needless to say, was exceeded.

I felt at ease, however, among the people with whom my wanderings brought me in contact; often they were disinterested and very interesting acquaintances, and although I was of course not an object of respect to them as I had been in my previous environment, I at least had no need to fear that they would look at me askance or ask me questions.

Occasionally my particular social accomplishments made me genuinely popular with the clientele of boarding-houses at which I stayed. I remember especially a scene in the public room at the Pensione

Minelli in Palermo. Amid a circle of Frenchmen of various ages I had somehow begun to play the piano and to improvise a music drama 'by Richard Wagner', with much tragic grimacing, declamatory song and rolling harmony. I had just finished, to thunderous applause, when an old gentleman hastened up to me. He was almost totally bald, with scanty white mutton-chop whiskers drooping over his grey travelling coat. He seized both my hands and exclaimed with tears in his eyes:

'But that was fantastic! That was fantastic, my dear sir! I swear I have not been so delightfully entertained for the last thirty years! Pray, sir, allow me to thank you from the bottom of my heart! But you must, yes you must, become an actor or a musician!'

I confess that on such occasions I felt something of the pride of genius, such as a great painter must feel who has condescended to scribble an absurd yet brilliant caricature on the top of a table at which he is sitting among friends. After dinner however I returned alone to the sitting-room and passed a solitary and wistful hour coaxing the instrument into a series of sustained chords, expressive, as I thought, of the mood inspired in me by the sight of Palermo.

From Sicily I had paid a fleeting visit to Africa, then I had gone on to Spain; and it was there, in the country near Madrid, on a dreary wet winter afternoon, that I first became conscious of a wish to return to Germany – and realized, moreover, that it was now necessary for me to do so. For apart from the fact that I was beginning to long for a quiet, regular and settled existence, it was not hard to calculate that by the time I reached Germany, however much I economized, I should have spent twenty thousand marks.

I began my slow return journey through France without over-much delay, but lingered for some time in this town and that, so that it took nearly six months. I remember with nostalgic clarity the summer evening on which my train drew into the main station of the provincial capital in central Germany which I had already selected as my destination before setting out. And now I had reached it – a little wiser, the richer by some experiences, equipped with some items of know-ledge, and full of childlike delight at the prospect of establishing myself here in carefree independence, subject of course to the limits of my modest means, and settling down to a life of untroubled, contemplative leisure.

At that time I was twenty-five years old.

# 8

It was not a bad choice of place. The town is an important centre, still free of the excessive noise and bustle and ugly industrialization of a very large city, but containing some quite spacious old squares and streets which lack neither liveliness nor a certain elegance. On its outskirts there are a number of pleasant spots, but my favourite among them has always been the so-called Lerchenberg promenade, a tastefully laid-out avenue traversing the long narrow hill on the side of which most of the town is built and from which one has an extensive view over the houses and churches, across the gently meandering river and into the distance. At certain points, especially on fine summer afternoons when a military band is playing and carriages and pedestrians are circulating, it is reminiscent of the Pincio. But I shall have occasion to refer again to this promenade . . .

I had rented a fair-sized room, with a small adjoining bedroom, in a lively district near the centre of the town, and I took an incredibly elaborate pleasure in furnishing it. Most of my parents' furniture, to be sure, had passed into my sisters' possession, but enough of it had come my way to suffice for my needs: handsome, solid pieces, which now arrived together with my books and the two family portraits, and above all the old grand piano, which my mother had specially bequeathed to me.

And in fact, when everything had been set up in its place – when every wall, the heavy mahogany desk and the commodious chest of drawers, had been adorned with the photographs I had collected during my travels –when with my arrangements made and all secure I let myself sink into an armchair by the window and proceeded by turns to look out into the streets and to survey my new lodging – I felt an undoubted sense of well-being. Yet nevertheless (for it was a moment I have not forgotten) amid all my contentment and confidence there was something else softly stirring within me: some slight misgiving and uneasiness, some half-conscious impulse of revolt and rebellion against a power that menaced me . . . It was the faintly depressing thought that my situation, which had hitherto never been more than merely provisional, must now for the first time be regarded as definitive and permanent . . .

I will not deny that I occasionally felt a recurrence of this and similar sensations. But how, after all, can any of us hope to avoid certain late-afternoon moods: those moments in which we gaze out into the gathering dusk, perhaps into a drizzle of rain as well, and are assailed by twinges of foreboding? I could at all events be certain that my future was fully provided for. I had entrusted the round sum of eighty thousand marks to the city bank; the interest – these are poor times, heaven knows! – amounted to about six hundred marks a quarter, and this was enough to permit me to live decently, to buy books, to go to the theatre now and then – not excluding an occasional lighter diversion.

From that time on I really did pass my days in a manner conforming to the ideal to which I had always aspired – I got up at ten, had breakfast, spent part of the morning at the piano and the rest of it reading a literary periodical or a book. At midday I strolled down the street to the little restaurant which I regularly patronized, and had lunch there; then I would go for a fairly long walk along the streets, round a gallery, through the outskirts of the town, up to the Lerchenberg. On returning home I would resume my morning's occupations: reading, making music, sometimes even drawing, after a fashion, to amuse myself, or writing a carefully penned letter. In the evening, if I was not going to a play or a concert after dinner, I sat on at the café reading the papers till bedtime. And I would assess the day as a good one, as one that had contained some pleasure and happiness, if I had succeeded in producing at the piano some effect which struck me as new and beautiful, or if in reading a short story or looking at a picture I had experienced some emotion which had lasted for a while . . .

I will, however, not omit to mention that there was a certain idealistic purposefulness in my arrangements, that I made it my serious business to ensure that each of my days should 'contain' as much as possible. I ate modestly, I usually had only one suit, in short I carefully limited my bodily needs in order to be able to afford a good seat at the opera or an expensive concert ticket, and to be in a position to buy the latest literary publications or visit an occasional art exhibition . . .

But the days went by, and they turned into weeks and months – was I bored? I will concede that one does not always have a book that will yield hour after hour of memorable experience; moreover one's attempts to improvise at the piano have at times been complete failures, and one has sat by the window, smoking cigarettes, while gradually and irresistibly a feeling of distaste creeps over one, distaste for oneself and for everything else. Once again one is assailed by misgiving, by that unpleasantly familiar misgiving – and one jumps from one's chair, one leaves the house and walks along the streets, watching those others go by: the people with jobs, the people with professions, at whom one can cheerfully shrug one's shoulders, in happy contempt for the intellectual inferiority and material misfortune which deprives them of leisure and of the capacity to enjoy it.

## 9

Is it possible for any man, at the age of twenty-seven, seriously to believe that his situation has been unalterably finalized, however depressingly probable this may in fact be? The twittering of a bird, a tiny gap of blue in the sky, some half-remembered dream when one wakes in the morning – all these are enough to flood one's heart with sudden vague hopes, to fill it with a festive expectation of some great unforeseen happiness . . . I drifted from one day to the next, meditatively, aimlessly, my mind busy with this or that trivial hope, even looking forward to such things as the next issue of an amusing periodical: I was filled with the resolute conviction that I was happy, but from time to time I felt the weariness of solitude.

If the truth were told, they were by no means rare, these moods of exasperation at the thought of my lack of friends and social intercourse; for this lack scarcely needs explaining. I had no connections with the best or even with the second-best local society; to get on a convivial footing with the *jeunesse dorée* I should have needed, God knows, a great deal more money than I possessed; and as for bohemian circles – why, damn it, I am a man of education, I wear clean linen and a decent suit: am I supposed to enjoy sitting with unkempt young men round tables sticky with absinthe, discussing anarchism? In brief: there was no specific social circle to which I obviously belonged, and such acquaintanceships as I happened in one way or another to make were few and far between, superficial and uncordial – this, I admit, was my own fault, for in these cases too I behaved with diffident reserve, disagreeably conscious of the fact that I was unable to tell even a down-at-heel painter, in brief clear words that would command his respect, who and what I actually was.

I had, of course, severed my ties with 'society' and renounced it, as soon as I had taken the liberty of going my own way instead of somehow making myself useful to it. Had I needed 'other people' in order to be happy? If so, then I was bound to ask myself whether I should not now have been busy enriching myself as a fairly successful entrepreneur, who would at the same time be serving the community and earning its envy and esteem.

Whereas – whereas! The fact remained that I was finding my philosophic isolation excessively vexing, and in the last resort quite inconsistent with my conception of 'happiness' – with my consciousness, my conviction, that I was happy. And that this conviction should be shaken was, of course, beyond any shadow of doubt quite out of the question. Not to be happy – to be unhappy – why, was this even thinkable? It was unthinkable. Thus I decided, and thus I disposed of the question – until the mood returned and I felt again that there was something wrong, something very far wrong, about my self-isolation, my retired seclusion, my outsider's life. And this thought put me most shockingly out of humour.

Is one 'out of humour' if one is happy? I remembered my earlier life in my native town, that restricted society in which I had moved, full of the gratifying consciousness of my artistic gifts and genius – sociable, charming, my eyes sparkling with high-spirited mockery and an air of benevolent superiority to everyone; people had thought me rather odd, but I had nevertheless been popular. I had been happy then, in spite of having to work in Herr Schlievogt's big timber firm. And what was I now?

But after all, an absolutely fascinating book has just been published, a new French novel which I have decided I can afford to buy and which I shall have leisure to enjoy, sitting comfortably in my armchair. Another three hundred pages, full of taste, *blague* and exquisite artistry! Come now, I have arranged my life the way I wanted it! Can I possibly not be happy? The question is ridiculous. The question is utterly absurd . . .

## 10

Another day has drawn to a close, a day which has undeniably, thank God, contained its quota of pleasure; darkness has fallen, I have drawn the curtains and lit the reading lamp; it is nearly midnight. I could go to bed; instead of which I sit on in my armchair, leaning right back with my hands folded on my lap, gazing at the ceiling, and attending submissively to the noiseless delving and gnawing of some scarcely identifiable distress which I have been unable to shake off.

Only a couple of hours ago I was allowing a great masterpiece to do its work on me – one of those monstrous, cruel masterpieces by an unprincipled dilettantistic genius, full of decadent splendours that shake and dumbfound the spectator, torture him to ecstasy and overwhelm him . . . My nerves are still quivering, my imagination has been violently stirred, strange moods are surging up and down within me, moods of passionate longing, of religious ardour, of exultation, of mystic peace – and mingled with all this is a craving, an impulse that constantly restimulates these moods, an impulse to work them out of my system: the need to express them, to communicate them, to 'make something of them' . . .

What if I really were an artist, capable of expressing myself in sound, or words, or visual images – or rather, as I should frankly prefer, in all three simultaneously? And yet it is true that I have all sorts of talents! For example, first and foremost, I can sit down at the piano and treat myself, in the intimacy of my own room, to a display of my beautiful feelings: surely that is enough? For if I needed 'other people' in order to be happy, then I – yes, well, all this I concede. But let us suppose that I did set some slight store by success, by fame, recognition, praise, envy, love? . . . Oh, God, if I so much as think of the scene at that inn in Palermo, I have to admit that it would be so indescribably encouraging and comforting if a similar incident were to happen now!

On careful reflection I feel bound to admit that there must be a distinction (sophistical and absurd though it seems) between internal and external happiness. 'External happiness'! What in fact is it? There is a certain class of human beings who seem to be the favourites of the gods, whose good fortune is their genius and whose genius is their good fortune: they are children of light, and with the sun's radiance mirrored in their eyes they move lightly, gracefully, charmingly, playfully through life, admiringly surrounded by everyone, praised and envied and loved by everyone, because even envy cannot bring itself to hate them. But they return the general gaze as rather spoiled children do, with a kind of whimsical irreverent mockery and unclouded goodwill, secure in their good fortune and in their genius, never for a moment entertaining the thought that things might be otherwise . . .

As for myself, I confess my weakness: I should dearly like to belong to that privileged category. And rightly or wrongly, I am still beset by the thought that once upon a time I did belong to it. Whether I am right or wrong in thinking so matters not a jot – for let us be candid: the important thing is what one thinks of oneself, the image one presents of oneself, the image of oneself that one has the confidence to present!

Perhaps in reality the situation is simply that I renounced this 'external happiness' by contracting out of the service of 'society' and arranging to live my life independently of 'other people'. But it goes without saying that I am content with such an arrangement: this is not for one moment to be doubted, it cannot be doubted, it must not be doubted. For let me repeat with desperate emphasis: I intend to be happy, and I must be happy! The conception of 'good fortune' as something meritorious, as a kind of genius, of aristocratic distinction, of special charm, and the contrary conception of 'misfortune' as something ugly, skulking, contemptible and in a word ridiculous, are both so deeply rooted in me that if I were unhappy I should inevitably lose my self-respect.

How could I possibly allow myself to be unhappy? What sort of a figure should I then cut in my own eyes? I should have to squat in outer darkness like some sort of bat or owl, blinking as I gazed enviously across the gulf at the happy, charming 'children of light'. I should have to hate them, with that hatred which is merely love turned sour – and I should have to despise myself!

'To squat in outer darkness'! Oh, it comes back to me now, all I have thought and felt, over and over again for many a month, about my 'outsider's life' and my 'philosophic isolation'! And the anxiety returns, that unpleasantly familiar anxiety! And that vague impulse of rebellion against some menacing power . . .

Needless to say, some consolation was to hand, some anodyne distraction, on this occasion and on the next, and again on the next. But the same reflections returned; all of them returned a thousand times in the course of the months and the years.

## 11

There are certain autumn days that are like a miracle. Summer is already over, the leaves began to turn yellow some time ago, and for days the wind has been whistling all round the streets and muddy water streaming down the gutters. One has resigned oneself to the change of season, one has so to speak taken one's seat by the fire, ready to submit to the coming of winter. But one morning one wakes up and cannot believe one's eyes: between the curtains a narrow strip of brilliant blue is shining into the room. In amazement one leaps out of bed and throws the window open: a flood of tremulous sunlight bursts over one, through all the street noise one can hear the birds happily twittering and chattering, and as one breathes in the light, fresh October air it seems to have exactly the aroma of the wind in May – so incomparably sweet, so incomparably full of promise. It is spring, quite obviously spring, despite the calendar; and one flings on one's clothes and hurries out into the streets, into the open, under this radiant sky . . .

About four months ago – we are now at the beginning of February – there was just such an unexpected and unusual day; and on that day I saw a quite remarkably pretty thing. I had set out in the morning before nine o'clock and was making my way towards the Lerchenberg, light of heart and high in spirits and full of a vague expectation that something or other was going to change, that something surprising and delightful was going to happen. I approached the hill from the right and walked all the way up it and along the top, keeping close to the edge of the main promenade, beside the low stone parapet: from here, for the whole length of the avenue – that is for something like half an hour's walk – I could have an unobstructed view across the town as it drops with a slightly terraced effect down the slope, and over the meandering links of the river as they gleamed in the sunlight, with the hills and greenery of the open countryside lost in a shimmering haze beyond them.

There was hardly anyone else up here yet. The seats on the far side of the promenade were empty, and here and there a statue looked out from among the trees, glittering white in the sun, although now and then a withered leaf would drift slowly down and settle on it. As I walked I watched the bright panorama to one side of me, and listened to the silence, which remained unbroken until I reached the end of the hill where the road begins to dip and is lined with old chestnut trees. But at this point I heard behind me the clatter of horses' hooves and wheels; a carriage was approaching at a brisk trot, and I had to make way for it about half-way down the hill. I stepped aside and paused to let it pass.

It was a small, quite light two-wheeled carriage, drawn by a pair of large, glossy, spirited, snorting bays. The reins were held by a young lady of about nineteen or twenty, and beside her sat an old gentleman of handsome and distinguished appearance, with white moustaches à la russe and bushy white eyebrows. The rear seat was occupied by a smart-looking groom in plain black and silver livery.

The horses had been reined back to a walk at the beginning of the descent, as one of them seemed nervous and refractory. It had pulled clear of the shaft right over to one side, holding its head against its chest, and its slender legs picked their way downhill in so restive and mettlesome a manner that the old gentleman was leaning forward rather anxiously, offering the young lady his elegantly gloved left hand to help her pull the reins tight. The driving seemed to have been entrusted to her only temporarily and only half in earnest: she appeared at any rate to be manoeuvring the vehicle with a mixture of childlike self-importance and inexperience. She was making a solemn, indignant little movement with her head as she tried to control the shying, stumbling animal.

She was dark and slender. Her hair was wound into a firm knot behind her neck but lay quite lightly and loosely over her forehead and temples, where an occasional light brown strand could be seen. On it was perched a round straw hat, dark in colour and decorated only with a modest arrangement of ribbons. For the rest, she was wearing a short dark blue jacket and a simple skirt of light grey material.

In her finely shaped oval face with its dark brown complexion slightly flushed in the morning air, the most attractive feature was undoubtedly her eyes: they were long and narrow, their scarcely visible irises were a glittering black, and the brows arched above them were extraordinarily even, as if traced with a pen. Her nose was perhaps a trifle long, and her mouth might well have been smaller, although her lips were clearly and finely cut. But at the moment it was looking particularly charming, for one could see her gleaming white, rather widely spaced teeth, and as she tugged at the horse the young lady pressed them hard on to her lower lip, giving a slight upward tilt to her almost childishly round chin.

It would be quite incorrect to say that this was a face of outstanding and admirable beauty. It had the charm of youth and freshness and high spirits, and this charm had so to speak been smoothed, refined and ennobled by easy affluence, gentle upbringing and luxurious care. There was no doubt that those narrow, sparkling eyes, which were now concentrated with fastidious petulance on the fractious horse, would in a minute or two resume an expression of secure happiness, of happiness taken for granted. The sleeves of her jacket, widely cut at the shoulders, fitted closely round her slender wrists, and I thought I had never seen anything so enchantingly, so exquisitely elegant as the way those tiny, pale, ungloved hands held the reins!

I stood quite unnoticed by the side of the road as the carriage passed, and walked slowly on as the horses quickened their pace again and rapidly drew out of sight. My feelings were, in the first instance, pleasure and admiration; but I simultaneously became conscious of a strange, burning pain, a bitter, insistent upsurge – of envy? of love? – I did not dare analyse it. Of self-contempt?

As I write, the image that occurs to me is that of a wretched beggar standing outside a jeweller's shop, staring at some precious glittering gem in the window. Such a man cannot let the desire to possess the jewel present itself clearly to his mind: for even the thought of such a desire would be an absurdity, an impossibility, a thought that would make him utterly ridiculous in his own eyes.

## 12

I will report that only a week later, by chance, I saw that young lady again: this time it was at the opera, at a performance of Gounod's *Faust*. I had just entered the brightly lit auditorium and was proceeding towards my seat in the stalls when I caught sight of her, sitting on the old gentleman's left, in a stage box at the other side of the house. I incidentally noticed, ludicrous though it seems, that this rather startled me and threw me into a kind of confusion, so that for some reason I at once averted my eyes and aimlessly surveyed the other boxes and rows of seats. Not until the overture began did I resolve to inspect the pair a little more closely.

The old gentleman, wearing a carefully fastened frock coat with a black silk necktie, was leaning back in his chair in a calm and dignified posture, resting one brown-gloved hand lightly on the plush balustrade of his box, and now and then slowly stroking his beard or his well trimmed grey hair with the other. But the young lady – who was no doubt his daughter – sat leaning forward with an air of lively interest; she had both hands on the balustrade and they were holding her fan. From time to time she made a slight movement with her head to toss back the loose, light brown hair from her forehead and temples.

She was wearing a very light pale silk blouse, with a posy of violets in the girdle; and in the bright lights her narrow eyes were gleaming still blacker than when I had seen her before. I also observed that the expression of her mouth which I had noticed a week ago was evidently a habit with her: not a moment passed but she pressed her lower lip with her little white regularly spaced teeth, and drew up her chin slightly. This innocent gesture in which there was not a trace of coquetry, those calmly yet gaily wandering eyes, that delicate white neck, which she wore uncovered except for a neatly fitting narrow silk ribbon the same colour as her bodice, and the way she turned now and then to draw the old gentleman's attention to something in the orchestra pit or some feature of the curtain or someone in another box – all this made an impression of ineffably subtle childlike charm which was at the same time entirely unsentimental and aroused no kind of 'compassionate' tenderness whatsoever. It was an aristocratic, measured childlikeness, coloured by the security and confidence that come of a refined and gracious way of living. Her evident happiness had nothing arrogant about it: it was the kind of quiet happiness that can be taken for granted.

Gounod's brilliant and tender music was, I thought, no bad accompaniment to this spectacle. As I listened to it I paid no attention to what was happening on the stage and became entirely absorbed in a reflective mood of gentle melancholy, which without this music would perhaps have been more acute. But in the very first interval, after Act I, a gentleman of, let us say, twenty-seven to thirty rose from his seat in the stalls, disappeared and immediately reappeared, with a deftly executed bow, in the box on which my eyes were fixed. The old man at once shook hands with him, and the young lady too, with a cordial inclination of the head, held out hers, which he gracefully raised to his lips; whereupon he was invited to take a seat.

I declare that I am willing to concede that this young man possessed the most incomparable shirt-front that I have ever in my life been privileged to see. It was a shirt-front completely exposed to view, for his waistcoat was no more than a narrow black band and his evening jacket, fastened by one button quite some way below his stomach, was cut out from the shoulders in an unusually sweeping curve. But the shirt-front — which ended in a tall, stiff, smartly turned down butterfly collar and a wide black bow-tie, and was fastened at regular intervals by two large square buttons, also black — was dazzlingly white, and although admirably starched it did not lack flexibility, for in the region of his stomach it formed a pleasing hollow, only to rise again, further up, to a satisfying and gleaming apex.

I need hardly say that it was this shirt that chiefly claimed one's attention; as for his head, however, which was completely spherical and covered with very blond hair cropped close to the skull, it was adorned with a pair of rimless and ribbonless eyeglasses, a none-too-thick blond moustache with slightly curled points, and a number of small duelling scars on one cheek, running right up to the temple. For the rest, this gentleman was of unexceptionable build and moved with an air of assurance.

In the course of the evening — for he remained in the box — I noticed two postures which seemed especially characteristic of him. On the one hand, if conversation with his companions flagged, he would lean comfortably back with his legs crossed and his opera-glasses on his lap, lower his head, energetically protrude the whole of his mouth and relapse into profound contemplation of both points of his moustache, evidently quite hypnotized by them, and slowly and silently turning his head to and fro. If on the other hand he was engaged in discourse with the young lady, he would respectfully modify the position of his legs, but lean back still further, grasping his chair with both hands; as he did so he would raise his head as high as possible and smile, opening his mouth rather wide, charmingly and a shade patronizingly down at his young neighbour. There could be no doubt that this gentleman rejoiced in a wonderfully happy conceit of himself . . .

I declare in all seriousness that these are characteristics which I fully appreciate. The nonchalance of his movements may have been a trifle daring, but not one of them gave rise to a moment's embarrassment; his self-confidence sustained him throughout. And why should it be otherwise? Here, clearly, was a man who while perhaps lacking any particular distinction had irreproachably made his way, and would pursue it to clear and profitable ends; who sheltered in the shade of agreement with all men, and basked in the sunshine of their general approval. And in the mean time there he sat in the box, chattering with a girl to whose pure and exquisite charm he was perhaps not unsusceptible, and whose hand, if this were so, he could with a good conscience request in marriage. Most assuredly, I have no wish to utter a single disrespectful word about this gentleman.

But what of myself? I sat on down here and was at liberty to observe from a distance, peering bitterly out of the darkness, that precious inaccessible creature as she chatted and joked with this contemptible wretch! Excluded, unheeded, unauthorized, a stranger, *hors ligne*, *déclassé*, a pariah, a pitiful object even in my own eyes . . .

I stayed till the end, and I met the trio again in the cloakroom, where they lingered a little as they donned their fur coats, exchanging a word here and there with some lady or some officer . . . The young gentleman accompanied the father and daughter as they left the theatre, and I followed them at a discreet interval across the foyer.

It was not raining, there were a few stars in the sky, and they did not take a carriage. They walked ahead of me at a leisurely pace, talking busily, and some way behind I timidly dogged their footsteps – crushed and tormented by a dreadful feeling of biting, mocking misery . . .

They had not far to walk; it was scarcely a street's length to where they stopped in front of the simple façade of an imposing-looking house, and a moment later the young lady and her father vanished into it after bidding a cordial good-night to their escort, who in turn quickened his pace and disappeared.

The heavy, carved front door of the house bore the title and name 'Justizrat Rainer'.

## 13

I am determined to complete this written record, despite the inner repugnance which constantly impels me to throw down my pen and rush out into the street. I have pondered this affair and brooded over it to the point of utter exhaustion! How sick to death, how nauseated I am by the whole thing! . . .

Not quite three months ago I learned from the papers that a 'bazaar' for charitable purposes had been arranged and would take place in the town hall; and that it would be attended by the best society. I read this announcement attentively and at once decided to go to the bazaar. She will be there, I thought, perhaps selling things at one of the stalls, and in that case there will be nothing to prevent my approaching her. When all is said and done I am a man of education and good family, and if I find this Fräulein Rainer attractive, then on an occasion of that sort I have as much right as the gentleman with the astonishing shirt-front to address her and exchange a few pleasantries with her . . .

It was a windy and rainy afternoon when I betook myself to the town hall; there was a throng of people and carriages in front of the entrance. I managed to penetrate into the building, paid the admission fee, deposited my coat and hat and made my way with some difficulty up the wide, crowded stair to the first floor and into the banqueting hall. The air in here was sultry and smelled heavily of wine, food, scent and pine needles, and there was a confused hubbub of laughter, conversation, music, vendors' cries and ringing gongs.

The vast hall with its enormously high ceiling was gaily festooned with flags and garlands of all colours, and there were vending stalls in the middle of the floor as well as all along the sides – open stalls and closed booths, with men in fantastic masks standing outside the latter and inviting custom at the tops of their voices. The ladies who were standing round selling flowers, needlework, tobacco and various refreshments were also wearing all kinds of costumes. The band was playing loudly at one end of the hall on a platform covered with potted plants; and a tightly packed procession of people was slowly advancing along the rather narrow passageway that had been left between the stalls.

Somewhat stunned by the noise of the music and by the high-spirited shouting from the booths and lottery tubs, I joined the general stream, and scarcely a minute has passed when I caught sight of the young lady I was looking for, a few paces to the left of the entrance. She was selling wine and lemonade at a little stall decorated with pine branches, and she had chosen an Italian costume: the brightly coloured skirt, the four-square white headdress and short bodice such as Albanese women wear, with the sleeves leaving her dainty arms bare to the elbow. She was leaning sideways against her serving-table, slightly flushed, toying with her colourful fan and chatting to a group of men who stood round the stall smoking. Among these I discerned at first glance the figure already familiar to me; he was standing close beside her, with four fingers of each hand in the side pockets of his jacket.

I pressed slowly past, resolving to approach her as soon as an opportunity should present itself, as soon as she was a little less busy. Now, by God, it would be seen whether I still had any remnant of happy self-possession, any pride and *savoir-faire* left in me, or whether my morose, half-desperate mood of the last few weeks had been justified! What on earth had been the matter with me? Why should the sight of this girl fill me with the agonizing miserable mixture of envy, love, shame and bitter resentment with which – I confess it – my cheeks were now once again burning? Single-mindedness! Charm! Lightness of heart, devil take it, and elegant self-complacency, as befits a gifted and fortunate man! And with nervous eagerness I rehearsed the jocular phrase, the *bon mot*, the Italian greeting with which I intended to address her . . .

It was some time before the crowd had clumsily squeezed its way round the room and brought me full circle – and sure enough, when I reached the little wine stall again, the group of gentlemen had dispersed, and only my familiar rival was still leaning against the table, in animated conversation with the young saleswoman. Well then, by his leave, I must take the liberty of interrupting this discussion . . . And with a brisk movement I disengaged myself from the stream and stepped up to the stall.

What happened? Why, nothing! Virtually nothing! The conversation broke off, my rival stepped aside, seized his rimless and ribbonless eyeglasses with all five fingers of one hand and inspected me through these fingers; while the young lady looked me calmly and critically up and down – she surveyed my suit and surveyed my boots. The suit was by no means a new one, and the boots were muddy; I was aware of that. In addition I was flushed, and I dare say it is quite possible that my hair was untidy. I was not cool, I was not at ease, I was not equal to the situation. I was overwhelmed by the feeling that I was intruding, that I was a stranger who had no rights here and did not belong and was making himself ridiculous. Insecurity, helplessness, hatred and pitiful mortification made it impossible for me to return her gaze – in a word, the upshot of my high-spirited intentions was that with darkly knitted brows and in a hoarse voice I said curtly and almost rudely:

'A glass of wine, please.'

It is not of the slightest consequence whether I was right or wrong in thinking that I noticed a fleeting exchange of derisive glances between the girl and her friend. None of us uttered a word as she handed me the wine, and without raising my eyes, red and distraught with rage and anguish, a wretched and ridiculous figure, I stood between the pair of them, gulped a mouthful or two, put the money down on the table, made a confused bow, left the hall and rushed out of the building.

Since that moment I have known that I am doomed; and it makes precious little difference to my story to add that a few days later I read the following notice in the papers:

'Justizrat Rainer has the honour to announce the engagement of his daughter Anna to Herr Assessor Dr Alfred Witznagel.'

## 14

Since that moment I have known that I am doomed. My last fugitive remnant of well-being and self-complacency has collapsed and disintegrated. I can bear no more. Yes, I confess it now: I am unhappy, and I see myself as a pitiful and ridiculous figure. But this is unendurable! It will kill me! Today or tomorrow I shall blow my brains out!

My first impulse, my first instinct, was to try to dramatize the affair and cunningly cloak my contemptible wretchedness in the aesthetic garb of 'unhappy love'. A puerile stratagem, I need hardly say. One does not die of unhappy love. Unhappy love is a pose, and quite a comfortable one. Unhappy love can be a source of self-satisfaction. But what is destroying me is the knowledge that all the self-satisfaction I once possessed is now for ever at an end!

And was I really – let me face the question – was I really in love with this girl? It may be so . . . but in what way and why? Was this love not a product of my already wounded, already sick vanity, my vanity which had flared up agonizingly at the first sight of this precious jewel so far beyond my reach, and had filled me with feelings of envy, hatred and self-contempt for which love had then been no more than a cover, a refuge, a lifeline?

Yes, it has all been vanity! Did my father not long ago call me a buffoon and joker?

What right did I have, I of all people, to hold myself aloof from 'society' and to turn my back on it, I who am too vain to bear its scorn and disregard, I who cannot live without society and without its approval! And yet was it really a matter of what I had or had not the right to do? Was it not a matter of necessity? Could my useless buffooning ever have earned me any social position? No: it was this very thing, this joker's talent, that was bound in any case to destroy me.

I realize that indifference would be happiness of a kind . . . But I am unable to feel that indifference about myself, I am unable to view myself except through the eyes of 'other people' and I am being destroyed by a bad conscience – although I feel in no way to blame! Is even a bad conscience nothing more than festering vanity? .

There is only one real misfortune: to forfeit one's own good opinion of oneself. To have lost one's self-respect: that is what unhappiness is. Oh,

I have always known that so well! Everything else is part of the game, an enrichment of one's life; in every other form of suffering one can feel such extraordinary self-satisfaction, one can cut such a fine figure. Only when one has fallen out with oneself and no longer suffers with a good conscience, only in the throes of stricken vanity – only then does one become a pitiful and repulsive spectacle.

An old acquaintance appeared on the scene, a gentleman of the name of Schilling: long ago, as employees of Herr Schlievogt's big timber firm, we had worked together in the service of society. He was briefly visiting the town on business, and he came to see me – a 'sceptical fellow', with his hands in his trouser pockets, black-rimmed pince-nez and a realistic, tolerant shrug of the shoulders. He arrived one evening and said: 'I shall be here for a few days.' We went and sat in a tavern.

He treated me as if I were still the happy, self-satisfied man he had once known, and thinking in all good faith that he was only echoing my own blithe self-esteem, he said:

'By God, my dear fellow, you've arranged your life very pleasantly! Independent, what? Free! You're right of course, damn it! We only live once, don't we? What does anything else matter, after all? You're the wiser of the two of us, I must say. Of course, you were always a genius . . .' And he continued most cordially, as he had done long ago, to express his respect for me and pay me compliments, little dreaming that I for my part was anxiously dreading his disapproval.

I made desperate efforts to sustain the role in which he had cast me, to keep up the appearance of success, of happiness, of self-complacency. It was useless! There was no resilience left in me, no aplomb, no self-possession. I could respond to him only with crestfallen embarrassment and cringing diffidence – and he was incredibly quick to sense this! It was frightening to watch how this man who had at first been fully prepared to recognize and respect me as a fortunate and superior person began to see through me, to look at me in astonishment, to grow cool, then superior, then impatient and irritated, and finally to treat me with undisguised contempt. It was still early when he got up to go, and next day he sent me a brief note saying that he had been obliged to leave town after all.

The fact is that everyone is much too busily preoccupied with himself to be able to form a serious opinion about another person. The indolent

world is all too ready to treat any man with whatever degree of respect
corresponds to his own self-confidence. Be what you please, live as you
please – but put a bold face on it, act with self-assurance and show no
qualms, and no one will be moralist enough to point the finger of scorn
at you. But once have the misfortune to forfeit your single-mindedness
and lose your self-complacency, once betray your own self-contempt –
and the world will unhesitatingly endorse it. As for me, I am past
hope . . .

At this point I stop writing. I cast my pen aside – full of disgust, of
disgust! Shall I make an end of it all? Surely that would be rather too
heroic for a 'buffoon and joker'! I am afraid the upshot of the matter will
be that I shall continue to live, to eat, to sleep, to dabble in this and
dabble in that; and gradually, as my apathy increases, I shall get used to
being a 'wretched and ridiculous figure'.

Oh, God, who would have supposed – who could have supposed –
that to be born a joker was so disastrous a fate!

# The Road to the Churchyard

*Der Weg zum Friedhof*

1900

# The Road to the Churchyard

The road to the churchyard ran parallel to the main highway, and kept close beside it until it reached the place to which it led, namely the churchyard. On the other side of it there was, at first, a row of human habitations – new suburban houses, some of them still under construction; and then came fields. As for the highway, it was lined with trees, gnarled beech trees of respectable age; and only one half of it was paved, the other was not. But the road to the churchyard was lightly strewn with gravel, and for this reason it was really more like a pleasant footpath. The two roads were separated by a narrow dry ditch, full of grass and meadow flowers.

It was spring, indeed it was already nearly summer. The world was smiling. The Lord God's blue sky was full of little round compact lumps of cloud, quaint little snow-white tufts scattered gaily all over it. The birds were twittering in the beeches, and a gentle breeze was blowing across the fields.

On the highway, a cart from the next village was crawling towards the town, half of it on the paved part of the road and half on the unpaved part. The carter was letting his legs hang down on either side of the shaft, and whistling very much out of tune. But at the far end of the cart, with its back to him, sat a little yellow dog with a little pointed nose over which it was gazing, with an indescribably solemn and meditative expression, back along the way it had come. It was an exquisite and highly amusing little dog, worth its weight in gold; unfortunately however it is irrelevant in the present context, and we must therefore ignore it. A troop of soldiers was passing. They were from the nearby barracks and they marched along through their own sweaty exhalations, singing as they marched. A second cart, coming from the direction of the town, was crawling towards the next village. The driver was asleep, and there was no dog on this vehicle, which is therefore of no interest whatsoever. Two apprentices came by, one of them a hunchback and the other gigantically tall. They walked barefoot, because they were carrying their boots over their shoulders; they called out some merry quip or other to the sleeping carter and proceeded on their way. Such was the moderate traffic, and it pursued its course without any complications or incidents.

Only one man was walking along the road to the churchyard; he was walking slowly, with bowed head and leaning on a black stick. This man's name was Piepsam – Lobgott Piepsam, believe it or not, and I expressly mention it on account of his subsequent extremely odd behaviour.

He was dressed in black, for he was on his way to visit the graves of his loved ones. He wore a rough-surfaced curved top hat, a frock coat shiny with age, trousers which were both too narrow and too short and black kid gloves with all the surface worn off. His neck, a long skinny neck with a prominent Adam's apple, rose out of a turn-down collar which was beginning to fray – yes, this collar was already rather ravelled at the edges. But when the man raised his head, which from time to time he did to see how far he was from the churchyard, then his face became visible, and this was a rare sight; for undoubtedly it was a face one would not forget again in a hurry.

It was clean-shaven and pale. But from between the hollow cheeks a bulbous nose protruded, a nose thicker at its tip than at its base, glowing with a monstrous and unnatural redness and closely covered, for good measure, with little insalubrious excrescences which gave it an irregular and fantastic appearance. There was something improbable and picturesque about this deeply flushed nose which stood out so sharply against the dull pallor of the rest of the face; it looked as if it had been stuck on like a carnival nose, in melancholy jest. But it had not . . . His mouth was wide, with drooping corners, and he kept it tight shut; his eyebrows were black but speckled with white, and when he looked up he would arch them almost to the brim of his hat, exposing to full view his woefully inflamed, dark-ringed eyes. In a word, it was a face which could not fail in the end to inspire the liveliest compassion.

Lobgott Piepsam's appearance was far from cheerful, it ill became this delightful morning, and even for a man about to visit the graves of his loved ones it was excessively woebegone. A glimpse of his state of mind, however, would have been enough to satisfy anyone that there was good cause for this. He was, shall we say, in rather low spirits . . . It is hard to explain these matters to happy people like yourselves . . . But yes, he had his little troubles, you know, he was rather badly done by. Alas, if the truth be told, his troubles were by no means little, but grievous in the highest degree – in fact, his condition could fairly be described as absolutely wretched.

To begin with, he drank. Well, we shall have occasion to refer to this again. Secondly he was a widower and a bereaved father, forsaken by everyone; he had not a soul left on earth to whom he was dear. His wife, whose maiden name had been Lebzelt, had been snatched from him six months ago when she had borne him a child; it was their third child, and it had been born dead. The other two had also died, one of diphtheria, the other of nothing in particular, perhaps just of general deficiency. As if this were not enough, he had shortly afterwards lost his job, he had been shamefully dismissed from his employment and livelihood, and this had been in consequence of the above-mentioned ruling passion, which was a passion stronger than Piepsam.

In the old days he had been able to resist it up to a point, despite periodic bouts of immoderate indulgence. But when he had been bereft of wife and children and stood alone in the world without guidance or support, deprived of all dependants, the vice had become his master, and had increasingly broken his resistance and his spirit. He had had a position on the staff of an insurance company, as a kind of superior clerk earning ninety marks a month. But he had been guilty, when in a condition of irresponsibility, of various acts of gross negligence, and in the end his employers, after repeatedly reprimanding him, had dismissed him as hopelessly unreliable.

It need hardly be said that this had in no way improved Piepsam's moral character; on the contrary he had now gone completely to pieces. The fact is, dear readers, that misfortune destroys human dignity. (And yet it is just as well, you know, to have a certain insight into these matters.) The truth in this case is strange and rather horrible. It is no use for a man to go on protesting his innocence to himself: he will usually despise himself simply for being unfortunate. But there is a dreadful reciprocal intimacy between self-contempt and vice – they nourish each other, they play into each other's hands in a way that is quite uncanny. And thus it was with Piepsam. He drank because he did not respect himself, and he respected himself less and less because his self-confidence was undermined by the ever-recurring collapse of all his good resolutions. At home in his wardrobe there stood a bottle of poisonous-looking yellow liquid, a ruinous liquid which we shall take the precaution of not identifying. In front of this wardrobe Lobgott Piepsam had before now literally fallen on his knees, with his clenched teeth nearly severing his tongue; and nevertheless he had finally succumbed to the temptation . . . We are reluctant to acquaint our readers with such matters; but they are after all very instructive. So now he was proceeding along the road to the churchyard, thrusting his black walking-stick before him. The gentle breeze played round his nose as it did round anyone else's, but he did not notice it. With eyebrows steeply arched he stared at the world with a hollow melancholy stare, like the lost wretched soul he was. Suddenly he heard behind him a sound that caught his attention: a soft whirr was approaching from a distance at high speed. He turned and stopped in his tracks . . . It was a bicycle: with its tyres crunching over the lightly gravelled surface, it was approaching at full tilt but presently slowed down, as Piepsam was standing in the middle of the road.

On the saddle sat a young man – a boy, a carefree tourist. He made no pretension to be counted among the great ones of this earth, oh dear me no! He was riding quite an inexpensive machine of no matter what make, a bicycle costing two hundred marks, just as it came. And on it he was out for a ride in the country, coming out of town for a bit of a spin, bowling along with his pedals glittering in the sunlight, into God's wide open spaces, hurrah! He was wearing a gaily coloured shirt with a grey jacket over it, sports gaiters and the sauciest little cap you ever saw – a joke of a cap, made of brown check material with a button at the top. But from under it came a thick tangled mop of blond hair, standing up round his forehead. His eyes were a gleaming blue. He sped towards Piepsam like Life itself, ringing his bicycle bell. But Piepsam did not budge an inch out of the way. He stood there and stared at Life, not a muscle of his face moving.

Life irritably returned his gaze and rode slowly past him, whereupon Piepsam likewise resumed his progress. But when Life was just in front of him he said slowly and with heavy emphasis:

'Number nine thousand seven hundred and seven.'

Then he pursed his lips and stared straight down at the road in front of him, aware that the eyes of Life were contemplating him in some perplexity.

Life had turned round, resting one hand on the back of the saddle and riding very slowly.

'What?' it asked . . .

'Number nine thousand seven hundred and seven,' repeated Piepsam. 'Oh, nothing. I shall report you.'

'Report me?' asked Life, turning round still further and pedalling still more slowly, which necessitated a strenuous balancing manoeuvre with the handlebars.

'Certainly,' replied Piepsam from a distance of five or six paces.

'What for?' asked Life, dismounting and standing still with an air of expectancy.

'You know perfectly well yourself.'

'No, I do not.'

'You must know.'

'But I do *not* know,' said Life, 'and what is more, I care even less!' Whereupon it prepared to remount its bicycle. Life was certainly not at a loss for words.

'I shall report you because you are riding here, not out there on the main road but here on the road to the churchyard,' said Piepsam.

'But my dear sir,' said Life with an exasperated impatient laugh, turning round again and stopping, 'you can see that there are bicycle tracks here all the way along . . . Everyone rides here . . .'

'That makes not the slightest difference to me,' answered Piepsam, 'I shall report you.'

'Oh well, then, do whatever you please!' exclaimed Life, and mounted its bicycle. It mounted well and truly, not disgracing itself by any fumbling of the operation, but with one thrust of the foot swung itself up into the saddle and there energetically prepared to resume its progress at the speed appropriate to its temperament.

'If you go on riding here on the road to the churchyard I shall most certainly report you,' said Piepsam, tremulously raising his voice. But Life paid precious little attention and simply rode on, gathering speed.

If you had seen Lobgott Piepsam's face at that moment you would have been profoundly startled. He compressed his lips so violently that his cheeks and even his fiery nose were pulled right out of shape; his brows were arched to a preternatural height, and under them his eyes stared insanely at the bicycle as it drew away from him. Suddenly he dashed forward. A short distance separated him from the vehicle; he covered it at a run, and seized the saddlebag. He clutched it with both hands, he positively clung to it: and, still pressing his lips together with superhuman force, speechless and wild-eyed, he tugged with all his strength at the unsteadily advancing machine. Anyone who had seen him might have wondered whether he maliciously intended to prevent the young man from riding on, or whether the fancy had suddenly taken him to be towed in the rider's wake, to mount up behind him and ride with him, bowling along with glittering pedals into God's wide open spaces, hurrah! . . . The bicycle could not support this monstrous load for long; it came to a stop, it tilted, it fell over.

But at this point Life lost its temper. It had ended up perching on one leg, and now, lunging out with its right arm, it fetched Herr Piepsam such a clout on the chest that he staggered back several paces. Then, with its voice rising in a threatening crescendo, it said:

'You must be drunk, man! You crazy old crackpot! Just you try once more to stop me and I'll knock your block off, do you understand? I give you fair warning, I'll break every bone in your body!' Thereupon it turned its back on Herr Piepsam, indignantly readjusted its little cap, and remounted the bicycle. Oh yes, it was certainly not lost for words. And it mounted just as skilfully and successfully as before. Just one thrust of the foot and it sat secure in the saddle and at once had the machine under control. Piepsam saw its back receding faster and faster into the distance.

There he stood, gasping, staring at Life as it left him behind . . . Life did not fall off, no accident occurred, no tyre burst, and there was no stone in its path; it sped resiliently away. And now Piepsam began to shriek and to curse – one might almost say to bellow: it was certainly no longer a human voice.

'Get off!' he yelled. 'Stop riding here! You are to ride out there on the main road and not on the road to the churchyard, do you hear me?! . . . Dismount! Dismount at once! Oh! Oh! I'll report you, I'll have you prosecuted! Oh, by God in heaven, why don't you fall, why don't you fall off, you riff-raff! I'd kick you! I'd trample your face in with my boot, you damned young puppy . . .'

Never had such a scene been witnessed! A man on the road to the churchyard screaming curses, a man swollen-faced and bellowing, a man dancing and capering in a frenzy of invective, flinging his arms and legs about, completely beside himself. The bicycle was away out of sight already, and Piepsam was still raging on the same spot.

'Stop him! Stop him! He's riding on the road to the churchyard! Pull him off his bicycle, the damned young monkey! Ah . . . ah . . . if I had you here, how I'd flay the hide off you, you brainless brute, you shallow hooligan, you clown, you ignorant fool! . . . Dismount! Dismount this instant! Will no one pull him down into the dust, the blackguard? . . . Ride your bicycle, will you? On the road to the churchyard, would you?! You scoundrel! You insolent lout! You damned popinjay! Bright blue eyes you have, haven't you! And what else? May the Devil claw them out of your head, you ignorant, ignorant, ignorant fool! . . .'

Piepsam now began to use expressions which cannot be repeated; he foamed at the mouth and hoarsely poured forth the vilest abuse, while his bodily movements became increasingly frenzied. A few children were walking along the main road with a basket and a pinscher dog: they came across, climbed the ditch, stood round the screaming man and gazed curiously at his distorted face. Some labourers, busy on the new building sites beyond him or just starting their lunch-break, now also took notice, and a number of them, accompanied by hod-women, advanced along the path towards the group. But Piepsam went on raving, in fact he got worse and worse. Blindly, wildly, he shook his fists at heaven and in all directions, kicked and thrashed with his legs, spun round and round, bent his knees and then jerked himself upright again, in a frantic effort to yell still louder. His flow of invective continued without pause, he scarcely left himself time to breathe, and his command of vocabulary was astonishing. His face was hideously swollen, his top hat had slid half-way down his neck and his shirt-front was hanging out from under his waistcoat. But he had long ago passed over into generalities and was uttering things which no longer had the remotest connection with the matter in hand. They included allusions to his life of vice, and religious intimations, all spluttered out in so very unsuitable a tone and disgracefully mingled with terms of abuse.

'Come hither, come here to me all of you!' he roared. 'Not you, not only you, but you others as well, you others with the caps and the bright blue eyes! I will shout truths into your ears that will make your flesh creep for ever and ever, you shallow *canaille*! . . . Do you grin? Do you shrug your shoulders? . . . I drink . . . yes, I drink! I even booze, if you want to know! What of that?! The end is not yet come! There shall be a day, you worthless vermin, when God shall weigh us all and find us wanting . . . Oh . . . Oh . . . the Son of Man shall come in the clouds of heaven, you innocent riff-raff, and his justice is not of this world! He shall cast you into outer darkness, you light-hearted rabble, and there shall be wailing and . . .'

He was now surrounded by a quite considerable assemblage of people. Some were laughing and some were staring at him with puckered brows. More labourers and hod-women had come up from the building sites. A driver had stopped his cart on the main road, dismounted, crossed the ditch and likewise approached, whip in hand. One man shook Piepsam by the arm, but this had no effect. A troop of soldiers craned their necks and laughed as they marched past him. The pinscher could contain itself no longer, braced its forepaws against the ground, wedged its tail between its hindquarters and howled up into his face.

Suddenly Lobgott Piepsam yelled once more at the top of his voice: 'Dismount, dismount at once, you ignorant puppy!' Then he described a wide semicircle with one arm, and collapsed. He lay there, abruptly silent, a black heap amid the curious crowd. His curved top hat had flown from his head, bounced once on the ground and then also lay still.

Two masons bent over the motionless Piepsam and discussed the case in the sensible straightforward language that working-men use. Then one of them set off at a run and disappeared. The remaining bystanders made a few further attempts to revive the senseless man. One of them sprinkled him with water from a pail, another took out a bottle of brandy, poured some of it into the hollow of his hand and rubbed Piepsam's temples with it. But these experiments proved unavailing.

Thus a short time elapsed. Then the sound of wheels was heard and a vehicle approached along the main road. It was an ambulance, and it stopped on the very spot. It was drawn by two neat little horses and had an enormous red cross painted on each side. Two men in smart uniforms got down from the driving seat, and while one of them went round to the back of the vehicle to open it and pull out the stretcher, the other crossed quickly to the road to the churchyard, pushed aside the staring onlookers and with the assistance of a labourer dragged Herr Piepsam to the ambulance. They loaded him on to the stretcher and slid him inside, like a loaf into an oven; whereupon the door clicked shut again and the two uniformed men remounted the box. The whole thing was done with great precision, with a few practised movements, swiftly and deftly, like something in a pantomime.

And then they drove Lobgott Piepsam away.

# Gladius Dei

## Gladius Dei

1902

# Gladius Dei

## 1

Munich was resplendent. A shining vault of silky blue sky stood above the festive squares, the white colonnades, the classicistic monuments and baroque churches, the leaping fountains, palaces and parks of the capital city, and its broad bright vistas, tree-lined and beautifully proportioned, basked in the shimmering haze of a fine early June day.

Over every little street the chatter of birds, an air of secret exultation . . . And across the squares, and past the rows of houses, the droll unhurried life of this beautiful leisurely town dawdles and trundles and rumbles along. Tourists of all nationalities are driving about in the slow little cabs, gazing with unselective curiosity at the house-fronts to right and left of them, or walking up the steps into museums . . .

Many windows stand open, and through many of them music floats out into the streets – the sound of pianos or violins or cellos being practised, of earnest and well-meant amateur endeavours. But from the Odeon a number of grand pianos can be heard simultaneously, on which serious study is in progress.

Young men whistling the Nothung motif, the kind of young men who fill the gallery of the modern Schauspielhaus every night, are strolling in and out of the University and the State Library, with literary periodicals in their side pockets. In front of the Academy of Fine Arts, which spreads its white wings between the Türkenstrasse and the Siegestor, a court carriage has stopped. And at the top of the ramp, standing, sitting and lounging in colourful groups, are the models – picturesque old men, children and women in the costume of peasants from the Alban Hills.

In the northern quarter, all the long streets are full of indolent, unhurrying, sauntering people . . . This place is not exactly the home of feverish cutthroat commercial competition: its inhabitants devote themselves to more agreeable pursuits. Young artists with small round hats perched on the backs of their heads, loosely tied cravats and no walking-sticks – carefree young men who pay their rent with an occasional sketch – are out walking, seeking moods of inspiration in the bright blue morning sky and letting their eyes stray after the girls: those pretty, rather dumpy little girls with their dark hair plaited *en bandeaux*, their slightly too large feet, and their accommodating morals . . . One house in five, here, has studio windows that gleam in the sun. Often, in a row of dull solid buildings, some artistic edifice stands out, the work of some young and imaginative architect: wide-fronted, with shallow arches and bizarre decorative motifs, full of style and inventive wit. Or suddenly, in some very boring façade, one door is framed by a saucy improvisation of flowing lines and luminous colours, Bacchantes, water nymphs and rose-pink nudes . . .

It is always unfailingly delightful to linger in front of a cabinet-maker's window display, or those of the large stores which sell modern luxury articles of all kinds. What sybaritic imagination, what humour there is in the lines and outlines of all these things! There are little shops everywhere selling sculptures and frames and antiques, and through their windows the busts of Florentine ladies of the quattrocento sublimely and suggestively confront one's gaze. And the owner of even the smallest and most modest of these establishments will talk to one about Donatello and Mino da Fiesole for all the world as if they had personally given him sole reproduction rights . . .

But up there on the Odeonsplatz, near the massive loggia with the wide expanse of mosaic pavement in front of it, diagonally opposite the Prince Regent's palace, there are always people pressing round the wide windows and showcases of one large art shop: the elaborate beauty emporium of Herr M. Blüthenzweig. What a sumptuous array of delightful exhibits it offers! There are reproductions of masterpieces from every gallery on earth, presented in expensive frames which have been subtly tinted and decorated in a taste combining simplicity with preciosity. There are facsimiles of modern paintings, gay sensuous fantasies in which the world of antiquity seems to have been brought back to life with humorous realism; perfect casts of Renaissance sculpture; bronze nudes and fragile ornamental glassware; tall earthenware vases which have emerged from baths of metal vapour clad in iridescent colours; volumes in exquisite bindings, triumphs of fine modern book production, lavish luxury editions of the works of fashionable lyric poets. And among all this the portraits of artists, musicians, philosophers, actors and writers are displayed to gratify the inquisitive public's taste for personal details . . . On an easel in the first window, the one nearest the adjacent bookshop, there is a large picture which particularly attracts the crowd: an excellent sepia photograph in a massive old-gold frame. It is a rather sensational item – a copy of the chief attraction in this year's great international exhibition, the exhibition so effectively publicized by the quaintly printed placards which are to be seen on every poster-pillar, in concert programmes and even in artistic advertisements for toilet preparations.

Look about you, survey the windows of the bookshops! Your eyes will encounter such titles as *Interior Decoration Since the Renaissance, Colour Sense and How to Train It, The Renaissance in Modern Applied Art, The Book as a Work of Art, The Art of Decoration, The Hunger for Art.* Reflect, too, that these stimulating publications are bought and read by the thousand, and that the very same topics are lectured on every evening to packed halls . . .

With any luck, you will also personally encounter one of the famous women already familiar to you through the medium of art – one of those rich, beautiful ladies with dyed Titian-blonde hair and diamond necklaces, whose bewitching features have been immortalized by some portrait-painter of genius, and whose love-life is the talk of the town. At carnival time they preside as queens over the artists' revels: slightly rouged, slightly painted, sublimely suggestive, flirtatious and adorable. And look! there goes a great painter with his mistress, driving up the Ludwigstrasse. People point at the carriage, people stop and gaze after the pair. Many salute them. The policemen all but stand to attention.

Art is flourishing, art rules the day, art with its rose-entwined sceptre holds smiling sway over the city. That it should continue so to thrive is a matter of general and reverent concern; on all sides diligent work and propaganda are devoted to its service; everywhere there is a pious cult of line, of ornament, of form, of the senses, of beauty . . . Munich is resplendent.

## 2

A young man was walking along the Schellingstrasse. Surrounded by cyclists ringing their bells, he was striding down the middle of the woodblock paving towards the broad façade of the Ludwigskirche. When one looked at him, a shadow seemed to pass across the sun or a memory of dark hours across the soul. Did he dislike the sun that was bathing this lovely city in festive light? Why did he keep his eyes fixed on the ground as he walked, engrossed in his own thoughts and heedless of the world?

He was hatless, which was no matter for comment amid the sartorial freedom of this easygoing town; instead of a hat he had pulled the hood of his wide black cloak over his head, so that it shaded his low, bony protruding forehead, covered his ears and surrounded his gaunt visage. What torment of conscience, what scruples and what self-inflicted hardships could have so hollowed out those cheeks? Is it not horrible to see care written on a man's sunken face on so beautiful a day? His dark eyebrows thickened sharply at the narrow base of his long, aquiline, overprominent nose, and his lips were full and fleshy. Each time he raised his rather close-set brown eyes, wrinkles formed on his angular forehead. His gaze betokened knowledge, narrowness of spirit and suffering. Seen in profile, this face exactly resembled an old portrait once painted by a monk and now preserved in Florence in a hard narrow cloister cell, from which long ago there issued forth a terrible and overwhelming protest against life and its triumphs . . .

Hieronymus strode along the Schellingstrasse, slowly and firmly, holding his wide cloak together from inside with both hands. Two young girls, two of those pretty, dumpy creatures with plaited hair, rather too large feet and accommodating morals, were strolling along arm in arm, out for adventure; as they passed him they nudged each other and giggled at the sight of his hood and his face, indeed they bent double with laughter and had to break into a run. But he paid no heed to this. With head bowed, and looking neither right nor left, he crossed the Ludwigstrasse and mounted the steps of the church.

The great central portal was wide open. In the dim religious light of the interior, cool and musty and heavy with the scent of incense, a faint red glow was visible from somewhere far within. An old woman with bloodshot eyes got up from a prayer-stool and dragged herself on crutches between the columns. Otherwise the church was empty.

Hieronymus sprinkled his brow and breast from the stoup, genuflected before the high altar and then remained standing in the nave. Somehow he seemed to have grown in stature here. He stood erect and motionless, holding his head high; his great hooked nose jutted out over his full lips with a masterful expression, and his eyes were no longer fixed on the ground but gazed boldly straight ahead towards the crucifix on the distant high altar. Thus he paused for a while without stirring; then he genuflected again as he stepped back, and left the church.

He strode up the Ludwigstrasse, slowly and firmly, with head bowed, walking in the middle of the broad unpaved carriageway, towards the massive loggia and its statues. But on reaching the Odeonsplatz he raised his eyes, and wrinkles formed on his angular forehead: he came to a halt, his attention drawn by the crowd in front of the great art shop, in front of the elaborate beauty emporium of M. Blüthenzweig.

People were moving from window to window, pointing out to each other the treasures there displayed, exchanging views and peering over each other's shoulders. Hieronymus mingled with them, and he too began to survey the various objects, to inspect them all, one by one.

He saw the reproductions of masterpieces from every gallery on earth; the expensive, artlessly bizarre frames; the Renaissance sculpture, the bronze nudes and ornamental glassware, the iridescent vases, the luxurious bookbindings, the portraits of artists, musicians, philosophers, actors and writers; he looked at them all, devoting a moment to every object. Holding his cloak firmly together from inside with both hands, he turned his hooded head with slight, curt movements from one thing to another; his dark eyebrows, thickening sharply at the base of his nose, were raised, and from under them his eyes rested for a while on every item in the display with a puzzled, cold, astonished stare. And so in due course he came to the first window, the one behind which the rather sensational picture stood. For some minutes he looked over the shoulders of the people who were crowding round it; then he managed to get to the front, and stood close to the glass.

The big sepia photograph, framed most tastefully in old gold, had been placed on an easel in the centre of the window. It was a Madonna, painted in a wholly modern and entirely unconventional manner. The sacred figure was ravishingly feminine, naked and beautiful. Her great sultry eyes were rimmed with shadow, and her lips were half parted in a strange and delicate smile. Her slender fingers were grouped rather nervously and convulsively round the waist of the Child, a nude boy of aristocratic, almost archaic slimness, who was playing with her breast and simultaneously casting a knowing sidelong glance at the spectator.

Two other young men were standing next to Hieronymus discussing the picture. They had books under their arms which they had just fetched from the State Library or were taking back to it; they were young men of classical education, well versed in the arts and other learning.

'Devil take me, but he's a lucky young fellow!' said one of them.

'And he clearly intends to make us envy him,' replied the other . . . 'A woman of parts, to be sure.'

'A woman to go crazy for! She does make one a bit doubtful about the dogma of the Immaculate Conception . . .'

'Oh, indeed, she doesn't look exactly *intacta*. Have you seen the original?'

'Of course. I found it most perturbing. She's even more *provoquante* in colour . . . especially the eyes.'

'It's certainly a very outspoken likeness.'

'How do you mean?'

'Don't you know the model? Why, he used that little milliner of his. It's almost a portrait of her, but with the depraved flavour deliberately emphasized . . . The girl herself is more innocent-looking.'

'I should hope so. Life would be rather a strain if there were many of them like this *mater amata* . . .'

'The Pinakothek has bought it.'

'Really? Well, well! They know what they're doing, of course. The treatment of the flesh and the flowing lines of the garment are certainly quite outstanding.'

'Yes, he's a fantastically talented chap.'

'Do you know him?'

'Slightly. There's no doubt that he'll have a successful career. He's been to dinner with the Prince Regent twice already . . .'

During this last exchange they had been preparing to take leave of each other.

'Shall we see you tonight at the theatre?' asked one of them. 'The Drama Club is putting on Machiavelli's *Mandragola*.'

'Oh, good! That's certain to be amusing. I was meaning to go to the Artists' Variety, but I dare say I shall give preference to our friend Niccolò after all. *Au revoir* . . .'

They separated, left the window and went off in different directions. New spectators took their place and gazed at the successful work of art. But Hieronymus stood on motionless; he stood with his head thrust forward, and his hands, as he grasped his cloak with them from inside and held it together on his breast, were seen to tighten convulsively. His brows were no longer raised as before in that expression of cold, rather resentful astonishment. They were lowered and frowning darkly; his cheeks, half hidden by the black hood, seemed more deeply sunken than ever, and his full lips had turned very pale. Slowly his head dropped further and further down, until finally his eyes were staring fixedly upward at the picture from well below it. The nostrils of his great nose were quivering.

He remained in this posture for about a quarter of an hour. A succession of different people stood round the window beside him, but he did not stir from the spot. Finally he turned round slowly, very slowly, on the balls of his feet, and walked away.

## 3

But the picture of the Madonna went with him. Continually, even as he sat in his small hard narrow room or knelt in the cool churches, it stood before his outraged soul with its sultry, dark-rimmed eyes, with a mysterious smile on its lips, naked and beautiful. And no prayer could exorcise it.

But on the third night it came to pass that Hieronymus received a command and a summons from on high, bidding him take action and raise his voice in protest against frivolous profligacy and the insolent, pretentious cult of beauty. In vain he pleaded, like Moses, that he was slow of speech and heavy of tongue: God's will remained inflexible, his bidding loud and clear. Faint-hearted or no, Hieronymus must go forth on this sacrificial mission among his mocking enemies.

And so in the morning he rose up and betook himself, since God so willed it, to the art shop – to M. Blüthenzweig's great beauty emporium. He wore his hood over his head and held his cloak together from inside with both hands as he walked.

## 4

It had grown sultry; the sky was livid and a storm was imminent. Once again, quite a multitude was besieging the windows of the art shop, especially the one in which the Madonna was exhibited. Hieronymus gave it only a cursory glance, and then pressed down the handle of the glass door hung with posters and art magazines. 'It is God's will!' he said, and entered the shop.

A young girl, a pretty, dark creature with plaited hair and rather too large feet who had been sitting somewhere at a desk writing in a ledger, approached and inquired politely how she could be of service to him.

'Thank you,' said Hieronymus, looking her gravely in the eyes and wrinkling his angular forehead, 'it is not to you I wish to speak, but to the owner of the shop, Herr Blüthenzweig.'

She hesitated a little, then withdrew and resumed her occupation. He remained standing in the middle of the shop.

All the objects exhibited singly outside were piled up here by the score, in a lavish display – an abundance of colour, line and form, of style, wit, taste and beauty. Hieronymus gazed slowly to his right and to his left, then drew the folds of his black cloak more tightly about him.

There were several people in the shop. At one of the broad tables that ran across the room sat a gentleman in a yellow suit with a black goatee, looking at a portfolio of French drawings, to which he occasionally reacted with a bleating laugh. A young man, who looked as if he were underpaid and lived on a vegetarian diet, was serving him and kept dragging further portfolios across for him to inspect. Diagonally opposite the bleating gentleman an important-looking elderly lady was examining some modern art needlework, huge fantastic flowers embroidered in pale colours, standing vertically side by side on long straight stalks. She too was being attended to by one of the assistants. An Englishman was sitting nonchalantly at another table, with his travelling cap on and a pipe in his mouth; cold, clean-shaven, of uncertain age and wearing solid durable clothes. He was in the act of choosing between a number of bronzes that were being offered to him by Herr Blüthenzweig in person. One of them was a graceful nude statuette of a young girl with an immature figure and delicate limbs, her little hands chastely and coquettishly crossed on her breast; he was holding her by the head, rotating her slowly and inspecting her in detail.

Herr Blüthenzweig, a man with short brown side-whiskers and moustaches and glistening eyes of the same colour, was hovering round him, rubbing his hands and praising the little girl with every adjective he could lay his tongue to.

'A hundred and fifty marks, sir,' he said in English. 'An example of Munich art, sir. Certainly quite enchanting. Full of charm, you know. The very embodiment of grace, sir. Really extremely pretty, very dainty, an admirable piece.' He added as an afterthought: 'Most attractive and seductive,' and then began again from the beginning.

His nose lay rather flat on his upper lip, so that he was constantly breathing into his moustache with a slight snorting sound; he also kept approaching the customer in a stooping posture, as if he were sniffing him. When Hieronymus entered, Herr Blüthenzweig briefly investigated him in exactly the same manner, but then turned back at once to the Englishman.

The aristocratic old lady had made her choice and left the shop. A new customer entered. Herr Blüthenzweig gave him a quick sniff as if to assess his purchasing power, and then handed him over to the young woman with the ledger. This gentleman merely bought a faience bust of Piero de' Medici, son of Lorenzo the Magnificent, and then departed. The Englishman now also prepared to leave. He had taken possession of the little nude girl and was shown to the door by Herr Blüthenzweig with much bowing and scraping. The art dealer then turned to Hieronymus and came up to him.

'What can I do for you?' he asked with scant deference.

Hieronymus held his cloak together from inside with both hands and looked Herr Blüthenzweig in the face almost without moving a muscle. Then he slowly parted his thick lips and said:

'I have come to you about the picture in that window, the big photograph, the Madonna.' His voice was husky and expressionless.

'Ah yes, of course,' said Herr Blüthenzweig with interest and began rubbing his hands. 'Seventy marks including the frame, sir. Guaranteed durability . . . a first-class reproduction. Most attractive and charming.'

Hieronymus was silent. He bowed his hooded head and seemed to shrink slightly as the art dealer spoke. Then he drew himself upright again and said:

'I must tell you in advance that I am not in a position to buy anything from you, nor do I in any case wish to do so. I regret to have to disappoint your expectations. If this upsets you, I am sorry. But in the first place I am poor, and in the second place I do not like the things you are offering for sale. No, I cannot buy anything.'

'You cannot . . . Oh, quite so,' said Herr Blüthenzweig, snorting loudly. 'Well, may I ask . . .'

'If I judge you right,' continued Hieronymus, 'you despise me because I am not able to buy anything from you . . .'

'Hm . . . not at all!' said Herr Blüthenzweig. 'But . . .'

'Nevertheless I beg you to listen to me and to give due weight to my words.'

'Give due weight. Hm. May I ask . . .'

'You may ask,' said Hieronymus, 'and I will answer you. I have come to request you to remove that picture, the big photograph, the Madonna, from your window immediately and never to exhibit it again.'

Herr Blüthenzweig stared at Hieronymus for a while in silence, as if expecting him to be covered with confusion by his own extraordinary speech. Since however no such thing happened, he snorted violently and delivered himself as follows:

'Will you be so good as to inform me whether you are here in some official capacity which authorizes you to dictate to me, or what exactly your business here is? . . .'

'Oh, no,' replied Hieronymus, 'I have no office or position under the State. The power of this world is not on my side, sir. What brings me here is solely my conscience.'

Herr Blüthenzweig, at a loss for a reply, wagged his head to and fro, snorted violently into his moustache and struggled to find words. Finally he said:

'Your conscience . . . Then will you kindly allow me . . . to inform you . . . that so far as we are concerned . . . your conscience is a thing of no importance whatsoever!'

With that he turned on his heel, walked quickly to his desk at the back of the shop and began to write. The two male assistants laughed heartily. The pretty young bookkeeper also giggled. As for the gentleman in yellow with the black beard, it became apparent that he was a foreigner, for he had obviously not understood a word, but went on studying the French drawings, uttering his bleating laugh from time to time.

'Will you please deal with the gentleman,' said Herr Blüthenzweig over his shoulder to his assistant. Then he went on writing. The young man with the ill-paid vegetarian look came up to Hieronymus, doing his best not to laugh, and the other assistant approached as well.

'Is there anything else we can do for you?' asked the ill-paid assistant gently. Hieronymus kept his sorrowful, obtuse yet penetrating gaze steadily fixed on him.

'No,' he said, 'there is not. I beg you to remove the picture of the Madonna from the window at once, and for ever.'

'Oh . . . Why?'

'It is the holy Mother of God . . .' said Hieronymus in hushed tones.

'Of course . . . But you have heard for yourself that Herr Blüthenzweig is not prepared to do as you request.'

'We must remember that it is the holy Mother of God,' said Hieronymus, his head trembling.

'That is so. But what follows? Is it wrong to exhibit Madonnas? Is it wrong to paint them?'

'Not like that! Not like that!' said Hieronymus almost in a whisper, straightening himself and shaking his head vehemently several times. The angular forehead under his hood was lined all over with long, deep furrows. 'You know very well that what has been painted there is vice itself, naked lust! I heard with my own ears two simple, unreflecting young men, as they looked at that picture, say that it made them doubt the dogma of the Immaculate Conception . . .'

'Oh, excuse me, that is quite beside the point,' said the young assistant with a superior smile. In his leisure hours he was writing a pamphlet on the modern movement in art, and was quite capable of conducting a cultured conversation. 'The picture is a work of art,' he continued, 'and as such it must be judged by the appropriate standards. It has been acclaimed by everyone. The State has bought it . . .'

'I know that the State has bought it,' said Hieronymus. 'I also know that the painter has dined twice with the Prince Regent. This is common talk among the people, and God knows what conclusions they draw from the fact that by a work of that sort a man can become famous! What does such a fact attest? It attests the blindness of the world, a blindness that is incomprehensible unless it is mere shameless hypocrisy. That picture was painted in sensual lust, and it is enjoyed in sensual lust . . . Is this true or not? Answer me! You too, Herr Blüthenzweig, answer me!'

A pause ensued. Hieronymus seemed in all seriousness to be expecting a reply, and his sorrowful penetrating brown eyes looked by turns at Herr Blüthenzweig's rounded back and at the two assistants, who stared at him with embarrassed curiosity. There was silence, broken only by the bleating laugh of the gentleman in yellow with the black beard as he pored over the French drawings.

'It *is* true!' continued Hieronymus, his husky voice trembling with profound indignation. 'You dare not deny it! But how then is it possible that the painter of that picture should be solemnly extolled as if he had contributed something to the spiritual enrichment of mankind? How is it possible to stand before that picture and enjoy the vile pleasure it gives, and to silence one's conscience with talk of beauty – indeed to persuade oneself in all seriousness that one is undergoing a noble and refined experience, an experience worthy of the dignity of man? Is this wicked ignorance or the basest hypocrisy? It passes my comprehension . . . the absurdity of this fact passes my comprehension! That a man can rise to high renown on this earth by a witless, brazen manifestation of his animal instincts! Beauty . . . What is beauty? What impulses beget beauty, and to what does it appeal? No one can possibly be ignorant of this, Herr Blüthenzweig! But how can one conceivably see through something in this way and yet not be filled with grief and revulsion at the thought of it! This exaltation and blasphemous idolatry of beauty is a crime, for it confirms and encourages the ignorance of shameless children, it strengthens them in their folly – the folly of impudence, the folly of the morally blind who know nothing of suffering and still less of the way to salvation! . . ."Who are you," you will ask me, "who see things so blackly?" I tell you, knowledge is the bitterest torment in this world; but it is the fire of purgatory, the purifying anguish without which no soul can be saved. It is not impudent naïvety or wicked heedlessness that will avail, Herr Blüthenzweig, but only understanding, that insight by which the passions of our loathsome flesh are consumed and extinguished.'

Silence. The gentleman in yellow with the black beard uttered a short bleat.

'It would really be better if you left now,' said the ill-paid assistant gently.

But Hieronymus showed no sign whatsoever of leaving. Erect in his hooded cloak, with his eyes burning, he stood there in the middle of the art shop, and in a harsh voice that seemed rusty with disuse his thick lips went on pouring forth words of condemnation . . .

'Art! they cry – pleasure! beauty! Wrap the world in a veil of beauty and set upon everything the noble imprint of style! . . . Enough of this infamy! Do you think gaudy colours can gloss over the misery of the world? Do you think loud orgies of luxurious good taste can drown the moans of the tortured earth? You are wrong, you shameless wretches! God is not mocked, and your insolent idolatry of the glistering surface of things is an abomination in His sight! . . . "Who are you," you will answer, "to be reviling Art?" You lie, I tell you; I am not reviling art! Art is not a cynical deception, a seductive stimulus to confirm and strengthen the lusts of the flesh! Art is the sacred torch that must shed its merciful light into all life's terrible depths, into every shameful and sorrowful abyss; art is the divine flame that must set fire to the world, until the world with all its infamy and anguish burns and melts way in redeeming compassion! . . . Remove it, Herr Blüthenzweig, remove that famous painter's work from your window – indeed, you would do well to burn it with hot fire and scatter its ashes to the winds, yes, to all four winds! . . .'

His unlovely voice broke off. He had taken a vehement step backwards, had snatched one arm from under the fold of his black cloak with a passionate movement and was holding it far outstretched; with a strangely contorted, convulsively trembling hand he pointed towards the window display, the showcase containing the sensational picture of the Madonna. He paused in this masterful posture. His great hooked nose seemed to jut out imperiously, his dark brows that thickened sharply at its base were arched so high that his angular forehead under the overshadowing hood was covered with broad furrows, and a hectic flush had spread over his sunken cheeks.

But at this point Herr Blüthenzweig turned round. Perhaps it was the fact of being called upon to burn a reproduction worth seventy marks that had so genuinely outraged him, or perhaps Hieronymus's speeches in general had finally exhausted his patience; at all events he was the very picture of righteous wrath. He gesticulated with his pen towards the door of the shop, snorted sharply several times into his moustache, struggled for words in his agitation and then declared with extreme emphasis:

'Now listen to me, you crazy fellow: unless you clear out of here this very instant, I'll get the packer to facilitate your exit, do you understand?!'

'Oh, no, you shall not intimidate me, you shall not drive me away, you shall not silence my voice!' cried Hieronymus, pulling his hood together above his chest with one clenched hand and fearlessly shaking his head. 'I know I am alone and powerless, and yet I will not have done until you hear me, Herr Blüthenzweig! Take that picture out of your window and burn it, this very day! Oh, burn not only it! Burn these statuettes and busts as well – the sight of them tempts men to sin! Burn these vases and ornaments, these shameless revivals of paganism! Burn these luxurious volumes of love poetry! Burn everything in your shop, Herr Blüthenzweig, for it is filth in the sight of God! Burn it, burn it, burn it!' he cried, quite beside himself, and making a wild, sweeping, circular gesture with his arm . . . 'The harvest is ripe for the reaper . . . The insolence of this age exceeds all bounds . . . But I say unto you . . .'

'Krauthuber!' shouted Herr Blüthenzweig, turning towards a door at the back of the shop and raising his voice, 'come in here at once!'

The response to this summons was the appearance on the scene of an enormous, overwhelming figure, a monstrous, swollen hulk of terrifyingly massive humanity with gross, teeming limbs thickly padded with flesh and all shapelessly merging into each other – a prodigious, gigantic presence, slowly and ponderously heaving itself across the floor and puffing heavily: a son of the people, malt-nourished, herculean and awe-inspiring! A fringe of walrus moustache was discernible on his face, a huge paste-smeared leather apron enveloped his body and yellow shirt-sleeves were rolled back from his heroic arms.

'Will you open the door for this gentleman, Krauthuber,' said Herr Blüthenzweig, 'and if he still cannot find his way to it, will you help him out into the street.'

'Huh?' said the man, shifting his little elephant eyes to and fro between Hieronymus and his enraged employer . . . It was a primitive grunt, expressing vast strength held laboriously in check. Then he strode, with steps that made everything round him tremble, to the door and opened it.

Hieronymus had turned very pale. 'Burn it –' he began to exclaim, but already a fearful superior force was upon him, and he felt himself being turned round: a bodily hulk against which there could be no conceivable resistance was slowly and inexorably thrusting him towards the door.

'I am weak,' he gasped . . . 'My flesh will not avail against force . . . it cannot stand firm . . . no! but what does that prove? Burn –'

He stopped short. He was outside the art shop. Herr Blüthenzweig's colossal henchman had released him with a slight shove and a final little flourish which had obliged him to collapse sideways on to the stone threshold, supporting himself on one hand. And the glass door was slammed shut behind him.

He rose to his feet. He stood upright, breathing heavily, pulling his hood together above his chest with one clenched hand and letting the other hang down inside the cloak. A grey pallor had gathered in his sunken cheeks; the nostrils of his great hooked nose twitched open and shut; his ugly lips were contorted into an expression of desperate hatred, and his eyes, aflame with a kind of mad ecstasy, roved to and fro across the beautiful square.

He did not see the bystanders who were looking at him with curiosity and amusement. Instead, on the mosaic paving in front of the great loggia, he saw the vanities of the world: the artists' carnival costumes, the ornaments, vases, jewellery and *objets d'art*, the naked statues, the busts of women, the painted revivals of paganism, the masterly portraits of famous beauties, the luxurious volumes of love poetry and the art publications – he saw them all piled up into a great pyramid, and saw the multitude, enthralled by his terrible words, consign them to crackling flames amid cries of jubilation . . . And there, against a yellow wall of cloud that had drifted across from the Theatinerstrasse with a soft roll of thunder, he saw the broad blade of a fiery sword, outstretched in the sulphurous sky above this light-hearted city . . .

'*Gladius Dei super terram*,' his thick lips whispered; and drawing himself to his full height in his hooded cloak, he shook his hanging, hidden fist convulsively and added in a quivering undertone: '*cito et velociter!*'

# Tristan

*Tristan*


1903

# Tristan

## 1

Here we are at 'Einfried', the well-known sanatorium! It is white and rectilinear, a long low-lying main building with a side wing, standing in a spacious garden delightfully adorned with grottoes, leafy arcades and little bark pavilions; and behind its slate roofs the massive pine-green mountains rear their softly outlined peaks and clefts into the sky.

The director of the establishment, as always, is Dr Leander. With his double-pointed black beard, curled as crisply as horse-hair stuffing, his thick flashing spectacles and his general air of one into whom science has instilled a certain coldness and hardness and silent tolerant pessimism, he holds sway in his abrupt and reserved manner over his patients – over all these people who are too weak to impose laws upon themselves and obey them, and who therefore lavish their fortunes on Dr Leander in return for the protection of his rigorous regime.

As for Fräulein von Osterloh, she manages all domestic matters here, and does so with tireless devotion. Dear me, what a whirl of activity! She hurries upstairs and downstairs and from one end of the institution to the other. She is mistress of the kitchen and store-rooms, she rummages about in the linen cupboards, she has the servants at her beck and call, she plans the clients' daily fare on principles of economy, hygiene, taste and elegance. She keeps house with fanatical thoroughness; and in her extreme efficiency there lies concealed a standing reproach to the entire male sex, not one member of which has ever taken it into his head to make her his wife. But in two round crimson spots on her cheeks there burns the inextinguishable hope that one day she will become Frau Dr Leander . . .

Ozone, and still, unstirring air . . . Einfried, whatever Dr Leander's envious detractors and rivals may say, is most warmly to be recommended for all tubercular cases. But not only consumptives reside here: there are patients of all kinds – ladies, gentlemen and even children; Dr Leander can boast of successes in the most varied fields. There are people with gastric disorders, such as Magistratsrätin Spatz, who is also hard of hearing; there are heart cases, paralytics, rheumatics and nervous sufferers of all sorts and conditions. There is a diabetic general, who grumbles continually as he consumes his pension. There are several gentlemen with lean, shrivelled faces, walking with that unruly dancing gait which is always a bad sign. There is a lady of fifty, Pastorin Höhlenrauch, who has had nineteen children and is now totally incapable of thought, despite which her mind is still not at peace: for a whole year now, driven by some restless nervous impulse, she has been wandering aimlessly all over the house – a staring, speechless, uncanny figure, leaning on the arm of her private attendant.

Occasionally a death occurs among the 'serious cases', those who are confined to their beds and do not appear at meals or in the drawing-room; and no one is ever aware of it, not even the patient next door. In the silence of night the waxen guest is removed, and Einfried pursues the even tenor of its way: the massage, the electrical treatment, the injections, douches, medicinal baths, gymnastics, exsudations and inhalations all continue, in premises equipped with every wonder of modern science . . .

Ah yes, this is a lively place. The establishment is flourishing. The porter at the entrance in the side wing sounds the great bell when new guests arrive, and all who leave are shown to the carriage with due formality by Dr Leander and Fräulein von Osterloh in person. Many an odd figure has lived under Einfried's hospitable roof. There is even a writer here, idling away his time – an eccentric fellow with a name reminiscent of some sort of mineral or precious stone . . .

Apart from Dr Leander there is, moreover, a second resident physician, who deals with those cases which are not serious at all and those which are hopeless. But his name is Müller and we need waste no time discussing him.

## 2

At the beginning of January Herr Klöterjahn the wholesale merchant, of the firm of A. C. Klöterjahn & Co., brought his wife to Einfried. The porter sounded the bell, and Fräulein von Osterloh came to greet the new arrivals after their long journey; she met them in the reception-room, which like almost all the rest of this elegant old house was furnished in remarkably pure *Empire* style. In a moment or two Dr Leander also appeared; he bowed, and an introductory, mutually informative conversation ensued.

Outside lay the wintry garden, its flower-beds covered with matting, its grottoes blocked with snow, its little temples isolated; and two porters were dragging in the new guests' luggage from the carriage which had stopped at the wrought-iron gate, for there was no drive up to the house.

'Take your time, Gabriele, take care, darling, and keep your mouth closed,' Herr Klöterjahn had said as he conducted his wife across the garden; and the moment one saw her one's heart trembled with such tender solicitude that one could not help inwardly echoing his words – though it must be admitted that Herr Klöterjahn's 'take care', which he had said in English, could equally well have been said in German.

The coachman who had driven the lady and gentleman from the station to the sanatorium was a plain, unsophisticated and unsentimental fellow; but he had positively bitten his tongue in an agony of helpless caution as the wholesale merchant assisted his wife down from the carriage. Indeed, even the two bay horses, as they stood steaming in the silent frosty air, had seemed to be rolling back their eyes and intently watching this anxious operation, full of concern for so much fragile grace and delicate charm.

The young lady had an ailment affecting her trachea, as was expressly stated in the letter which Herr Klöterjahn had dispatched from the shores of the Baltic to the medical director of Einfried, announcing their intended arrival; the trachea, and not, thank God, the lungs! And yet – even if it had been the lungs, this new patient could scarcely have looked more enchantingly remote, ethereal and insubstantial than she did now, as she sat by her burly husband, leaning softly and wearily back in her straight, white-lacquered armchair, listening to his conversation with the doctor.

Her beautiful pale hands, bare of jewellery except for a simple wedding ring, were resting in her lap among the folds of a dark, heavy cloth skirt, above which she wore a close-fitting silver-grey bodice with a stand-up collar and a pattern of cut velvet arabesques. But these warm and weighty materials made her ineffably delicate, sweet, languid little head look all the more touching, unearthly and lovely. Her light brown hair was brushed smoothly back and gathered in a knot low down on her neck; only one stray curl drooped towards her right temple, not far from the spot where a strange, sickly little pale blue vein branched out above one of her well marked eyebrows and across the clear, unblemished, almost translucent surface of her forehead. This little blue vein over one eye rather disturbingly dominated the whole of her delicate oval face. It stood out more strongly as soon as she began to speak, indeed as soon as she even smiled; and when this happened it gave her a strained look, an expression almost of anxiety, which filled the onlooker with obscure foreboding. And nevertheless she spoke, and she smiled. She spoke with candour and charm in her slightly husky voice, and smiled with her eyes, although she seemed to find it a little difficult to focus them, indeed they sometimes showed a slight uncontrollable unsteadiness. At their corners, on each side of her slender nose, there were deep shadows. She smiled with her mouth as well, which was wide and beautiful and seemed to shine despite its pallor, perhaps because the lips were so very sharply and clearly outlined. Often she would clear her throat a little. When she did so, she would put her handkerchief to her mouth and then look at it.

'Now, Gabriele, don't clear your throat,' said Herr Klöterjahn. 'You know Dr Hinzpeter at home particularly told you not to do that, darling, and it's merely a matter of pulling oneself together, my dear. As I said, it's the trachea,' he repeated. 'I really did think it was the lungs when it began; bless my soul, what a fright I got! But it's not the lungs – good God, no, we're not standing for any of that sort of thing, are we, Gabriele, what? Oh-ho, no!'

'Indubitably not,' said Dr Leander, flashing his spectacles at them.

Whereupon Herr Klöterjahn asked for coffee – coffee and buttered rolls; and the guttural northern way he pronounced 'coffee' and 'butter' was expressive enough to give anyone an appetite.

He was served with the desired refreshments, rooms were provided for him and his wife and they made themselves at home.

We should add that Dr Leander personally took charge of the case, without availing himself of the services of Dr Müller.

# 3

The personality of the new patient caused a considerable stir in Einfried; and Herr Klöterjahn, accustomed to such successes, accepted with satisfaction all the homage that was paid to her. The diabetic general stopped grumbling for a moment when he first caught sight of her; the gentlemen with the shrivelled faces, when they came anywhere near her, smiled and made a great effort to keep their legs under control; and Magistratsrätin Spatz immediately appointed herself her friend and chaperon. Ah yes, this lady who bore Herr Klöterjahn's name most certainly made an impression! A writer who had for a few weeks been passing his time in Einfried – an odd fish with a name reminiscent of some kind of precious stone – positively changed colour when she passed him in the corridor: he stopped short and was still standing as if rooted to the spot long after she had disappeared.

Not two days had passed before her story was known to every inmate of the sanatorium. She had been born in Bremen, a fact in any case attested by certain charming little peculiarities of her speech; and there, some two years since, she had consented to become the wedded wife of Herr Klöterjahn the wholesale merchant. She had gone with him to his native town up there on the Baltic coast, and about ten months ago she had borne him a child – an admirably lively and robust son and heir, born under quite extraordinarily difficult and dangerous circumstances. But since these terrible days she had never really recovered her strength, if indeed she had ever had any strength to recover. She had scarcely risen from her confinement, utterly exhausted, her vital powers utterly impoverished, when in a fit of coughing she had brought up a little blood – oh, not much, just an insignificant little drop; but it would of course have been better if there had been none at all. And the disturbing thing was that before long the same unpleasant little incident recurred. Well, this was a matter that could be dealt with, and Dr Hinzpeter, the family physician, took the appropriate measures. Complete rest was ordered, little pieces of ice were swallowed, morphine was prescribed to check the coughing and all possible steps were taken to tranquillize the heart. Nevertheless the patient's condition failed to improve; and whereas the child, that magnificent infant Anton Klöterjahn Jr, won and held his place in life with colossal energy and ruthlessness, his young mother seemed to be gently fading away, quietly burning herself out . . . It was, as we have mentioned, the trachea; and this word, when Dr Hinzpeter used it, had a remarkably soothing, reassuring, almost cheering effect upon all concerned. But even though it was not the lungs, the doctor had in the end strongly recommended a milder climate, and a period of residence in a sanatorium, to hasten the patient's recovery; and the reputation of Einfried and of its director had done the rest.

Thus matters stood; and Herr Klöterjahn himself would tell the whole story to anyone sufficiently interested to listen. He had a loud, slovenly, good-humoured way of talking, like a man whose digestion is as thoroughly sound as his finances. He spoke with extravagant movements of the lips, broadly yet fluently, as people from the north coast do; many of his words were spluttered out with a minor explosion in every syllable, and he would laugh at this as if at a successful joke.

He was of medium height, broad, strongly built, with short legs, a round red face, watery blue eyes, pale blond eyelashes, wide nostrils and moist lips. He wore English side-whiskers and a complete outfit of English clothes, and was delighted to encounter an English family at Einfried – father, mother and three attractive children with their nurse, who were here simply and solely because they could not think of anywhere else to live. Herr Klöterjahn ate an English breakfast with them every morning. He had a general predilection for eating and drinking plentifully and well; he displayed a real connoisseur's knowledge of food and wine, and would entertain the inmates of the sanatorium with highly stimulating accounts of dinners given by his friends at home, describing in particular certain choice dishes unknown in these southern parts. As he did so his eyes would narrow benevolently, while his speech became increasingly palatal and nasal and was accompanied by slight munching sounds at the back of his throat. He was also not altogether averse to certain other worldly pleasures, as was made evident one evening when one of the patients at

Einfried, a writer by profession, saw him flirting rather disgracefully with a chambermaid in the corridor – a trifling, humorous incident to which the writer in question reacted with a quite ludicrous grimace of disapproval.

As for Herr Klöterjahn's wife, it was plain for all to see that she was deeply attached to him. She watched his every movement and smiled at all he said. Her manner showed no trace of that patronizing indulgence with which many sick people treat those who are well; on the contrary she behaved as kindly and good-natured patients do, taking genuine pleasure in the hearty self-assurance of persons blessed with good health.

Herr Klöterjahn did not remain at Einfried for long. He had escorted his wife here; but after a week, having assured himself that she was well provided for and in good hands, he saw no reason to prolong his stay. Equally pressing duties – his flourishing child and his no less flourishing business – recalled him to his native town; they obliged him to depart, leaving his wife behind to enjoy the best of care.

4

The name of the writer who had been living in Einfried for several weeks was Spinell – Detlev Spinell; and his appearance was rather extraordinary.

Let us imagine a tall, well built man in his early thirties, with dark hair already beginning to turn distinctly grey about the temples, and a round, white, rather puffy face on which there was not the slightest sign of any growth of beard. It had not been shaved – that would have been noticeable; it was soft, indistinctly outlined and boyish, with nothing on it but an occasional little downy hair. And this really did look very odd. He had gentle, glistening, chestnut brown eyes and a thick, rather too fleshy nose. He also had an arched, porous, Roman-looking upper lip, large carious teeth and feet of remarkable dimensions. One of the gentlemen with the unruly legs, a cynic and would-be wit, had christened him behind his back 'the putrefied infant'; but this was malicious and wide of the mark. He dressed well and fashionably, in a long dark coat and a waistcoat with coloured spots.

He was unsociable and kept company with no one. Only occasionally was he seized by a mood of affability and exuberant friendliness, and this always happened when his aesthetic sensibilities were aroused – when the sight of something beautiful, a harmonious combination of colours, a vase of noble shape or the light of the setting sun on the mountains, transported him to articulate expressions of admiration. 'What beauty!' he would then exclaim, tilting his head to one side, raising his shoulders, spreading out his hands and curling back his nose and lips. 'Ah, dear me, pray observe, how beautiful that is!' And in the emotion of such moments Herr Spinell was capable of falling blindly upon the neck of no matter who might be at hand, whatever their status or sex . . .

On his desk, permanently on view to anyone who entered his room, lay the book he had written. It was a novel of moderate length with a completely baffling cover design, printed on the kind of paper one might use for filtering coffee, in elaborate typography with every letter looking like a Gothic cathedral. Fräulein von Osterloh had read it in an idle quarter of an hour and had declared it to be 'refined', which was her polite way of saying 'unconscionably tedious'. Its scenes were set in fashionable drawing-rooms and luxurious boudoirs full of exquisite *objets d'art*, full of Gobelin tapestries, very old furniture, priceless porcelain, rare materials and artistic treasures of every sort. They were all described at length and with loving devotion, and as one read one constantly seemed to see Herr Spinell curling back his nose and exclaiming: 'What beauty! Ah, dear me, pray observe, how beautiful that is!' It was, to be sure, rather surprising that he had not written any other books than this one, since his passion for writing was evidently extreme. He spent most of the time in his room doing so, and sent an extraordinary number of letters to the post, one or two almost every day – though the odd and amusing thing was that he himself very rarely received any . . .

## 5

Herr Spinell sat opposite Herr Klöterjahn's wife at table. On the occasion of the new guests' first appearance in the great dining-room on the ground floor of the side wing, he arrived a minute or two late, murmured a greeting to the company generally and took his seat, whereupon Dr Leander, without much ceremony, introduced him to the new arrivals. He bowed and began to eat, evidently a trifle embarrassed, and manoeuvring his knife and fork in a rather affected manner with his large, white, well formed hands which emerged from very narrow coat sleeves. Later he seemed less ill at ease and looked calmly by turns at Herr Klöterjahn and at his wife. Herr Klöterjahn too, in the course of the meal, addressed one or two questions and remarks to him about the topography and climate of Einfried; his wife also interspersed a few charming words, and Herr Spinell answered politely. His voice was soft and really quite agreeable, though he had a slightly impeded, dragging way of speaking, as if his teeth were getting in the way of his tongue.

After the meal, when the company had moved over to the drawing-room and Dr Leander was uttering the usual courtesies to the new guests in particular, Herr Klöterjahn's wife inquired about the gentleman who had sat opposite.

'What is his name?' she asked . . . 'Spinelli? I didn't quite catch it.'

'Spinell – not Spinelli, madam. No, he's not an Italian, merely a native of Lemberg, so far as I know . . .'

'Did you say he was a writer, or something like that?' asked Herr Klöterjahn. His hands were in the pockets of his easy-fitting English trousers; he tilted one ear towards the doctor, and opened his mouth to listen, as some people do.

'Yes, I don't know – he writes . . .' answered Dr Leander. 'He has published a book, I believe, some kind of novel; I really don't know . . .'

These repeated declarations of ignorance indicated that Dr Leander had no very high opinion of the writer and declined all responsibility for him.

'But that is extremely interesting!' said Herr Klöterjahn's wife. She had never yet met a writer face to face.

'Oh, yes,' replied Dr Leander obligingly. 'I am told he has a certain reputation . . .' After that no more was said about the writer.

But a little later, when the new guests had withdrawn and Dr Leander too was just about to leave the drawing-room, Herr Spinell detained him and made inquiries in his turn.

'What is the name of the couple?' he asked . . . 'I didn't catch it, of course.'

'Klöterjahn,' answered Dr Leander, already turning to go.

'*What* is his name?' asked Herr Spinell . . .

'Their name is *Klöterjahn*,' said Dr Leander, and walked away. He really had no very high opinion of the writer.

## 6

I think we had reached the point at which Herr Klöterjahn had returned home. Yes – he was back on the shores of the Baltic with his business and his baby, that ruthless vigorous little creature who had cost his mother so much suffering and a slight defect of the trachea. She herself, the young wife, remained behind at Einfried, and Magistratsrätin Spatz appointed herself as her friend and chaperon. This however did not prevent Herr Klöterjahn's wife from being on friendly terms with the other inmates of the sanatorium – for example, with Herr Spinell, who to everyone's astonishment (for hitherto he had kept company with no one) treated her from the outset in an extraordinarily devoted and courteous manner; and she for her part, during the few leisure hours permitted by her rigorous daily regime, seemed by no means averse to his conversation.

He would approach her with extreme circumspection and deference, and always talked to her in a carefully muted voice, so that Rätin Spatz, who was hard of hearing, usually did not catch a word of what he said. He would tiptoe on his great feet up to the armchair in which Herr Klöterjahn's wife reclined, fragile and smiling; at a distance of two paces he would stop, with one leg poised a little way behind the other and bowing from the waist; and in this posture he would talk to her in his rather impeded, dragging way, softly and intensely, but ready at any moment to withdraw and disappear as soon as her face should show the slightest sign of fatigue or annoyance. But she was not annoyed; she would invite him to sit down beside her and Frau Spatz; she would ask him some question or other and then listen to him with smiling curiosity, for often he said amusing and strange things such as no one had ever said to her before.

'Why actually are you at Einfried?' she asked. 'What treatment are you taking, Herr Spinell?'

'Treatment? . . . Oh, I am having a little electrical treatment. It's really nothing worth mentioning. I will tell you, dear madam, why I am here: it is on account of the style.'

'Ah?' said Herr Klöterjahn's wife, resting her chin on her hand and turning towards him with an exaggerated show of interest, as one does to children when they want to tell one something.

'Yes. Einfried is pure *Empire*; I am told it used to be a royal residence, a summer palace. This side wing of course is a later addition, but the main building is old and genuine. Now, there are times when I simply cannot do without *Empire*, times when it is absolutely necessary to me if I am to achieve even a modest degree of well-being. You will appreciate that one's state of mind when one is surrounded by voluptuously soft and luxurious furniture differs entirely from the mood inspired by the straight lines of these tables and chairs and draperies . . . This brightness and hardness, this cold, austere simplicity, this rigorous reserve imparts its composure and dignity to the beholder: prolonged contact with it has an inwardly purifying and restoring effect on me – there is no doubt that it raises my moral tone.'

'Really, how remarkable,' she said. 'And I think I can understand what you mean, if I make an effort.'

Whereupon he replied that what he meant was certainly not worth making an effort to understand, and they both laughed. Rätin Spatz also laughed and thought it remarkable; but she did not say that she understood what he meant.

The drawing-room was large and beautiful. A tall white double door, standing wide open, led to the adjacent billiard-room in which the gentlemen with the unruly legs and some others were playing. On the other side was a glass door through which one could see into the wide terrace and the garden. Near it stood a piano. There was a card-table with a green top at which the diabetic general and a few other gentlemen were playing whist. Ladies sat reading or doing needlework. The room was heated by an iron stove, but in front of the elegant fireplace with its pieces of imitation coal pasted over with glowing red paper, there were comfortable places to sit and talk.

'You are an early riser, Herr Spinell. I have already quite by chance seen you two or three times leaving the house at half-past seven in the morning.'

'An early riser? . . . Ah, only in a rather special sense, dear madam. The fact is that I rise early because I am really a late sleeper.'

'Now, that you must explain, Herr Spinell!' – Rätin Spatz also desired an explanation.

'Well . . . if one is an early riser, then it seems to me that one does not really need to get up so early. Conscience, dear lady – conscience is a terrible thing! I and my kind spend all our lives battling with it, and we have our hands full trying from time to time to deceive it and to satisfy it in cunning little ways. We are useless creatures, I and my kind, and apart from our few good hours we do nothing but chafe ourselves sore and sick against the knowledge of our own uselessness. We hate everything that is useful, we know that it is vulgar and ugly, and we defend this truth fanatically, as one only defends truths that are absolutely necessary to one's existence. And nevertheless our bad conscience so gnaws at us that it leaves not one spot on us unscathed. In addition, matters are made worse by the whole character of our inner life, by our outlook, our way of working – they are terribly unwholesome, they undermine us, they exhaust us. And so one has recourse to certain little palliatives, without which it would all be quite unendurable. For example, some of us feel the need for a well conducted outward existence, for a certain hygienic austerity in our habits. To get up early, cruelly early; to take a cold bath and a walk out into the snow . . . That makes us feel moderately satisfied with ourselves for perhaps an hour or so. If I were to act in accordance with my true nature, I should lie in bed until well into the afternoon, believe me. My early rising is really hypocrisy.'

'Why, not at all, Herr Spinell! I call it self-discipline . . . Don't you, Frau Rätin?' Rätin Spatz also called it self-discipline.

'Hypocrisy or self-discipline – whichever word you prefer! I have a melancholically honest disposition, and consequently . . .'

'That's just it. I am sure you are much too melancholic.'

'Yes, dear madam, I am melancholic.'

The fine weather continued. Everything was bright, hard and clean, windless and frosty; the house and garden, the surrounding countryside and the mountains, lay mantled in dazzling whiteness and pale blue shadows; and over it all stood a vaulted sky of delicate azure and utter purity, in which a myriad shimmering light particles and dazzling crystals seemed to be dancing. At this period Herr Klöterjahn's wife seemed to be in tolerably good health; she had no fever, scarcely coughed at all, and had not too bad an appetite. Often she would sit out on the terrace for hours in the frost and the sun, as her doctor had prescribed. She sat in the snow, warmly wrapped in blankets and furs, hopefully breathing in the pure icy air for the benefit of her trachea. Sometimes she would see Herr Spinell walking in the garden; he too was warmly dressed and wore fur boots which made his feet look absolutely enormous. He walked through the snow with a tentative gait and a careful, prim posture of the arms; when he reached the terrace he would greet her very respectfully and mount the steps to engage her in a little conversation.

'I saw a beautiful woman on my morning walk today . . . Ah, dear me, how beautiful she was!' he said, tilting his head to one side and spreading out his hands.

'Really, Herr Spinell? Do describe her to me!'

'No, that I cannot do. Or if I did, I should be giving you an incorrect picture of her. I only glanced fleetingly at the lady as I passed, I did not really see her. But that uncertain glimpse was sufficient to stir my imagination, and I received and took away with me a vision of beauty . . . ah, of what beauty!'

She laughed. 'Is that your way of looking at beautiful women, Herr Spinell?'

'Yes, dear madam; and it is a better way than if I were to stare them in the face with a crude appetite for reality, and imprint their actual imperfections on my mind . . .'

' "Appetite for reality" . . . what a strange phrase! That really is a phrase only a writer could have used. Herr Spinell! But I must confess that it impresses me. It suggests something to me that I partly understand, a certain feeling of independence and freedom, even a certain disrespect for reality – although I know that reality is more deserving of respect than anything else, indeed that it is the only truly respectable thing . . . And then I realize that there is something beyond what we can see and touch, something more delicate . . .'

'I know only one face,' he said suddenly, speaking with a strange exaltation, raising his clenched hands to his shoulders and showing his carious teeth in an ecstatic smile . . . 'I know only one face which even in reality is so noble and spiritual that any attempt by my imagination to improve upon it would be blasphemy – a face at which I could gaze, which I long to contemplate, not for minutes, not for hours, but for the whole of my life, for in it I should lose myself utterly and forget all earthly things . . .'

'Yes, quite, Herr Spinell. But Fräulein von Osterloh's ears stick out rather far, don't you think?'

He made no reply and bowed deeply. When he raised his eyes again, they rested with an expression of embarrassment and sadness on the strange, sickly little pale blue vein that branched out across the clear, almost translucent surface of her forehead.

# 7

A strange fellow, a really very odd fellow! Herr Klöterjahn's wife sometimes thought about him, for she had plenty of time for thinking. Perhaps the beneficial effect of the change of air had begun to wear off, or perhaps some positively harmful influence was at work upon her: at all events her state of health had deteriorated, the condition of her trachea seemed to leave much to be desired, she felt weak and weary, she had lost her appetite and was often feverish. Dr Leander had most emphatically urged her to rest, not to talk too much, to exercise the utmost care. And so, when she was allowed up at all, she would sit with Rätin Spatz, not talking too much, holding her needlework idly in her lap and thinking her thoughts as they came and went.

Yes, this curious Herr Spinell made her think and wonder; and the remarkable thing was that he made her think not so much about him as about herself; somehow he awakened in her a strange curiosity about her own nature, a kind of interest in it she had never felt before. One day, in the course of conversation, he had remarked:

'Yes, women are certainly very mysterious . . . the facts are nothing new, and yet they are a perpetual source of astonishment. One is confronted, let us say, with some wonderful creature – a sylph, a figure from a dream, a fairy's child. And what does she do? She goes off and marries some fairground Hercules, some butcher's apprentice. And there she comes, leaning on his arm, perhaps even with her head on his shoulder, and looking about her with a subtle smile as if to say: "Well, here's a phenomenon to make you all rack your brains!" And we rack them, we do indeed.'

This was a speech which Herr Klöterjahn's wife had repeatedly pondered.

On another occasion, to the astonishment of Rätin Spatz, the following dialogue took place between them:

'I am sure, dear madam, that it is very impertinent of me, but may I ask you what your name is – what it really is?'

'But my name is Klöterjahn, Herr Spinell, as you know!'

'Hm. Yes, that I know. Or rather: that I deny. I mean of course your own name, your maiden name. You must in all fairness concede, dear madam, that if anyone were to address you as "Frau Klöterjahn" he would deserve to be horsewhipped.'

She laughed so heartily that the little blue vein over her eyebrow stood out alarmingly clearly and gave her sweet delicate face a strained, anxious expression that was deeply disturbing.

'Why, good gracious, Herr Spinell! Horsewhipped? Do you find "Klöterjahn" so appalling?'

'Yes, dear madam, I have most profoundly detested that name ever since I first heard it. It is grotesque, it is unspeakably ugly; and to insist on social convention to the point of calling you by your husband's name is barbaric and outrageous.'

'Well, what about "Eckhof"? Is Eckhof any better? My father's name is Eckhof.'

'Ah, there now, you see! "Eckhof" is quite another matter! There was once even a great actor called Eckhof. Eckhof is appropriate. You only mentioned your father. Is your mother . . .'

'Yes; my mother died when I was little.'

'I see. Please tell me a little more about yourself; do you mind my asking? If it tires you, then do not do it. Just rest, and I will go on describing Paris to you, as I did the other day. But you could talk very softly, you know; you could even whisper, and it would make what you tell me all the more beautiful . . . You were born in Bremen?' He uttered this question almost voicelessly, with an expression of reverent awe, as if he were asking something momentous, as if Bremen were some city beyond compare, full of ineffable excitements and hidden beauties, and as if to have been born there conferred some kind of mysterious distinction.

'Yes, just fancy!' she said involuntarily. 'I was born in Bremen.'

'I was there once,' he remarked meditatively.

'Good gracious, you've been there, too? Why, Herr Spinell, I do believe you've seen everything there is to see between Tunis and Spitzbergen!'

'Yes, I was there once,' he repeated. 'For a few short hours, one evening. I remember an old, narrow street with gabled houses and the moon slanting strangely down on them. And then I was in a vaulted basement room that smelled of wine and decay. How vividly I recall it . . .'

'Really? I wonder where that was. Yes, I was born in a grey gabled house like that, an old patrician merchant's house with an echoing front hall and a white-painted gallery.'

'Then your father is a man of business?' he asked a little hesitantly.

'Yes. But in addition, or perhaps I should really say in the first place, he is an artist.'

'Ah! Ah! What kind of artist?'

'He plays the violin. But that is not saying much. It is *how* he plays it that matters, Herr Spinell! I have never been able to listen to certain notes without tears coming to my eyes – such strange, hot tears! No other experience has ever moved me like that. I dare say you will scarcely believe me . . .'

'I believe you! Oh, I believe you indeed! . . . Tell me, dear lady: surely your family is an old one? Surely, in that grey gabled house, many generations have already lived and laboured and been gathered to their forefathers?'

'Yes. But why do you ask?'

'Because it often happens that an old family, with traditions that are entirely practical, sober and bourgeois, undergoes in its declining days a kind of artistic transfiguration.'

'Is that so? Well, so far as my father is concerned he is certainly more of an artist than many a man who calls himself one and is famous for it. I only play the piano a little. Of course, now they have forbidden me to play; but I still did in those days, when I was at home. Father and I used to play together . . . Yes, all those years are a precious memory to me; especially the garden, our garden behind the house. It was terribly wild and overgrown, and the walls round it were crumbling and covered with moss; but that was just what gave it its great charm. It had a fountain in the middle, surrounded by a dense border of flag irises. In summer I used to sit there for hours with my friends. We would all sit on little garden chairs round the fountain . . .'

'What beauty!' said Herr Spinell, raising his shoulders. 'You sat round it singing?'

'No, we were usually crocheting.'

'Ah, nevertheless . . . nevertheless . . .'

'Yes, we crocheted and gossiped, my six friends and I . . .'

'What beauty! Ah, dear me, how beautiful that is!' cried Herr Spinell, with his face quite contorted.

'But what is so particularly beautiful about that, Herr Spinell?'

'Oh, the fact that there were six young ladies besides yourself, the fact that you were not one of their number, but stood out amongst them like a queen . . . You were singled out from your six friends. A little golden crown, quite inconspicuous yet full of significance, gleamed in your hair . . .'

'Oh, what nonsense, there was no such crown . . .'

'Ah, but there was: it gleamed there in secret. I should have seen it, I should have seen it in your hair quite plainly, if I had been standing unnoticed among the bushes on one of those occasions . . .'

'Heaven knows what you would have seen. But you were not standing there, on the contrary it was my husband, as he now is, who one day stepped out of the bushes with my father beside him. I'm afraid they had even been listening to a lot of our chatter . . .'

'So that, dear madam, was where you first met your husband?'

'Yes, that was where I met him!' Her voice was firm and happy, and as she smiled the little delicate blue vein stood out strangely and strenuously above her brow. 'He was visiting my father on business, you see. He came to dinner the following evening, and only three days later he asked for my hand.'

'Really! Did it all happen so very fast?'

'Yes . . . Or rather, from then on it went a little more slowly. You see, my father was not at all keen on the marriage, and insisted on our postponing it for quite a long time to think it over properly. It was partly that he would have preferred me to go on living with him, and he had other reservations about it as well. But . . .'

'But?'

'But *I* was quite determined,' she said with a smile, and once more the little pale blue vein overshadowed her sweet face with an anxious, sickly expression.

'Ah, you were determined.'

'Yes, and I made my wishes quite clear and stood my ground, as you see . . .'

'As I see. Yes.'

'. . . so that my father had to give his consent in the end.'

'And so you forsook him and his violin, you forsook the old house and the overgrown garden and the fountain and your six friends, and followed after Herr Klöterjahn.'

' "And followed after" . . . How strangely you put things, Herr Spinell! It sounds almost biblical! Yes, I left all that behind me, for after all, that is the law of nature.'

'Of nature, yes, I dare say it is.'

'And after all, my future happiness was at stake.'

'Of course. And you came to know that happiness . . .'

'I came to know it, Herr Spinell, when they first brought little Anton to me, our little Anton, and when I heard him crying so noisily with his healthy little lungs, the strong, healthy little creature . . .'

'I have heard you mention the good health of your little Anton before, dear lady. He must be a quite exceptionally healthy child?'

'Yes, he is. And he looks so absurdly like my husband!'

'Ah! I see. So that was how it happened. And now your name is no longer Eckhof, but something else, and you have your healthy little Anton and a slight defect of the trachea.'

'Yes. And as for *you*, Herr Spinell, you are a most mysterious person, I do assure you . . .'

'Yes, God bless my soul, so you are!' said Rätin Spatz, who was, after all, still there.

But this conversation too was one to which Herr Klöterjahn's wife afterwards frequently reverted in her thoughts. Insignificant though it had been, there had nevertheless been several things latent in it which gave her food for reflection about herself. Could *this* be the harmful influence that was affecting her? Her weakness increased, and her temperature often rose: she would lie in a quiet feverish glow, in a state of mild euphoria to which she surrendered herself pensively, fastidiously, complacently, with a faintly injured air. When she was not confined to her bed, Herr Spinell would approach her, tiptoeing up to her on his great feet with extreme circumspection, stopping at a distance of two paces with one leg poised a little way behind the other, and bowing from the waist: he would talk to her in a deferentially muted voice, as if he were raising her gently aloft with reverent awe, and laying her down on soft cushioning clouds where no strident noise nor earthly contact should reach her. At such moments she would remember Herr Klöterjahn's way of saying 'Careful, Gabriele, take care, darling, and keep your mouth closed!' in a voice as hard as a well-meant slap on the back. But then she would at once put this memory aside and lie back weakly and euphorically on the cloudy cushions which Herr Spinell so assiduously spread out beneath her.

One day, apropos of nothing at all, she suddenly reverted to the little conversation they had had about her background and earlier life.

'So it is really true, Herr Spinell,' she asked, 'that you would have seen the crown?'

And although it was already a fortnight since they had talked of this, he at once knew what she meant and ardently assured her that if he had been there then, as she sat with her six friends by the fountain, he would have seen the little golden crown gleaming – would have seen it secretly gleaming in her hair.

A few days later one of the patients politely inquired whether her little Anton at home was in good health. She exchanged a fleeting glance with Herr Spinell who was nearby, and answered with a slightly bored expression:

'Thank you, he is quite well; why should he not be? And so is my husband.'

# 8

One frosty day at the end of February, a day purer and more brilliant than any that had preceded it, high spirits prevailed at Einfried. The heart cases chattered away to each other with flushed cheeks, the diabetic general hummed and chirruped like a boy, and the gentlemen with the unruly legs were quite beside themselves with excitement. What was it all about? A communal outing had been planned, nothing less: an excursion into the mountains in several sleighs, with jingling bells and cracking whips. Dr Leander had decided upon this diversion for his patients.

Of course, the 'serious cases' would have to stay at home, poor things! With much meaningful nodding it was tacitly agreed that the entire project must be concealed from them, and the opportunity to exercise this degree of compassion and consideration filled everyone with a glow of self-righteousness. But even a few of those who might very well have taken part in the treat declined to do so. Fräulein von Osterloh was of course excused in any case. No one so overburdened with duties as herself could seriously contemplate going on sleigh excursions. The tasks of the household imperatively required her presence – and in short, at Einfried she remained. But there was general disappointment when Herr Klöterjahn's wife also declared her intention of staying at home. In vain Dr Leander urged upon her the benefits of the refreshing trip; she insisted that she was not in the mood, that she had a headache, that she felt tired; and so there was no more to be said. But the cynical would-be wit took occasion to observe:

'Mark my words, now the Putrefied Infant won't come either.'

And he was right, for Herr Spinell let it be known that he intended to spend the afternoon working – he was very fond of describing his dubious activity as 'work'. The prospect of his absence was in any case regretted by no one, and equally little dismay was caused by Rätin Spatz's decision to remain behind and keep her young friend company, since (as she said) sleigh-riding made her feel seasick.

There was an early lunch that day, at about noon, and immediately after it the sleighs drew up in front of Einfried. The patients, warmly wrapped up, made their way across the garden in animated groups, full of excitement and curiosity. The scene was watched by Herr

Klöterjahn's wife and Rätin Spatz from the glass door leading out to the terrace, and by Herr Spinell from the window of his room. There was a certain amount of playful and hilarious fighting about who should sit where; Fräulein von Osterloh, with a fur boa round her neck, darted from sleigh to sleigh pushing hampers of food under the seats; finally Dr Leander, wearing a fur cap above his flashing spectacles, sat down himself after a last look round, and gave the signal for departure . . . The horses drew away, a few ladies shrieked and fell over backwards, the bells jangled, the short-shafted whips cracked and their long lashes trailed across the snow beside the runners; and Fraülein von Osterloh stood at the garden gate waving her handkerchief until the vehicles slid out of sight round a bend in the road and the merry noise died away. Then she hurried back through the garden to set about her tasks again; the two ladies left the glass door, and almost simultaneously Herr Spinell retired from his vantage-point.

Silence prevailed in Einfried. The expedition was not expected back before evening. The 'serious cases' lay in their rooms and suffered. Herr Klöterjahn's wife and her companion took a short walk and then withdrew to their rooms. Herr Spinell, too, was in his room, occupied after his fashion. At about four o'clock half a litre of milk was brought to each of the ladies, and Herr Spinell was served with his usual weak tea. Shortly after this Herr Klöterjahn's wife tapped on the wall between her room and that of Magistratsrätin Spatz and said:

'Shall we go down to the drawing-room, Frau Rätin? I really can't think of anything else to do here.'

'Certainly, my dear, I'll come at once,' answered Frau Spatz. 'I'll just put on my boots, if you don't mind, because I've just been taking a bit of a rest, as a matter of fact.'

As might have been expected, the drawing-room was empty. The ladies sat down by the fireplace. Rätin Spatz was embroidering flowers on a piece of canvas; Herr Klöterjahn's wife, too, began a little needlework, but presently let it drop into her lap and gazed dreamily over the arm of her chair at nothing in particular. Finally she made a remark which was really not worth opening one's mouth to reply to. But Rätin Spatz nevertheless asked: 'What did you say?' so that to her humiliation she had to repeat the whole sentence. Rätin Spatz again asked: 'What?' But just at this moment they heard steps in the lobby, the door opened and Herr Spinell came into the room.

'Do I disturb you?' he asked softly, pausing on the threshold, looking only at Herr Klöterjahn's wife, and executing a kind of delicately hovering half-bow from the waist . . . She replied: 'Why, not at all, Herr Spinell! In the first place this room is supposed to be open to all comers, as you know, and in any case what is there to disturb? I have a very strong suspicion that I am boring Frau Spatz . . .'

He could think of no answer to this, but merely smiled, showing his carious teeth. The eyes of the two ladies followed him as with a certain air of embarrassment he walked to the glass door, where he stopped and stood looking out, rather ill-manneredly turning his back on them. Then he half turned towards them, but continued to gaze out into the garden as he said:

'The sun has disappeared. The sky has imperceptibly clouded over. It's beginning to get dark already.'

'Yes, indeed, there are shadows everywhere,' replied Herr Klöterjahn's wife. 'I should think it may well be snowing before our sleighing party gets back. Yesterday at this time it was still broad daylight, and now dusk is falling.'

'Oh,' he said, 'what a relief it is to the eyes! There has been too much brightness these last few weeks – too much of this sun which glares with such obtrusive clarity on everything, whether beautiful or vulgar . . . I am really thankful that it is hiding its face for a little at last.'

'Do you not like the sun, Herr Spinell?'

'Well, I am no painter, you know . . . When there is no sun one feels more spiritual. There is a thick, pale grey layer of cloud all over the sky. Perhaps it means there will be a thaw tomorrow. Incidentally I would not advise you, dear madam, to go on gazing at your needlework over there.'

'Oh, you need not worry, I've stopped it in any case. But what else is there to do?'

He had sat down on the revolving stool in front of the piano, leaning on the lid of the instrument with one arm.

'Music . . .' he said. 'If only there were a chance to hear a little music nowadays! Sometimes the English children sing little Negro songs, and that is all.'

'And yesterday afternoon Fräulein von Osterloh gave a high-speed rendering of "The Monastery Bells",' remarked Herr Klöterjahn's wife.

'But dear lady, you play, do you not?' he said pleadingly, and rose to his feet . . . 'There was a time when you used to make music every day with your father.'

'Yes, Herr Spinell, that was in the old days! The days of the fountain in the garden, you know . . .'

'Do it today!' he begged. 'Play a few bars just this once! If you knew how I craved to hear them . . .'

'Our family doctor and Dr Leander have both expressly forbidden me to play, Herr Spinell.'

'They are not here; neither of them is here! We are free . . . you are free, dear lady! A few trifling little chords . . .'

'No, Herr Spinell, it's no use your trying to persuade me. Heaven knows what sort of marvels you expect of me! And I have forgotten everything, I assure you. I can play scarcely a note by heart.'

'Oh, then play that! Play scarcely a note! Besides, there is some music here too – here it is, on the top of the piano. No, this is nothing. But here is some Chopin . . .'

'Chopin?'

'Yes, the nocturnes. And now all that remains is for us to light the candles . . .'

'Don't imagine that I am going to play, Herr Spinell! I must not play! What if it were to do me harm?'

He was silent. With his great feet, his long black coat, his grey hair and his beardless face with its indistinctly outlined features, he stood there in the light of the two piano candles, letting his hands hang down by his sides.

Finally he said in a soft voice: 'In that case I cannot ask it of you. If you are afraid it will do you harm, dear madam, then let the beauty that might come to life under your fingers remain dead and mute. You were not always so very prudent; not, at least, when you were asked to make the opposite decision and renounce beauty. You were not concerned about your bodily welfare then, you showed less hesitation and a stronger will when you left the fountain and took off the little golden crown . . . Listen!' he said after a pause, dropping his voice still lower. 'If you sit here now and play as you once did, when your father was still standing beside you and drawing those notes out of his violin that brought tears to your eyes – then perhaps it will be seen again, gleaming secretly in your hair, the little golden crown . . .'

'Really?' she said, with a smile. It somehow happened that her voice failed her on this word, which came out huskily and half in a whisper. She cleared her throat and asked:

'Are those really Chopin's nocturnes you have there?'

'Indeed they are. They are open and everything is ready.'

'Well, then, in God's name, I will play one of them,' she said. 'But only one, do you understand? In any case, after one you certainly won't want to hear any more.'

So saying she rose, put down her needlework and came across to the piano. She sat down on the revolving stool, on which two or three bound volumes of music lay; she adjusted the lights, and began turning over the pages of the Chopin album. Herr Spinell had drawn up a chair, and sat beside her like a music master.

She played the Nocturne in E-flat major, Opus 9, no. 2. If it was really true that she had forgotten anything of what she had once learned, then she must in those days have been a consummate artist. The piano was only a mediocre one, but after the very first notes she was able to handle it with perfect taste and control. She showed a fastidious ear for differences of timbre, and her enthusiastic command of rhythmic mobility verged on the fantastic. Her touch was both firm and gentle. Under her hands the melody sang forth its uttermost sweetness, and the figurations entwined themselves round it with diffident grace.

She was wearing the dress she had worn the day of her arrival, the one with the dark heavy bodice and the thick cut-velvet arabesques, which gave to her head and her hands a look of such unearthly delicacy. The expression of her face did not change as she played, but her lips seemed to grow more clear-cut than ever and the shadows seemed to deepen in the corners of her eyes. When she had finished she lowered her hands to her lap and went on gazing at the music. Herr Spinell sat on motionless, without saying a word.

She played another nocturne, she played a second and a third. Then she rose, but only to look for some more music on the top of the piano.

It occurred to Herr Spinell to examine the black bound albums on the piano stool. Suddenly he uttered an unintelligible sound, and his great white hands passionately fingered one of the neglected volumes.

'It's not possible! . . . It can't be true! . . . And yet there is no doubt

of it! . . . Do you know what this is? . . . Do you realize what has been
lying here – what I have in my hands? . . .'

'What is it?' she asked.

Speechlessly he pointed to the title page. He had turned quite pale; he
lowered the volume and looked at her with trembling lips.

'Indeed? I wonder how that got here? Well, give it to me,' she said
simply. She put it on the music stand, sat down, and after a moment's
silence began to play the first page.

He sat beside her, leaning forward, with his hands between his knees
and his head bowed. She played the opening at an extravagantly,
tormentingly slow tempo, with a disturbingly long pause between each
of the phrases. The *Sehnsucht* motif, a lonely wandering voice in the
night, softly uttered its tremulous question. Silence followed, a silence
of waiting. And then the answer: the same hesitant, lonely strain, but
higher in pitch, more radiant and tender. Silence again. And then, with
that wonderful muted sforzando which is like an upsurging, uprearing
impulse of joy and passion, the love motif began: it rose, it climbed
ecstatically to a mingling sweetness, reached its climax and fell away,
while the deep song of the cellos came into prominence and continued
the melody in grave, sorrowful rapture . . .

Despite the inferiority of her instrument the performer tried with
some success to suggest the appropriate orchestral effects. She rendered
with brilliant precision the violin scales in the great crescendo. She
played with fastidious reverence, lingering faithfully over every significant detail of the structure, humbly and ceremoniously exhibiting it,
like a priest elevating the sacred host. What story did the music tell? It
told of two forces, two enraptured lovers reaching out towards each other
in suffering and ecstasy and embracing in a convulsive mad desire for
eternity, for the absolute . . . The prelude blazed to its consummation
and died down. She stopped at the point where the curtain parts and
continued to gaze silently at the music.

The boredom of Rätin Spatz had by this time reached that degree of
intensity at which it causes protrusion of the eyes and a terrifying,
corpse-like disfigurement of the human countenance. In addition this
kind of music affected her stomach nerves, it threw her dyspeptic
organism into a turmoil of anxiety, and Frau Spatz began to fear that she
was about to have a fit.

'I'm afraid I must go to my room,' she said in a faint voice. 'Goodbye, I shall be back presently.'

And she departed. The evening dusk was already far advanced. Outside on the terrace, thick snow was silently falling. The two candles gave a close and flickering light.

'The second act,' he whispered; and she turned the pages and began playing the second act.

The sound of horns dying away in the distance . . . or was it the wind in the leaves? The soft murmuring of the stream? Already the night had flooded the grove with its stillness and hushed the castle halls, and no warning entreaty availed now to stem the tide of overmastering desire. The sacred mystery was enacted. The torch was extinguished; the descending notes of the death-motif spoke with a strange, suddenly clouded sonority; and in tumultuous impatience the white veil was passionately waved, signalling to the beloved as he approached with outspread arms through the darkness.

Oh boundless, oh unending exultation of this meeting in an eternal place beyond all visible things! Delivered from the tormenting illusion, set free from the bondage of space and time, self and not-self blissfully mingling, 'thine' and 'mine' mystically made one! The mocking falsehoods of day could divide them, but its pomp and show no longer had power to deceive them, for the magic potion had opened their eyes: it had made them initiates and visionaries of night. He who has gazed with love into the darkness of death and beheld its sweet mystery can long for one thing only while daylight still holds him in its delusive thrall: all his desire and yearning is for the sacred night which is eternal and true, and which unifies all that has been separated.

Oh sink down, night of love, upon them; give them that forgetfulness they long for, enfold them utterly in your joy and free them from the world of deception and division! 'See, the last lamp has been extinguished! Thought and the vanity of thinking have vanished in the holy twilight, the world-redeeming dusk outspread over all illusion and all woe. And then, as the shining phantasm fades and my eyes fail with passion: then this world from which the falsehood of day debarred me, which to my unquenchable torment it held out before me as the object of my desire – then I myself, oh wonder of wishes granted! then *I myself* am the world . . .' And there followed

Brangäne's warning call, with those rising violin phrases that pass all understanding.

'I am not always sure what it means, Herr Spinell; I can only guess at some of it. What is "then I myself am the world"?'

He explained it to her, softly and briefly.

'Yes, I see. But how can you understand it all so well, and yet not be able to play it?'

Strangely enough, this simple question quite overwhelmed him. He coloured, wrung his hands and seemed to sink into the floor, chair and all. Finally he answered in stricken tones:

'The two seldom go together. No, I cannot play. But please continue.'

And the drunken paeans of the mystery drama continued. 'Can love ever die? Tristan's love? The love of thy Isolde, of my Isolde? Oh, it is everlasting, death cannot assail it! What could perish by death but the powers that interfere, the pretences that part us, we who are two and one?' By the sweet word 'and' love bound them together – and if death should sunder that bond, how could death come to either of them and not bring with it the other's own life? . . . And thus they sang their mysterious duo, sang of their nameless hope, their death-in-love, their union unending, lost for ever in the embrace of night's magic kingdom. O sweet night, everlasting night of love! Land of blessedness whose frontiers are infinite! What visionary once has dreamed of you and does not dread to wake again into desolate day? O grace of death, cast out that dread! Set free these lovers utterly from the anguish of waking! Ah, this miraculous tempest of rhythms, this chromatic uprushing ecstasy, this metaphysical revelation! 'A rapture beyond knowing, beyond foregoing, far from the pangs of the light that parts us, a tender longing with no fear or feigning, a ceasing in beauty with no pain, an enchanted dreaming in immensity! Thou art Isolde, I am Isolde no longer; I am Tristan no longer, thou art Tristan –'

At this point there was a startling interruption. The pianist suddenly stopped playing and shaded her eyes with her hand to peer into the darkness; and Herr Spinell swung round on his chair. At the far side of the room the door that led into the passage had opened, and a shadowy figure entered, leaning on the arm of a second figure. It was one of the Einfried patients, one who had also been unable to join in the sleigh ride, but had chosen this evening hour for one of her pathetic instinctive tours round the institution: it was the lady who had had nineteen children and was no longer capable of thought – it was Pastorin Höhlenrauch on the arm of her attendant. She did not raise her eyes, but wandered with groping steps across the background of the room and disappeared through the opposite door, like a sleepwalker, dumb and staring and conscious of nothing. All was silent.

'That was Pastorin Höhlenrauch,' he said.

'Yes, that was poor Frau Höhlenrauch,' she replied. Then she turned the pages and played the closing passage of the whole work, the *Liebestod*, Isolde's death-song.

How pale and clear her lips were, and how the shadows deepened in the corners of her eyes! The little pale blue vein over one eyebrow, which gave her face such a disturbingly strained look, stood out more and more prominently on her translucent forehead. Under her rapidly moving hands the fantastic crescendo mounted to its climax, broken by that almost shameless, sudden pianissimo in which the ground seems to slide away under our feet and a sublime lust to engulf us in its depths. The triumph of a vast release, a tremendous fulfilment, a roaring tumult of immense delight, was heard and heard again, insatiably repeated, flooding back and reshaping itself; when it seemed on the point of ebbing away it once more wove the *Sehnsucht*-motif into its harmony, then breathed out its uttermost breath and died, faded into silence, floated into nothingness. A profound stillness reigned.

They both sat listening, tilting their heads to one side and listening.

'That's the sound of bells,' she said.

'It's the sleighs,' he said. 'I shall go.'

He rose and walked across the room. When he came to the door at the far end he stopped, turned round and stood for a moment, uneasily shifting his weight from one foot to the other. And then, fifteen or twenty paces from her, he suddenly sank down on his knees – down on both knees, without a word. His long black frock coat spread out round him on the floor. His hands were clasped across his mouth and his shoulders twitched convulsively.

She sat with her hands in her lap, leaning forward away from the piano, and looked at him. She was smiling with a strained, uncertain smile, and her eyes gazed pensively into the half-darkness, focusing themselves with difficulty, with a slight uncontrollable unsteadiness.

From some way off the jangle of sleigh-bells, the crack of whips and a babel of human voices could be heard approaching.

# 9

The sleigh excursion, which remained the chief topic of conversation for a considerable time, had taken place on the twenty-sixth of February. On the twenty-seventh a thaw set in, everything turned soft and slushy and dripped and dribbled, and on that day Herr Klöterjahn's wife was in excellent health. On the twenty-eighth she coughed up a little blood – oh, hardly any to speak of; but it was blood. At the same time she began to feel weaker than ever before, and took to her bed.

Dr Leander examined her, and his face as he did so was cold and hard. He then prescribed the remedies indicated by medical science: little pieces of ice, morphine, complete rest. It also happened that on the following day he declared himself unable to continue the treatment personally owing to pressure of work, and handed it over to Dr Müller, who meekly undertook it, as his contract required. He was a quiet, pale, insignificant, sad-looking man, whose modest and unapplauded function it was to care for those patients who were scarcely ill at all and for those whose cases were hopeless.

The opinion expressed by Dr Müller, first and foremost, was that the separation between Herr Klöterjahn and his wedded wife had now lasted rather a long time. It was, in his view, extremely desirable that Herr Klöterjahn – if, of course, his prosperous business could possibly spare him – should pay another visit to Einfried. One might write to him, one might even send him a little telegram . . . And it would, Dr Müller thought, undoubtedly cheer and strengthen the young mother if he were to bring little Anton with him – quite apart from the fact that it would be of considerable interest to the doctors to make the acquaintance of this very healthy little child.

And lo and behold, Herr Klöterjahn came. He had received Dr Müller's little telegram and had arrived from the Baltic coast. He dismounted from the carriage, ordered coffee and buttered rolls and looked extremely put out.

'Sir,' he said, 'what is the matter? Why have I been summoned to her?'

'Because it is desirable,' answered Dr Müller, 'that you should be near your wife at the present time.'

'Desirable . . . desirable . . .! But is it *necessary?* I have to consider my money, sir – times are bad and railway fares are high. Was this lengthy journey really indispensable? I'd say nothing if for example it were her lungs; but since, thank God, it's only her trachea . . .'

'Herr Klöterjahn,' said Dr Müller gently, 'in the first place the trachea is an important organ . . .' He said 'in the first place', although this was incorrect, since he did not then mention any second place.

But simultaneously with Herr Klöterjahn a buxom young woman appeared at Einfried, clad entirely in red and tartan and gold, and it was she who on one arm carried Anton Klöterjahn Jr, little healthy Anton. Yes – he was here, and no one could deny that he was in fact a prodigy of good health. Pink and white, cleanly and freshly clothed, fat and fragrant, he reposed heavily upon the bare red arm of his gold-braided nurse, devoured enormous quantities of milk and chopped meat, screamed and abandoned himself in all respects to his instincts.

From the window of his room, the writer Spinell had observed the arrival of the Klöterjahn child. Through half-closed eyes, with a strange yet penetrating scrutiny, he had watched him being lifted out of the carriage and conveyed into the house; and he had then stood on motionless for some time with his expression unchanged.

Thereafter, so far as was feasible, he avoided all contact with Anton Klöterjahn Jr.

10

Herr Spinell was sitting in his room 'working'.

It was a room like all the others in Einfried, furnished in a simple and elegant period style. The massive chest of drawers had metal lion's-head mountings; the tall pier-glass was not one smooth sheet, but composed of numerous small panes framed in lead; the gleaming floor was uncarpeted and the stiff legs of the furniture seemed to extend as light shadows into its bluish, varnished surface. A large writing-table stood near the window, across which the novelist had drawn a yellow curtain, presumably to make himself feel more spiritual.

In a yellowish twilight he was sitting bowed over the desk and writing – he was writing one of those numerous letters which he sent to the post every week and to which, comically enough, he usually received no reply. A large thick sheet of writing-paper lay before him, and in its top left-hand corner, under an intricately vignetted landscape, the name 'Detlev Spinell' was printed in letters of an entirely novel design. He was covering this sheet with tiny handwriting, with a neat and most carefully executed calligraphy.

'Sir!' he had written, 'I am addressing the following lines to you because I simply cannot help it – because my heart is so full of what I have to say to you that it aches and trembles, and the words come to me in such a rush that they would choke me if I could not unburden myself of them in this letter . . .'

To be strictly correct, this statement about the words coming to him in a rush was quite simply untrue, and God knows what foolish vanity induced Herr Spinell to make such an assertion. Rushing was the very last thing his words seemed to be doing; indeed, for one whose profession and social status it was to be a writer, he was making miserably slow progress, and no one could have watched him without reaching the conclusion that a writer is a man to whom writing comes harder than to anyone else.

Between two fingertips he held one of the strange little downy hairs that grew on his face and went on twirling it for periods of a quarter of an hour or more, at the same time staring into vacancy and adding not a line to his composition; he would then daintily pen a few words and come to a halt once more. On the other hand it must be admitted that what he finally produced did give the impression of smooth spontaneity and vigour, notwithstanding its odd and dubious and often scarcely intelligible content.

'I am', the letter continued, 'under an inescapable compulsion to make you see what I see, to make you share the inextinguishable vision that has haunted me for weeks, to make you see it with my eyes, illuminated by the language in which I myself would express what I inwardly behold. An imperative instinct bids me communicate my experiences to the world, to communicate them in unforgettable words each chosen and placed with burning accuracy; and this is an instinct which it is my habit to obey. I ask you, therefore, to hear me.

'I merely wish to tell you about something as it was and as it now is. It is a quite short and unspeakably outrageous story, and I shall tell it without comment, accusation or judgement, but in my own words. It is the story of Gabriele Eckhof, sir, the lady whom you call your wife . . . and please note: although the experience was yours, it is nevertheless I whose words will for the first time raise it for you to the level of a significant event.

'Do you remember the garden, sir, the old neglected garden behind the grey patrician house? Green moss grew in the crevices of the weather-beaten walls that surrounded this wild and dreaming place. And do you remember the fountain in the centre? Lilac-coloured sword-lilies drooped over its crumbling edge, and its silvery jet murmured mysteriously as it played upon the riven stonework. The summer day was drawing to its close.

'Seven maidens were sitting in a circle round the fountain; but in the hair of the seventh, the one and chiefest among them all, the sunset's rays seemed secretly to be weaving a glittering emblem of royal rank. Her eyes were like troubled dreams, and yet her bright lips were parted in a smile . . .

'They were singing. Lifting their slender faces they watched the leaping jet, they gazed up at the point where it wearily and nobly curved into its fall, and their soft clear voices hovered around its graceful dance. Their delicate hands, perhaps, were clasped about their knees as they sang . . .

'Do you remember this scene, sir? Did you even see it? No, you did not. It was not for your eyes, and yours were not the ears to hear the chaste sweetness of that melody. Had you seen it, you would not have dared to draw breath, and your heart would have checked its beat. You would have had to withdraw, go back into life, back to your own life, and preserve what you had beheld as something untouchable and inviolable, as a sacred treasure within your soul, to the end of your earthly days. But what did you do?

'That scene, sir, was the end of a tale. Why did you have to come and destroy it, why give the story so vulgar and ugly and painful a sequel? It had been a moving, tranquil apotheosis, immersed in the transfiguring sunset glow of decline and decay and extinction. An old family, already grown too weary and too noble for life and action, had reached the end of its history, and its last utterances were sounds of music: a few violin notes, full of the sad insight which is ripeness for death . . . Did you look into the eyes that were filled with tears by those notes? It may be that the souls of her six companions belonged to life – but not hers, the soul of their sister and queen: for on it beauty and death had set their mark.

'You saw it, that death-doomed beauty: you looked upon it to lust after it. No reverence, no awe touched your heart at the sight of something so moving and holy. You were not content to look upon it: you had to possess it, to exploit it, to desecrate it . . . What a subtle choice you made! You are a gourmet, sir, a plebeian gourmet, a peasant with taste.

'Please note that I have no wish whatever to offend you. What I have said is not abuse: I am merely stating the formula, the simple psychological formula of your simple, aesthetically quite uninteresting personality; and I am stating it solely because I feel the need to shed a little light for you on your own nature and behaviour – because it is my ineluctable vocation on this earth to call things by their names, to make them articulate, and to illuminate whatever is unconscious. The world is full of what I call "the unconscious type", and all these unconscious types are what I cannot bear! I cannot bear all this primitive, ignorant life, all this naïve activity, this world of infuriating intellectual blindness all round me! I am possessed by a tormenting irresistible impulse to analyse all these human lives in my vicinity, to do my utmost to give to each its correct definition and bring it to consciousness of itself – and I am unrestrained by consideration of the consequences of doing so, I care not whether my words help or hinder, whether they carry comfort and solace or inflict pain.

'You, sir, as I have said, are a plebeian gourmet, a peasant with taste. Although in fact your natural constitution is coarse and your position on the evolutionary scale extremely low, your wealth and your sedentary habits have enabled you to achieve a certain barbarian corruption of the nervous system, sudden and historically quite inappropriate, but lending a certain lascivious refinement to your appetites. I dare say your throat muscles began to contract automatically, as if stimulated by the prospect of swallowing some delicious soup or masticating some rare dish, when you decided to take possession of Gabriele Eckhof . . .

'And so indeed you did: interrupting her dream and imposing your misguided will upon hers, leading her out of the neglected garden into life and ugliness, giving her your vulgar name and making her a married woman, a housewife, a mother. You degraded that weary diffident beauty, which belonged to death and was blossoming in sublime uselessness, by harnessing it to the service of everyday triviality and of that mindless, gross and contemptible idol which is called "nature"; and your peasant conscience has never stirred with the slightest inkling of how profound an outrage you committed.

'Once again: what in fact has happened? She, with those eyes that are like troubled dreams, has borne you a child; to that creature, that mere continuation of its begetter's crude existence, she at the same time gave every particle of vitality and viability she possessed – and now she dies. She is dying, sir! And if nevertheless her departure is not vulgar and trivial, if at the very end she has risen from her degradation and perishes proudly and joyfully under the deadly kiss of beauty, then it is *I* who have made it my business to bring that about. You, I dare say, were in the mean time diverting yourself in quiet corridors with chambermaids.

'But her son, Gabriele Eckhof's son, is living and thriving and triumphant. Perhaps he will continue his father's career and become an active trading citizen, paying his taxes and eating well; perhaps he will be a soldier or an official, an unenlightened and efficient pillar of society; in any case he will be a normally functioning philistine type, unscrupulous and self-assured, strong and stupid.

'Let me confess to you, sir, that I hate you, you and your child, as I hate life itself – the vulgar, absurd and nevertheless triumphant life which you represent, and which is the eternal antithesis and arch-enemy of beauty. I cannot say that I despise you. I am unable to despise you. I honestly admit this. You are the stronger man. In our struggle I have only one thing to turn against you, the sublime avenging weapon of the weak: intellect and the power of words. Today I have used this weapon. For this letter – here too let me make an honest admission – is nothing but an act of revenge; and if it contains even a single phrase that is biting and brilliant and beautiful enough to strike home, to make you aware of an alien force, to shake your robust

equanimity even for one moment, then I shall exult in that dis-
comfiture. – DETLEV SPINELL.'

And Herr Spinell put this piece of writing in an envelope, added a
stamp, daintily penned an address, and delivered it to the post.

## 11

Herr Klöterjahn knocked at the door of Herr Spinell's room; he held a
large, neatly written sheet of paper in one hand, and wore the air of a
man determined upon energetic measures. The post had done its duty,
the letter had completed its curious journey from Einfried to Einfried
and had duly reached its intended recipient. The time was four o'clock
in the afternoon.

When Herr Klöterjahn entered, Herr Spinell was sitting on the sofa
reading his own novel, the book with the baffling cover design. He rose
to his feet with a surprised and interrogative glance at his visitor, while at
the same time colouring perceptibly.

'Good afternoon,' said Herr Klöterjahn. 'Pardon my intrusion upon
your occupations. But may I ask whether you wrote this?' So saying he
held up the large, neatly written sheet in his left hand and struck it with
the back of his right, making it crackle sharply. He then pushed his right
hand into the pocket of his wide, easy-fitting trousers, tilted his head to
one side and opened his mouth to listen, as some people do.

Oddly enough Herr Spinell smiled; with an obliging, rather confused
and half-apologetic smile he raised one hand to his forehead as if he
were trying to recollect what he had done, and said:

'Ah yes . . . that is so . . . I took the liberty . . .'

The fact was that on this particular day he had acted in accordance
with his true nature and slept until noon. Consequently he was suffering
from a bad conscience, his head was not clear, he felt nervous and his
resistance was low. In addition there was now a touch of spring in the
air, which he found fatiguing and deeply depressing. This must all be
mentioned in extenuation of the pitifully silly figure he cut throughout
the following scene.

'Did you indeed? Ah-ha! Very well!' Herr Klöterjahn, having got this opening formality out of the way, thrust his chin down against his chest, raised his eyebrows, flexed his arms and gave various other indications that he was about to come mercilessly to the point. His exuberant self-satisfaction was such that he slightly overdid these preparatory antics, so that what eventually followed did not quite live up to the elaborate menace of the preliminary pantomime. But Herr Spinell had turned several shades paler.

'Very well, my dear sir!' repeated Herr Klöterjahn. 'Then I shall answer it by word of mouth, if you don't mind, having regard to the fact that I consider it idiotic to write letters several pages long to a person to whom one can speak at any hour of the day . . .'

'Well . . . idiotic perhaps . . .' said Herr Spinell with an apologetic, almost humble smile.

'Idiotic!' repeated Herr Klöterjahn, energetically shaking his head in token of the utter unassailability of his position. 'And I'd not be wasting words now on this scribbled piece of trash, frankly I'd not even have kept it to use for wrapping up sandwiches, but for the fact that it has opened my eyes and clarified certain matters which I had not understood, certain changes . . . however, that's no concern of yours and it's beside the point. I am a busy man, I have more important things to think about than your indistinguishable visions . . .'

'I wrote "inextinguishable vision",' said Herr Spinell, drawing himself up to his full height. During this whole scene it was the one moment in which he displayed a minimum of dignity.

'Inextinguishable . . . indistinguishable . . .!' retorted Herr Klöterjahn, glancing at the manuscript. 'Your handwriting's wretched, my dear sir; you'd not get a job in my office. At first sight it seems decent enough, but when you look at it closely it's full of gaps and all of a quiver. However, that's your affair and not mine. I came here to tell you that in the first place you are a fool and a clown – well, let's hope you're aware of that already. But in addition you are a damned coward, and I dare say I don't need to prove that to you in detail either. My wife once wrote to me that when you meet women you don't look them square in the face but just give them a sort of squint from the side, because you're afraid of reality and want to carry away a beautiful impression in your mind's eye. Later on unfortunately she stopped mentioning you in her letters, or I'd have heard some more fine stories about you. But that's the sort of man you are. It's 'beauty' and 'beauty' in every sentence you speak, but the basis of it all is cringing cowardice and envy, and I suppose that also explains your impudent allusion to "quiet corridors". I dare say that remark was intended to knock me absolutely flat, and all it did was to give me a good laugh. A damned good laugh! Well, now have I told you a few home truths? Have I – let me see – "shed a little light for you on your nature and behaviour", you miserable specimen? Not, of course, that it's my "indestructible vocation" to do so, heh, heh! . . .'

'I wrote "ineluctable vocation",' said Herr Spinell; but he let the point go. He stood there crestfallen and helpless, like a great pathetic grey-haired scolded schoolboy.

'Indestructible . . . ineluctable . . . I tell you you are a contemptible cowardly cur. Every day you see me at table. You bow to me and smile, you pass me dishes and smile, you say the polite things and smile. And one fine day you fling this screed of abusive drivel into my face. Ho, yes, you're bold enough on paper! And this ridiculous letter's not the whole story. You've been intriguing against me behind my back, I see that now quite clearly . . . Although you needn't imagine you've had any success. If you flatter yourself that you've put any fancy notions into my wife's head, then you're barking up the wrong tree, my fine friend! My wife has too much common sense! Or if you should even be thinking that when I got here with the child her behaviour towards us was in any way different from what it used to be, then you're even more of a half-wit than I supposed! It's true she didn't kiss the little fellow, but that was a precaution, because just lately the suggestion's been made that the trouble isn't with her trachea but with her lungs, and if that's so one can't be too . . . but anyhow they're still a long way from proving their lung theory, and as for you and your "she is dying, sir" – why, you crazy ninny, you . . .!'

Here Herr Klöterjahn struggled a little to recover his breath. By now he had worked himself up into a passionate rage; he kept stabbing the air with his right forefinger and crumpling the manuscript with his left hand till it was scarcely fit to be seen. His face, between its blond English side-whiskers, had turned terribly red, and swollen veins ran like streaks of wrathful lightning across his clouded brow.

'You hate me,' he went on, 'and you would despise me if I were not the stronger man . . . Yes, and so I am, by God! My heart's in the right place; and where's yours? In your boots most of the time I suppose, and if it were not forbidden by law I'd knock you to pieces, with your "intellect and power of words" and all, you blithering snake in the grass! But that does not mean, my fine fellow, that I intend to put up with your insults lying down, and when I get back and show my lawyer that bit about my "vulgar name" – then we'll see whether you don't get the shock of your life. My name is good, sir, and it's my own hard work that made it good. Just you ask yourself whether anyone will lend you a brass farthing on yours, you idle tramp from God knows where! The law of the land is for dealing with people like you! You're a public danger! You drive people crazy! . . . But I'll have you know that you've not got away with your little tricks this time, my very smart friend! I'm not the man to let your sort get the better of me, oh no! My heart's in the right place . . .'

Herr Klöterjahn was now in a real fury. He was positively bellowing, and kept on repeating that his heart was in the right place.

' "They were singing". Full stop. They were doing nothing of the sort! They were knitting. What's more, from what I overheard, they were discussing a recipe for potato pancakes; and when I show this passage about "decline and decay" to my father-in-law, he'll take you to court too, you may be sure of that! . . . "Do you remember that scene, did you see it?" Of course I saw it, but what I don't see is why I should have held my breath at the sight and run away. I don't squint and leer at women from the side, I look them in the face, and if I like the look of them and they like me, I go ahead and get them. My heart's in the right pl . . .'

Someone was knocking. Knocking at the door of the room, nine or ten times in rapid succession, in an urgent, frantic little tattoo which stopped Herr Klöterjahn in mid-sentence; and a voice exclaimed, panic-stricken and stumbling with distress and haste:

'Herr Klöterjahn, Herr Klöterjahn – oh, is Herr Klöterjahn there?'

'Keep out!' said Herr Klöterjahn rudely. 'What's the matter? I'm busy here talking.'

'Herr Klöterjahn,' said the tremulous, gasping voice, 'you must come . . . the doctors are there too . . . oh, it's so dreadfully sad . . .'

He was at the door with one stride and snatched it open. Rätin Spatz was standing outside. She was holding her handkerchief to her mouth, and great long tears were rolling down into it from both her eyes.

'Herr Klöterjahn,' she managed to say, '. . . .it's so terribly sad . . .
She brought up so much blood, such a dreadful lot . . . She was sitting
up quite quietly in her bed humming a little snatch of music to herself,
and then it came – oh, God, there was such a lot, you never saw such a
lot . . .'

'Is she dead?' shrieked Herr Klöterjahn, seizing Frau Spatz by the arm
and dragging her to and fro on the threshold . . . 'No, not quite, what?
Not quite dead yet, she can still see me, can't she? Brought up a little
blood again, has she? From the lungs, was it? Maybe it does come from
the lungs, I admit that it may . . . Gabriele!' he cried suddenly, tears
starting to his eyes, and the warm, kindly, honest, human emotion that
welled up from within him was plain to see. 'Yes, I'm coming!' he said,
and with long strides he dragged Frau Spatz out of the room and away
along the corridor. From far in the distance his rapidly receding voice
could still be heard: 'Not quite, what? . . . From her lungs, you say?'

## 12

Herr Spinell went on standing exactly where he had stood throughout
Herr Klöterjahn's so abruptly terminated visit. He stared at the open
door; finally he advanced a few steps into the passage and listened. But in
the distance all was silent; and so he returned to his room, closing the
door behind him.

He contemplated himself in the mirror for several minutes, then went
to his desk, took a small flask and a glass from somewhere inside it and
swallowed a brandy – for which in the circumstances he could scarcely
be blamed. Then he lay down on the sofa and closed his eyes.

The window was open at the top. Outside in the garden of Einfried
the birds were twittering; and somehow the whole of spring was
expressed in those subtle, tender, penetrating, insolent little notes. At
one point Herr Spinell muttered the phrase 'indestructible vocation . . .!' to himself, and shook his head from side to side, sucking the
breath in between his teeth as if afflicted by acute nervous discomfort.

To regain calm and composure was out of the question. One's
constitution is really quite unsuited to these coarse experiences! By a

psychological process the analysis of which would carry us too far afield, Herr Spinell reached the decision to get up and take a little exercise, a short walk in the open air. Accordingly he picked up his hat and left his room.

As he stepped out of the house into the balmy, fragrant air he turned his head back towards the building and slowly raised his eyes until they reached a certain window, a window across which the curtains had been drawn: he gazed fixedly at it for a while, and his expression was grave and sombre. Then, with his hands on his back, he went on his way along the gravel path. He was deep in thought as he walked.

The flower-beds were still covered with matting, the trees and bushes were still bare; but the snow had gone, and there were only a few damp patches here and there on the paths. The spacious garden with its grottoes, leafy arcades and little pavilions was bathed in the splendid intense colours of late afternoon, full of strong shadows and a rich golden light, and intricate patterns of dark branches and twigs stood sharply and finely silhouetted against the bright sky.

It was the time of day at which the sun's outline becomes clear, when it is no longer a shapeless brilliant mass but a visibly sinking disc whose richer, milder glow the eye can bear to behold. Herr Spinell did not see the sun; he walked with his head bowed, humming a little snatch of music to himself, a brief phrase, a few anguished, plaintively rising notes: the *Sehnsucht*-motif . . . But suddenly, with a start, with a quick convulsive intake of breath, he stood still as if rooted to the spot and stared straight ahead of him, wide-eyed, with sharply contracted brows and an expression of horrified repugnance . . .

The path had turned; it now led straight towards the setting sun, which stood large and low in the sky, its surface intersected by two narrow wisps of gleaming cloud with gilded edges, its warm yellow radiance flooding the garden and setting the tree-tops on fire. And in the very midst of this golden transfiguration, erect on the path, with the sun's disc surrounding her head like a mightly halo, stood a buxom young woman clad entirely in red and gold and tartan. She was resting her right hand on her well-rounded hip, while with her left she lightly rocked a graceful little perambulator to and fro. But in front of her, in this perambulator, sat the child – sat Anton Klöterjahn Jr, Gabriele Eckhof's fat son!

There he sat among his cushions, in a white woolly jacket and a big white hat – chubby, magnificent and robust; and his eyes, unabashed and alive with merriment, looked straight into Herr Spinell's. The novelist was just on the point of pulling himself together; after all, he was a grown man, he would have had the strength to step right past this unexpected sight, this resplendent phenomenon, and continue his walk. But at that very moment the appalling thing happened: Anton Klöterjahn began to laugh – he screamed with laughter, he squealed, he crowed: it was inexplicable. It was positively uncanny.

God knows what had come over him, what had set him off into this wild hilarity: the sight of the black-clad figure in front of him perhaps, or some sudden spasm of sheer animal high spirits. He had a bone teething ring in one hand and a tin rattle in the other, and he held up these two objects triumphantly into the sunshine, brandishing them and banging them together, as if he were mockingly trying to scare someone off. His eyes were almost screwed shut with pleasure, and his mouth gaped open so wide that his entire pink palate was exposed. He even wagged his head to and fro in his exultation.

And Herr Spinell turned on his heel and walked back the way he had come. Pursued by the infant Klöterjahn's jubilant shrieks, he walked along the gravel path, holding his arms in a careful, prim posture; and something in his gait suggested that it cost him an effort to walk slowly – the effort of a man intent upon concealing the fact that he is inwardly running away.

# Tonio Kröger

## Tonio Kröger

1903

# Tonio Kröger

## 1

The winter sun was no more than a feeble gleam, milky and wan behind layers of cloud above the narrow streets of the town. Down among the gabled houses it was damp and draughty, with occasional showers of a kind of soft hail that was neither ice nor snow.

School was over. The hosts of liberated pupils streamed across the cobbled yard and out through the wrought-iron gate, where they dispersed and hastened off in opposite directions. The older ones held their bundles of books in a dignified manner, high up against their left shoulders, and with their right arms to windward steered their course towards dinner; the little ones trotted merrily off with their feet splashing in the icy slush and the paraphernalia of learning rattling about in their sealskin satchels. But now and then they would one and all snatch off their caps with an air of pious awe as some senior master with the beard of Jove and the hat of Wotan strode solemnly by . . .

'Are you coming now, Hans?' said Tonio Kröger; he had been waiting in the street for some time. With a smile he approached his friend, who had just emerged from the gate, chattering to some other boys and about to move off with them . . . 'What?' he asked, looking at Tonio . . . 'Oh yes, of course! All right, let's walk a little.'

Tonio did not speak, and his eyes clouded over with sadness. Had Hans forgotten, had he only just remembered that they had arranged to walk home together this afternoon? And he himself, ever since Hans had promised to come, had been almost continuously looking forward to it!

'Well, so long, you fellows,' said Hans Hansen to his companions.

'I'm just going for a walk now with Kröger.' And the two of them turned to the left, while the others sauntered off to the right.

Hans and Tonio had time to take a walk after school, because they both came from families in which dinner was not served until four o'clock. Their fathers were important men of business, who held public office in the town and wielded considerable influence. The Hansens had for many generations owned the big timber yard down by the river, where powerful mechanical saws hissed and spat as they cut up the tree trunks. But Tonio was the son of Consul Kröger, whose sacks of grain could be seen any day being driven through the streets, with his firm's name stamped on them in great black letters; and his spacious old ancestral house was the grandest in the whole town . . . The two friends were constantly having to doff their caps to their numerous acquaintances; indeed, although they were only fourteen, many of those they met were the first to greet them . . .

Both had slung their satchels across their shoulders, and both were well and warmly dressed: Hans in a short reefer jacket with the broad blue collar of his sailor's suit hanging out over his back, and Tonio in a grey, belted overcoat. Hans wore a Danish sailor's cap with black ribbons, and a shock of his flaxen blond hair stood out from under it. He was extraordinarily good-looking and well built, broad in the shoulders and narrow in the hips, with keen, steely blue eyes set wide apart. But Tonio's complexion, under his round fur cap, was swarthy, his features were sharply cut and quite southern in character, and the look in his dark heavy-lidded eyes, ringed with delicate shadows, was dreamy and a little hesitant . . . The outlines of his mouth and chin were unusually soft. His gait was nonchalant and unsteady, whereas Hans's slender black-stockinged legs moved with a springy and rhythmic step . . .

Tonio was walking in silence. He was suffering. He had drawn his rather slanting brows together and rounded his lips as if to whistle, and was gazing into vacancy with his head tilted to one side. This attitude and facial expression were characteristic of him.

Suddenly Hans pushed his arm under Tonio's with a sidelong glance at him, for he understood very well what was the matter. And although Tonio still did not speak during the next few steps, he suddenly felt very moved.

'I hadn't forgotten, you know, Tonio,' said Hans, gazing down at the sidewalk, 'I just thought we probably wouldn't be having our walk after all today, because it's so wet and windy. But I don't mind the weather of course, and I think it's super of you to have waited for me all the same. I'd already decided you must have gone home, and I felt cross . . .'

Everything in Tonio began to dance with joy at these words.

'Well, then, let's go round along the promenade!' he said, in a voice full of emotion. 'Along the Mühlenwall and the Holstenwall, and that'll take us as far as your house, Hans . . . Oh, of course not, it doesn't matter, I don't mind walking home by myself afterwards; you can walk me home next time.'

In his heart he was not really convinced by what Hans had said, and sensed very clearly that his friend attached only half as much importance as he did to this tête-à-tête walk. But he perceived nevertheless that Hans was sorry for his forgetfulness and was going out of his way to conciliate him. And Tonio was very far from wishing to resist these conciliatory advances . . .

The fact was that Tonio loved Hans Hansen, and had already suffered a great deal on his account. Whoever loves the more is at a disadvantage and must suffer – life had already imparted this hard and simple truth to his fourteen-year-old soul; and his nature was such that when he learned something in this way he took careful note of it, inwardly writing it down, so to speak, and even taking a certain pleasure in it – though without, of course, modifying his own behaviour in the light of it or turning it to any practical account. He had, moreover, the kind of mind that found such lessons much more important and interesting than any of the knowledge that was forced on him at school; indeed, as he sat through the hours of instruction in the vaulted Gothic classrooms, he would chiefly be occupied in savouring these insights to their very depths and thinking out all their implications. And this pastime would give him just the same sort of satisfaction as he felt when he wandered round his own room with his violin (for he played the violin) and drew from it notes of such tenderness as only he could draw, notes which he mingled with the rippling sound of the fountain down in the garden as it leapt and danced under the branches of the old walnut tree . . .

The fountain, the old walnut tree, his violin and the sea in the distance, the Baltic Sea to whose summer reveries he could listen when he visited it in the holidays: these were the things he loved, the things which, so to speak, he arranged around himself and among which his inner life evolved – things with the names that may be employed in poetry to good effect, and which did indeed very frequently recur in the poems that Tonio Kröger from time to time composed.

The fact that he possessed a notebook full of poems written by himself had by his own fault become public knowledge, and it very adversely affected his reputation both with his schoolmates and with the masters. Consul Kröger's son on the one hand thought their disapproval stupid and contemptible, and consequently despised his fellow pupils as well as his teachers, whose ill-bred behaviour in any case repelled him and whose personal weaknesses had not escaped his uncommonly penetrating eye. But on the other hand he himself felt that there was something extravagant and really improper about writing poetry, and in a certain sense he could not help agreeing with all those who considered it a very odd occupation. Nevertheless this did not prevent him from continuing to write . . .

Since he frittered away his time at home and was lethargic and inattentive in class and out of favour with the masters, he continually brought back absolutely wretched reports, to the great annoyance and distress of his father, a tall, carefully dressed man with pensive blue eyes who always wore a wild flower in his buttonhole. To Tonio's mother, however – his beautiful dark-haired mother whose first name was Consuelo and who was in every way so unlike the other ladies of the city, his father having in days gone by fetched her up as his bride-to-be from somewhere right at the bottom of the map – to his mother these school reports did not matter in the least . . .

Tonio loved his dark, fiery mother, who played the piano and the mandolin so enchantingly, and he was glad that his dubious standing in human society did not grieve her. But on the other hand he felt that his father's anger was much more dignified and *comme il faut*, and though scolded by him he basically agreed with his father's view of the matter and found his mother's blithe unconcern slightly disreputable. Often his thoughts would run rather like this: 'It's bad enough that I am as I am, that I won't and can't change and am careless and stubborn and that my mind's full of things no one else thinks about. It's at least only right and proper that I should be seriously scolded and punished for it, instead of having it all passed over with kisses and music. After all, we're not gypsies in a green caravan, but respectable people – the Krögers, Consul Kröger's family . . .' And occasionally he would reflect: 'But why am I peculiar, why do I fight against everything, why am I in the masters' bad books and a stranger among the other boys? Just look at them, the good pupils and the solid mediocre ones! They don't find the masters ridiculous, they don't write poetry and they only think the kind of thoughts that one does and should think, the kind that can be spoken aloud. How decent they must feel, how at peace with everything and everyone! It must be good to be like that . . . But what is the matter with me, and what will come of it all?'

This way of thinking, this view of himself and of how he stood to life, was an important factor in Tonio's love for Hans Hansen. He loved him firstly because he was beautiful; but secondly because he saw him as his own counterpart and opposite in all respects. Hans Hansen was an outstanding pupil as well as being a fine fellow, a first-class rider and gymnast and swimmer who enjoyed universal popularity. The masters almost doted on him, called him by his first name and promoted his interests in every way; his schoolmates vied for his favour; ladies and gentlemen stopped him in the street, seized him by the shock of flaxen blond hair that stood out from under his Danish sailor's cap, and said: 'Good morning, Hans Hansen, with your nice head of hair! Still top of the class? That's a fine lad! Remember me to your father and mother . . .'

Such was Hans Hansen, and ever since they had first met the very sight of him had filled Tonio Kröger with longing, an envious longing which he could feel as a burning sensation in his chest. 'If only one could have blue eyes like yours,' he thought, 'if only one could live so normally and in such happy harmony with all the world as you do! You are always doing something suitable, something that everyone respects. When you have finished your school tasks you take riding lessons or work at things with your fretsaw, and even when you go down to the sea in the holidays you are busy rowing and sailing and swimming, while I lounge about forlornly on the sand, gazing at the mysterious changing expressions that fleet across the face of the sea. But that is why your eyes are so clear. If I could be like you . . .'

He made no attempt to become like Hans Hansen, indeed his wish to be like him was perhaps even hardly serious. But he did most painfully desire that Hans should love him for what he was; and so he sought his love, wooing him after his fashion – patiently and ardently and devotedly. It was a wooing full of anguish and sadness, and this sadness burned deeper and sharper than any impulsive passion such as might have been expected from someone of Tonio's exotic appearance.

And his wooing was not entirely in vain; for Hans, who in any case respected in Tonio a certain superiority, a certain gift of speech, a talent for expressing complicated things, sensed very clearly that he had roused in him an unusually strong and tender feeling. He was grateful for this, and responded in a way that gave Tonio much happiness – but also cost him many a pang of jealousy and disappointment in his frustrated efforts to establish intellectual companionship between them. For oddly enough, although Tonio envied Hans Hansen for being the kind of person he was, he constantly strove to entice him into being like Tonio; and the success of such attempts could at best be only momentary and even then only apparent . . .

'I've just been reading something wonderful, something quite splendid . . .' he was saying. They were walking along eating by turns out of a paper bag of fruit lozenges which they had purchased at Iwersen's store in the Mühlenstrasse for ten pfennigs. 'You must read it, Hans. It's *Don Carlos* by Schiller, actually . . . I'll lend it to you if you like . . .'

'Oh, no,' said Hans Hansen, 'don't bother, Tonio, that isn't my kind of thing. I'd rather stick to my horse books, you know. The illustrations in them are really super. Next time you're at my house I'll show you them. They're instantaneous photographs, so you can see the horses trotting and galloping and jumping, in all the positions – you can never see them like that in real life because they move so fast . . .'

'In all the positions?' asked Tonio politely. 'Yes, that must be nice. But *Don Carlos*, you know, it's quite unbelievable. There are passages in it, you'll find, they're so beautiful they give you a jolt, it's like a kind of explosion . . .'

'An explosion?' asked Hans Hansen . . . 'How do you mean?'

'For example, the passage where the king has wept because the marquis has betrayed him . . . but the marquis, you see, has only betrayed him to help the prince, he's sacrificing himself for the prince's sake. And then word is brought from the king's study into the ante-room that the king has wept. "Wept?" "The king wept?" All the courtiers are absolutely amazed, and it pierces you through and through, because he's a frightfully strict and stern king. But you can understand so well why he weeps, and actually I feel sorrier for him than for the prince and the marquis put together. He's always so very alone, and no one loves him, and then he thinks he has found someone, and that's the very man who betrays him . . .'

Hans Hansen glanced sideways at Tonio's face, and something in it must have aroused his interest in the subject, for he suddenly linked arms with him again and asked:

'Why, how does he betray him, Tonio?'

Tonio's heart leapt.

'Well, you see,' he began, 'all the dispatches for Brabant and Flanders . . .'

'Here comes Erwin Jimmerthal,' said Hans.

Tonio fell silent. If only, he thought, the earth would open and swallow that fellow Jimmerthal up! Why does he have to come and interrupt us? If only he doesn't join us and spend the whole walk talking about their riding lessons! For Erwin Jimmerthal took riding lessons too. He was the bank manager's son and lived out here beyond the city wall. He had already got rid of his satchel and was advancing towards them along the avenue with his bandy legs and slit-like eyes.

'Hullo, Jimmerthal,' said Hans. 'I'm going for a bit of a walk with Kröger . . .'

'I've got to go into town and get something,' said Jimmerthal. 'But I'll walk along with you for a little way . . . Are those fruit lozenges you've got there? Yes, thanks, I'll have a couple. It's our lesson again tomorrow, Hans.' He was referring to the riding lesson.

'Super!' said Hans. 'I'm going to be given my leather gaiters now, you know, because I was top in the essay the other day . . .'

'You don't take riding lessons, I suppose, Kröger?' asked Jimmerthal, and his eyes were just a pair of glinting slits . . .

'No . . .' replied Tonio in uncertain accents.

Hans Hansen remarked: 'You should ask your father to let you have lessons too, Kröger.'

'Yes . . .' said Tonio, hastily and without interest, his throat suddenly contracting because Hans had called him by his surname; Hans seemed to sense this and added by way of explanation:

143

'I call you Kröger because you've got such a crazy first name, you know; you mustn't mind my saying so, but I really can't stand it. Tonio . . . why, it isn't a name at all! Though of course it's not your fault, goodness me!'

'No, I suppose they called you that mainly because it sounds so foreign and special . . .' said Jimmerthal, with an air of trying to say something nice.

Tonio's mouth twitched. He pulled himself together and said:

'Yes, it's a silly name, God knows I'd rather it were Heinrich or Wilhelm, I can assure you. But it's all because I was christened after one of my mother's brothers whose name's Antonio; my mother comes from abroad, you know . . .'

Then he was silent and let the others talk on about horses and leather equipment. Hans had linked arms with Jimmerthal and was speaking with a fluent enthusiasm which *Don Carlos* could never have inspired in him . . . From time to time Tonio felt the tears welling up inside him, his nose tingled, and his chin kept trembling so that he could hardly control it . . .

Hans could not stand his name, and there was nothing to be done about it. His own name was Hans, and Jimmerthal's was Erwin – two good names which everyone recognized, to which no one could object. But 'Tonio' was something foreign and special. Yes, he was a special case in every way, whether he liked it or not; he was isolated, he did not belong among decent normal people – notwithstanding the fact that he was no gypsy in a green caravan, but Consul Kröger's son, a member of the Kröger family . . . But why did Hans always call him Tonio when they were alone together, if he felt ashamed of him as soon as anyone else appeared? Sometimes indeed there was a closeness between them, he was temporarily won over. 'Why, how does he betray him, Tonio?' he had asked, and had taken his arm. But the moment Jimmerthal had turned up he had breathed a sigh of relief nevertheless, he had dropped him and gratuitously criticized him for his foreign first name. How it hurt to have to understand all this so well! . . . He knew that in fact Hans Hansen did like him a little, when they were by themselves; but when anyone else was there he would feel ashamed and throw him over. And Tonio would be alone again. He thought of King Philip. The king wept . . .

'Oh, God,' said Erwin Jimmerthal, 'I really must go into town now.

Goodbye, you two – thanks for the fruit lozenges!' Whereupon he jumped on to a wooden seat at the side of the avenue, ran along it with his bandy legs and trotted away.

'I like Jimmerthal!' said Hans emphatically. Privileged as he was, he had a self-assured way of declaring his likes and dislikes, of graciously conferring them, so to speak . . . And then, having warmed to the theme, he went on talking about his riding lessons. In any case they were by now quite near the Hansens' house; it did not take long to reach it by the promenade along the old fortifications. They clutched their caps and bent their heads before the wind, the strong damp breeze that moaned and jarred among the leafless branches. And Hans Hansen talked, with Tonio merely interjecting an occasional insincere 'Ah!' or 'Oh, yes', and getting no pleasure from the fact that Hans, in the excitement of his discourse, had again linked arms with him; for it was merely a superficial and meaningless contact . . .

Presently, not far from the station, they turned off the promenade; they watched a train bustling and puffing past, counted the coaches just for fun, and as the last one went by, waved to the man who sat up there wrapped in his fur overcoat. Then they stopped in the Lindenplatz in front of the villa of Herr Hansen the wholesale timber merchant, and Hans demonstrated in detail what fun it was to stand on the bottom rail of the garden gate and swing oneself to and fro on its creaking hinges. But after that he took his leave.

'Well, I must go in now,' he said. 'Goodbye, Tonio. Next time I'll walk *you* home, I promise.'

'Goodbye, Hans,' said Tonio. 'It was a nice walk.'

Their hands, as they touched, were all wet and rusty from the garden gate. But when Hans glanced into Tonio's eyes he seemed to recollect himself, and a look of contrition came over his handsome face.

'And by the way, I'll read *Don Carlos* sometime soon,' he said quickly. 'That bit about the king in his study must be super!' Whereupon he hitched his satchel under his arm and ran off through the front garden. Before disappearing into the house he turned round and nodded once more.

And Tonio Kröger sped off homeward, joy lending him wings. The wind was behind him, but it was not only the wind that bore him so lightly along.

Hans was going to read *Don Carlos*, and then they would have something in common, something they could talk about, and neither Jimmerthal nor anyone else would be able to join in! How well they understood each other! Perhaps – who could say? – he would one day even be able to get him to write poetry, like Tonio himself . . . No, no, he didn't want that to happen. Hans must never become like Tonio, but stay as he was, with his strength and his sun-like happiness which made everyone love him, and Tonio most of all! But still, it would be no bad thing if he read *Don Carlos* . . . And Tonio walked under the low arch of the old gate, he walked along the quayside and up the steep, draughty, damp little street with its gabled buildings, till he reached his parents' house. His heart was alive in those days; in it there was longing, and sad envy, and just a touch of contempt, and a whole world of innocent delight.

## 2

Ingeborg Holm, the daughter of Dr Holm who lived in the market square with its tall pointed complicated Gothic fountain – the fair-haired Inge it was whom Tonio Kröger loved at the age of sixteen.

How did it come about? He had seen her hundreds of times; but one evening he saw her in a certain light. As she talked to a friend he saw how she had a certain way of tossing her head to one side with a saucy laugh, and a certain way of raising her hand – a hand by no means particularly tiny or delicately girlish – to smooth her hair at the back, letting her sleeve of fine white gauze slide away from her elbow. He heard her pronounce some word in a certain way, some quite insignificant word, but with a certain warm timbre in her voice. And his heart was seized by a rapture far more intense than the rapture he had sometimes felt at the sight of Hans Hansen, long ago, when he had still been a silly little boy.

That evening her image remained imprinted on his mind: her thick blond tresses, her rather narrowly cut laughing blue eyes, the delicate hint of freckles across the bridge of her nose. The timbre of her voice haunted him and he could not sleep; he tried softly to imitate the particular way she had pronounced that insignificant word, and a tremor ran through him as he did so. He knew from experience that this was love. And he knew only too well that love would cost him much pain, distress and humiliation; he knew also that it destroys the lover's peace of mind, flooding his heart with music and leaving him no time to form and shape his experience, to recollect it in tranquillity and forge it into a whole. Nevertheless he accepted this love with joy, abandoning himself to it utterly and nourishing it with all the strength of his spirit; for he knew that it would enrich him and make him more fully alive – and he longed to be enriched and more fully alive, rather than to recollect things in tranquillity and forge them into a whole . . .

It was thus that Tonio Kröger had lost his heart to blithe Inge Holm; and it had happened in Frau Consul Husteede's drawing-room, from which the furniture had been removed that evening, because it was the Frau Consul's turn to have the dancing class at her house. It was a private class, attended only by members of the best families, and the parents took turns in inviting all the young people together to receive their instruction in dancing and deportment. The dancing master, Herr Knaak, came once a week specially from Hamburg for this purpose.

François Knaak was his name, and what a character he was! '*J'ai l'honneur de me vous présenter,*' he would say, '*mon nom est Knaak* . . . And we say this not during our bow but after it, when we are standing up straight again. Quietly, but distinctly. It does not happen every day that we have to introduce ourselves in French, but if we can do it correctly and faultlessly in that language then we are all the more likely to get it right in German.' How magnificently his silky black tailcoat clung to his plump hips! His trousers fell in soft folds over his patent leather shoes with their wide satin bows, and his brown eyes gazed round with an air of wearily satisfied consciousness of their own beauty . . .

His self-assurance and urbanity were absolutely overwhelming. He would walk – and no one but he could walk with so rhythmic, so supple, so resilient, so royal a tread – up to the lady of the house, bow to her and wait for her to extend her hand. When she had done so he would murmur his thanks, step buoyantly back, turn on his left heel, smartly raise his right foot from the ground, pointing it outward and downward, and walk away with his hips swaying to and fro.

When one left a party one stepped backwards out of the door, with a bow; when one fetched a chair, one did not seize it by one leg and drag it across the floor, but carried it lightly by the back and set it down noiselessly. One did not stand with one's hands crossed on one's stomach and one's tongue in the corner of one's mouth; if anyone did do so, Herr Knaak had a way of imitating the posture that put one off it for the rest of one's life . . .

So much for deportment. As for dancing, Herr Knaak's mastery of that was possibly even more remarkable. The empty drawing-room was lit by a gas chandelier and by candles over the fireplace. Talcum powder had been strewn on the floor and the pupils stood round in a silent semicircle; and in the adjacent room, beyond the curtained doorways, their mothers and aunts sat on plush-covered chairs watching Herr Knaak through their lorgnettes, as with a forward inclination of the body, two fingers of each hand grasping his coat-tails, he capered elastically through a step-by-step demonstration of the mazurka. But when he wished to dumbfound his audience utterly, he would all of a sudden and for no good reason leap vertically off the floor, whirling his legs round each other in the air with bewildering rapidity as though he were executing a trill with them, and then return to terra firma with a discreet but earth-shaking thump . . .

'What a preposterous monkey!' thought Tonio Kröger to himself. But he could not fail to notice that Inge, blithe Inge Holm, would often watch Herr Knaak's every movement with rapt and smiling attention; and this was not the only reason why, in the last resort, he could not help feeling a certain grudging admiration for the dancing-master's impressively controlled physique. How calm and imperturbable was Herr Knaak's gaze! His eyes did not look deeply into things, they did not penetrate to the point at which life becomes complex and sad; all they knew was that they were beautiful brown eyes. But that was why he had such a proud bearing! Yes, it was necessary to be stupid in order to be able to walk like that; and then one was loved, for then people found one charming. How well he understood why Inge, sweet fair-haired Inge, gazed at Herr Knaak the way she did. But would no girl ever look that way at Tonio?

Oh yes, it did happen. There was the daughter, for instance, of Dr Vermehren the lawyer – Magdalena Vermehren, with her gentle mouth and her big, dark, glossy eyes so full of solemn enthusiasm. She often fell over when she danced. But when it was the ladies' turn to choose partners she always came to him; for she knew that he wrote poems, she had twice asked him to show them to her and she would often sit with her head drooping and gaze at him from a distance. But what good was that to Tonio? *He* loved Inge Holm, blithe, fair-haired Inge, who certainly despised him for his poetic scribblings . . . He watched her, he watched her narrow blue eyes so full of happiness and mockery; and an envious longing burned in his heart, a bitter insistent pain at the thought that to her he would always be an outsider and a stranger . . .

'First couple *en avant!*' said Herr Knaak, and words cannot describe how exquisitely he enunciated the nasal vowel. They were practising quadrilles, and to Tonio Kröger's profound alarm he was in the same set as Inge Holm. He avoided her as best he could, and yet constantly found himself near her; he forced his eyes not to look at her, and yet they constantly wandered in her direction . . . And now, hand-in-hand with the red-haired Ferdinand Matthiessen, she came gliding and running towards him, tossed her head back and stopped opposite him, recovering her breath. Herr Heinzelmann, the pianist, attacked the keyboard with his bony hands, Herr Knaak called out his instructions and the quadrille began.

She moved to and fro in front of him, stepping and turning, forwards and backwards; often he caught a fragrance from her hair or from the delicate white material of her dress, and his eyes clouded over with ever-increasing pain. 'I love you, dear, sweet Inge,' he said to himself, and the words contained all the anguish he felt as he saw her so eagerly and happily concentrating on the dance and paying no attention to him. A wonderful poem by Theodor Storm came into his mind: 'I long to sleep, to sleep, but you must dance.' What a torment, what a humiliating contradiction it was to have to dance when one's heart was heavy with love . . .

'First couple *en avant!*' said Herr Knaak; the next figure was beginning. '*Compliment! Moulinet des dames! Tour de main!*' And no words can do justice to his elegant muting of the *e* in '*de*'.

'Second couple *en avant!*' Tonio Kröger and his partner were the second couple. '*Compliment!*' And Tonio Kröger bowed. '*Moulinet des dames!*' And Tonio Kröger, with bent head and frowning brows, laid his hand on the hands of the four ladies, on Inge Holm's hand, and danced the *moulinet*.

All round him people began to titter and laugh. Herr Knaak struck a ballet-dancer's pose expressing stylized horror. 'Oh dear, oh dear!' he exclaimed. 'Stop, stop! Kröger has got mixed up with the ladies! *En arrière*, Miss Kröger, get back, *fi donc!* Everyone but you understands the steps by now. *Allons, vite!* Begone! *Retirez-vous!*' And he drew out his yellow silk handkerchief and flapped it at Tonio Kröger, chasing him back to his place.

Everyone laughed, the boys and the girls and the ladies in the next room, for Herr Knaak had turned the incident to such comical account; it was as entertaining as a play. Only Herr Heinzelmann, with a dry professional air, waited for the signal to go on playing; he was inured against Herr Knaak's devices.

And the quadrille continued. Then there was an interval. The parlourmaid entered with a tray of wine jellies in clinking glass cups, closely followed by the cook with a load of plum cake. But Tonio Kröger slipped unobtrusively out of the room into the corridor, and stood with his hands on his back gazing at a window, regardless of the fact that since the venetian blind was down one could see nothing and it was therefore absurd to stand in front of this window pretending to be looking out of it.

But it was inwards he was looking, inwards at his own grief and longing. Why, why was he here? Why was he not sitting at the window in his own room, reading Storm's *Immensee* and occasionally glancing out into the garden where it lay in the evening light, with the old walnut tree and its heavy creaking branches? That was where he should have been. Let the others dance and enjoy themselves and be good at it! . . . But no, no, this was his place nevertheless – here where he knew he was near Inge, even if all he could do was to stand by himself in the distance, listening to the hum and the clatter and the laughter and trying to pick out her voice from among it all, her voice so full of warmth and life. Dear, fair-haired Inge, with your narrow-cut, laughing blue eyes! Only people who do not read *Immensee* and never try to write anything like it can be as beautiful and light-hearted as you; that is the tragedy! . . .

Surely she would come! Surely she would notice that he had left the room, and feel what he was suffering, and slip out after him – even if it were only pity that brought her – and put her hand on his shoulder and say: 'Come back and join us, don't be sad, I love you!' And he listened to the voices behind him, waiting in senseless excitement for her to come. But she did not come. Such things did not happen on earth.

Had she laughed at him too, like all the others? Yes, she had, however much he would have liked to deny it for her sake and his. And yet he had only joined in the *moulinet des dames* because he had been so engrossed by her presence. And what did it matter anyway? One day perhaps they would stop laughing. Had he not recently had a poem accepted by a periodical – even if the periodical had gone out of business before the poem could appear? The day was coming when he would be famous and when everything he wrote would be printed; and then it would be seen whether that would not impress Inge Holm . . . No; it would *not* impress her; that was just the point. Magdalena Vermehren, the girl who was always falling over – yes, she would be impressed. But not Inge Holm, not blithe blue-eyed Inge, never. So what was the good of it all? . . .

Tonio Kröger's heart contracted in anguish at the thought. How it hurt to feel the upsurge of wonderful, sad, creative powers within one, and yet to know that they can mean nothing to those happy people at whom one gazes in love and longing across a gulf of inaccessibility! And yet – alone and excluded though he was, standing hopelessly with his distress in front of a drawn blind pretending to be looking through it – he was nevertheless happy. For his heart was alive in those days. Warmly and sorrowfully it throbbed for you, Ingeborg Holm, and in blissful self-forgetfulness his whole soul embraced your blond, radiant, exuberantly normal little personality.

More than once he stood thus by himself, with flushed cheeks, in out-of-the-way corners where the music, the scent of flowers and the clink of glasses could only faintly be heard, trying to pick out the timbre of your voice from among the other distant festive sounds; he stood there and pined for you, and was nevertheless happy. More than once it mortified him that he should be able to talk to Magdalena Vermehren, the girl who was always falling over – that she should understand him and laugh with him and be serious with him, whereas fair-haired Inge, even when he was sitting beside her, seemed distant and alien and embarrassed by him, for they did not speak the same language. And nevertheless he was happy. For happiness, he told himself, does not consist in being loved; that merely gratifies one's vanity and is mingled with repugnance. Happiness consists in loving – and perhaps snatching a few little moments of illusory nearness to the beloved. And he inwardly noted down this reflection, thought out all its implications and savoured it to its very depths.

'*Fidelity!*' thought Tonio Kröger. 'I will be faithful and love you, Ingeborg, for the rest of my life.' For he had a well-meaning nature. And nevertheless there was a sad whisper of misgiving within him, reminding him that he had, after all, quite forgotten Hans Hansen too, although he saw him daily. And the hateful, pitiable thing was that this soft, slightly mocking voice turned out to be right. Time went by, and the day came when Tonio Kröger was no longer so unreservedly ready as he had once been to lay down his life for blithe Inge; for he now felt within himself the desire and the power to achieve something of his own in this world, indeed to achieve in his own way much that would be remarkable.

And he hovered watchfully round the sacrificial altar on which his love burned like a pure, chaste flame; he knelt before it and did all he could to fan it and feed it and remain faithful. And he found that after a time, imperceptibly, silently and without fuss, the flame had nevertheless gone out.

But Tonio Kröger stood on for a while before the cold altar, full of astonishment and disillusionment as he realized that in this world fidelity is not possible. Then he shrugged his shoulders and went his way.

## 3

He went the way he had to go; rather nonchalantly and unsteadily, whistling to himself, gazing into vacancy with his head tilted to one side. And if it was the wrong way, then that was because for certain people no such thing as a right way exists. When he was asked what on earth he intended to do with his life, he would give various answers; for he would often remark (and had already written the observation down) that he carried within himself a thousand possible ways of life, although at the same time privately aware that none of them was possible at all . . .

Even before he left his native city and its narrow streets, the threads and bonds that held him to it had been quietly severed. The old Kröger family had gradually fallen into a state of decay and disintegration, and Tonio Kröger's own existence and nature were with good reason generally regarded as symptomatic of this decline. His father's mother, the family's senior and dominant member, had died; and his father, that tall, pensive, carefully dressed man with the wild flower in his buttonhole, had not been long in following her. The great Kröger mansion with all its venerable history was put up for sale and the firm was liquidated. But Tonio's mother, his beautiful fiery mother who played the piano and the mandolin so enchantingly and to whom nothing really mattered, got married again a year later – to a musician, a virtuoso with an Italian name, with whom she departed to live under far-off blue skies. Tonio Kröger thought this slightly disreputable; but who was he to set himself against it? He wrote poetry and could not even give an answer when asked what on earth he intended to do with his life . . .

So he left his home town with its gabled houses and the damp wind whistling round them; he left the fountain and the old walnut tree in the garden, those faithful companions of his youth; he left the sea too, his beloved sea, and left it all without a pang. For he was grown-up and enlightened now, he understood his situation and was full of contempt for the crude and primitive way of life that had enveloped him for so long.

He surrendered himself utterly to that power which he felt to be the sublimest power on earth, to the service of which he felt called and which promised him honour and renown: the power of intellect and words, a power that sits smilingly enthroned above mere inarticulate, unconscious life. He surrendered to it with youthful passion, and it rewarded him with all that it has to give, while inexorably exacting its full price in return.

It sharpened his perceptions and enabled him to see through the high-sounding phrases that swell the human breast, it unlocked for him the mysteries of the human mind and of his own, it made him clear-sighted, it showed him life from the inside and revealed to him the fundamental motives behind what men say and do. But what did he see? Absurdity and wretchedness – absurdity and wretchedness.

And with the torment and the pride of such insight came loneliness; for he could not feel at ease among the innocent, among the light of heart and dark of understanding, and they shrank from the sign on his brow. But at the same time he savoured ever more sweetly the delight of words and of form, for he would often remark (and had already written the observation down) that mere knowledge of human psychology would in itself infallibly make us despondent if we were not cheered and kept alert by the satisfaction of expressing it . . . .

He lived in large cities in the south, for he felt that his art would ripen more lushly in the southern sun; and perhaps it was heredity on his mother's side that drew him there. But because his heart was dead and had no love in it, he fell into carnal adventures, far into the hot guilty depths of sensuality, although such experiences cost him intense suffering. Perhaps it was because of something inside him inherited from his father – from the tall, pensive, neatly dressed man with the wild flower in his buttonhole – that he suffered so much there: something that often stirred within him the faint nostalgic recollection of a more heartfelt joy he had once known and which now, amid these other pleasures, he could never recapture.

He was seized by revulsion, by a hatred of the senses, by a craving for purity and decency and peace of mind; and yet he was breathing the atmosphere of art, the mild, sweet, heavily fragrant air of a continual spring in which everything sprouts and burgeons and germinates in mysterious procreative delight. And so he could do no more than let himself be cast helplessly to and fro between gross extremes, between icy intellectuality on the one hand and devouring feverish lust on the other. The life he lived was exhausting, tormented by remorse, extravagant, dissipated and monstrous, and one which Tonio Kröger himself in his heart of hearts abhorred. 'How far astray I have gone!' he would sometimes think. 'How was it possible for me to become involved in all these eccentric adventures? After all, I wasn't born a gypsy in a green caravan . . .'

But as his health suffered, so his artistry grew more refined: it became fastidious, exquisite, rich, subtle, intolerant of banality and hyper-sensitive in matters of tact and taste. His first publication was received by the competent critics with considerable acclaim and appreciation, for it was a well-made piece of work, full of humour and the knowledge of suffering. And very soon his name – the same name that had once been shouted at him by angry schoolmasters, the name with which he had signed his first verses addressed to the sea and the walnut tree and the fountain, this mixture of southern and northern sounds, this respectable middle-class name with an exotic flavour – became a formula betokening excellence. For the profound painfulness of his experience of life was allied to a rare capacity for hard, ambitious, unremitting toil; and of this perseverance, joined in anguished combat with his fastidiously sensitive taste, works of quite unusual quality were born.

He worked, not like a man who works in order to live, but like one who has no desire but to work, because he sets no store by himself as a living human being, seeks recognition only as a creative artist, and spends the rest of his time in a grey incognito, like an actor with his make-up off, who has no identity when he is not performing. He worked in silence, in invisible privacy, for he utterly despised those minor hacks who treated their talent as a social ornament – who, whether they were poor or rich, whether they affected an unkempt and shabby appearance or sumptuous individualistic neckwear, aimed above all clse at living happily, charmingly and artistically, little suspecting that good work is brought forth only under the pressure of a bad life, that living and working are incompatible and that one must have died if one is to be wholly a creator.

# 4

'Do I disturb you?' asked Tonio Kröger, pausing at the studio door. He had his hat in his hand and even bowed slightly, although Lisaveta Ivanovna was an intimate friend and he could talk to her about anything.

'For pity's sake, Tonio Kröger, come in and never mind the politeness,' she answered in her jerky accent. 'We all know that you were well brought up and taught how to behave.' So saying, she transferred her brush to the same hand as her palette, held out her right hand to him and gazed at him laughingly, shaking her head.

'Yes, but you're working,' he said. 'Let me see . . . Oh but you've made progress.' And he looked by turns at the colour sketches propped against chair-backs on either side of the easel, and at the big canvas marked off in squares and covered with a confused schematic charcoal sketch on which the first patches of colour were beginning to appear.

They were in Munich, in a rear apartment on Schellingstrasse, several floors up. Outside the wide north-facing window the sky was blue, the birds twittered and the sun shone; and the young sweet spring air, streaming in through an open pane, mingled in the large studio with the smell of fixative and oil paint. The bright golden afternoon light flooded unhindered all over the bare spacious room, frankly showing up the rather worn floor-boards, falling on the rough window-table covered with brushes and tubes and little bottles, and on the unframed studies that hung on the unpapered walls; it fell on the torn silk screen that enclosed a tastefully furnished little living corner near the door; it fell on the work that was gradually taking shape on the easel, and on the painter and the writer as they looked at it.

She was about the same age as himself, rather over thirty. In her dark blue paint-stained overall she sat on a low stool, propping her chin in her hand. Her brown hair was firmly set, greying a little at the sides already, and slightly waved over the temples; it framed a dark, very charming face of Slav cut, with a snub nose, prominent cheekbones and little shiny black eyes. Tensely, sceptically, with an air almost of irritation, she scrutinized her work from the side, with her eyes half-closed.

He stood beside her with his right hand on his hip and his left hand rapidly twirling his brown moustache. His slanting brows were frowning and working energetically, and he whistled softly to himself as usual. He was very carefully and punctiliously dressed, in a quiet grey suit of reserved cut. But his forehead, under the dark hair with its exceedingly correct and simple parting, twitched nervously, and his southern features were already sharp, clear-cut and traced as if with a hard chisel, although his mouth and chin were so gently and softly outlined . . . Presently he drew his hand across his forehead and eyes and turned away.

'I shouldn't have come,' he said.

'Why not, Tonio Kröger?'

'I've just been working, Lisaveta, and inside my head everything looks just as it does on this canvas. A skeleton, a faint sketch, a mess of corrections, and a few patches of colour, to be sure; and now I come here and see the same thing. And the same contradiction is here too,' he said, sniffing the air, 'the same conflict that was bothering me at home. It's odd. Once a thought has got hold of you, you find expressions of it everywhere, you even *smell* it in the wind, don't you? Fixative and the scent of spring! Art and – well, what is the opposite? Don't call it "nature", Lisaveta, "nature" isn't an adequate term. Oh, no, I dare say I ought to have gone for a walk instead, though it's doubtful whether that would have made me feel any better. Five minutes ago, quite near here, I met a colleague – Adalbert, the short-story writer. "God damn the spring!" he said in his aggressive way. "It is and always was the most abominable season of the year! Can you think a single thought that makes sense, Kröger? Have you peace of mind enough to work out any little thing, anything pointed and effective, with all this indecent itching in your blood and a whole swarm of irrelevant sensations pestering you, which turn out when you examine them to be absolutely trivial, unusable rubbish? As for me, I'm off to a café. It's neutral territory, you know, untouched by change of season; it so to speak symbolizes literature – that remote and sublime sphere in which one is incapable of grosser thoughts . . ." And off he went into the café; and perhaps I should have followed him.'

Lisaveta was amused.

'Very good, Tonio Kröger! "Indecent itching" – that's good. And he's not far wrong, because one really doesn't get much work done in spring. But now listen to me, I am now, in spite of the spring, going to do this little piece here – work out this pointed little effect, as Adalbert would say – and then we shall go into my "salon" and have some tea, and you shall tell me all; for I can see well enough that you have a lot on your mind today. Until then please arrange yourself somewhere – on that chest, for example, unless you think your aristocratic garments will be the worse for it . . .'

'Oh, stop going on at me about my clothes, Lisaveta Ivanovna! Would you like me to be running around in a torn velvet jacket or a red silk waistcoat? As an artist I'm already enough of an adventurer in my inner life. So far as outward appearances are concerned one should dress decently, damn it, and behave like a respectable citizen . . . No, I haven't got a lot on my mind,' he went on, watching her mix some colours on her palette. 'As I told you, I'm just preoccupied with a certain problem and contradiction, and it's been preventing me from working . . . What were we talking about just now? Yes: Adalbert, the short-story writer – he's a proud man and knows his own mind. "Spring is the most abominable season," he said, and went into a café. One must know what one wants, mustn't one? You see, I get nervous in spring too; I get distracted by the sweet trivial memories and feelings it revives in me. The difference is that I can't bring myself to put the blame on the spring and to despise it; for the fact is that the spring makes me feel ashamed. I am put to shame by its pure naturalness, its triumphant youthfulness. And I don't know whether to envy or despise Adalbert for not having any such reaction . . .

'One certainly does work badly in spring: and why? Because one's feelings are being stimulated. And only amateurs think that a creative artist can afford to have feelings. It's a naïve amateur illusion; any genuine honest artist will smile at it. Sadly, perhaps, but he will smile. Because, of course, *what* one says must never be one's main concern. It must merely be the raw material, quite indifferent in itself, out of which the work of art is made; and the act of making must be a game, aloof and detached, performed in tranquillity. If you attach too much importance to what you have to say, if it means too much to you emotionally, then you may be certain that your work will be a complete fiasco. You will become solemn, you will become sentimental, you will produce something clumsy, ponderous, pompous, ungainly, unironical, insipid, dreary and commonplace; it will be of no interest to anyone, and you yourself will end up disillusioned and miserable . . . For that is how it is, Lisaveta: emotion, warm, heartfelt emotion, is invariably commonplace and unserviceable – only the stimulation of our corrupt nervous system, its cold ecstasies and acrobatics, can bring forth art. One simply has to be something inhuman, something standing outside humanity, strangely remote and detached from its concerns, if one is to have the ability or indeed even the desire to play this game with it, to play with men's lives, to portray them effectively and tastefully. Our stylistic and formal talent, our gift of expression, itself presupposes this cold-blooded, fastidious attitude to mankind, indeed it presupposes a certain human impoverishment and stagnation. For the fact is: all healthy emotion, all strong emotion lacks taste. As soon as an artist becomes human and begins to feel, he is finished as an artist. Adalbert knew this, and that is why he retreated into a café, into the "remote sphere" – ah yes!'

'Well, God be with him, *batushka*,' said Lisaveta, washing her hands in a tin basin. 'After all, there's no need for you to follow him.'

'No, Lisaveta, I shall not follow him; and the only reason I shall not is that I am occasionally capable, when confronted with spring, of feeling slightly ashamed of being an artist. You know, I sometimes get letters from complete strangers, from appreciative and grateful readers, expressions of admiration from people whom my work has moved. I read these communications and am touched by the warm, clumsy emotions stirred up by my art – I am overcome by a kind of pity for the enthusiastic naïvety that speaks from every line, and I blush to think what a sobering effect it would have on the honest man who wrote such a letter if he could ever take a look behind the scenes, if his innocent mind could ever grasp the fact that the last thing any proper, healthy, decent human being ever does is to write or act or compose . . . Though needless to say all this does not stop me using his admiration for my genius as an enrichment and a stimulus; I still take it uncommonly seriously and ape the solemn airs of a great man . . . Oh, don't start contradicting me, Lisaveta! I tell you I am often sick to death of being a portrayer of humanity and having no share in human experience . . . Can one even say that an artist *is* a man? Let Woman answer that! I think we artists are all in rather the same situation as those artificial papal sopranos . . . Our voices are quite touchingly beautiful. But –'

'Be ashamed of yourself, Tonio Kröger. Come along and have tea. The water will be boiling in a minute, and here are some *papirosi*. Now, you stopped at the soprano singers; so please continue from that point. But you ought to be a little ashamed of what you are saying. If I did not know how passionately devoted to your profession and how proud of it you are . . .'

'Don't speak to me of my "profession", Lisaveta Ivanovna! Literature isn't a profession at all, I'll have you know – it's a curse. And when do we first discover that this curse has come upon us? At a terribly early age. An age when by rights one should still be living at peace and harmony with God and the world. You begin to feel that you are a marked man, mysteriously different from other people, from ordinary normal folk; a gulf of irony, of scepticism, of antagonism, of awareness, of sensibility, is fixed between you and your fellow men – it gets deeper and deeper, it isolates you from them, and in the end all communication with them becomes impossible. What a fate! Always supposing, of course, that you still have enough feeling, enough *love* left in your heart to know how appalling it is . . . You develop an exacerbated self-consciousness, because you are well aware of being marked out among thousands by a sign on your brow which no one fails to notice. I once knew an actor of genius who, as a man, had to struggle against a morbid instability and lack of confidence. This was how his overstimulated consciousness of himself affected him when he was not actually engaged in performing a part. He was a consummate artist and an impoverished human being . . . A real artist is not one who has taken up art as his profession, but a man predestined and foredoomed to it; and such an artist can be picked out from a crowd by anyone with the slightest perspicacity. You can read in his face that he is a man apart, a man who does not belong, who feels that he is recognized and is being watched; there is somehow an air of royalty about him and at the same time an air of embarrassment. A prince walking incognito among the people wears a rather similar expression. But the incognito doesn't work, Lisaveta! Disguise yourself, put on civilian costume, dress up like an attaché or a guards lieutenant on leave – you will hardly have raised your eyes and uttered a word before everyone will know that you are not a human being but something strange, something alien, something different . . .

'But what *is* an artist? I know of no other question to which human complacency and incuriosity has remained so impervious. "That sort of thing is a gift," say average decent folk humbly, when a work of art has produced its intended effect upon them; and because in the goodness of their hearts they assume that exhilarating and noble effects must necessarily have exhilarating and noble causes, it never enters their heads that the origins of this so-called "gift" may well be extremely dubious and extremely disreputable . . . It's well known that artists are easily offended; and it's also well known that this is not usually the case with people who have a good conscience and solidly grounded self-confidence . . . You see, Lisaveta, I harbour in my very soul a rooted suspicion of the artist as a type – I suspect him no less deeply, though in a more intellectual way, than every one of my honourable ancestors up there in that city of narrow streets would have suspected any sort of mountebank or performing adventurer who had strolled into his house. Listen to this. I know a banker, a middle-aged man of business, who has a talent for writing short stories. He exercises this talent in his spare time, and what he writes is often quite first-class. Despite – I call it "despite" – this admirable gift he is a man of not entirely blameless reputation: on the contrary he has already served quite a heavy prison sentence, and for good reason. In fact it was actually in gaol that he first became aware of his talents, and his experiences as a prisoner are the basic theme in all his work. One might draw the rather fanciful conclusion from this that it is necessary to have been in some kind of house of correction if one is to become a writer. But can one help suspecting that in its roots and origins his artistic tendency had less to do with his experiences in gaol than with *what got him sent there*? A banker who writes short stories: that's an oddity, isn't it? But a banker with no criminal record and no stain on his character who writes short stories – *there's no such phenomenon* . . . Yes, you may laugh, but I am half serious nevertheless. There's no problem on earth so tantalizing as the problem of what an artist is and what art does to human beings. Take the case of the most remarkable masterpiece of the most typical and therefore mightiest of all artists – take a morbid, profoundly equivocal work like *Tristan and Isolde*, and observe the effects of this work on a young, healthy listener of entirely normal sensibility. He will be filled with exaltation, animation, warm, honest enthusiasm, perhaps even inspired to "artistic" creative efforts of his own . . . Poor, decent dilettante! We artists have an inner life very different from what our "warm-hearted" admirers in their "genuine enthusiasm" imagine. I have seen artists with women and young men crowding round them, applauding and idolizing them, artists about whom *I knew the truth* . . . The sources and side-effects and preconditions of artistic talent are something about which one constantly makes the most curious discoveries . . .'

'Discoveries, Tonio Kröger – forgive my asking – about other artists? Or not only about others?'

He did not reply. He contracted his slanting brows in a frown and whistled to himself.

'Give me your cup, Tonio. The tea's not strong. And have another cigarette. And in any case you know very well that it is not necessary to take such a view of things as you are taking . . .'

'That's Horatio's answer, isn't it, my dear Lisaveta. " 'Twere to consider too curiously to consider so." '

'I mean, Tonio Kröger, that they can be considered just as curiously from another angle. I am only a stupid painting female, and if I can manage to make any reply to you, and offer some sort of defence of your own profession against you, I am sure there will be nothing new to you in what I say; I can only remind you of things you know very well yourself . . . Of the purifying, sanctifying effect of literature, for example; of the way our passions dissolve when they are grasped by insight and expressed in words; of literature as a path to understanding, to forgiveness and love. Think of the redeeming power of language, of the literary intellect as the sublimest manifestation of all human intellect, of the writer as supreme humanity, the writer as saint – to consider things so, is that not to consider them curiously enough?'

'You have a right to talk that way, Lisaveta Ivanovna, and it is conferred upon you by your national literature, by the sublime writers of Russia; their work I will willingly worship as the sacred literature of which you speak. But I have not left your objections out of account, on the contrary they too are part of what I have got on my mind today . . . Look at me. I don't look exactly bursting with high spirits, do I? Rather old and sharp-featured and weary, don't I? Well, to revert to the subject of "insight": can you not imagine someone with an innately unsceptical disposition, placid and well-meaning and a bit sentimental, being quite literally worn out and destroyed by psychological enlightenment? Not to let oneself be overwhelmed by the sadness of everything; to observe and study it all, to put even anguish into a category, and to remain in a good humour into the bargain, if only because of one's proud consciousness of moral superiority over the abominable invention of existence – oh, yes, indeed! But there are times, notwithstanding all the delights of expression, when the whole thing becomes a little too much for one. *"Tout comprendre, c'est tout pardonner"*? I'm not so sure. There is something that I call the nausea of knowledge, Lisaveta: a state of mind in which a man has no sooner seen through a thing than so far from feeling reconciled to it he is immediately sickened to death by it. This was how Hamlet felt, Hamlet the Dane, that typical literary artist. He knew what it was like to be called upon to bear a burden of knowledge for which one was not born. To be clear-sighted even through the mist of tears – even then to have to understand, to study, to observe and ironically discard what one has seen – even at moments when hands clasp and lips touch and eyes fail, blinded by emotion – it's infamous, Lisaveta, it's contemptible and outrageous . . . But what good does it do to feel outraged?

'Another equally charming aspect of the matter, of course, is the way one becomes sophisticated and indifferent to truth, blasé and weary of it all. It's well known that you'll never find such mute hopelessness as among a gathering of intellectuals, all of them thoroughly hagridden already. All insights are old and stale to them. Try telling them about some truth you have discovered, in the acquisition and possession of which you perhaps feel a certain youthful pride, and their response to your vulgar knowledgeableness will be a very brief expulsion of air through the nose . . . Oh yes, Lisaveta, literature wears people out! I assure you that in ordinary human society, by sheer scepticism and suspension of judgement, one can give the impression of being stupid, whereas in fact one is merely arrogant and lacking in courage . . . So much for "insight". As for "words", I wonder if they really redeem our passions: is it not rather that they refrigerate them and put them in cold storage? Don't you seriously think that there is a chilling, outrageous effrontery in the instant, facile process by which literary language eliminates emotion? What does one do when one's heart is too full, when some sweet or sublime experience has moved one too deeply? The answer is simple! Apply to a writer: the whole thing will be settled in a trice. He will analyse it all for you, formulate it, name it, express it and make it articulate, and so far as you are concerned the entire affair will be eliminated once and for all: he will have turned it for you into a matter of total indifference, and he'll not even expect you to thank him for doing so. But you will go home with your heart lightened, all warmth and all mystery dispelled, wondering why on earth you were distraught with such delicious excitement only a moment ago. Can we seriously defend this vain cold-hearted charlatan? Anything that has been expressed has thereby been eliminated – that is his creed. When the whole world has been expressed, it too will have been eliminated, redeemed, abolished . . . *Très bien!* But I am not a nihilist . . .'

'You are not a –' said Lisaveta . . . She was just about to take a sip of tea and stopped dead with the spoon near her mouth.

'Well, of course not . . . What's the matter with you, Lisaveta! I tell you I am not a nihilist inasmuch as I affirm the value of living emotion. Don't you see, what the literary artist basically fails to grasp is that life goes on, that it is not ashamed to go on living, even after it has been expressed and "eliminated". Lo and behold! Literature may redeem it as much as it pleases, it just carries on in its same old sinful way; for to the intellectual eye all activity is sinful . . .

'I'm nearly finished, Lisaveta. Listen to me. I love life – that is a confession. I present it to you for safe keeping; you are the first person to whom I have made it. It has been said, it has even been written and printed, that I hate or fear or despise or abominate life. I enjoy this suggestion, I have always felt flattered by it; but it is none the less false. I love life . . . You smile, Lisaveta, and I know why. But I implore you not to mistake what I am saying for mere literature! Do not think of Cesare Borgia or of any drunken philosophy that makes him its hero! This Cesare Borgia is nothing to me, I feel not a particle of respect for him, and I shall never be able to understand this idealization and cult of the extraordinary and the demonic. No: "life" confronts intellect and art as their eternal opposite – but not as a vision of bloodstained greatness and savage beauty. We who are exceptions do not see life as something exceptional; on the contrary! Normality, respectability, decency – these are our heart's desire, this to us is life, life in its seductive banality! No one, my dear, has a right to call himself an artist if his profoundest craving is for the refined, the eccentric and the satanic – if his heart knows no longing for innocence, simplicity and living warmth, for a little friendship and self-surrender and familiarity and human happiness – if he is not secretly devoured, Lisaveta, by this longing for the bliss of the commonplace! . . .

'A human friend! Will you believe me when I say that it would make me proud and happy to win the friendship of a human being? But until now all my friends have been demons, hobgoblins, phantoms struck dumb by the ghoulish profundity of their insight – in other words, men of letters.

'Sometimes I find myself on some public platform, facing a roomful of people who have come to listen to me. Do you know, it can happen on such occasions that I find myself surveying the audience, I catch myself secretly peering round the hall, and in my heart there is a question: Who are these who have come to me, whose is this grateful applause I hear, with whom have I achieved this spiritual union through my art? . . . I don't find what I am looking for, Lisaveta. I find my own flock, my familiar congregation, a sort of gathering of early Christians: people with clumsy bodies and refined souls, the kind of people, so to speak, who are always falling over when they dance, if you see what I mean; people to whom literature is a quiet way of taking their revenge on life – all of them sufferers, all repining and impoverished: never once is there one of the others among them, Lisaveta, one of the blue-eyed innocents who don't need intellect! . . .

'And after all it would be deplorably inconsistent, wouldn't it, to be glad if things were otherwise! It is absurd to love life and nevertheless to be trying with all the skill at one's command to entice it from its proper course, to interest it in our melancholy subtleties, in this whole sick aristocracy of literature. The kingdom of art is enlarging its frontiers in this world, and the realm of health and innocence is dwindling. What is left of it should be most carefully preserved: we have no right to try to seduce people into reading poetry when they would much rather be looking at books full of snapshots of horses!

'For when all's said and done, can you imagine a more pitiable spectacle than that of life attempting to be artistic! There is no one whom we artists so utterly despise as the dilettante, the living human being who thinks he can occasionally try his hand at being an artist as well. I assure you this particular kind of contempt is very familiar to me from personal experience. I am a guest, let us say, at a party, among members of the best society; we are eating and drinking and talking, and all getting on famously, and I am feeling glad and grateful to have escaped for a while into the company of simple, conventionally decent people who are treating me as an equal. And suddenly (this actually happened to me once) an officer rises to his feet, a lieutenant, a good-looking, fine, upstanding man whom I should never have believed capable of any conduct unbecoming his uniform, and asks in so many words for permission to recite to us a few lines of verse which he has composed. The permission is granted, with some smiling and raising of eyebrows, and he carries out his intention: he produces a piece of paper which he has hitherto been concealing in his coat-tail pocket, and he reads us his work. It was something or other about music and love, deeply felt and totally inept. I ask you: a lieutenant! A member of polite society! What need was there for him to do it, good heavens above! . . . Well, there was the predictable result: long faces, silence, a little polite applause and everyone feeling thoroughly uncomfortable. The first psychological effect upon myself of which I became aware was a feeling that I too, and not only this rash young man, was to blame for spoiling the party; and sure enough there were some mocking and unfriendly glances in my direction as well, for it was my trade he had bungled. But my second reaction was that this man, for whose character and way of life I had only a moment ago felt the sincerest respect, suddenly began to sink and sink and sink in my esteem . . . I felt sorry for him, I was filled with benevolent indulgence towards him. I and one or two other good-natured guests plucked up heart to approach him with a few encouraging words. "Congratulations, lieutenant!" I said. "What a charming talent you have! That was really very pretty!" And I very nearly patted him on the shoulder. But is indulgence a proper thing to feel towards a lieutenant? . . . It was his own fault! There he stood, in utter embarrassment, suffering the penalty of having supposed that one may pluck even a single leaf from the laurel tree of art and not pay for it with one's life. Oh, no! Give me my colleague, the banker with the criminal record . . . But don't you think, Lisaveta, that my eloquence today is worthy of Hamlet?'

'Have you finished now, Tonio Kröger?'

'No. But I shall say no more.'

'Well, you have certainly said enough. Are you expecting an answer?'

'Have you got one for me?'

'I certainly have. I have listened to you carefully, Tonio, from beginning to end, and I will now tell you what the answer is to everything you have said this afternoon, and what the solution is to the problem that has been worrying you so much. So! The solution is quite simply that you are, and always will be, a bourgeois.'

'Am I?' he asked, with a somewhat crestfallen air . . .

'That's a hard home truth for you, isn't it. And I don't wonder. So I don't mind modifying it a little, for it so happens that I can. You are a bourgeois who has taken the wrong turning, Tonio Kröger – a bourgeois *manqué*.'

There was silence. Then he got up resolutely and seized his hat and walking-stick.

'Thank you, Lisaveta Ivanovna; now I can go home with a good conscience. *I have been eliminated*.'

## 5

Near the end of the summer Tonio Kröger said to Lisaveta Ivanovna:

'Well, I'm leaving now, Lisaveta; I must have a change of air, a change of scene, I must get away from it all.'

'So, *batushka*, I suppose you will honour Italy with another visit?'

'Oh God, Lisaveta, don't talk to me of Italy! I am bored with Italy to the point of despising it! It's a long time since I thought I felt at home there. The land of art! Velvet-blue skies, heady wine and sweet sensuality . . . No thank you, that's not for me. I renounce it. All that *bellezza* gets on my nerves. And I can't stand all that dreadful southern vivacity, all those people with their black animal eyes. They've no conscience in their eyes, those Latin races . . . No, this time I'm going for a little trip to Denmark.'

'Denmark?'

'Yes. And I think I shall benefit from it. It so happens that I've never yet got round to going there, although I was so near the frontier during the whole of my youth, and yet it's a country I've always known about and loved. I suppose I must get this northern predilection from my father, for my mother really preferred the *bellezza*, you know, that is in so far as anything mattered to her at all. But think of the books they write up there in the north, Lisaveta, books of such depth and purity and humour – there's nothing like them, I love them. Think of the Scandinavian meals, those incomparable meals, only digestible in a strong salty air – in fact, I doubt if I shall be able to digest them at all now; I know them too from my childhood, the food's just like that even where I come from. And just think of the names, the names they christen people by up there – you'll find a lot of them in my part of the world as well: names like "Ingeborg", for instance – three syllables plucked on a harp of purest poetry. And then there's the sea – one is on the Baltic Sea up there! . . . Anyway, that's where I'm going, Lisaveta. I want to see the Baltic again, to hear those names again, to read those books in the country where they were written; and I want to stand on the battlements at Kronborg, where the "spirit"* came to Hamlet and brought anguish and death to the poor noble youth . . .'

'How shall you travel, Tonio, if I may ask? What route will you be taking?'

'The usual route,' he said, shrugging his shoulders and blushing visibly. 'Yes, I shall be passing through my – my point of departure, Lisaveta, after these thirteen years, and I dare say it may be a rather odd experience.'

She smiled.

'That's what I wanted to hear, Tonio Kröger. Well, be off with you, in God's name. And be sure you write to me, won't you? I'm looking forward to an eventful description of your journey to – Denmark . . .'

# 6

And Tonio Kröger travelled north. He travelled first-class (for he would often say that a man whose psychological problems are so much more difficult than those of other people has a right to a little external comfort) and he continued without a halt until the towers of his native town, that town of narrow streets, rose before him into the grey sky. There he made a brief and singular sojourn . . .

It was a dreary afternoon, already almost evening, when the train steamed into the little smoke-stained terminus which he remembered with such strange vividness; under its dirty glass roof the smoke was still rolling up into clouds or drifting to and fro in straggling wisps, just as it had done long ago when Tonio Kröger had left this place with nothing but mockery in his heart. He saw to his luggage, gave instructions that it was to be sent to his hotel and left the station.

*Mann here untranslatably plays upon two different meanings of the word 'Geist' ('intellect' and 'ghost'). (Translator's note.)

There stood the cabs, black and absurdly tall and wide, each drawn by a pair of horses, the cabs that had always been used in this town, waiting in a row outside the station! He did not take one; he merely looked at them, and he looked at everything else as well: the narrow gables and pointed towers that looked back at him over the nearby roofs, the fair-haired, easygoing unsophisticated people with their broad yet rapid way of talking – there they were, all round him, and laughter welled up within him, strangely hysterical laughter that was not far from tears. He went on foot, walking slowly, feeling the steady pressure of the damp wind on his face; he crossed the bridge, with its parapets decorated by mythological statues, and walked a little way along the quayside.

Great heavens, what a tiny, nookshotten place it all seemed! Had it been like this all these years, with these narrow gabled streets, climbing so steeply and quaintly up into the town? The ships' funnels and masts swayed gently in the dusk as the wind swept across the dull grey river. Should he walk up that street now, that street that led to the house he remembered so well? No, he would go tomorrow. He was feeling so sleepy now. The journey had made him drowsy, and his head was full of drifting nebulous thoughts.

Occasionally during these thirteen years, when suffering from indigestion, he had dreamed he was at home again in the old, echoing house on the slanting street, and that his father was there again too, indignantly upbraiding him for his degenerate way of life; and he had always felt that this was entirely as it should be. And he could in no way distinguish his present impressions from one of these delusive and compelling fabrications of the dreaming mind during which one asks oneself whether this is fantasy or reality and is driven firmly to the latter conclusion, only to end by waking up after all . . . He advanced through the half-empty, draughty streets, bending his head before the breeze, moving like a sleepwalker towards the hotel where he had decided to spend the night, the best hotel in the town. Ahead of him, a bow-legged man with a rolling nautical gait was carrying a pole with a little flame at the top, and lighting the gas-lamps with it.

What was he really feeling? Under the ashes of his weariness something was glowing, obscurely and painfully, not flickering up into a clear flame: what was it? Hush, he must not say it! He must not put it into words! He would have liked to stroll on indefinitely, in the wind and the dusk, along these familiar streets of his dreams. But it was all so close, so near together. One reached one's destination at once.

In the upper part of the town there were arc-lamps, and they were just coming alight. There was the hotel, and there were the two black lions couched in front of it; as a child he had always been afraid of them. They were still staring at each other, looking as if they were just about to sneeze; but they seemed to have grown much smaller now. Tonio Kröger walked between them into the hotel.

As a guest arriving on foot he was received without much ceremony. He encountered the inquiring gaze of the porter and of a very smartly dressed gentleman in black who was doing the honours, and who had a habit of constantly pushing his shirt-cuffs back into his coat-sleeves with his little fingers. They both looked him carefully up and down from head to foot, obviously trying hard to place him, to assign him an approximate position in the social hierarchy which would determine the degree of respect that was his due; they were unable, however, to reach a satisfactory conclusion on this point, and therefore decided in favour of a moderate show of politeness. A mild-mannered waiter with sandy side-whiskers, a frock coat shiny with age and rosettes on his noiseless shoes, conducted him two floors up to a neatly furnished, old-fashioned room. From its window, in the twilight, there was a picturesque medieval view of courtyards, gables and the bizarre massive outlines of the church near which the hotel was situated. Tonio Kröger stood for a while looking out of this window; then he sat with folded arms on the commodious sofa, frowning and whistling to himself.

Lights were brought, and his luggage arrived. At the same time the mild-mannered waiter laid the registration form on the table, and Tonio Kröger, with his head tilted to one side, scrawled something on it that would pass for his name and status and place of origin. He then ordered some supper and continued to stare into vacancy from the corner of his sofa. When the food had been placed before him he left it untouched for a long time, then finally ate a morsel or two and walked up and down in the room for another hour, occasionally stopping and closing his eyes. Then he slowly undressed and went to bed. He slept for a long time and had confused, strangely nostalgic dreams.

When he woke up his room was full of broad daylight. In some haste and confusion he recalled where he was, and got up to draw the curtains. The blue of the late-summer sky was already rather pale, and covered with wind-reft wisps of cloud; but the sun was shining over his native town.

He devoted more care than usual to his toilet, washed and shaved meticulously until he was as fresh and immaculate as if he were about to pay a call on a conventional, well bred family with whom he would have to look his best and be on his best behaviour; and as he went through the processes of dressing he listened to the anxious beating of his heart.

How bright it was outside! He would have felt better if the streets had been dusky like yesterday; but now he would have to walk through clear sunlight exposed to the public gaze. Would he meet people he knew, would they stop him and call him to account by asking him how he had spent the last thirteen years? No, thank God, no one knew him now, and anyone who remembered him would not recognize him, for he had indeed somewhat changed in the mean time. He inspected himself attentively in the mirror, and suddenly felt safer behind his mask, behind his face on which experience had laid its mark early, his face that was older than his years . . . He sent for breakfast, and then he left the hotel, crossing the front hall under the calculating gaze of the porter and the elegant gentleman in black, and passing out into the street between the two lions.

Where was he going? He scarcely knew. He had the same sensation as yesterday. No sooner was he surrounded again by this strangely dignified and long-familiar complex of gables, turrets, arcades and fountains – no sooner did he feel again on his face the pressure of the wind, this strong fresh wind full of the delicate sharp flavour of distant dreams – than a misty veil of fantasy benumbed his senses . . . The muscles of his face relaxed; and his eyes as he gazed at people and things had grown calm. Perhaps, at the next corner, just over there, he would wake up after all . . .

Where was he going? He had an impression that the route he chose was not unconnected with last night's sad and strangely rueful dreams . . . He walked to the market square, under the arcades of the town hall; here were the butchers, weighing their wares with blood-stained hands, and here on the square was the tall, pointed, complicated Gothic fountain. Here he paused in front of a certain house, a simple narrow house much like any of the others, with an ornamental pierced gable. He stood gazing at it, read the name on the plate by the door, and let his eyes rest for a little on each of the windows in turn. Then he turned slowly away.

Where was he going? He was going home. But he made a detour, he took a walk outside the old city walls, for he had plenty of time. He walked along the Mühlenwall and the Holstenwall, clutching his hat before the wind that rustled and jarred among the trees. Presently, not far from the station, he turned off the promenade, watched a train bustling and puffing past, counted the coaches just for fun and gazed after the man who sat up there on the last one as it went by. But in the Lindenplatz he stopped in front of one of its handsome villas, stared for a long time into the garden and up at the windows, and finally took to swinging the iron gate to and fro on its creaking hinges. He gazed for a few moments at his hands, cold now and stained with rust; then he went on his way, he walked under the low arch of the old gate, along the harbour and up the steep draughty little street to his parents' house.

There it stood, surrounded by the neighbouring buildings, its gable rising above them: it was as grey and solemn as it had been for the last three hundred years, and Tonio Kröger read the pious motto engraved over the doorway in letters now half obliterated. Then he took a deep breath and went in.

His heart was beating anxiously, for it would not have surprised him if his father had thrown open one of the doors on the ground floor as he passed them, emerging in his office coat and with his pen behind his ear to confront him and take him severely to task for his dissolute life; and Tonio would have felt that this was just as it should be. But he got past without being interfered with by anyone. The inner door of the porch was not closed, only left ajar, a fact which he noted with disapproval, although at the same time he had the sensation of being in one of those elated dreams in which obstacles dissolve before one of their own accord and one advances unimpeded, favoured by some miraculous good fortune . . . The wide entrance hall, paved with great square flagstones, re-echoed with the sound of his footsteps. Opposite the kitchen, which was silent now, the strange, clumsy but neatly painted wooden cubicles still projected from high up in the wall as they had always done: these had been the maids' rooms, only accessible from the hall by a kind of open flight of steps. But the great cupboards and the carved chest that had once stood here were gone . . . The son of the house began to climb the imposing main stairway, resting his hand on the white-painted openwork balustrade; with every step he took he raised it and gently let it fall again, as if he were diffidently trying to discover whether his former familiarity with this solid old handrail could be re-established . . . But on the landing he stopped. At the entrance to the intermediate floor was a white board with black lettering which said: 'Public Library'.

Public library? thought Tonio Kröger, for in his opinion this was no place either for the public or for literature. He knocked on the door . . . He was bidden to enter, and did so. Tense and frowning, he beheld before him a most unseemly transformation.

There were three rooms on this intermediate floor, and their communicating doors stood open. The walls were covered almost up to the ceiling with uniformly bound books, standing in long rows on dark shelves. In each of the rooms a seedy-looking man was sitting writing at a sort of counter. Two of them merely turned their heads towards Tonio Kröger, but the first rose hastily to his feet, placed both hands on the desk to support himself, thrust his head forwards, pursed his lips, raised his eyebrows and surveyed the visitor with rapidly blinking eyes . . .

'Excuse me,' said Tonio Kröger, still staring at the multitude of books. 'I am a stranger here, I am making a tour of the town. So this is the public library? Would you allow me to take a short look at your collection?'

'Certainly!' said the official, blinking more vigorously than ever . . . 'Certainly, anyone may do so. Please take a look round . . . Would you like a catalogue?'

'No, thank you,' answered Tonio Kröger. 'I shall find my way about quite easily.' And he began to walk slowly along the walls, pretending to be studying the titles of the books. Finally he took down a volume, opened it, and stationed himself with it at the window.

This had been the morning-room. They had always had breakfast here, not upstairs in the big dining-room, with its blue wallpaper boldly decorated with the white figures of Greek gods . . . The adjoining room had been used as a bedroom. His father's mother had died there, and her death-struggle had been terrible, old as she was, for she had been a woman of the world who enjoyed life and clung to it. And later in that same room his father too had breathed his last, the tall, correct, rather sad and pensive gentleman with the wild flower in his buttonhole . . . Tonio had sat at the foot of his deathbed, his eyes hot with tears, in sincere and utter surrender to an inarticulate intense emotion of love and grief. And his mother too had knelt by the bed, his beautiful fiery mother, weeping her heart out; whereupon she had departed with that artist from the south to live under far-off blue skies . . . But the third room, the little one at the back, now fully stocked with books like the other two, with a seedy-looking attendant to supervise them – this for many years had been his own room. This was the room to which he had returned from school, perhaps after just such a walk as he had taken just now; there was the wall where his desk had stood, with its drawer where he had kept his first heartfelt clumsy efforts at verse composition . . . The walnut tree . . . He felt a sharp pang of grief. He glanced sideways through the window. The garden was neglected and overgrown, but the old walnut tree was still there, heavily creaking and rustling in the wind. And Tonio Kröger let his eyes wander back to the book he was holding in his hand, an outstanding work of literature which he knew well. He looked down at the black lines of print and groups of sentences, followed the elegant flow of the text for a little, observing its passionate stylization, noting how effectively it rose to a climax and fell away from it again . . .

Yes, that's well done, he said to himself; he replaced the work on the shelf and turned away. And he noticed that the official was still on his feet, still blinking hard, with a mingled expression of eager servility and puzzled suspicion.

'I see you have an excellent collection,' said Tonio Kröger. 'I have already formed a general impression of it. I am most grateful to you. Good-day.' Whereupon he left the room; but it was not a very successful exit, and he had the strong impression that the library attendant was so disconcerted by his visit that he would still be standing there blinking several minutes later.

He felt disinclined to explore further. He had visited his home. The large rooms upstairs, beyond the pillared hall, were now obviously occupied by strangers; for the staircase ended in a glass door which had not previously been there, and there was some kind of name-plate beside it. He turned away, walked downstairs and across the echoing entrance hall and left the house of his fathers. He went to a restaurant and sat at a corner table, deep in thought, eating a rich, heavy meal; then he returned to his hotel.

'I have finished my business,' he said to the elegant gentleman in black. 'I shall leave this afternoon.' And he asked for his bill, at the same time ordering a cab which would take him down to the harbour to board the steamer for Copenhagen. Then he went to his room and sat upright and in silence, resting his cheek on his hand and gazing down at the desk with unseeing eyes. Later he settled his bill and packed his luggage. At the appointed time the cab was announced and Tonio Kröger went downstairs, ready for his journey.

At the foot of the staircase the elegant gentleman in black was waiting for him.

'Excuse me!' he said, pushing his cuffs back into his sleeves with his little fingers . . . 'I beg your pardon, sir, but we must just detain you for one moment. Herr Seehaase – the proprietor of the hotel – would like to have a word with you. A mere formality . . . He's just over there . . . Would you be so kind as to come with me . . . It's *only* Herr Seehaase, the proprietor.'

And with polite gestures he ushered Tonio Kröger to the back of the hall. There, to be sure, stood Herr Seehaase. Tonio Kröger knew him by sight, from days gone by. He was short, plump and bow-legged. His clipped side-whiskers were white now; but he still wore a low-cut frock coat and a little velvet cap embroidered with green. He was, moreover, not alone. Beside him, at a small high desk fixed to the wall, stood a policeman with his helmet on and his gloved right hand resting on a complicated-looking document which lay before him on the desk. He was looking straight at Tonio Kröger with his honest soldierly eyes as if he expected him to sink right into the ground at the sight of him.

Tonio Kröger looked from one to the other and decided to await developments.

'You have come here from Munich?' asked the policeman eventually in a slow, good-natured voice.

Tonio Kröger answered this question in the affirmative.

'You are travelling to Copenhagen?'

'Yes, I am on my way to a Danish seaside resort.'

'Seaside resort? Well, you must let me see your papers,' said the policeman, uttering the last word with an air of special satisfaction.

'Papers . . .?' He had no papers. He took out his pocket-book and glanced at its contents; but apart from some money it contained only the proofs of a short story, which he intended to correct at his destination. He did not like dealing with officials, and had never yet had a passport issued to him . . .

'I am sorry,' he said, 'but I have no papers with me.'

'Indeed!' said the policeman . . . 'None at all? What is your name?'

Tonio Kröger answered him.

'Is that the truth?' asked the policeman, drawing himself up to his full height and suddenly opening his nostrils as wide as he could.

'Certainly,' replied Tonio Kröger.

'And what's your occupation, may I ask?'

Tonio Kröger swallowed and in a firm voice named his profession. Herr Seehaase raised his head and looked up at him with curiosity.

'Hm!' said the policeman. 'And you allege that you are not identical with an individial of the name of –' He said 'individial', and proceeded to spell out from the complicated document a highly intricate and romantic name which seemed to have been bizarrely compounded from the languages of various races; Tonio Kröger had no sooner heard it than he had forgotten it. 'An individial,' the policeman continued, 'of unknown parentage and dubious domicile, who is wanted by the Munich police in connection with various frauds and other offences and is probably trying to escape to Denmark?'

'I do not merely "allege" this,' said Tonio Kröger, with a nervous movement of his shoulders. That made a certain impression.

'What? Oh, quite, yes, of course!' said the policeman. 'But you can't identify yourself in any way, can you!'

Herr Seehaase attempted a conciliatory intervention.

'The whole thing is a formality,' he said, 'nothing more! You must realize that the officer is merely doing his duty. If you could show some kind of identification . . . some document . . .'

They all fell silent. Should he make an end of the matter by disclosing who he was, by informing Herr Seehaase that he was not an adventurerer of dubious domicile, not born a gypsy in a green caravan, but the son of Consul Kröger, a member of the Kröger family? No, he had no wish to say anything of the sort. And were they not right, in a way, these representatives of bourgeois society? In a certain sense he entirely agreed with them . . . He shrugged his shoulders and said nothing.

'What have you got there?' asked the policeman. 'There, in your pocket-book?'

'Here? Nothing. Only a proof,' answered Tonio Kröger.

'Proof? Proof of what? Let's have a look.'

And Tonio Kröger handed him his work. The policeman spread it out on the desk and began to read it. Herr Seehaase, stepping closer, did the same. Tonio Kröger glanced over their shoulders to see what part of the text they had reached. It was a good passage, pointed and effective; he had taken pains with it and got it exactly right. He was pleased with himself.

'You see!' he said. 'There is my name. I wrote this, and now it is being published, you understand.'

'Well, that's good enough!' said Herr Seehaase decisively. He put the sheets together, folded them and returned them to their author. 'It must be good enough, Petersen,' he repeated curtly, surreptitiously closing his eyes and shaking his head to forestall any objections. 'We must not delay the gentleman any longer. His cab is waiting. I hope, sir, you will excuse this slight inconvenience. The officer was of course only doing his duty, though I told him at once that he was on the wrong track . . .'

'Did you, now?' thought Tonio Kröger.

The policeman did not seem entirely satisfied; he raised some further query about 'individial' and 'identification'. But Herr Seehaase conducted his guest back through the foyer, with repeated expressions of regret; he accompanied him out between the two lions to his cab and saw him into it, closing the door himself with a great display of respect. Whereupon the absurdly tall, broad vehicle, rumbling and stumbling, noisily and clumsily rolled down the steep narrow streets to the harbour . . .

And that was Tonio Kröger's curious visit to the city of his fathers.

# 7

Night was falling, and the moon was rising, its silver radiance floating up the sky, as Tonio Kröger's ship moved out into the open sea. He stood in the bows, warmly wrapped against the mounting wind, and gazed down at the dark restless wandering of the great smooth waves beneath him, watching them slithering round each other, dashing against each other, darting away from each other in unexpected directions with a sudden glitter of foam . . .

His heart was dancing with silent elation. The experience of being nearly arrested in his native town as a criminal adventurer had somewhat damped his spirits, to be sure – even although in a certain sense he had felt that this was just as it should be. But then he had come on board and stood, as he had sometimes done with his father as a boy, watching the freight being loaded on to the boat: its capacious hold had been stuffed with bales and crates, amid shouts in a mixture of Danish and Plattdeutsch, and even a polar bear and a Bengal tiger had been lowered into it in cages with strong iron bars; evidently they had been sent from Hamburg for delivery to some Danish menagerie. And all this had cheered him up. Later, as the steamer had slipped downstream between the flat embankments, he had completely forgotten his interrogation by Constable Petersen, and all his previous impressions had revived again in his mind: his sweet, sad, rueful dreams, his walk, the sight of the walnut tree. And now, as they passed out of the estuary, he saw in the distance the shore where as a boy he had listened to the sea's summer reveries, he saw the flash of the lighthouse and the lighted windows of the resort's principal hotel at which he and his parents had stayed . . . The Baltic Sea! He bent his head before the strong salt wind which was blowing now with full unimpeded force; it enveloped him, drowning all other sounds, making him feel slightly giddy, half numbed with a blissful lethargy which swallowed up all his unpleasant memories, all his sufferings and errors and efforts and struggles. And in the clashing, foaming, moaning uproar all round him he thought he heard the rustling and jarring of the old walnut tree, the creaking of a garden gate . . . The darkness was thickening.

'The sstars, my God, just look at the sstars!' said a voice suddenly. It spoke in a plaintively singsong northern accent and seemed to come from the interior of a large barrel. He had heard it already; it belonged to a sandy-haired, plainly dressed man with reddened eyelids and a chilled, damp look, as if he had just been bathing. He had sat next to

Tonio Kröger at dinner in the saloon and had consumed, in a modest and hesitant manner, astonishing quantities of lobster omelette. He was now standing beside him leaning against the rail, staring up at the sky and holding his chin between his thumb and forefinger. He was obviously in one of those exceptional, festive and contemplative moods in which the barriers between oneself and one's fellow men are lowered, one's heart is laid bare to strangers and one's tongue speaks of matters on which it would normally preserve an embarrassed silence . . .

'Look, sir, just look at the sstars! Twinkling away up there; by God, the whole sky's full of them. And when you look up at it all and consider that a lot of them are supposed to be a hundred times the size of the earth, well, I ask you, how does it make one feel! We men have invented the telegraph and the telephone and so many wonders of modern times, yes, so we have. But when we look up there we have to realize nevertheless that when all's said and done we are just worms, just miserable little worms and nothing more – am I right or am I wrong, sir? Yes,' he concluded, answering his own question, 'that's what we are: worms!' And he nodded towards the firmament in abject contrition.

Oh, Lord, thought Tonio Kröger. No, he's got no literature in his system. And at once he recalled something he had recently read by a famous French writer, an essay on the cosmological and the psychological world view; it had been quite a clever piece of verbiage.

He made some kind of reply to the young man's heartfelt observation, and they then continued to converse, leaning over the rail and gazing into the flickering, stormy dusk. It turned out that Tonio Kröger's travelling companion was a young businessman from Hamburg who was devoting his holiday to this excursion . . .

'I thought: why not take the ssteamer and pop up to Copenhagen?' he explained. 'So here I am, and so far so good, I must say. But those lobster omelettes were a misstake, sir, I can tell you, because there's going to be a gale tonight, the captain said so himself, and that's no joke with indigestible food like that in your sstomach . . .'

Tonio Kröger listened with a certain secret sympathy to these foolish familiar overtures.

'Yes,' he said, 'the food's generally too heavy up in these parts. It makes one sluggish and melancholy.'

'Melancholy?' repeated the young man, looking at him in some puzzlement, then suddenly added: 'You're a sstranger here, sir, I suppose?'

'Oh yes, I'm from a long way away!' answered Tonio Kröger with a vague and evasive gesture.

'But you're right,' said the young man. 'God knows, you're right about feeling melancholy! I'm nearly always melancholy, but especially on evenings like this when there are sstars in the sky.' And he rested his chin again on his thumb and forefinger.

He probably writes poetry, thought Tonio Kröger; deeply felt, honest, businessman's poetry . . .

It was getting late, and the wind was so high now that it made conversation impossible. So they decided to retire, and bade each other good-night.

Tonio Kröger lay down on the narrow bunk in his cabin, but could not sleep. The strong gale with its sharp tang had strangely excited him, and his heart beat anxiously, as if troubled by the expectation of some sweet experience. He also felt extremely seasick, for the ship was in violent motion, sliding down one steep wave after another with its propeller lifting right out of the water and whirring convulsively. He put on all his clothes again and returned to the deck.

Clouds were racing across the moon. The sea was dancing. The waves were not rounded and rolling in ordered succession, they were being lashed and torn and churned into frenzy as far as the eye could reach. In the pallid, flickering light they licked and leapt upwards like gigantic pointed tongues of flame: between foam-filled gulfs, jagged and incredible shapes were hurled on high: the sea seemed to be lifting mighty arms, tossing its spume into the air in wild, monstrous exhilaration. The ship was having a hard passage: pitching and rolling, thudding and groaning, it struggled on through the tumult, and from time to time the polar bear and the tiger could be heard roaring miserably from below decks. A man in an oilskin, with the hood over his head and a lantern strapped round his waist, was pacing the deck with straddled legs, keeping his balance with difficulty. But there in the stern, leaning far overboard, stood the young man from Hamburg, woefully afflicted.

'My God,' he remarked in hollow, unsteady tones when he caught sight of Tonio Kröger, 'just look at the uproar of the elements, sir!' But at this point he was interrupted and turned away hastily.

Tonio Kröger clutched the first taut piece of rope he could find and stood gazing out into all this mad, exuberant chaos. His spirits soared in an exultation that felt mighty enough to outshout the storm and the waves. Inwardly he began to sing a song of love, a paean of praise to the sea. Friend of my youth, ah wild sea weather, once more we meet, once more together . . . But there the poem ended. It was not a finished product, not an experience formed and shaped, recollected in tranquillity and forged into a whole. His heart was alive . . .

Thus he stood for a long time; then he lay down on a bench beside the deck-house and looked up at the sky with its glittering array of stars. He even dozed off for a while. And when the cold foam sprayed his face as he lay there half asleep, he felt it as a caress.

Vertical chalk cliffs loomed ghostly in the moonlight and drew nearer; it was the island of Møn. And again he dozed off, wakened from time to time by salt showers of spray which bit into his face and numbed his features . . . By the time he was fully awake it was already broad daylight, a fresh pale grey morning, and the green sea was calmer. At breakfast he again encountered the young businessman, who blushed scarlet, obviously ashamed of having said such discreditably poetical things under cover of darkness. He readjusted his small reddish moustache, stroking it upwards with all five fingers, barked out a brisk military 'Good morning!' to Tonio Kröger and then carefully steered clear of him.

And Tonio Kröger landed in Denmark. He arrived in Copenhagen, gave a tip to everyone who showed signs of expecting him to do so and then spent three days exploring the city from his hotel, holding his guidebook open in front of him and in general behaving like a well bred foreigner intent on improving his mind. He inspected Kongens Nytorv and the 'Horse' in its midst, glanced up respectfully at the columns of the Fruekirke, paused long before Thorwaldsen's noble and charming sculptures, climbed the Round Tower, visited various palaces and passed two colourful evenings at Tivoli. Yet all this was not really what he saw.

He saw houses which often exactly resembled those of his native town, houses with ornamental pierced gables, and the names by their front doors were names familiar to him from long ago, names symbolizing for him something tender and precious, and containing at the same time a kind of reproach, the sorrowful nostalgic reminder of something lost. And everywhere he went, slowly and pensively breathing in the damp sea air, he saw eyes just as blue, hair just as blond, faces just like those that had filled the strange sad rueful dreams of that night in his native town. As he walked these streets he would suddenly encounter a look, a vocal inflection, a peal of laughter, that pierced him to the heart . . .

The lively city did not hold him for long. He felt driven from it by a certain restlessness, by mingled memory and expectancy, and because he longed to be able to lie quietly somewhere on the sea-shore and not have to play the part of a busily circulating tourist. And so he embarked once more and sailed northwards, on a dull day, over an inky sea, up the coast of Zealand to Elsinore. From there he at once continued his journey for another few miles by coach along the main road, which also ran close to the sea, until he reached his final and true destination. It was a little white seaside hotel with green shutters, surrounded by a cluster of low-lying houses and looking out with its wooden-shingled tower across the sound towards the Swedish coast. Here he stopped, took possession of the bright sunny room they had reserved for him, filled its shelves and cupboards with his belongings and settled down to live here for a while.

# 8

It was late September already; there were not many visitors left in Aalsgaard. Meals were served in the big dining-room on the ground floor, which had a beamed ceiling and tall windows overlooking the glazed veranda and the sea; they were presided over by the proprietress, an elderly spinster with white hair, colourless eyes, faintly pink cheeks and a vague twittering voice, who always tried to arrange her reddened hands on the tablecloth in a manner that would display them to their best advantage. One of the guests was a short-necked old gentleman with a hoary sailor's beard and a dark bluish complexion; he was a fish dealer from the capital and could speak German. He seemed to be completely congested and inclined to apoplexy, for he breathed in short gasps and occasionally lifted a ringed index finger to his nose, pressed it against one nostril and blew hard through the other as if to clear it a little. Notwithstanding this he addressed himself continually to a bottle of aquavit which stood before him at breakfast, lunch and dinner. The only other members of the company were three tall American boys with their tutor or director of studies, who played football with them day in and day out and otherwise merely fidgeted with his spectacles and said nothing. The three youths had reddish fair hair parted in the middle, and elongated expressionless faces. 'Will you pass me some of that *Wurst*, please,' one of them would say in English. 'It's not *Wurst*, it's *Schinken*,' the other would reply; and that was the extent of their contribution to the conversation; for the rest of the time they and their tutor sat in silence drinking hot water.

Such were Tonio Kröger's neighbours at table, and they could not have been more to his liking. He was left in peace, and sat listening to the Danish glottal stops and front and back vowels in the speeches which the fish dealer and the proprietress now and then addressed to each other; with the former he would exchange an occasional simple remark about the state of the weather; he would then take his leave, pass through the veranda and walk down again to the beach, where he had already spent most of the morning.

Sometimes it was all summer stillness there. The sea lay idle and smooth, streaked with blue and bottle-green and pale red, and the light played over it in glittering silvery reflections. The seaweed withered like hay in the sun, and the stranded jellyfish shrivelled. There was a slight smell of decay, and a whiff of tar from the fishing boat against which Tonio Kröger leaned as he sat on the sand, facing away from the Swedish coast and towards the open horizon; but over it all swept the pure, fresh, gentle breath of the sea.

And then there would be grey, stormy days. The waves curved downwards like bulls lowering their horns for a charge, and dashed themselves furiously against the shore, which was strewn with shining wet sea-grass, mussel-shells and pieces of driftwood, for the water rushed far inland. Under the overcast sky the wave troughs were foaming green, like long valleys between ranges of watery hills; but where the sun shone down from beyond the clouds, the sea's surface shimmered like white velvet.

Tonio Kröger would stand there enveloped in the noise of the wind and the surf, immersed in this perpetual, ponderous, deafening roar he loved so much. When he turned and moved away, everything all round him suddenly seemed calm and warm. But he always knew that the sea was behind him, calling, luring, beckoning. And he would smile.

He would walk far inland, along solitary paths across meadows, and would soon find himself surrounded by the beech trees which covered most of the low, undulating coastland. He would sit on the mossy ground, leaning against a tree trunk, at a point from which a strip of the sea was still visible through the wood. Sometimes the clash of the surf, like wooden boards falling against each other in the distance, would be carried to him by the breeze. Crows cawed above the tree-tops, hoarse and desolate and forlorn . . . He would sit with a book on his knees, but reading not a word of it. He was experiencing a profound forgetfulness, floating as if disembodied above space and time, and only at certain moments did he feel his heart stricken by a pang of sorrow, a brief, piercing, nostalgic or remorseful emotion which in his lethargic trance he made no attempt to define or analyse.

Thus many days passed; he could not have told how many, and had no desire to know. But then came one on which something happened; when the sun was shining and many people were there, and Tonio Kröger did not even find it particularly surprising.

There was something festive and delightful about that day from its very beginning. Tonio Kröger woke unusually early and quite suddenly; he was gently and vaguely startled out of his sleep and at once confronted with an apparently magical spectacle, an elfin miracle of morning radiance. His room had a glass door and balcony facing out over the sound; it was divided into a sleeping and a living area by a white gauze curtain, and papered and furnished lightly in delicate pale shades, so that it always looked bright and cheerful. But now, before his sleep-dazed eyes, it had undergone an unearthly transfiguration and illumination, it was completely drenched in an indescribably lovely and fragrant rose-coloured light: the walls and furniture shone golden and the gauze curtain was a glowing pink . . . For some time Tonio Kröger could not understand what was happening. But when he stood by the glass door and looked out, he saw that the sun was rising.

It had been dull and rainy for several days on end, but now, over land and sea, the sky was like tight-stretched pale blue silk, bright and glistening; and the sun's disc, traversed and surrounded by resplendent red and gold clouds, was mounting in triumph above the shimmering, wrinkled water, which seemed to quiver and catch fire beneath it . . . Thus the day opened, and in joy and confusion Tonio Kröger threw on his clothes; he had breakfast down in the veranda before anyone else, then swam some way out into the sound from the little wooden bathing hut, then walked for an hour along the beach. When he got back to the hotel there were several horse-drawn omnibuses standing in front of it, and from the dining-room he could see that a large number of visitors had arrived: both in the adjoining parlour where the piano stood, and on the veranda and on the terrace in front of it, they were sitting at round tables consuming beer and sandwiches and talking excitedly. They were visitors in simple middle-class attire, whole families, young people and older people, even a few children.

At mid-morning lunch – the table was heavily laden with cold food, smoked and salted delicacies and pastries – Tonio Kröger inquired what was afoot.

'Day visitors!' declared the fish dealer. 'A party from Elsinore; they're having a dance here. Yes, God help us, we'll not sleep a wink tonight. There'll be dancing and music, and you can depend on it, they'll go on till all hours. It's some sort of subscription affair with various families taking part, an excursion in the country with a ball afterwards to make the most of the fine day. They came by boat and by road and now they're having lunch. Afterwards they'll go for another drive, but they'll be back in the evening, and then it'll be dancing and fun and games here in the dining-room. Yes, damn and confound it, we'll not shut an eye this night . . .'

'It makes an agreeable change,' said Tonio Kröger.

Whereupon silence was resumed. The proprietress sorted out her red fingers, the fish dealer snorted through his right nostril to clear it a little and the Americans drank hot water and made long faces.

Then suddenly it happened: *Hans Hansen and Ingeborg Holm walked through the dining-room.*

Tonio Kröger, pleasantly weary after his swim and his rapid walk, was leaning back in his chair eating smoked salmon on toast; he was facing the veranda and the sea. And suddenly the door opened and the two of them sauntered in, unhurried, hand-in-hand. Ingeborg, the fair-haired Inge, was wearing a light-coloured frock, just as she had done at Herr

Knaak's dancing lessons. It was made of thin material with a floral pattern, and reached down only to her ankles; round her shoulders was a broad white tulle collar cut well down in front and exposing her soft, supple neck. She had tied the ribbons of her hat together and slung it over one arm. She had perhaps grown up a little since he had last seen her, and her wonderful blonde tresses were wound round her head now; but Hans Hansen was just as he had always been. He was wearing his reefer jacket with the gold buttons and with the broad blue collar hanging out over his back; in his free hand he held his sailor's cap with its short ribbons, carelessly dangling it to and fro. Ingeborg kept her narrow-cut eyes averted, feeling perhaps a little shy under the gaze of the people sitting over their lunch. But Hans Hansen, as if in defiance of all and sundry, turned his head straight towards the table, and his steely blue eyes inspected each member of the company in turn, with a challenging and slightly contemptuous air; he even let go of Ingeborg's hand and swung his cap more vigorously to and fro, to show what a fine fellow he was. Thus the pair of them passed by before Tonio Kröger's eyes, against the background of the calm blue sea; they walked the length of the dining-room and disappeared through the door at the far end, into the parlour.

This happened at half-past eleven, and while the residents were still eating, the visiting party next door and on the veranda set out on their excursion; no one else came into the dining-room, they left the hotel by the side entrance. Outside, they could be heard getting into their omnibuses, amid much laughter and joking, and then there was the sound of one vehicle after another rumbling away . . .

'So they're coming back?' asked Tonio Kröger.

'They are indeed!' said the fish dealer. 'And God damn the whole thing, I say. They've engaged a band, and I sleep right over this room.'

'It makes an agreeable change,' said Tonio Kröger again. Then he got up and left.

He spent that day as he had spent the others, on the beach and in the woods, holding a book on his knee and blinking in the sunlight. There was only one thought in his mind: that they would be coming back and holding a dance in the dining-room as the fish dealer had predicted, and he did nothing all day but look forward to this, with a sweet apprehensive excitement such as he had not felt throughout all these long, dead years. Once, by some associative trick of thought, he fleetingly remembered a far-off acquaintance: Adalbert, the short-story writer, the man who knew what he wanted and had retreated into a café to escape the spring air. And he shrugged his shoulders at the thought of him . . .

Dinner was earlier than usual; supper was also served in advance of the normal time and in the parlour, because preparations for the dance were already being made in the dining-room: the whole normal programme was delightfully disarranged for so festive an occasion. Then, when it was already dark and Tonio Kröger was sitting in his room, there were signs of life again on the road and in the hotel. The party was returning; there were even new guests arriving from Elsinore by bicycle or by carriage, and already he could hear, down below, a violin being tuned and the nasal tones of a clarinet practising scales . . . There was every indication that it would be a magnificent ball.

And now the little orchestra began playing: a march in strict time, muted but clearly audible upstairs. The dancing began with a polonaise. Tonio Kröger sat on quietly for a while and listened. But when the march tempo changed to a waltz rhythm, he rose and slipped quietly out of his room.

From his corridor there was a subsidiary flight of stairs leading down to the side entrance of the hotel, and from there one could reach the glazed veranda without passing through any of the rooms. He went this way, walking softly and stealthily as if he had no business to be there, groping cautiously through the darkness, irresistibly drawn towards the foolish, happily lilting music; he could hear it now quite loudly and distinctly.

The veranda was empty and unlit, but in the dining-room the two large paraffin lamps with their polished reflectors were shining brightly, and the glass door stood open. He crept noiselessly up to it; here he could stand in the dark unobserved, watching the dancers in the lighted room, and this furtive pleasure made his skin tingle. Quickly and eagerly he glanced round for the pair he sought . . .

The festivity was already in full swing, although the dancing had begun less than half an hour ago; but the participants had of course been already warmed up and excited by the time they had got back here, having spent the whole day together in happy and carefree companionship. In the parlour, into which Tonio Kröger could see if he ventured forward a little, several older men had settled down to smoke and drink and play cards; others again were sitting with their wives on the plush-upholstered chairs in the foreground or along the walls of the dining-room, watching the dance. They sat resting their hands on their outspread knees, with prosperous puffed-out faces; the mothers, wearing bonnets high up on their parted hair, looked on at the whirl of young people, with their hands folded in their laps and their heads tilted sideways. A platform had been erected against one of the longer walls, and on it the musicians were doing their best. There was even a trumpeter among them, blowing on his instrument rather diffidently and cautiously – it seemed to be afraid of its own voice, which despite all efforts kept breaking and tripping over itself . . . The dancing couples circled round each other, swaying and gyrating, while others walked about the room hand-in-hand. The company was not properly dressed for a ball, merely for a summer Sunday outing in the country: the young beaux wore suits of provincial cut which they obviously used only at weekends, and the girls were in light pale frocks with bunches of wild flowers on their bosoms. There were even some children present, dancing with each other after their fashion, even when the band was not playing. The master of ceremonies appeared to be a long-legged man in a swallow-tailed coat, some kind of small-town dandy with a monocle and artificially curled hair, an assistant postmaster perhaps – a comic character straight out of a Danish novel. He devoted himself heart and soul to his task, positively perspiring with officiousness; he was everywhere at once, curvetting busily round the room with a mincing gait, setting his toes down first and artfully criss-crossing his feet, which were clad in shining pointed half-boots of military cut. He waved his arms, issued instructions, called for music and clapped his hands; as he moved, the ribbons of the gaily coloured bow which had been pinned to his shoulder in token of his office fluttered behind him, and from time to time he glanced lovingly round at it.

Yes, there they were, the pair who had walked past Tonio Kröger that morning in the sunlight: he saw them again, his heart suddenly leaping with joy as he caught sight of them almost simultaneously. There stood Hans Hansen, quite near him, not far from the door; with outspread legs and leaning forward slightly, he was slowly and carefully devouring a large slice of sponge cake, holding one hand cupped under his chin to catch the crumbs. And there by the wall sat Ingeborg Holm, the fair-haired Inge; at that very moment the assistant postmaster minced up to her and invited her to dance with a stilted bow, placing one hand on the small of his back and gracefully inserting the other into his bosom, but she shook her head and indicated that she was too much out of breath and must rest for a little, whereupon the assistant postmaster sat down beside her.

Tonio Kröger looked at them both, those two for whom long ago he had suffered love: Hans and Ingeborg. For that was who they were – not so much by virtue of particular details of their appearance or similarities of dress, but by affinity of race and type: they too had that radiant blondness, those steely blue eyes, that air of untroubled purity and lightness of heart, of proud simplicity and unapproachable reserve . . . He watched them, watched Hans Hansen standing there in his sailor suit, bold and handsome as ever, broad in the shoulders and narrow in the hips; he watched Ingeborg's way of tossing her head to one side with a saucy laugh, her way of raising her hand – a hand by no means particularly tiny or delicately girlish – to smooth her hair at the back, letting her light sleeve slide away from the elbow; and suddenly his heart was pierced by such an agony of homesickness that he instinctively shrank further back into the shadows to hide the twitching of his face.

'Had I forgotten you?' he asked. 'No, never! I never forgot you, Hans, nor you, sweet fair-haired Inge! It was for you I wrote my works, and when I heard applause I secretly looked round the room to see if you had joined in it . . . Have you read *Don Carlos* yet, Hans Hansen, as you promised me at your garden gate? Don't read it! I no longer want you to. What has that lonely weeping king to do with you? You must not make your bright eyes cloudy and dreamy and dim by peering into poetry and sadness . . . If I could be like you! If only I could begin all over again and grow up like you, decent and happy and simple, normal and *comme il faut*, at peace with God and the world, loved by the innocent and light of heart – and marry you, Ingeborg Holm, and have a son like you, Hans Hansen! If only I could be freed from the curse of insight and the creative torment, and live and love and be thankful and blissfully commonplace! . . . Begin all over again? It would be no good. It would all turn out the same – all happen again just as it has happened. For certain people are bound to go astray because for them no such thing as a right way exists.'

The music had stopped; there was an interval, and refreshments were being handed round. The assistant postmaster in person was tripping about with a trayful of herring salad, offering it to the ladies; but before

Ingeborg Holm he even went down on one knee as he handed her the dish, and this made her blush with pleasure.

The spectator by the glass door of the dining-room was now beginning to attract attention after all, and from handsome flushed faces uncordial and inquiring looks were cast in his direction; but he stood his ground. Ingeborg and Hans glanced at him too, almost simultaneously, with that air of utter indifference so very like contempt. But suddenly he became conscious that a gaze from some other quarter had sought him out and was resting on him . . . He turned his head, and his eyes at once met those whose scrutiny he had sensed. Not far from him a girl was standing, a girl with a pale, slender delicate face whom he had noticed before. She had not been dancing much, the gentlemen had paid scant heed to her, and he had seen her sitting alone by the wall with tightly pursed lips. She was standing by herself now too. She wore a light-coloured frock like the other girls, but through its transparent gossamer-like material one could glimpse bare shoulders which were thin and pointed, and between these meagre shoulders her thin neck sat so low that this quiet girl almost gave the impression of being slightly deformed. She had thin short gloves on, and held her hands against her flat breasts with their fingers just touching. She had lowered her head and was gazing up at Tonio Kröger with dark, melting eyes. He turned away . . .

Here, quite near him, sat Hans and Ingeborg. Possibly they were brother and sister; Hans had sat down next to her, and surrounded by other young people with healthy pink complexions they were eating and drinking, chattering and enjoying themselves and exchanging pleasantries, and their bright clear voices and laughter rang through the air. Could he not perhaps approach them for a moment? Could he not speak to one or other of them, make whatever humorous remark occurred to him, and would they not at least have to answer with a smile? It would give him such pleasure; he longed for it to happen; he would go back to his room contented, in the knowledge of having established some slight contact with them both. He thought out something he might say to them; but he could not nerve himself to go forward and say it. After all, the situation was as it had always been: they would not understand, they would listen to his words in puzzled embarrassment. For they did not speak the same language.

The dancing, apparently, was on the point of beginning again. The assistant postmaster burst into ubiquitous activity. He hurried to and fro, urged everyone to choose a partner, helped the waiter to clear chairs and glasses out of the way, issued instructions to the musicians and pushed a few awkward uncomprehending dancers into place, steering them by the shoulders. What was about to happen? Squares were being formed, of four couples each . . . A dreadful memory made Tonio Kröger blush. They were going to dance quadrilles.

The music began; the couples bowed and advanced and interchanged. The assistant postmaster directed the dance; great heavens, he was actually directing it in French, and pronouncing the nasal vowels with incomparable distinction! Ingeborg Holm was dancing just in front of Tonio Kröger, in the set nearest to the glass door. She moved to and fro in front of him, stepping and turning, forwards and backwards; often he caught a fragrance from her hair or from the delicate white material of her dress, and he closed his eyes, filled with an emotion so long familiar to him: during all these last days he had been faintly aware of its sharp enchanting flavour, and now it was welling up once more inside him in all its sweet urgency. What was it? Desire, tenderness? envy? self-contempt? . . . *Moulinet des dames!* Did you laugh, fair-haired Inge, did you laugh at me on that occasion, when I danced the *moulinet* and made such a miserable fool of myself? And would you still laugh today, even now when I have become, in my own way, a famous man? Yes you would – and you would be a thousand times right to do so, and even if I, single-handed, had composed the Nine Symphonies and written *The World as Will and Idea* and painted the *Last Judgement* – you would still be right to laugh, eternally right . . . He looked at her, and remembered a line of poetry, a line he had long forgotten and which was nevertheless so close to his mind and heart: 'I long to sleep, to sleep, but you must dance.' He knew so well the melancholy northern mood it expressed, awkward and half-articulate and heartfelt. To sleep . . . To long to be able to live simply for one's feelings alone, to rest idly in sweet self-sufficient emotion, uncompelled to translate it into activity, unconstrained to dance – and to have to dance nevertheless, to have to be alert and nimble and perform the difficult, difficult and perilous sword-dance of art, and never to be able quite to forget the humiliating paradox of having to dance when one's heart is heavy with love . . .

Suddenly, all round him, a wild extravagant whirl of movement developed. The sets had broken up, and everyone was leaping and gliding about in all directions: the quadrille was finishing with a gallopade. The couples, keeping time to the music's frantic prestissimo, were darting past Tonio Kröger, *chassé*ing, racing, overtaking each other with little gasps of laughter. One of them, caught up and swept forward by the general rush, came spinning towards him. The girl had a delicate pale face and thin, hunched shoulders. And all at once, directly in front of him, there was a slipping and tripping and stumbling . . . The pale girl had fallen over. She fell so hard and heavily that it looked quite dangerous, and her partner collapsed with her. He had evidently hurt himself so badly that he completely forgot the lady and began in a half-upright posture to grimace with pain and rub his knee; the girl seemed quite dazed by her fall and was still lying on the floor. Whereupon Tonio Kröger stepped forward, took her gently by both arms and lifted her to her feet. She looked up at him, exhausted, bewildered and wretched, and suddenly a pink flush spread over her delicate face.

'*Tak! O, mange tak!*' she said, and looked up at him with dark melting eyes.

'You had better not dance again, Fräulein,' he said gently. Then he glanced round until once more he saw *them*, Hans and Ingeborg; and turned away. He left the veranda and the ball and went back up to his room.

He was elated by these festivities in which he had not shared, and wearied by jealousy. It had all been the same as before, so exactly the same! With flushed face he had stood in the darkness, his heart aching for you all, you the fair-haired, the happy, the truly alive; and then he had gone away, alone. Surely someone would come now! Surely Ingeborg would come now, surely she would notice that he had left, and slip out after him, put her hand on his shoulder and say: 'Come back and join us! Don't be sad! I love you!' But she did not come. Such things do not happen. Yes, it was all as it had been long ago, and he was happy as he had been long ago. For his heart was alive. But what of all those years he had spent in becoming what he now was? Paralysis; barrenness; ice; and intellect! and art! . . .

He undressed and got into bed and put out the light. He whispered two names into his pillow, whispered those few chaste northern syllables which symbolized his true and native way of loving and suffering and being happy – which to him meant life and simple heartfelt emotion and home. He looked back over the years that had passed between then and now. He remembered the dissolute adventures in which his senses, his nervous system and his mind had indulged; he saw himself corroded by irony and intellect, laid waste and paralysed by insight, almost exhausted by the fevers and chills of creation, helplessly and contritely tossed to and fro between gross extremes, between saintly austerity and lust – oversophisticated and impoverished, worn out by cold, rare, artificial ecstasies, lost, ravaged, racked and sick – and he sobbed with remorse and nostalgia.

Round about him there was silence and darkness. But lilting up to him from below came the faint music, the sweet trivial waltz rhythm of life.

## 9

Tonio Kröger sat in the north writing to his friend Lisaveta Ivanovna, as he had promised he would do.

'My dear Lisaveta down there in Arcadia,' he wrote, 'to which I hope soon to return: here is a letter of sorts, but I am afraid it may disappoint you, for I propose to write in rather general terms. Not that I have nothing to tell you, or have not, after my fashion, undergone one or two experiences. At home, in my native town, I was even nearly arrested . . . but of that you shall hear by word of mouth. I sometimes now have days on which I prefer to attempt a well formulated general statement, rather than narrate particular events.

'I wonder if you still remember, Lisaveta, once calling me a bourgeois *manqué*? You called me that on an occasion on which I had allowed myself to be enticed, by various indiscreet confessions I had already let slip, into avowing to you my love for what I call "life"; and I wonder if you realized how very right you were, and how truly my bourgeois nature and my love for "life" are one and the same. My journey here has made me think about this point . . .

'My father, as you know, was of a northern temperament: contemplative, thorough, puritanically correct, and inclined to melancholy. My mother was of a vaguely exotic extraction, beautiful, sensuous, naïve, both reckless and passionate, and given to impulsive, rather disreputable behaviour. There is no doubt that this mixed heredity contained extraordinary possibilities – and extraordinary dangers. Its result was a bourgeois who went astray into art, a bohemian homesick for his decent background, an artist with a bad conscience. For after all it is my bourgeois conscience that makes me see the whole business of being an artist, of being any kind of exception or genius, as something profoundly equivocal, profoundly dubious, profoundly suspect; and it too has made me fall so foolishly in love with simplicity and naïvety, with the delightfully normal, the respectable and mediocre.

'I stand between two worlds, I am at home in neither, and this makes things a little difficult for me. You artists call me a bourgeois, and the bourgeois feel they ought to arrest me . . . I don't know which of the two hurts me more bitterly. The bourgeois are fools; but you worshippers of beauty, you who say I am phlegmatic and have no longing in my soul, you should remember that there is a kind of artist so profoundly, so primordially fated to be an artist that no longing seems sweeter and more precious to him than his longing for the bliss of the commonplace.

'I admire those proud, cold spirits who venture out along the paths of grandiose, demonic beauty and despise "humanity" – but I do not envy them. For if there is anything that can turn a *littérateur* into a true writer, then it is this bourgeois love of mine for the human and the living and the ordinary. It is the source of all warmth, of all kind-heartedness and of all humour, and I am almost persuaded it is that very love without which, as we are told, one may speak with the tongues of men and of angels and yet be a sounding brass and a tinkling cymbal.

'What I have achieved so far is nothing, not much, as good as nothing. I shall improve on it, Lisaveta – this I promise you. As I write this, I can hear below me the roar of the sea, and I close my eyes. I gaze into an unborn, unembodied world that demands to be ordered and shaped, I see before me a host of shadowy human figures whose gestures implore me to cast upon them the spell that shall be their deliverance: tragic and comic figures, and some who are both at once – and to these I am strongly drawn. But my deepest and most secret love belongs to the fair-haired and the blue-eyed, the bright children of life, the happy, the charming and the ordinary.

'Do not disparage this love, Lisaveta; it is good and fruitful. In it there is longing, and sad envy, and just a touch of contempt, and a whole world of innocent delight.'

# Death in Venice

*Der Tod in Venedig*

1912

# Death in Venice

## 1

On a spring afternoon in 19—, the year in which for months on end so grave a threat seemed to hang over the peace of Europe, Gustav Aschenbach, or von Aschenbach as he had been officially known since his fiftieth birthday, had set out from his apartment on the Prinzregentenstrasse in Munich to take a walk of some length by himself. The morning's writing had overstimulated him: his work had now reached a difficult and dangerous point which demanded the utmost care and circumspection, the most insistent and precise effort of will, and the productive mechanism in his mind – that *motus animi continuus* which according to Cicero is the essence of eloquence – had so pursued its reverberating rhythm that he had been unable to halt it even after lunch, and had missed the refreshing daily siesta which was now so necessary for him as he became increasingly subject to fatigue. And so, soon after taking tea, he had left the house hoping that fresh air and movement would set him to rights and enable him to spend a profitable evening.

It was the beginning of May, and after a succession of cold, wet weeks a premature high summer had set in. The Englischer Garten, although still only in its first delicate leaf, had been as sultry as in August, and at its city end full of traffic and pedestrians. Having made his way to the Aumeister along less and less frequented paths, Aschenbach had briefly surveyed the lively scene at the popular open-air restaurant, around which a few cabs and private carriages were standing; then, as the sun sank, he had started homewards across the open meadow beyond the park, and since he was now tired and a storm seemed to be brewing over

Föhring, he had stopped by the Northern Cemetery to wait for the tram that would take him straight back to the city.

As it happened, there was not a soul to be seen at or near the tram-stop. Not one vehicle passed along the Föhringer Chaussee or the paved Ungererstrasse on which solitary gleaming tram-rails pointed towards Schwabing; nothing stirred behind the fencing of the stonemasons' yards, where crosses and memorial tablets and monuments, ready for sale, composed a second and untenanted burial-ground; across the street, the mortuary chapel with its Byzantine styling stood silent in the glow of the westering day. Its façade, adorned with Greek crosses and brightly painted hieratic motifs, is also inscribed with symmetrically arranged texts in gilt lettering, selected scriptural passages about the life to come, such as: 'They shall go in unto the dwelling-place of the Lord', or 'May light perpetual shine upon them'. The waiting Aschenbach had already been engaged for some minutes in the solemn pastime of deciphering the words and letting his mind wander in contemplation of the mystic meaning that suffused them, when he noticed something that brought him back to reality: in the portico of the chapel, above the two apocalyptic beasts that guard the steps leading up to it, a man was standing, a man whose slightly unusual appearance gave his thoughts an altogether different turn.

It was not entirely clear whether he had emerged through the bronze doors from inside the chapel or had suddenly appeared and mounted the steps from outside. Aschenbach, without unduly pondering the question, inclined to the former hypothesis. The man was moderately tall, thin, beardless and remarkably snub-nosed; he belonged to the red-haired type and had its characteristic milky, freckled complexion. He was quite evidently not of Bavarian origin; at all events he wore a straw hat with a broad straight brim which gave him an exotic air, as of someone who had come from distant parts. It is true that he also had the typical Bavarian rucksack strapped to his shoulders and wore a yellowish belted outfit of what looked like frieze, as well as carrying a grey rain-cape over his left forearm which was propped against his waist, and in his right hand an iron-pointed walking-stick which he had thrust slantwise into the ground, crossing his feet and leaning his hip against its handle. His head was held high, so that the Adam's apple stood out stark and bare on his lean neck where it rose from the open shirt; and there were two pronounced vertical furrows, rather strangely ill-matched to his turned-up nose, between the colourless red-lashed eyes with which he peered sharply into the distance. There was thus – and perhaps the raised point of vantage on which he stood contributed to this impression – an air of imperious survey, something bold or even wild about his posture; for whether it was because he was dazzled into a grimace by the setting sun or by reason of some permanent facial deformity, the fact was that his lips seemed to be too short and were completely retracted from his teeth, so that the latter showed white and long between them, bared to the gums.

Aschenbach's half absent-minded, half inquisitive scrutiny of the stranger had no doubt been a little less than polite, for he suddenly became aware that his gaze was being returned: the man was in fact staring at him so aggressively, so straight in the eye, with so evident an intention to make an issue of the matter and outstare him, that Aschenbach turned away in disagreeable embarrassment and began to stroll along the fence, casually resolving to take no further notice of the fellow. A minute later he had put him out of his mind. But whether his imagination had been stirred by the stranger's itinerant appearance, or whether some other physical or psychological influence was at work, he now became conscious, to his complete surprise, of an extraordinary expansion of his inner self, a kind of roving restlessness, a youthful craving for far-off places, a feeling so new or at least so long unaccustomed and forgotten that he stood as if rooted, with his hands clasped behind his back and his eyes to the ground, trying to ascertain the nature and purport of his emotion.

It was simply a desire to travel; but it had presented itself as nothing less than a seizure, with intensely passionate and indeed hallucinatory force, turning his craving into vision. His imagination, still not at rest from the morning's hours of work, shaped for itself a paradigm of all the wonders and terrors of the manifold earth, of all that it was now suddenly striving to envisage: he saw it, saw a landscape, a tropical swampland under a cloud-swollen sky, moist and lush and monstrous, a kind of primeval wilderness of islands, morasses and muddy alluvial channels; far and wide around him he saw hairy palm-trunks thrusting upwards from rank jungles of fern, from among thick fleshy plants in exuberant flower; saw strangely misshapen trees with roots that arched through the air before sinking into the ground or into stagnant, shadowy-green, glassy waters where milk-white blossoms floated as big as plates, and among them exotic birds with grotesque beaks stood hunched in the shallows, their heads tilted motionlessly sideways; saw between the knotted stems of the bamboo thicket the glinting eyes of a crouching tiger; and his heart throbbed with terror and mysterious longing. Then the vision faded; and with a shake of his head Aschenbach resumed his perambulation along the fencing of the gravestone yards.

His attitude to foreign travel, at least since he had had the means at his disposal to enjoy its advantages as often as he pleased, had always been that it was nothing more than a necessary health precaution, to be taken from time to time however disinclined to it one might be. Too preoccupied with the tasks imposed upon him by his own sensibility and by the collective European psyche, too heavily burdened with the compulsion to produce, too shy of distraction to have learned how to take leisure and pleasure in the colourful external world, he had been perfectly well satisfied to have no more detailed a view of the earth's surface than anyone can acquire without stirring far from home, and he had never even been tempted to venture outside Europe. This had been more especially the case since his life had begun its gradual decline and his artist's fear of not finishing his task – the apprehension that his time might run out before he had given the whole of himself by doing what he had it in him to do – was no longer something he could simply dismiss as an idle fancy; and during this time his outward existence had been almost entirely divided between the beautiful city which had become his home and the rustic mountain retreat he had set up for himself and where he passed his rainy summers.

And sure enough, the sudden and belated impulse that had just overwhelmed him very soon came under the moderating and corrective influence of common sense and of the self-discipline he had practised since his youth. It had been his intention that the book to which his life was at present dedicated should be advanced to a certain point before he moved to the country, and the idea of a jaunt in the wide world that would take him away from his work for months now seemed too casual, too upsetting to his plans to be considered seriously. Nevertheless, he knew the reason for the unexpected temptation only too well. This relaxation and forgetfulness – it had been, he was bound to admit, an urge to escape, to run away from his writing, away from the humdrum scene of his cold, inflexible, passionate duty. True, it was a duty he loved, and by now he had almost even learned to love the enervating daily struggle between his proud, tenacious, tried and tested will and that growing weariness which no one must be allowed to suspect nor his finished work betray by any tell-tale sign of debility or lassitude. Nevertheless, it would be sensible, he decided, not to span the bow too far and wilfully stifle a desire that had erupted in him with such vivid force. He thought of his work, thought of the passage at which he had again, today as yesterday, been forced to interrupt it – that stubborn problem which neither patient care could solve nor a decisive *coup de main* dispel. He reconsidered it, tried to break or dissolve the inhibition, and, with a shudder of repugnance, abandoned the attempt. It was not a case of very unusual difficulty, he was simply paralysed by a scruple of distaste, manifesting itself as a perfectionistic fastidiousness which nothing could satisfy. Perfectionism, of course, was something which even as a young man he had come to see as the innermost essence of talent, and for its sake he had curbed and cooled his feelings; for he knew that feeling is apt to be content with high-spirited approximations and with work that falls short of supreme excellence. Could it be that the enslaved emotion was now avenging itself by deserting him, by refusing from now on to bear up his art on its wings, by taking with it all his joy in words, all his appetite for the beauty of form? Not that he was writing badly: it was at least the advantage of his years to be master of his trade, a mastery of which at any moment he could feel calmly confident. But even as it brought him national honour he took no pleasure in it himself, and it seemed to him that his work lacked that element of sparkling and joyful improvisation, that quality which surpasses any intellectual substance in its power to delight the receptive world. He dreaded spending the summer in the country, alone in that little house with the maid who prepared his meals and the servant who brought them to him; dreaded the familiar profile of the mountain summits and mountain walls which would once again surround his slow discontented toil. So what did he need? An interlude, some impromptu living, some *dolce far niente*, the invigoration of a distant climate, to make his summer bearable and fruitful. Very well then – he would travel. Not all that far, not quite to where the tigers were. A night in the wagon-lit and a siesta of three or four weeks at some popular holiday resort in the charming south . . .

Such were his thoughts as the tram clattered towards him along the Ungererstrasse, and as he stepped into it he decided to devote that evening to the study of maps and timetables. On the platform it occurred to him to look round and see what had become of the man in the straw hat, his companion for the duration of this not inconsequential wait at a tram-stop. But the man's whereabouts remained a mystery, for he was no longer standing where he had stood, nor was he to be seen anywhere else at the stop or in the tramcar itself.

## 2

The author of the lucid and massive prose epic about the life of Frederic of Prussia; the patient artist who with long toil had woven the great tapestry of the novel called *Maya*, so rich in characters, gathering so many human destinies together under the shadow of one idea; the creator of that powerful tale entitled A *Study in Abjection*, which earned the gratitude of a whole younger generation by pointing to the possibility of moral resolution even for those who have plumbed the depths of knowledge; the author (lastly but not least in this summary enumeration of his maturer works) of that passionate treatise *Intellect and Art* which in its ordering energy and antithetical eloquence has led serious critics to place it immediately alongside Schiller's disquisition *On Naïve and Reflective Literature*: in a word, Gustav Aschenbach, was born in L—, an important city in the province of Silesia, as the son of a highly-placed legal official. His ancestors had been military officers, judges, government administrators; men who had spent their disciplined, decently austere life in the service of the King and the state. A more inward spirituality had shown itself in one of them who had been a preacher; a strain of livelier, more sensuous blood had entered the family in the previous generation with the writer's mother, the daughter of a director of music from Bohemia. Certain exotic racial characteristics in his external appearance had come to him from her. It was from this marriage between hard-working, sober conscientiousness and darker, more fiery impulses that an artist, and indeed this particular kind of artist, had come into being.

With his whole nature intent from the start upon fame, he had displayed not exactly precocity, but a certain decisiveness and personal trenchancy in his style of utterance, which at an early age made him ripe for a life in the public eye and well suited to it. He had made a name for himself at little more than school age. Ten years later he had learned to perform, at his writing desk, the social and administrative duties entailed by his reputation; he had learned to write letters which, however brief they had to be (for many claims beset the successful man who enjoys the confidence of the public), would always contain something kindly and pointed. By the age of forty he was obliged, wearied though he might be by the toils and vicissitudes of his real work, to deal with a daily correspondence that bore postage stamps from every part of the globe.

His talent, equally remote from the commonplace and from the eccentric, had a native capacity both to inspire confidence in the general public and to win admiration and encouragement from the discriminating connoisseur. Ever since his boyhood the duty to achieve – and to achieve exceptional things – had been imposed on him from all sides, and thus he had never known youth's idleness, its carefree negligent ways. When in his thirty-fifth year he fell ill in Vienna, a subtle observer remarked of him on a social occasion: 'You see, Ashenbach has always only lived like *this*' – and the speaker closed the fingers of his left hand tightly into a fist – 'and never like *this*' – and he let his open hand hang comfortably down along the back of the chair. It was a correct observation; and the morally courageous aspect of the matter was that Aschenbach's native constitution was by no means robust, that the constant harnessing of his energies was something to which he had been called, but not really born.

As a young boy, medical advice and care had made school attendance impossible and obliged him to have his education at home. He had grown up by himself, without companions, and had nevertheless had to recognize in good time that he belonged to a breed not seldom talented, yet seldom endowed with the physical basis which talent needs if it is to fulfil itself – a breed that usually gives of its best in youth, and in which the creative gift rarely survives into mature years. But he would 'stay the course' – it was his favourite motto, he saw his historical novel about Frederic the Great as nothing if not the apotheosis of this, the king's word of command, '*durchhalten!*', which to Aschenbach epitomized a manly ethos of suffering action. And he dearly longed to grow old, for it had always been his view that an artist's gift can only be called truly great and wide-ranging, or indeed truly admirable, if it has been fortunate enough to bear characteristic fruit at all the stages of human life.

They were not broad, the shoulders on which he thus carried the tasks laid upon him by his talent; and since his aims were high, he stood in great need of discipline – and discipline, after all, was fortunately his inborn heritage on his father's side. At the age of forty or fifty, and indeed during those younger years in which other men live prodigally and dilettantishly, happily procrastinating the execution of great plans, Aschenbach would begin his day early by dashing cold water over his chest and back, and then, with two tall wax candles in silver candlesticks placed at the head of his manuscript, he would offer up to art, for two or three ardently conscientious morning hours, the strength he had garnered during sleep. It was a pardonable error, indeed it was one that betokened as nothing else could the triumph of his moral will, that uninformed critics should mistake the great world of *Maya*, or the massive epic unfolding of Frederic's life, for the product of solid strength and long stamina, whereas in fact they had been built up to their impressive size from layer upon layer of daily opuscula, from a hundred or a thousand separate inspirations; and if they were indeed so excellent, wholly and in every detail, it was only because their creator, showing that same constancy of will and tenacity of purpose as had once conquered his native Silesia, had held out for years under the pressure of one and the same task, and had devoted to actual composition only his best and worthiest hours.

For a significant intellectual product to make a broad and deep immediate appeal, there must be a hidden affinity, indeed a congruence, between the personal destiny of the author and the wider destiny of his generation. The public does not know why it grants the accolade of fame to a work of art. Being in no sense connoisseurs, readers imagine they perceive a hundred good qualities in it which justify their admiration; but the real reason for their applause is something imponderable, a sense of sympathy. Hidden away among

Aschenbach's writings was a passage directly asserting that nearly all the great things that exist owe their existence to a defiant despite: it is despite grief and anguish, despite poverty, loneliness, bodily weakness, vice and passion and a thousand inhibitions, that they have come into being at all. But this was more than an observation, it was an experience, it was positively the formula of his life and his fame, the key to his work; is it surprising then that it was also the moral formula, the outward gesture, of his work's most characteristic figures?

The new hero-type favoured by Aschenbach, and recurring in his books in a multiplicity of individual variants, had already been remarked upon at an early stage by a shrewd commentator, who had described his conception as that of 'an intellectual and boyish manly virtue, that of a youth who clenches his teeth in proud shame and stands calmly on as the swords and spears pass through his body'. That was well put, perceptive and precisely true, for all its seemingly rather too passive emphasis. For composure under the blows of fate, grace in the midst of torment – this is not only endurance: it is an active achievement, a positive triumph, and the figure of Saint Sebastian is the most perfect symbol if not of art in general, then certainly of the kind of art here in question. What did one see if one looked in any depth into the world of this writer's fiction? Elegant self-control concealing from the world's eyes until the very last moment a state of inner disintegration and biological decay; sallow ugliness, sensuously marred and worsted, which nevertheless is able to fan its smouldering concupiscence to a pure flame, and even to exalt itself to mastery in the realm of beauty; pallid impotence, which from the glowing depths of the spirit draws strength to cast down a whole proud people at the foot of the Cross and set its own foot upon them as well; gracious poise and composure in the empty austere service of form; the false, dangerous life of the born deceiver, his ambition and his art which lead so soon to exhaustion – to contemplate all these destinies, and many others like them, was to doubt if there is any other heroism at all but the heroism of weakness. In any case, what other heroism could be more in keeping with the times? Gustav Aschenbach was the writer who spoke for all those who work on the brink of exhaustion, who labour and are heavy-laden, who are worn out already but still stand upright, all those moralists of achievement who are slight of stature and scanty of resources, but who yet, by some ecstasy of the will and by wise husbandry, manage at least for a time to force their work into a semblance of greatness. There are many such, they are the heroes of our age. And they all recognized themselves in his work, they found that it confirmed them and raised them on high and celebrated them; they were grateful for this, and they spread his name far and wide.

He had been young and raw with the times: ill advised by fashion, he had publicly stumbled, blundered, made himself look foolish, offended in speech and writing against tact and balanced civility. But he had achieved dignity, that goal towards which, as he declared, every great talent is innately driven and spurred; indeed it can be said that the conscious and defiant purpose of his entire development had been, leaving all the inhibitions of scepticism and irony behind him, an ascent to dignity.

Lively, clear-outlined, intellectually undemanding presentation is the delight of the great mass of the middle-class public, but passionate radical youth is interested only in problems: and Aschenbach had been as problematic and as radical as any young man ever was. He had been in thrall to intellect, had exhausted the soil by excessive analysis and ground up the seed-corn of growth; he had uncovered what is better kept hidden, made talent seem suspect, betrayed the truth about art – indeed, even as the sculptural vividness of his descriptions was giving pleasure to his more naïve devotees and lifting their minds and hearts, he, this same youthful artist, had fascinated twenty-year-olds with his breath-taking cynicisms about the questionable nature of art and of the artist himself.

But it seems that there is nothing to which a noble and active mind more quickly becomes inured than that pungent and bitter stimulus, the acquisition of knowledge; and it is very sure that even the most gloomily conscientious and radical sophistication of youth is shallow by comparison with Aschenbach's profound decision as a mature master to repudiate knowledge as such, to reject it, to step over it with head held high – in the recognition that knowledge can paralyse the will, paralyse and discourage action and emotion and even passion, and rob all these of their dignity. How else is the famous short story A *Study in Abjection* to be understood but as an outbreak of disgust against an age indecently undermined by psychology and represented by the figure of that

spiritless, witless semi-scoundrel who cheats his way into a destiny of
sorts when, motivated by his own ineptitude and depravity and ethical
whimsicality, he drives his wife into the arms of a callow youth –
convinced that his intellectual depths entitle him to behave with
contemptible baseness? The forthright words of condemnation which
here weighed vileness in the balance and found it wanting – they
proclaimed their writer's renunciation of all moral scepticism, of every
kind of sympathy with the abyss; they declared his repudiation of the
laxity of that compassionate principle which holds that to understand all
is to forgive all. And the development that was here being anticipated,
indeed already taking place, was that 'miracle of reborn naïvety' to
which, in a dialogue written a little later, the author himself had referred
with a certain mysterious emphasis. How strange these associations!
Was it an intellectual consequence of this 'rebirth', of this new dignity
and rigour, that, at about the same time, his sense of beauty was
observed to undergo an almost excessive resurgence, that his style took
on the noble purity, simplicity and symmetry that were to set upon all
his subsequent works that so evident and evidently intentional stamp of
the classical master? And yet: moral resoluteness at the far side of
knowledge, achieved in despite of all corrosive and inhibiting insight –
does not this in its turn signify a simplification, a morally simplistic view
of the world and of human psychology, and thus also a resurgence of
energies that are evil, forbidden, morally impossible? And is form not
two-faced? Is it not at one and the same time moral and immoral – moral
as the product and expression of discipline, but immoral and even anti-
moral inasmuch as it harbours within itself an innate moral indifference,
and indeed essentially strives for nothing less than to bend morality
under its proud and absolute sceptre?

Be that as it may! A development is a destiny; and one that is
accompanied by the admiration and mass confidence of a wide public
must inevitably differ in its course from one that takes place far from the
limelight and from the commitments of fame. Only the eternal
intellectual vagrant is bored and prompted to mockery when a great
talent grows out of its libertinistic chrysalis-stage, becomes an expressive
representative of the dignity of mind, takes on the courtly bearing of that
solitude which has been full of hard, uncounselled, self-reliant
sufferings and struggles, and has achieved power and honour among

men. And what a game it is too, how much defiance there is in it and how much satisfaction, this self-formation of a talent! As time passed, Gustav Aschenbach's presentations took on something of an official air, of an educator's stance; his style in later years came to eschew direct audacities, new and subtle nuances, it developed towards the exemplary and definitive, the fastidiously conventional, the conservative and formal and even formulaic; and as tradition has it of Louis XIV, so Aschenbach as he grew older banned from his utterance every unrefined word. It was at this time that the education authority adopted selected pages from his works for inclusion in the prescribed school readers. And when a German ruler who had just come to the throne granted personal nobilitation to the author of *Frederic of Prussia* on his fiftieth birthday, he sensed the inner appropriateness of this honour and did not decline it.

After a few restless years of experimental living in different places, he soon chose Munich as his permanent home and lived there in the kind of upper-bourgeois status which is occasionally the lot of certain intellectuals. The marriage which he had contracted while still young with the daughter of an academic family had been ended by his wife's death after a short period of happiness. She had left him a daughter, now already married. He had never had a son.

Gustav von Aschenbach was of rather less than average height, dark and clean-shaven. His head seemed a little too large in proportion to his almost delicate stature. His brushed-back hair, thinning at the top, very thick and distinctly grey over the temples, framed a high, deeply lined, scarred-looking forehead. The bow of a pair of gold spectacles with rimless lenses cut into the base of his strong, nobly curved nose. His mouth was large, often relaxed, often suddenly narrow and tense; the cheeks were lean and furrowed, the well-formed chin slightly cleft. Grave visitations of fate seemed to have passed over this head, which usually inclined to one side with an air of suffering. And yet it was art that had here performed that fashioning of the physiognomy which is usually the work of a life full of action and stress. The flashing exchanges of the dialogue between Voltaire and the king on the subject of war had been born behind this brow; these eyes that looked so wearily and deeply through their glasses had seen the bloody inferno of the Seven Years War sick-bays. Even in a personal sense, after all, art is an intensified life. By art one is more deeply satisfied and more rapidly used up. It engraves on the countenance of its servant the traces of imaginary and intellectual adventures, and even if he has outwardly existed in cloistral tranquillity, it leads in the long term to overfastidiousness, over-refinement, nervous fatigue and overstimulation, such as can seldom result from a life full of the most extravagant passions and pleasures.

## 3

Mundane and literary business of various kinds delayed Aschenbach's eagerly awaited departure until about a fortnight after that walk in Munich. Finally he gave instructions that his country house was to be made ready for occupation in four weeks' time, and then, one day between the middle and end of May, he took the night train to Trieste, where he stayed only twenty-four hours, embarking on the following morning for Pola.

What he sought was something strange and random, but in a place easily reached, and accordingly he took up his abode on an Adriatic island which had been highly spoken of for some years: a little way off the Istrian coast, with colourful, ragged inhabitants speaking a wild unintelligible dialect, and picturesque fragmented cliffs overlooking the open sea. But rain and sultry air, a self-enclosed provincial Austrian hotel clientele, the lack of that restful intimate contact with the sea which can only be had on a gentle, sandy coast, filled him with vexation and with a feeling that he had not yet come to his journey's end. He was haunted by an inner impulse that still had no clear direction; he studied shipping timetables, looked up one place after another – and suddenly his surprising yet at the same time self-evident destination stared him in the face. If one wanted to travel overnight to somewhere incomparable, to a fantastic mutation of normal reality, where did one go? Why, the answer was obvious. What was he doing here? He had gone completely astray. *That* was where he had longed to travel. He at once gave notice of departure from his present, mischosen stopping-place. Ten days after his arrival on the island, in the early-morning mist, a rapid motor-launch carried him and his luggage back over the water to the naval base, and here he landed only to re-embark immediately, crossing the gangway on to the damp deck of a ship that was waiting under steam to leave for Venice.

It was an ancient Italian boat, out of date and dingy and black with soot. Aschenbach was no sooner aboard than a grubby hunchbacked seaman, grinning obsequiously, conducted him to an artificially lit cave-like cabin in the ship's interior. Here, behind a table, with his cap askew and a cigarette-end in the corner of his mouth, sat a goat-bearded man with the air of an old-fashioned circus director and a slick caricatured business manner, taking passengers' particulars and issuing their tickets. 'To Venice!' he exclaimed, echoing Aschenbach's request, and extending his arm he pushed his pen into some coagulated leftover ink in a tilted inkstand. 'One first class to Venice. Certainly, sir!' He scribbled elaborately, shook some blue sand from a box over the writing and ran it off into an earthenware dish, then folded the paper with his yellow bony fingers and wrote on it again. 'A very happily chosen destination!' he chattered as he did so. 'Ah, Venice! A splendid city! A city irresistibly attractive to the man of culture, by its history no less than by its present charms!' There was something hypnotic and distracting about the smooth facility of his movements and the glib empty talk with which he accompanied them, almost as if he were anxious that the traveller might have second thoughts about his decision to go to Venice. He hastily took Aschenbach's money and with the dexterity of a croupier dropped the change on the stained tablecloth. '*Buon divertimento, signore,*' he said, bowing histrionically. 'It is an honour to serve you . . . Next, please, gentlemen!' he exclaimed with a wave of the arm, as if he were doing a lively trade, although in fact there was no one else there to be dealt with. Aschenbach returned on deck.

Resting one elbow on the handrail, he watched the idle crowd hanging about the quayside to see the ship's departure, and watched the passengers who had come aboard. Those with second-class tickets were squatting, men and women together, on the forward deck, using boxes and bundles as seats. The company on the upper deck consisted of a group of young men, probably shop or office workers from Pola, a high-spirited party about to set off on an excursion to Italy. They were making a considerable exhibition of themselves and their enterprise, chattering, laughing, fatuously enjoying their own gesticulations, leaning overboard and shouting glibly derisive ribaldries at their friends in the harbour-side street, who were hurrying about their business with briefcases under their arms and waved their sticks peevishly at the holiday-makers. One of the party, who wore a light yellow summer suit of extravagant cut, a scarlet necktie and a rakishly tilted Panama hat, was the most conspicuous of them all in his shrill hilarity. But as soon as Aschenbach took a slightly closer look at him, he realized with a kind of horror that the man's youth was false. He was old, there was no mistaking it. There were wrinkles round his eyes and mouth. His cheeks' faint carmine was rouge, the brown hair under his straw hat with its coloured ribbon was a wig, his neck was flaccid and scrawny, his small stuck-on moustache and the little imperial on his chin were dyed, his yellowish full complement of teeth, displayed when he laughed, were a cheap artificial set, and his hands, with signet rings on both index fingers, were those of an old man. With a spasm of distaste Aschenbach watched him as he kept company with his young friends. Did they not know, did they not notice that he was old, that he had no right to be acting as if he were one of them? They seemed to be tolerating his presence among them as something habitual and to be taken for granted, they treated him as an equal, reciprocated without embarrassment when he teasingly poked them in the ribs. How was this possible? Aschenbach put his hand over his forehead and closed his eyes, which were hot from too little sleep. He had a feeling that something not quite usual was beginning to happen, that the world was undergoing a dreamlike alienation, becoming increasingly deranged and bizarre, and that perhaps this process might be arrested if he were to cover his face for a little and then take a fresh look at things. But at that moment he had the sensation of being afloat, and starting up in irrational alarm, he noticed that the dark heavy hulk of the steamer was slowly parting company with the stone quayside. Inch by inch, as the engine pounded and reversed, the width of the dirty glinting water between the hull and the quay increased, and after clumsy manoeuvrings the ship turned its bows towards the open sea. Aschenbach crossed to the starboard side, where the hunchback had set up a deck-chair for him and a steward in a grease-stained frock coat offered his services.

The sky was grey, the wind damp. The port and the islands had been left behind, and soon all land was lost to view in the misty panorama.

Flecks of sodden soot drifted down on the washed deck, which never seemed to get dry. After only an hour an awning was set up, as it was beginning to rain.

Wrapped in his overcoat, a book lying on his lap, the traveller rested, scarcely noticing the hours as they passed him by. It had stopped raining; the canvas shelter was removed. The horizon was complete. Under the turbid dome of the sky the desolate sea surrounded him in an enormous circle. But in empty, unarticulated space our mind loses its sense of time as well, and we enter the twilight of the immeasurable. As Aschenbach lay there, strange and shadowy figures, the foppish old man, the goat-bearded purser from the ship's interior, passed with uncertain gestures and confused dream-words through his mind, and he fell asleep.

At midday he was requested to come below for luncheon in the long, narrow dining-saloon, which ended in the doors to the sleeping-berths; here he ate at the head of the long table, at the other end of which the group of apprentices, with the old man among them, had been quaffing since ten o'clock with the good-humoured ship's captain. The meal was wretched and he finished it quickly. He needed to be back in the open air, to look at the sky: perhaps it would clear over Venice.

It had never occurred to him that this would not happen, for the city had always received him in its full glory. But the sky and the sea remained dull and leaden, from time to time misty rain fell, and he resigned himself to arriving by water in a different Venice, one he had never encountered on the landward approach. He stood by the foremast, gazing into the distance, waiting for the sight of land. He recalled that poet of plangent inspiration who long ago had seen the cupolas and bell-towers of his dream rise before him out of these same waters; inwardly he recited a few lines of the measured music that had been made from that reverence and joy and sadness, and effortlessly moved by a passion already shaped into language, he questioned his grave and weary heart, wondering whether some new inspiration and distraction, some late adventure of the emotions, might yet be in store for him on his leisured journey.

And now, on his right, the flat coastline rose above the horizon, the sea came alive with fishing vessels, the island resort appeared: the steamer left it on its port side, glided at half-speed through the narrow channel named after it, entered the lagoon, and presently, near some shabby miscellaneous buildings, came to a complete halt, as this was where the launch carrying the public health inspector must be awaited.

An hour passed before it appeared. One had arrived and yet not arrived; there was no hurry, and yet one was impelled by impatience. The young men from Pola had come on deck, no doubt also patriotically attracted by the military sound of bugle calls across the water from the direction of the Public Gardens; and elated by the Asti they had drunk, they began cheering the *bersaglieri* as they drilled there in the park. But the dandified old man, thanks to his spurious fraternization with the young, was now in a condition repugnant to behold. His old head could not carry the wine as his sturdy youthful companions had done, and he was lamentably drunk. Eyes glazed, a cigarette between his trembling fingers, he stood swaying, tilted to and fro by inebriation and barely keeping his balance. Since he would have fallen at his first step he did not dare move from the spot, and was nevertheless full of wretched exuberance, clutching at everyone who approached him, babbling, winking, sniggering, lifting his ringed and wrinkled forefinger as he uttered some bantering inanity, and licking the corners of his mouth with the tip of his tongue in a repellently suggestive way. Aschenbach watched him with frowning disapproval, and once more a sense of numbness came over him, a feeling that the world was somehow, slightly yet uncontrollably, sliding into some kind of bizarre and grotesque derangement. It was a feeling on which, to be sure, he was unable to brood further in present circumstances, for at this moment the thudding motion of the engine began again, and the ship, having stopped short so close to its destination, resumed its passage along the San Marco Canal.

Thus it was that he saw it once more, that most astonishing of all landing-places, that dazzling composition of fantastic architecture which the Republic presented to the admiring gaze of approaching seafarers: the unburdened splendour of the Ducal Palace, the Bridge of Sighs, the lion and the saint on their two columns at the water's edge, the magnificently projecting side wing of the fabulous basilica, the vista beyond it of the gate tower and the Giants' Clock; and as he contemplated it all he reflected that to arrive in Venice by land, at the station, was like entering a palace by a back door: that only as he was now doing, only by ship, over the high sea, should one come to this most extraordinary of cities.

The engine stopped, gondolas pressed alongside, the gangway was let down, customs officers came on board and perfunctorily discharged their duties; disembarkation could begin. Aschenbach indicated that he would like a gondola to take him and his luggage to the stopping-place of the small steamboats that ply between the city and the Lido, since he intended to stay in a hotel by the sea. His wishes were approved, his orders shouted down to water-level, where the gondoliers were quarrelling in Venetian dialect. He was still prevented from leaving the ship, held up by his trunk which at that moment was being laboriously dragged and manoeuvred down the ladder-like gangway; and thus, for a full minute or two, he could not avoid the importunate attentions of the dreadful old man, who on some obscure drunken impulse felt obliged to do this stranger the parting honours. 'We wish the signore a most enjoyable stay!' he bleated, bowing and scraping. 'We hope the signore will not forget us! *Au revoir, excusez* and *bon jour*, your Excellency!' He drooled, he screwed up his eyes, licked the corners of his mouth, and the dyed imperial on his senile underlip reared itself upward. 'Our compliments,' he drivelled, touching his lips with two fingers, 'our compliments to your sweetheart, to your most charming, beautiful sweetheart . . .' And suddenly the upper set of his false teeth dropped half out of his jaw. Aschenbach was able to escape. 'Your sweetheart, your pretty sweetheart!' he heard from behind his back, in gurgling, cavernous, encumbered tones, as he clung to the rope railing and descended the gangway.

Can there be anyone who has not had to overcome a fleeting sense of dread, a secret shudder of uneasiness, on stepping for the first time or after a long interval of years into a Venetian gondola? How strange a vehicle it is, coming down unchanged from times of old romance, and so characteristically black, the way no other thing is black except a coffin – a vehicle evoking lawless adventures in the plashing stillness of night, and still more strongly evoking death itself, the bier, the dark obsequies, the last silent journey! And has it been observed that the seat of such a boat, that armchair with its coffin-black lacquer and dull black upholstery, is the softest, the most voluptuous, most enervating seat in the world? Aschenbach became aware of this when he had settled down at the gondolier's feet, sitting opposite his luggage, which was neatly assembled at the prow. The oarsmen were still quarrelling; raucously, unintelligibly, with threatening gestures. But in the peculiar silence of this city of water their voices seemed to be softly absorbed, to become bodiless, dissipated above the sea. It was sultry here in the harbour. As the warm breath of the sirocco touched him, as he leaned back on cushions over the yielding element, the traveller closed his eyes in the enjoyment of this lassitude as sweet as it was unaccustomed. It will be a short ride, he thought; if only it could last for ever! In a gently swaying motion he felt himself gliding away from the crowd and the confusion of voices.

How still it was growing all round him! There was nothing to be heard except the plashing of the oar, the dull slap of the wave against the boat's prow where it rose up steep and black and armed at its tip like a halberd, and a third sound also: that of a voice speaking and murmuring – it was the gondolier, whispering and muttering to himself between his teeth, in intermittent grunts pressed out of him by the labour of his arms. Aschenbach looked up and noticed with some consternation that the lagoon was widening round him and that his gondola was heading out to sea. It was thus evident that he must not relax too completely, but give some attention to the proper execution of his instructions.

'Well! To the *vaporetto* stop!' he said, half turning round. The muttering ceased, but no answer came.

'I said to the *vaporetto* stop!' he repeated, turning round completely and looking up into the face of the gondolier, who was standing behind him on his raised deck, towering between him and the pale sky. He was a man of displeasing, indeed brutal appearance, wearing blue seaman's clothes, with a yellow scarf round his waist and a shapeless, already fraying straw hat tilted rakishly on his head. To judge by the cast of his face and the blond curling moustache under his snub nose, he was quite evidently not of Italian origin. Although rather slightly built, so that one would not have thought him particularly well suited to his job, he plied his oar with great energy, putting his whole body into every stroke. Occasionally the effort made him retract his lips and bare his white teeth. With his reddish eyebrows knitted, he stared right over his passenger's head as he answered peremptorily, almost insolently:

'You are going to the Lido.'

Aschenbach replied:

'Of course. But I only engaged this gondola to row me across to San Marco. I wish to take the *vaporetto*.'

'You cannot take the *vaporetto*, signore.'

'And why not?'

'Because the *vaporetto* does not carry luggage.'

That was correct, as Aschenbach now remembered. He was silent. But the man's abrupt, presumptuous manner, so uncharacteristic of the way foreigners were usually treated in this country, struck him as unacceptable. He said:

'That is my affair. I may wish to deposit my luggage. Will you kindly turn round.'

There was silence. The oar plashed, the dull slap of the water against the bow continued, and the talking and muttering began again: the gondolier was talking to himself between his teeth.

What was to be done? Alone on the sea with this strangely contumacious, uncannily resolute fellow, the traveller could see no way of compelling him to obey his instructions. And in any case, how luxurious a rest he might have here if he simply accepted the situation! Had he not wished the trip were longer, wished it to last for ever? It was wisest to let things take their course, and above all it was very agreeable to do so. A magic spell of indolence seemed to emanate from his seat, from this low black-upholstered armchair, so softly rocked by the oarstrokes of the high-handed gondolier behind him. The thought that he had perhaps fallen into the hands of a criminal floated dreamily across Aschenbach's mind – powerless to stir him to any active plan of self-defence. There was the more annoying possibility that the whole thing was simply a device for extorting money from him. A kind of pride or sense of duty, a recollection, so to speak, that there are precautions to be taken against such things, impelled him to make one further effort. He asked:

'What is your charge for the trip?'

And looking straight over his head, the gondolier answered:

'You will pay, signore.'

The prescribed retort to this was clear enough. Aschenbach answered mechanically:

'I shall pay nothing, absolutely nothing, if you take me where I do not want to go.'

'The signore wants to go to the Lido.'

'But not with you.'

'I can row you well.'

True enough, thought Aschenbach, relaxing. True enough, you will row me well. Even if you are after my cash and dispatch me to the house of Hades with a blow of your oar from behind, you will have rowed me well.

But nothing of the sort happened. He was even provided with company: a boat full of piratical musicians, men and women singing to the guitar or mandolin, importunately travelling hard alongside the gondola and for the foreigner's benefit filling the silence of the waters with mercenary song. Aschenbach threw some money into the outheld hat, whereupon they fell silent and moved off. And the gondolier's muttering became audible again, as in fits and starts he continued his self-colloquy.

And so in due course one arrived, bobbing about in the wake of a *vaporetto* bound for the city. Two police officers, with their hands on their backs, were pacing up and down the embankment and looking out over the lagoon. Aschenbach stepped from the gondola on to the gangway, assisted by the old man with a boat-hook who turns up for this purpose at every landing-stage in Venice; and having run out of small change, he walked across to the hotel opposite the pier, intending to change money and pay off the oarsman with some suitable gratuity. He was served at the hall desk, and returned to the landing-stage to find his luggage loaded on to a trolley on the embankment: the gondola and the gondolier had vanished.

'He cleared off,' said the old man with the boat-hook. 'A bad man, a man without a licence, signore. He is the only gondolier who has no licence. The others telephoned across to us. He saw the police waiting for him. So he cleared off quick.'

Aschenbach shrugged his shoulders.

'The signore has had a free trip,' said the old man, holding out his hat. Aschenbach threw coins into it. He directed that his luggage should be taken to the Hotel des Bains, and followed the trolley along the avenue, that white-blossoming avenue, bordered on either side by taverns and bazaars and guest-houses, which runs straight across the island to the beach.

He entered the spacious hotel from the garden terrace at the back, passing through the main hall and the vestibule to the reception office.

As his arrival had been notified in advance, he was received with obsequious obligingness. A manager, a soft-spoken, flatteringly courteous little man with a black moustache and a frock coat of French cut, accompanied him in the lift to the second floor and showed him to his room, an agreeable apartment with cherry-wood furniture, strongly scented flowers put out to greet him, and a view through tall windows to the open sea. He went and stood by one of them when the manager had withdrawn, and as his luggage was brought in behind him and installed in the room, he gazed out over the beach, uncrowded at this time of the afternoon, and over the sunless sea which was at high tide, its long low waves beating with a quiet regular rhythm on the shore.

The observations and encounters of a devotee of solitude and silence are at once less distinct and more penetrating than those of the sociable man; his thoughts are weightier, stranger, and never without a tinge of sadness. Images and perceptions which might otherwise be easily dispelled by a glance, a laugh, an exchange of comments, concern him unduly, they sink into mute depths, take on significance, become experiences, adventures, emotions. The fruit of solitude is originality, something daringly and disconcertingly beautiful, the poetic creation. But the fruit of solitude can also be the perverse, the disproportionate, the absurd and the forbidden. And thus the phenomena of his journey to this place, the horrible old made-up man with his maudlin babble about a sweetheart, the illicit gondolier who had been done out of his money, were still weighing on the traveller's mind. Without in any way being rationally inexplicable, without even really offering food for thought, they were nevertheless, as it seemed to him, essentially strange, and indeed it was no doubt this very paradox that made them disturbing. In the mean time he saluted the sea with his gaze and rejoiced in the knowledge that Venice was now so near and accessible. Finally he turned round, bathed his face, gave the room-maid certain instructions for the enhancement of his comfort, and then had himself conveyed by the green-uniformed Swiss lift-attendant to the ground floor.

He took tea on the front terrace, then went down to the esplanade and walked some way along it in the direction of the Hotel Excelsior. When he returned, it was already nearly time to be changing for dinner. He did so in his usual leisurely and precise manner, for it was his custom to work when performing his toilet; despite this, he arrived a little early in the foyer, where he found a considerable number of the hotel guests assembled, unacquainted with each other and affecting a studied mutual indifference, yet all united in expectancy by the prospect of their evening meal. He picked up a newspaper from the table, settled down in a leather armchair and took stock of the company, which differed very agreeably from what he had encountered at his previous hotel.

A large horizon opened up before him, tolerantly embracing many elements. Discreetly muted, the sounds of the major world languages mingled. Evening dress, that internationally accepted uniform of civilization, imparted a decent outward semblance of unity to the wide variations of mankind here represented. One saw the dry elongated visages of Americans, many-membered Russian families, English ladies, German children with French nurses. The Slav component seemed to predominate. In his immediate vicinity he could hear Polish being spoken.

It was a group of adolescent and barely adult young people, sitting round a cane table under the supervision of a governess or companion: three young girls, of fifteen to seventeen as it seemed, and a long-haired boy of perhaps fourteen. With astonishment Aschenbach noticed that the boy was entirely beautiful. His countenance, pale and gracefully reserved, was surrounded by ringlets of honey-coloured hair, and with its straight nose, its enchanting mouth, its expression of sweet and divine gravity, it recalled Greek sculpture of the noblest period; yet despite the purest formal perfection, it had such unique personal charm that he who now contemplated it felt he had never beheld, in nature or in art, anything so consummately successful. What also struck him was an obvious contrast of educational principles in the way the boy and his sisters were dressed and generally treated. The system adopted for the three girls, the eldest of whom could be considered to be grown-up, was austere and chaste to the point of disfigurement. They all wore exactly the same slate-coloured half-length dresses, sober and of a deliberately unbecoming cut, with white turnover collars as the only relieving feature, and any charm of figure they might have had was suppressed and negated from the outset by this cloistral uniform. Their hair, smoothed and stuck back firmly to their heads, gave their faces a nun-like emptiness and expressionlessness. A mother was clearly in charge here; and it had not even occurred to her to apply to the boy the same pedagogic strictness as she thought proper for the girls. In his life, softness and tenderness were evidently the rule. No one had ever dared to cut short his beautiful hair; like that of the *Boy Extracting a Thorn* it fell in curls over his forehead, over his ears, and still lower over his neck. The English sailor's suit, with its full sleeves tapering down to fit the fine wrists of his still childlike yet slender hands, and with its lanyards and bows and embroideries, enhanced his delicate shape with an air of richness and indulgence. He was sitting, in semi-profile to Aschenbach's gaze, with one foot in its patent leather shoe advanced in front of the other, with one elbow propped on the arm of his basket chair, with his cheek nestling against the closed hand, in a posture of relaxed dignity, without a trace of the almost servile stiffness to which his sisters seemed to have accustomed themselves. Was he in poor health? For his complexion was white as ivory against the dark gold of the surrounding curls. Or was he simply a pampered favourite child, borne up by the partiality of a capricious love? Aschenbach was inclined to think so. Inborn in almost every artistic nature is a luxuriant, tell-tale bias in favour of the injustice that creates beauty, a tendency to sympathize with aristocratic preference and pay it homage.

A waiter circulated and announced in English that dinner was served. Gradually the company disappeared through the glass door into the dining-room. Latecomers passed, emerging from the vestibule or the lifts. The service of dinner had already begun, but the young Poles were still waiting round their cane table, and Aschenbach, comfortably ensconced in his deep armchair, and additionally having the spectacle of beauty before his eyes, waited with them.

The governess, a corpulent and rather unladylike, red-faced little woman, finally gave the signal for them to rise. With arched brows she pushed back her chair and bowed as a tall lady, dressed in silvery grey and very richly adorned with pearls, entered the hall. This lady's attitude was cool and poised, her lightly powdered coiffure and the style of her dress both had that simplicity which is the governing principle of taste in circles where piety is regarded as one of the aristocratic values. In Germany she might have been the wife of a high official. The only thing that did give her appearance a fantastic and luxurious touch was her jewellery, which was indeed beyond price, consisting of earrings as well as a very long three-stranded necklace of gently shimmering pearls as big as cherries.

The brother and sisters had quickly risen to their feet. They bowed over their mother's hand to kiss it, while she, with a restrained smile on her well maintained but slightly weary and angular face, looked over their heads and addressed a few words in French to the governess. Then she walked towards the glass door. Her children followed her: the girls in order of age, after them the governess, finally the boy. For some reason or other he turned round before crossing the threshold, and as there was now no one else in the hall, his strangely twilight-grey eyes met those of Aschenbach, who with his paper in his lap, lost in contemplation, had been watching the group leave.

What he had seen had certainly not been remarkable in any particular. One does not go in to table before one's mother, they had waited for her, greeted her respectfully, and observed normal polite precedence in entering the dining-room. But this had all been carried out with such explicitness, with such a strongly accented air of discipline, obligation and self-respect, that Aschenbach felt strangely moved. He lingered for another few moments, then he too crossed into the dining-room and had himself shown to his table – which, as he noticed with a brief stirring of regret, was at some distance from that of the Polish family.

Tired and yet intellectually stimulated, he beguiled the long and tedious meal with abstract and indeed transcendental reflections. He meditated on the mysterious combination into which the canonical and the individual must enter for human beauty to come into being, proceeded from this point to general problems of form and art, and concluded in the end that his thoughts and findings resembled certain seemingly happy inspirations that come to us in dreams, only to be recognized by the sober senses as completely shallow and worthless. After dinner he lingered for a while, smoking and sitting and walking about, in the evening fragrance of the hotel garden, then retired early and passed the night in sleep which was sound and long, though dream images enlivened it from time to time.

Next day the weather did not seem to be improving. The wind was from landward. Under a pallid overcast sky the sea lay sluggishly still and shrunken-looking, with the horizon in prosaic proximity and the tide so far out that several rows of long sand-bars lay exposed. When Aschenbach opened his window, he thought he could smell the stagnant air of the lagoon.

Vexation overcame him. The thought of leaving occurred to him then and there. Once before, years ago, after fine spring weeks, this same weather had come on him here like a visitation, and so adversely affected his health that his departure from Venice had been like a precipitate escape. Were not the same symptoms now presenting themselves again, that unpleasant feverish sensation, the pressure in the temples, the heaviness in the eyelids? To move elsewhere yet again would be tiresome; but if the wind did not change, then there was no question of his staying here. As a precaution he did not unpack completely. At nine he breakfasted in the buffet between the hall and the main restaurant which was used for serving breakfast.

The kind of ceremonious silence prevailed here which a large hotel always aims to achieve. The serving waiters moved about noiselessly. A clink of crockery, a half-whispered word, were the only sounds audible. In one corner, obliquely opposite the door and two tables away from his own, Aschenbach noticed the Polish girls with their governess. Perched very upright, their ash-blond hair newly brushed and with reddened eyes, in stiff blue linen dresses with little white turnover collars and cuffs, they sat there passing each other a jar of preserves. They had almost finished their breakfast. The boy was missing.

Aschenbach smiled. Well, my little Phaeacian! he thought. You seem, unlike these young ladies, to enjoy the privilege of sleeping your fill. And with his spirits suddenly rising, he recited to himself the line: 'Varied garments to wear, warm baths and restful reposing.'

He breakfasted unhurriedly, received some forwarded mail from the porter who came into the breakfast-room with his braided cap in hand, and opened a few letters as he smoked a cigarette. Thus it happened that he was still present to witness the entry of the lie-abed they were waiting for across the room.

He came through the glass door and walked in the silence obliquely across the room to his sisters' table. His walk was extraordinarily graceful, in the carriage of his upper body, the motion of his knees, the placing of his white-shod foot; it was very light, both delicate and proud, and made still more beautiful by the childlike modesty with which he twice, turning his head towards the room, raised and lowered his eyes as he passed. With a smile and a murmured word in his soft liquescent language, he took his seat; and now especially, as his profile was exactly turned to the watching Aschenbach, the latter was again amazed, indeed startled, by the truly god-like beauty of this human creature. Today the boy was wearing a light casual suit of blue and white striped linen material with a red silk breast-knot, closing at the neck in a simple white stand-up collar. But on this collar – which did not even match the rest of the suit very elegantly – there, like a flower in bloom, his head was gracefully resting. It was the head of Eros, with the creamy lustre of Parian marble, the brows fine-drawn and serious, the temples and ear darkly and softly covered by the neat right-angled growth of the curling hair.

Good, good! thought Aschenbach, with that cool professional approval in which artists confronted by a masterpiece sometimes cloak their ecstasy, their rapture. And mentally he added: Truly, if the sea and the shore did not await me, I should stay here as long as you do! But as it was, he went, went through the hall accompanied by the courteous attentions of the hotel staff, went down over the wide terrace and straight along the wooden passageway to the enclosed beach reserved for hotel guests. Down there, a barefooted old man with linen trousers, sailor's jacket and straw hat functioned as bathing attendant: Aschenbach had himself conducted by him to his reserved beach cabin, had his table and chair set up on the sandy wooden platform in front of it, and made himself comfortable in the deck-chair which he had drawn further out towards the sea on to the wax-yellow sand.

The scene on the beach, the spectacle of civilization taking its carefree sensuous ease at the brink of the element, entertained and delighted him as much as ever. Already the grey, shallow sea was alive with children wading, with swimmers, with assorted figures lying on the sand-bars, their crossed arms under their heads. Others were rowing little keelless boats painted red and blue, and capsizing with shrieks of laughter. In front of the long row of *capanne*, with their platforms like little verandahs to sit on, there was animated play and leisurely sprawling repose, there was visiting and chattering, there was punctilious morning elegance as well as unabashed nakedness contentedly enjoying the liberal local conventions. Further out, on the moist firm sand, persons in white bathing-robes, in loose-fitting colourful shirt-wear, wandered to and fro. On the right, a complicated sandcastle built by children was bedecked by flags in all the national colours. Vendors of mussels, cakes and fruit knelt to display their wares. On the left, in front of one of the huts in the row that was set at right angles to the others and to the sea, forming a boundary to the beach at this end, a Russian family was encamped: men with beards and big teeth, overripe indolent women, a Baltic spinster sitting at an easel and painting the sea with exclamations of despair, two good-natured hideous children, an old nanny in a head-cloth who behaved in the caressingly deferential manner of the born serf. There they all were, gratefully enjoying their lives, tirelessly shouting the names of their disobediently romping children, mustering a few Italian words to joke at length with the amusing old man who sold them sweets, kissing each other on the cheeks and caring not a jot whether anyone was watching their scene of human solidarity.

Well, I shall stay, thought Aschenbach. What better place could I find? And with his hands folded in his lap, he let his eyes wander in the sea's wide expanse, let his gaze glide away, dissolve and die in the monotonous haze of this desolate emptiness. There were profound reasons for his attachment to the sea: he loved it because as a hard-working artist he needed rest, needed to escape from the demanding complexity of phenomena and lie hidden on the bosom of the simple and tremendous; because of a forbidden longing deep within him that ran quite contrary to his life's task and was for that very reason seductive, a longing for the unarticulated and immeasurable, for eternity, for nothingness. To rest in the arms of perfection is the desire of any man intent upon creating excellence; and is not nothingness a form of perfection? But now, as he mused idly on such profound matters, the horizontal line of the sea-shore was suddenly intersected by a human figure, and when he had retrieved his gaze from limitless immensity and concentrated it again, he beheld the beautiful boy, coming from the left and walking past him across the sand. He walked barefoot, ready for wading, his slender legs naked to above the knees; his pace was leisured, but as light and proud as if he had long been used to going about without shoes. As he walked he looked round at the projecting row of huts: but scarcely had he noticed the Russian family, as it sat there in contented concord and going about its natural business, than a storm of angry contempt gathered over his face. He frowned darkly, his lips pouted, a bitter grimace pulled them to one side and distorted his cheek; his brows were contracted in so deep a scowl that his eyes seemed to have sunk right in under their pressure, glaring forth a black message of hatred. He looked down, looked back again menacingly, then made with one shoulder an emphatic gesture of rejection as he turned his back and left his enemies behind him.

A kind of delicacy or alarm, something like respect and embarrassment, moved Aschenbach to turn away as if he had seen nothing; for no serious person who witnesses a moment of passion by chance will wish to make any use, even privately, of what he has observed. But he was at one and the same time entertained and moved, that is to say he was filled with happiness. Such childish fanaticism, directed against so harmless a piece of good-natured living – it gave a human dimension to mute divinity, it made a statuesque masterpiece of nature, which had hitherto merely delighted the eyes, seem worthy of a profounder appreciation as well; and it placed the figure of this adolescent, remarkable already by his beauty, in a context which enabled one to take him seriously beyond his years.

With his head still averted, Aschenbach listened to the boy's voice, his high, not very strong voice, as he called out greetings to his playmates working at the sandcastle, announcing his arrival when he was still some way from them. They answered, repeatedly shouting his name or a diminutive of his name, and Aschenbach listened for this with a certain curiosity, unable to pick up anything more precise than two melodious syllables which sounded something like 'Adgio' or still oftener 'Adgiu', called out with a long *u* at the end. The sound pleased him, he found its euphony befitting to its object, repeated it quietly to himself and turned again with satisfaction to his letters and papers.

With his travelling writing-case on his knees, he took out his fountain pen and began to deal with this and that item of correspondence. But after no more than a quarter of an hour he felt that it was a great pity to turn his mind away like this from the present situation, this most enjoyable of all situations known to him, and to miss the experience of it for the sake of an insignificant activity. He threw his writing materials aside, he returned to the sea; and before long, his attention attracted by the youthful voices of the sandcastle builders, he turned his head comfortably to the right against the back of his chair, to investigate once more the whereabouts and doings of the excellent Adgio.

His first glance found him; the red breast-knot was unmistakable. He and some others were busy laying an old plank as a bridge across the damp moat of the sandcastle, and he was supervising this work, calling out instructions and motioning with his head. With him were about ten companions, both boys and girls, of his age and some of them younger, all chattering together in tongues, in Polish, in French and even in Balkan languages. But it was his name that was most often heard. It was obvious that he was sought after, wooed, admired. One boy in particular, a Pole like him, a sturdy youngster whom they called 'Yashu' or rather 'Jasiu', with glossy black hair and wearing a belted linen suit, seemed to be his particular vassal and friend. When the work on the sandcastle ended for the time being, they walked along the beach with their arms round each other, and the boy they called 'Jasiu' kissed his beautiful companion.

Aschenbach was tempted to shake his finger at him. 'But I counsel you, Critobulus,' he thought with a smile, 'to go travelling for a year! You will need that much time at least before you are cured.' And he then breakfasted on some large, fully ripe strawberries which he bought from a vendor. It had grown very warm, although the sun was unable to break through the sky's layer of cloud. Even as one's senses enjoyed the tremendous and dizzying spectacle of the sea's stillness, lassitude paralysed the mind. To the mature and serious Aschenbach it seemed an appropriate, fully satisfying task and occupation for him to guess or otherwise ascertain what name this could be that sounded approximately like 'Adgio'. And with the help of a few Polish recollections he established that what was meant must be 'Tadzio', the diminutive of 'Tadeusz' and changing in the vocative to 'Tadziu'.

Tadzio was bathing. Aschenbach, who had lost sight of him, identified his head and his flailing arm far out to sea; for the water was evidently still shallow a long way out. But already he seemed to be giving cause for alarm, already women's voices were calling out to him from the bathing huts, again shrieking this name which ruled the beach almost like a rallying-cry, and which with its soft consonants, its long drawn-out u-sound at the end, had both a sweetness and a wildness about it: 'Tadziu! Tadziu!' He returned, he came running, beating the resisting water to foam with his feet, his head thrown back, running through the waves. And to behold this living figure, lovely and austere in its early masculinity, with dripping locks and beautiful as a young god, approaching out of the depths of the sky and the sea, rising and escaping from the elements – this sight filled the mind with mythical images, it was like a poet's tale from a primitive age, a tale of the origins of form and of the birth of the gods. Aschenbach listened with closed eyes to this song as it began its music deep within him, and once again he reflected that it was good to be here and that here he would stay.

Later on, Tadzio lay in the sand resting from his bathe, wrapped in his white bathing-robe which he had drawn through under his right shoulder, and cradling his head on his naked arm; and even when Aschenbach was not watching him but reading a few pages of his book, he almost never forgot that the boy was lying there, and that he needed only to turn his head slightly to the right to have the admired vision again in view. It almost seemed to him that he was sitting here for the purpose of protecting the half-sleeping boy – busy with doings of his own and yet nevertheless constantly keeping watch over this noble human creature there on his right, only a little way from him. And his heart was filled and moved with a paternal fondness, the tender concern by which he who sacrifices himself to beget beauty in the spirit is drawn to him who possesses beauty.

After midday he left the beach, returned to the hotel and took the lift up to his room. Here he spent some time in front of the looking-glass studying his grey hair, his weary sharp-featured face. At that moment he thought of his fame, reflected that many people recognized him in the streets and would gaze at him respectfully, saluting the unerring and graceful power of his language – he recalled all the external successes he could think of that his talent had brought him, even calling to mind his elevation to the nobility. Then he went down to the restaurant and took lunch at his table. When he had finished and was entering the lift again, a group of young people who had also just been lunching crowded after him into the hovering cubicle, and Tadzio came with them. He stood quite near Aschenbach, so near that for the first time the latter was not seeing him as a distant image, but perceiving and taking precise cognizance of the details of his humanity. The boy was addressed by someone, and as he replied, with an indescribably charming smile, he was already leaving the lift again as it reached the first floor, stepping out backwards with downcast eyes. The beautiful are modest, thought

Aschenbach, and began to reflect very intensively on why this should be so. Nevertheless, he had noticed that Tadzio's teeth were not as attractive as they might have been: rather jagged and pale, lacking the lustre of health and having that peculiar brittle transparency which is sometimes found in cases of anaemia. 'He's very delicate, he's sickly,' thought Aschenbach, 'he'll probably not live to grow old.' And he made no attempt to explain to himself a certain feeling of satisfaction or relief that accompanied this thought.

He spent two hours in his room, and in mid-afternoon took the *vaporetto* across the stale-smelling lagoon to Venice. He got out at San Marco, took tea on the Piazza, and then, in accordance with the daily programme he had adopted for his stay here, set off on a walk through the streets. But it was this walk that brought about a complete change in his mood and intentions.

An unpleasant sultriness pervaded the narrow streets; the air was so thick that the exhalations from houses and shops and hot food stalls, the reek of oil, the smell of perfume and many other odours hung about in clouds instead of dispersing. Cigarette-smoke lingered and was slow to dissipate. The throng of people in the alleyways annoyed him as he walked instead of giving him pleasure. The further he went, the more overwhelmingly he was afflicted by that appalling condition sometimes caused by a combination of the sea air with the sirocco, a condition of simultaneous excitement and exhaustion. He began to sweat disagreeably. His eyes faltered, his chest felt constricted, he was feverish, the blood throbbed in his head. He fled from the crowded commercial thoroughfares, over bridges, into the poor quarters. There he was besieged by beggars, and the sickening stench from the canals made it difficult to breathe. In a silent square, one of those places in the depths of Venice that seem to have been forgotten and put under a spell, he rested on the edge of a fountain, wiped the sweat from his brow and realized that he would have to leave.

For the second time, and this time definitively, it had become evident that this city, in this state of the weather, was extremely injurious to him. To stay on wilfully would be contrary to good sense, the prospect of a change in the wind seemed quite uncertain. He must make up his mind at once. To return straight home was out of the question. Neither his summer nor his winter quarters were ready to receive him. But this was not the only place with the sea and a beach, and elsewhere they were to be had without the harmful additional ingredient of this lagoon with its mephitic vapours. He remembered a little coastal resort not far from Trieste which had been recommended to him. Why not go there? And he must do so without delay, if it was to be worth while changing to a different place yet again. He declared himself resolved and rose to his feet. At the next gondola stop he took a boat and had himself conveyed back to San Marco through the murky labyrinth of canals, under delicate marble balconies flanked with carved lions, round the slimy stone corners of buildings, past the mournful façades of *palazzi* on which boards bearing the names of commercial enterprises were mirrored in water where refuse bobbed up and down. He had some trouble getting to his destination, as the gondolier was in league with lace factories and glassworks and tried to land him at every place where he might view the wares and make a purchase; and whenever this bizarre journey through Venice might have cast its spell on him, he was effectively and irksomely disenchanted by the cutpurse mercantile spirit of the sunken queen of the Adriatic.

Back in the hotel, before he had even dined, he notified the office that unforeseen circumstances obliged him to leave on the following morning. Regret was expressed, his bill was settled. He took dinner and spent the warm evening reading newspapers in a rocking-chair on the back terrace. Before going to bed he packed completely for departure.

He slept fitfully, troubled by his impending further journey. When he opened his windows in the morning, the sky was still overcast, but the air seemed fresher, and – he began even now to regret his decision. Had he not given notice too impulsively, had it not been a mistake, an action prompted by a mere temporary indisposition? If only he had deferred it for a little, if only, without giving up so soon, he had taken a chance on acclimatizing himself to Venice or waiting for the wind to change, then he would now have before him not the hurry and flurry of a journey, but a morning on the beach like that of the previous day. Too late. What he had wanted yesterday he must go on wanting now. He got dressed and took the lift down to breakfast at eight o'clock.

When he entered the breakfast-room it was still empty of guests. A few came in as he was sitting waiting for what he had ordered. As he sipped his tea he saw the Polish girls arrive with their companion: strict and matutinal, with reddened eyes, they proceeded to their table in the window corner. Shortly after this the porter approached with cap in hand and reminded him that it was time to leave. The motor coach was standing ready to take him and other passengers to the Hotel Excelsior, from which point the motor-launch would convey the ladies and gentlemen through the company's private canal and across to the station. Time is pressing, signore. – In Aschenbach's opinion time was doing nothing of the sort. There was more than an hour till his train left. He found it extremely annoying that hotels should make a practice of getting their departing clients off the premises unnecessarily early, and indicated to the porter that he wished to have his breakfast in peace. The man hesitantly withdrew, only to reappear five minutes later. It was impossible, he said, for the automobile to wait any longer. Aschenbach retorted angrily that in that case it should leave, and take his trunk with it. He himself would take the public steamboat when it was time, and would they kindly leave it to him to deal with the problem of his own departure. The hotel servant bowed. Aschenbach, glad to have fended off these tiresome admonitions, finished his breakfast unhurriedly, and even got the waiter to hand him a newspaper. It was indeed getting very late by the time he rose. It so happened that at that same moment Tadzio entered through the glass door.

As he walked to his family's table his path crossed that of the departing guest. Meeting this grey-haired gentleman with the lofty brow, he modestly lowered his eyes, only to raise them again at once in his enchanting way, in a soft and full glance; and then he had passed. Goodbyë, Tadzio! thought Aschenbach. How short our meeting was. And he added, actually shaping the thought with his lips and uttering it aloud to himself, as he normally never did: 'May God bless you!' – He then went through the routine of departure, distributed gratuities, received the parting courtesies of the soft-spoken little manager in the French frock coat, and left the hotel on foot as he had come, walking along the white-blossoming avenue with the hotel servant behind him carrying his hand luggage, straight across the island to the *vaporetto* landing-stage. He reached it, he took his seat on board – and what followed was a voyage of sorrow, a grievous passage that plumbed all the depths of regret.

It was the familiar trip across the lagoon, past San Marco, up the

Grand Canal. Aschenbach sat on the semicircular bench in the bows, one arm on the railing, shading his eyes with his hand. The Public Gardens fell away astern, the Piazzetta revealed itself once more in its princely elegance and was left behind, then came the great flight of the *palazzi*, with the splendid marble arch of the Rialto appearing as the waterway turned. The traveller contemplated it all, and his heart was rent with sorrow. The atmosphere of the city, this slightly mouldy smell of sea and swamp from which he had been so anxious to escape – he breathed it in now in deep, tenderly painful draughts. Was it possible that he had not known, had not considered how deeply his feelings were involved in all these things? What had been a mere qualm of compunction this morning, a slight stirring of doubt as to the wisdom of his behaviour, now became grief, became real suffering, an anguish of the soul, so bitter that several times it brought tears to his eyes, and which as he told himself he could not possibly have foreseen. What he found so hard to bear, what was indeed at times quite unendurable, was evidently the thought that he would never see Venice again, that this was a parting for ever. For since it had become clear a second time that this city made him ill, since he had been forced a second time to leave it precipitately, he must of course from now on regard it as an impossible and forbidden place to which he was not suited, and which it would be senseless to attempt to revisit. Indeed, he felt that if he left now, shame and pride must prevent him from ever setting eyes again on this beloved city which had twice physically defeated him; and this contention between his soul's desire and his physical capacities suddenly seemed to the ageing Aschenbach so grave and important, the bodily inadequacy so shameful, so necessary to overcome at all costs, that he could not understand the facile resignation with which he had decided yesterday, without any serious struggle, to tolerate that inadequacy and to acknowledge it.

In the mean time the *vaporetto* was approaching the station, and Aschenbach's distress and sense of helplessness increased to the point of distraction. In his torment he felt it to be impossible to leave and no less impossible to turn back. He entered the station torn by this acute inner conflict. It was very late, he had not a moment to lose if he was to catch his train. He both wanted to catch it and wanted to miss it. But time was pressing, lashing him on; he hurried to get his ticket, looking round in the crowded concourse for the hotel company's employee who would be on duty here. The man appeared and informed him that his large trunk had been sent off as registered baggage. Sent off already? Certainly – to Como. To Como? And from hasty comings and goings, from angry questions and embarrassed replies, it came to light that the trunk, before even leaving the luggage room in the Hotel Excelsior, had been put with some quite different baggage and dispatched to a totally incorrect address.

Aschenbach had some difficulty preserving the facial expression that would be the only comprehensible one in these circumstances. A wild joy, an unbelievable feeling of hilarity, shook him almost convulsively from the depths of his heart. The hotel employee rushed to see if it was still possible to stop the trunk, and needless to say returned without having had any success. Aschenbach accordingly declared that he was not prepared to travel without his luggage, that he had decided to go back and wait at the Hotel des Bains for the missing article to turn up again. Was the company's motor-launch still at the station? The man assured him that it was waiting immediately outside. With Italian eloquence he prevailed upon the official at the booking office to take back Aschenbach's already purchased ticket. He swore that telegrams would be sent, that nothing would be left undone and no effort spared to get the trunk back in no time at all – and thus it most strangely came about that the traveller, twenty minutes after arriving at the station, found himself on the Grand Canal again and on his way back to the Lido.

How unbelievably strange an experience it was, how shaming, how like a dream in its bizarre comedy: to be returning, by a quirk of fate, to places from which one has just taken leave for ever with the deepest sorrow – to be sent back and to be seeing them again within the hour! With spray tossing before its bows, deftly and entertainingly tacking to and fro between gondolas and *vaporetti*, the rapid little boat darted towards its destination, while its only passenger sat concealing under a mask of resigned annoyance the anxiously exuberant excitement of a truant schoolboy. From time to time he still inwardly shook with laughter at this mishap, telling himself that even a man born under a lucky star could not have had a more welcome piece of ill luck. There would be explanations to be given, surprised faces to be confronted –

and then, as he told himself, everything would be well again, a disaster would have been averted, a grievous mistake corrected, and everything he thought he had turned his back on for good would lie open again for him to enjoy, would be his for as long as he liked . . . And what was more, did the rapid movement of the motor-launch deceive him, or was there really now, to crown all else, a breeze blowing from the sea?

The bow waves dashed against the concrete walls of the narrow canal that cuts across the island to the Hotel Excelsior. There a motor omnibus was waiting for the returning guest and conveyed him along the road above the rippling sea straight to the Hotel des Bains. The little manager with the moustache and the fancily cut frock coat came down the flight of steps to welcome him.

In softly flattering tones he expressed regret for the incident, described it as highly embarrassing for himself and for the company, but emphatically endorsed Aschenbach's decision to wait here for his luggage. His room, to be sure, had been relet, but another, no less comfortable, was immediately at his disposal. *'Pas de chance, monsieur!'* said the Swiss lift-attendant as they glided up. And thus the fugitive was once more installed in a room situated and furnished almost exactly like the first.

Exhausted and numbed by the confusion of this strange morning, he had no sooner distributed the contents of his hand luggage about the room than he collapsed into a reclining chair at the open window. The sea had turned pale green, the air seemed clearer and purer, the beach with its bathing cabins and boats more colourful, although the sky was still grey. Aschenbach gazed out, his hands folded in his lap, pleased to be here again but shaking his head with displeasure at his irresolution, his ignorance of his own wishes. Thus he sat for about an hour, resting and idly daydreaming. At midday he caught sight of Tadzio in his striped linen suit with the red breast-knot, coming from the sea, through the beach barrier and along the boarded walks back to the hotel. From up here at his window Aschenbach recognized him at once, before he had even looked at him properly, and some such thought came to him as: Why, Tadzio, there you are again too! But at the same instant he felt that casual greeting die on his lips, stricken dumb by the truth in his heart – he felt the rapturous kindling of his blood, the joy and the anguish of his soul, and realized that it was because of Tadzio that it had been so hard for him to leave.

He sat quite still, quite unseen at his high vantage-point, and began to search his feelings. His features were alert, his eyebrows rose, an attentive, intelligently inquisitive smile parted his lips. Then he raised his head, and with his arms hanging limply down along the back of his chair, described with both of them a slowly rotating and lifting motion, the palms of his hands turning forward, as if to sketch an opening and outspreading of the arms. It was a gesture that gladly bade welcome, a gesture of calm acceptance.

# 4

Now day after day the god with the burning cheeks soared naked, driving his four fire-breathing steeds through the spaces of heaven, and now, too, his yellow-gold locks fluttered wide in the outstorming east wind. Silk-white radiance gleamed on the slow-swelling deep's vast waters. The sand glowed. Under the silvery quivering blue of the ether, rust-coloured awnings were spread out in front of the beach cabins, and one spent the morning hours on the sharply defined patch of shade they provided. But exquisite, too, was the evening, when the plants in the park gave off a balmy fragrance, and the stars on high moved through their dance, and the softly audible murmur of the night-surrounded sea worked its magic on the soul. Such an evening carried with it the delightful promise of a new sunlit day of leisure easily ordered, and adorned with countless close-knit possibilities of charming chance encounter.

The guest whom so convenient a mishap had detained here was very far from seeing the recovery of his property as a reason for yet another departure. For a couple of days he had had to put up with some privations and appear in the main dining-room in his travelling clothes. Then, when finally the errant load was once more set down in his room, he unpacked completely and filled the cupboards and drawers with his possessions, resolving for the present to set no time-limit on his stay; he was glad now to be able to pass his hours on the beach in a tussore suit and to present himself again in seemly evening attire at the dinner-table.

The lulling rhythm of this existence had already cast its spell on him;

he had been quickly enchanted by the indulgent softness and splendour of this way of life. What a place this was indeed, combining the charms of a cultivated seaside resort in the south with the familiar ever-ready proximity of the strange and wonderful city! Aschenbach did not enjoy enjoying himself. Whenever and wherever he had to stop work, have a breathing-space, take things easily, he would soon find himself driven by restlessness and dissatisfaction – and this had been so in his youth above all – back to his lofty travail, to his stern and sacred daily routine. Only this place bewitched him, relaxed his will, gave him happiness. Often in the forenoon, under the awning of his hut, gazing dreamily at the blue of the southern sea, or on a mild night perhaps, reclining under a star-strewn sky on the cushions of a gondola that carried him back to the Lido from the Piazza where he had long lingered – and as the bright lights, the melting sounds of the serenade dropped away behind him – often he recalled his country house in the mountains, the scene of his summer labours, where the low clouds would drift through his garden, violent evening thunderstorms would put out all the lights, and the ravens he fed would take refuge in the tops of the pine trees. Then indeed he would feel he had been snatched away now to the Elysian land, to the ends of the earth, where lightest of living is granted to mortals, where no snow is nor winter, no storms and no rain down-streaming, but where Oceanus ever causes a gentle cooling breeze to ascend, and the days flow past in blessed idleness, with no labour or strife, for to the sun alone and its feasts they are all given over.

Aschenbach saw much of the boy Tadzio, he saw him almost constantly; in a confined environment, with a common daily pro-gramme, it was natural for the beautiful creature to be near him all day, with only brief interruptions. He saw him and met him everywhere: in the ground-floor rooms of the hotel, on their cooling journeys by water to the city and back, in the sumptuous Piazza itself, and often elsewhere from time to time, in alleys and byways, when chance had played a part. But it was during the mornings on the beach above all, and with the happiest regularity, that he could devote hours at a time to the contemplation and study of this exquisite phenomenon. Indeed, it was precisely this ordered routine of happiness, this equal daily repetition of favourable circumstances, that so filled him with contentment and zest for life, that made this place so precious to him, that allowed one sunlit day to follow another in such obligingly endless succession.

He rose early, as he would normally have done under the insistent compulsion of work, and was down at the beach before most of the other guests, when the sun's heat was still gentle and the sea lay dazzling white in its morning dreams. He greeted the barrier attendant affably, exchanged familiar greetings also with the barefooted, white-bearded old man who had prepared his place for him, spread the brown awning and shifted the cabin furniture out to the platform where Aschenbach would settle down. Three hours or four were then his, hours in which the sun would rise to its zenith and to terrible power, hours in which the sea would turn a deeper and deeper blue, hours in which he might watch Tadzio.

He saw him coming, walking along from the left by the water's edge, saw him from behind as he emerged between the cabins, or indeed would sometimes look up and discover, gladdened and startled, that he had missed his arrival and that the boy was already there, already in the blue and white bathing costume which now on the beach was his sole attire. There he would be, already busy with his customary activities in the sun and the sand – this charmingly trivial, idle yet ever-active life that was both play and repose, a life of sauntering, wading, digging, snatching, lying about and swimming, under the watchful eyes and at the constant call of the women on their platform, who with their high-pitched voices would cry out his name: 'Tadziu! Tadziu!' and to whom he would come running with eager gesticulation, to tell them what he had experienced, to show them what he had found, what he had caught: jellyfish, little sea-horses, and mussels, and crabs that go sideways. Aschenbach understood not a word of what he said, and commonplace though it might be, it was liquid melody in his ears. Thus the foreign sound of the boy's speech exalted it to music, the sun in its triumph shed lavish brightness all over him, and the sublime perspective of the sea was the constant contrasting background against which he appeared.

Soon the contemplative beholder knew every line and pose of that noble, so freely displayed body, he saluted again with joy each already familiar perfection, and there was no end to his wonder, to the delicate delight of his senses. The boy would be summoned to greet a guest who was making a polite call on the ladies in their cabin; he would run up, still wet perhaps from the sea, throw back his curls, and as he held out his hand, poised on one leg with the other on tiptoe, he had an enchanting way of turning and twisting his body, gracefully expectant, charmingly shamefaced, seeking to please because good breeding required him to do so. Or he would be lying full-length, his bathing-robe wrapped round his chest, his finely chiselled arm propped on the sand, his hand cupping his chin; the boy they called·'Jasiu' would squat beside him caressing him, and nothing could be more bewitching than the way the favoured Tadzio, smiling with his eyes and lips, would look up at this lesser and servile mortal. Or he would be standing at the edge of the sea, alone, some way from his family, quite near Aschenbach, standing upright with his hands clasped behind his neck, slowly rocking to and fro on the balls of his feet and dreamily gazing into the blue distance, while little waves ran up and bathed his toes. His honey-coloured hair nestled in ringlets at his temples and at the back of his neck, the sun gleamed in the down on his upper spine, the subtle outlining of his ribs and the symmetry of his breast stood out through the scanty covering of his torso, his armpits were still as smooth as those of a statue, the hollows of his knees glistened and their bluish veins made his body seem composed of some more translucent material. What discipline, what precision of thought was expressed in that outstretched, youthfully perfect physique! And yet the austere pure will that had here been darkly active, that had succeeded in bringing this divine sculptured shape to light – was it not well known and familiar to Aschenbach as an artist? Was it not also active in him, in the sober passion that filled him as he set free from the marble mass of language that slender form he had beheld in the spirit, and which he was presenting to mankind as a mirror and sculptured image of intellectual beauty?

A mirror and sculptured image! His eyes embraced that noble figure at the blue water's edge, and in rising ecstasy he felt he was gazing on Beauty itself, on Form as a thought of God, on the one and pure perfection that dwells in the spirit and of which a human similitude and likeness had here been lightly and graciously set up for him to worship. Such was his emotional intoxication; and the ageing artist welcomed it unhesitatingly, even greedily. His mind was in labour, its store of culture was in ferment, his memory threw up thoughts from ancient tradition which he had been taught as a boy, but which had never yet come alive in his own fire. Had he not read that the sun turns our attention from spiritual things to the things of the senses? He had read that it so numbs and bewitches our intelligence and memory that the soul, in its joy, quite forgets its proper state and clings with astonished admiration to that most beautiful of all the things the sun shines upon: yes, that only with the help of a bodily form is the soul then still able to exalt itself to a higher vision. That Cupid, indeed, does as mathematicians do, when they show dull-witted children tangible images of the pure Forms: so too the Love-god, in order to make spiritual things visible, loves to use the shapes and colours of young men, turning them into instruments of Recollection by adorning them with all the reflected splendour of Beauty, so that the sight of them truly sets us on fire with pain and hope.

Such were the thoughts the god inspired in his enthusiast, such were the emotions of which he grew capable. And a delightful vision came to him, spun from the sea's murmur and the glittering sunlight. It was the old plane tree not far from the walls of Athens – that place of sacred shade, fragrant with chaste-tree blossoms, adorned with votive statues and pious gifts in honour of the nymphs and of Acheloüs. The stream trickled crystal-clear over smooth pebbles at the foot of the great spreading tree; the crickets made their music. But on the grass, which sloped down gently so that one could hold up one's head as one lay, there reclined two men, sheltered here from the heat of the noonday: one elderly and one young, one ugly and one beautiful, the wise beside the desirable. And Socrates, wooing him with witty compliments and jests, was instructing Phaedrus on desire and virtue. He spoke to him of the burning tremor of fear which the lover will suffer when his eye perceives a likeness of eternal Beauty; spoke to him of the lusts of the profane and base who cannot turn their eyes to Beauty when they behold its image and are not capable of reverence; spoke of the sacred terror that visits the noble soul when a god-like countenance, a perfect body appears to him – of how he trembles then and is beside himself and hardly dares look at the possessor of beauty, and reveres him and would even sacrifice to him as to a graven image, if he did not fear to seem foolish in the eyes of men. For Beauty, dear Phaedrus, only Beauty is at one and the same time divinely desirable and visible: it is, mark well, the only form of the spiritual that we can receive with our senses and endure with our senses. For what would become of us if other divine things, if Reason and Virtue and Truth were to appear to us sensuously? Should we not perish in a conflagration of love, as once upon a time Semele did before Zeus? Thus Beauty is the lover's path to the spirit – only the path, only a means, little Phaedrus . . . And then he uttered the subtlest thing of all, that sly wooer: he who loves, he said, is more divine than the beloved, because the god is in the former, but not in the latter – this, the tenderest perhaps and the most mocking thought ever formulated, a thought alive with all the mischievousness and most secret voluptuousness of the heart.

The writer's joy is the thought that can become emotion, the emotion that can wholly become a thought. At that time the solitary Aschenbach took possession and control of just such a pulsating thought, just such a precise emotion: namely, that Nature trembles with rapture when the spirit bows in homage before Beauty. He suddenly desired to write. Eros indeed, we are told, loves idleness and is born only for the idle. But at this point of Aschenbach's crisis and visitation his excitement was driving him to produce. The occasion was almost a matter of indifference. An inquiry, an invitation to express a personal opinion on a certain important cultural problem, a burning question of taste, had been circulated to the intellectual world and had been forwarded to him on his travels. The theme was familiar to him, it was close to his experience; the desire to illuminate it in his own words was suddenly irresistible. And what he craved, indeed, was to work on it in Tadzio's presence, to take the boy's physique for a model as he wrote, to let his style follow the lineaments of this body which he saw as divine, and to carry its beauty on high into the spiritual world, as the eagle once carried the Trojan shepherd boy up into the ether. Never had he felt the joy of the word more sweetly, never had he known so clearly that Eros dwells in language, as during those perilously precious hours in which, seated at his rough table under the awning, in full view of his idol and with the music of his voice in his ears, he shaped upon Tadzio's beauty his brief essay – that page and a half of exquisite prose which with its limpid nobility and vibrant controlled passion was soon to win the admiration of many. It is as well that the world knows only a fine piece of work and not also its origins, the conditions under which it came into being; for knowledge of the sources of an artist's inspiration would often confuse readers and shock them, and the excellence of the writing would be of no avail. How strange those hours were! How strangely exhausting that labour! How mysterious this act of intercourse and begetting between a mind and a body! When Aschenbach put away his work and left the beach, he felt worn out, even broken, and his conscience seemed to be reproaching him as if after some kind of debauch.

On the following morning, just as he was leaving the hotel, he noticed from the steps that Tadzio, already on his way to the sea – and alone – was just approaching the beach barrier. The wish to use this opportunity, the mere thought of doing so, and thereby lightly, light-heartedly, making the acquaintance of one who had unknowingly so exalted and moved him: the thought of speaking to him, of enjoying his answer and his glance – all this seemed natural, it was the irresistibly obvious thing to do. The beautiful boy was walking in a leisurely fashion, he could be overtaken, and Aschenbach quickened his pace. He reached him on the boarded way behind the bathing cabins, he was just about to lay his hand on his head or his shoulder, and some phrase or other, some friendly words in French were on the tip of his tongue – when he felt his heart, perhaps partly because he had been walking fast, hammering wildly inside him, felt so breathless that he would only have been able to speak in a strangled and trembling voice. He hesitated, struggled to control himself, then was suddenly afraid that he had already been walking too long close behind the beautiful boy, afraid that Tadzio would notice this, that he would turn and look at him questioningly; he made one more attempt, failed, gave up, and hurried past with his head bowed.

Too late! he thought at that moment. Too late! But was it too late? This step he had failed to take would very possibly have been all to the good, it might have had a lightening and gladdening effect, led perhaps to a wholesome disenchantment. But the fact now seemed to be that the ageing lover no longer wished to be disenchanted, that the intoxication was too precious to him. Who shall unravel the mystery of an artist's nature and character! Who shall explain the profound instinctual fusion of discipline and licence on which it rests! For not to be able to desire wholesome disenchantment is to be licentious. Aschenbach was no longer disposed to self-criticism; taste, the intellectual mould of his years, self-respect, maturity and late simplicity all disinclined him to analyse his motives and decide whether what had prevented him from carrying out his intention had been a prompting of conscience or a disreputable weakness. He was confused, he was afraid that someone, even if only the bathing attendant, might have witnessed his haste and his defeat; he was very much afraid of exposure to ridicule. For the rest, he could not help inwardly smiling at his comic-sacred terror. 'Crestfallen,' he thought, 'spirits dashed, like a frightened cock hanging its wings in a fight! Truly this is the god who at the sight of the desired beauty so breaks our courage and dashes our pride so utterly to the ground . . .' He toyed with the theme, gave rein to his enthusiasm, plunged into emotions he was too proud to fear.

He was no longer keeping any tally of the leisure time he had allowed himself; the thought of returning home did not even occur to him. He had arranged for ample funds to be made available to him here. His one anxiety was that the Polish family might leave; but he had surreptitiously learned, by a casual question to the hotel barber, that these guests had begun their stay here only very shortly before his own arrival. The sun was browning his face and hands, the stimulating salty breeze heightened his capacity for feeling, and whereas formerly, when sleep or food or contact with nature had given him any refreshment, he would always have expended it completely on his writing, he now, with high-hearted prodigality, allowed all the daily revitalization he was receiving from the sun and leisure and sea air to burn itself up in intoxicating emotion.

He slept fleetingly; the days of precious monotony were punctuated by brief, happily restless nights. To be sure, he would retire early, for at nine o'clock, when Tadzio had disappeared from the scene, he judged his day to be over. But at the first glint of dawn a pang of tenderness would startle him awake, his heart would remember its adventure, he could bear his pillows no longer, he would get up, and lightly wrapped against the early-morning chill he would sit down at the open window to wait for the sunrise. His soul, still fresh with the solemnity of sleep, was filled with awe by this wonderful event. The sky, the earth and the sea still wore the glassy paleness of ghostly twilight; a dying star still floated in the void. But a murmur came, a winged message from dwelling-places no mortal may approach, that Eos was rising from her husband's side; and now it appeared, that first sweet blush at the furthest horizon of the sky and sea, which heralds the sensuous disclosure of creation. The goddess approached, that ravisher of youth, who carried off Cleitus and

Cephalus and defied the envy of all the Olympians to enjoy the love of the beautiful Orion. A scattering of roses began, there at the edge of the world, an ineffably lovely shining and blossoming; childlike clouds, transfigured and transparent with light, hovered like serving *amoretti* in the vermilion and violet haze; crimson light fell across the waves, which seemed to be washing it landwards; golden spears darted from below into the heights of heaven, the gleam became a conflagration, noiselessly and with overwhelming divine power the glow and the fire and the blazing flames reared upwards, and the sacred steeds of the goddess's brother Helios, tucking their hooves, leapt above the earth's round surface. With the splendour of the god irradiating him, the lone watcher sat; he closed his eyes and let the glory kiss his eyelids. Feelings he had had long ago, early and precious dolours of the heart, which had died out in his life's austere service and were now, so strangely transformed, returning to him – he recognized them with a confused and astonished smile. He meditated, he dreamed, slowly a name shaped itself on his lips, and still smiling, with upturned face, his hands folded in his lap, he fell asleep in his chair once more.

With such fiery ceremony the day began, but the rest of it, too, was strangely exalted and mythically transformed. Where did it come from, what was its origin, this sudden breeze that played so gently and speakingly around his temples and ears, like some higher insufflation? Innumerable white fleecy clouds covered the sky, like the grazing flocks of the gods. A stronger wind rose, and the horses of Poseidon reared and ran; his bulls too, the bulls of the blue-haired sea-god, roared and charged with lowered horns. But among the rocks and stones of the more distant beach the waves danced like leaping goats. A sacred deranged world, full of Panic life, enclosed the enchanted watcher, and his heart dreamed tender tales. Sometimes, as the sun was sinking behind Venice, he would sit on a bench in the hotel park to watch Tadzio, dressed in white with a colourful sash, at play on the rolled-gravel tennis court; and in his mind's eye he was watching Hyacinthus, doomed to perish because two gods loved him. He could even feel Zephyr's grievous envy of his rival, who had forgotten his oracle and his bow and his zither to be forever playing with the beautiful youth; he saw the discus, steered by cruel jealousy, strike the lovely head; he himself, turning pale too, caught the broken body in his arms, and the flower that sprang from that sweet blood bore the inscription of his undying lament.

Nothing is stranger, more delicate, than the relationship between people who know each other only by sight – who encounter and observe each other daily, even hourly, and yet are compelled by the constraint of convention or by their own temperament to keep up the pretence of being indifferent strangers, neither greeting nor speaking to each other. Between them is uneasiness and overstimulated curiosity, the nervous excitement of an unsatisfied, unnaturally suppressed need to know and to communicate; and above all, too, a kind of strained respect. For man loves and respects his fellow man for as long as he is not yet in a position to evaluate him, and desire is born of defective knowledge.

It was inevitable that some kind of relationship and acquaintance should develop between Aschenbach and the young Tadzio, and with a surge of joy the older man became aware that his interest and attention were not wholly unreciprocated. Why, for example, when the beautiful creature appeared in the morning on the beach, did he now never use the boarded walk behind the bathing cabins, but always take the front way, through the sand, passing Aschenbach's abode and often passing unnecessarily close to him, almost touching his table or his chair, as he sauntered towards the cabin where his family sat? Was this the attraction, the fascination exercised by a superior feeling on its tender and thoughtless object? Aschenbach waited daily for Tadzio to make his appearance and sometimes pretended to be busy when he did so, letting the boy pass him seemingly unnoticed. But sometimes, too, he would look up, and their eyes would meet. They would both be deeply serious when this happened. In the cultured and dignified countenance of the older man, nothing betrayed an inner emotion; but in Tadzio's eyes there was an inquiry, a thoughtful questioning, his walk became hesitant, he looked at the ground, looked sweetly up again, and when he had passed, something in his bearing seemed to suggest that only good breeding restrained him from turning to look back.

But once, one evening, it was different. The Poles and their governess had been absent from dinner in the main restaurant – Aschenbach had noticed this with concern. After dinner, very uneasy about where they might be, he was walking in evening dress and a straw hat in front of the hotel, at the foot of the terrace, when suddenly he saw the nun-like sisters appearing with their companion, in the light of the arc-lamps, and four paces behind them was Tadzio. Obviously they had come from the *vaporetto* pier, having for some reason dined in the city. The crossing had been chilly perhaps; Tadzio was wearing a dark blue reefer jacket with gold buttons and a naval cap to match. The sun and sea air never burned his skin, it was marble-pale as always; but today he seemed paler than usual, either because of the cool weather or in the blanching moonlight of the lamps. His symmetrical eyebrows stood out more sharply, his eyes seemed much darker. He was more beautiful than words can express, and Aschenbach felt, as so often already, the painful awareness that language can only praise sensuous beauty, but not reproduce it.

He had not been prepared for the beloved encounter, it came unexpectedly, he had not had time to put on an expression of calm and dignity. Joy no doubt, surprise, admiration, were openly displayed on his face when his eyes met those of the returning absentee – and in that instant it happened that Tadzio smiled: smiled at him, speakingly, familiarly, enchantingly and quite unabashed, with his lips parting slowly as the smile was formed. It was the smile of Narcissus as he bows his head over the mirroring water, that profound, fascinated, protracted smile with which he reaches out his arms towards the reflection of his own beauty – a very slightly contorted smile, contorted by the hopelessness of his attempt to kiss the sweet lips of his shadow; a smile that was provocative, curious and imperceptibly troubled, bewitched and bewitching.

He who had received this smile carried it quickly away with him like a fateful gift. He was so deeply shaken that he was forced to flee the lighted terrace and the front garden and hurry into the darkness of the park at the rear. Words struggled from his lips, strangely indignant and tender reproaches: 'You mustn't smile like that! One mustn't, do you hear, mustn't smile like that at anyone!' He sank down on one of the seats, deliriously breathing the nocturnal fragrance of the flowers and trees. And leaning back, his arms hanging down, overwhelmed, trembling, shuddering all over, he whispered the standing formula of the heart's desire – impossible here, absurd, depraved, ludicrous and sacred nevertheless, still worthy of honour even here: 'I love you!'

# 5

During the fourth week of his stay at the Lido Gustav von Aschenbach began to notice certain uncanny developments in the outside world. In the first place it struck him that as the height of the season approached, the number of guests at his hotel was diminishing rather than increasing, and in particular that the German language seemed to be dying away into silence all round him, so that in the end only foreign sounds fell on his ear at table and on the beach. Then one day the hotel barber, whom he visited frequently now, let slip in conversation a remark that aroused his suspicions. The man had mentioned a German family who had just left after only a brief stay, and in his chattering, flattering manner he added: 'But you are staying on, signore; you are not afraid of the sickness.' Aschenbach looked at him. 'The sickness?' he repeated. The fellow stopped his talk, pretended to be busy, had not heard the question. And when it was put to him again more sharply, he declared that he knew nothing and tried with embarrassed loquacity to change the subject.

That was at midday. In the afternoon, with the sea dead calm and the sun burning, Aschenbach crossed to Venice, for he was now driven by a mad compulsion to follow the Polish boy and his sisters, having seen them set off towards the pier with their companion. He did not find his idol at San Marco. But at tea, sitting at his round wrought-iron table on the shady side of the Piazza, he suddenly scented in the air a peculiar aroma, one which it now seemed to him he had been noticing for days without really being conscious of it – a sweetish, medicinal smell that suggested squalor and wounds and suspect cleanliness. He scrutinized it, pondered and identified it, finished his tea and left the Piazza at the far end opposite the basilica. In the narrow streets the smell was stronger. At corners, printed notices had been pasted up in which the civic authorities, with fatherly concern, gave warning to the local population that since certain ailments of the gastric system were normal in this weather, they should refrain from eating oysters and mussels and indeed from using water from the canals. The euphemistic character of the announcement was obvious. Groups of people were standing about silently on bridges or in squares, and the stranger stood among them, brooding and scenting the truth.

He found a shopkeeper leaning against his vaulted doorway, surrounded by coral necklaces and trinkets made of imitation amethyst, and asked him about the unpleasant smell. The man looked him over with heavy eyes, and hastily gathered his wits. 'A precautionary measure, signore,' he answered, gesticulating. 'The police have laid down regulations, and quite right too, it must be said. This weather is oppressive, the sirocco is not very wholesome. In short, the signore will understand – an exaggerated precaution no doubt . . .' Aschenbach thanked him and walked on. Even on the *vaporetto* taking him back to the Lido he now noticed the smell of the bactericide.

Back at the hotel, he went at once to the table in the hall where the newspapers were kept, and carried out some research. In the foreign papers he found nothing. Those in his own language mentioned rumours, quoted contradictory statistics, reported official denials and questioned their veracity. This explained the withdrawal of the German and Austrian clientele. Visitors of other nationalities evidently knew nothing, suspected nothing, still had no apprehensions. 'They want it kept quiet!' thought Aschenbach in some agitation, throwing the newspapers back on the table. 'They're hushing this up!' But at the same time his heart filled with elation at the thought of the adventure in which the outside world was about to be involved. For to passion, as to crime, the assured everyday order and stability of things is not opportune, and any weakening of the civil structure, any chaos and disaster afflicting the world, must be welcome to it, as offering a vague hope of turning such circumstances to its advantage. Thus Aschenbach felt an obscure sense of satisfaction at what was going on in the dirty alleyways of Venice, cloaked in official secrecy – this guilty secret of the city, which merged with his own innermost secret and which it was also so much in his own interests to protect. For in his enamoured state his one anxiety was that Tadzio might leave, and he realized with a kind of horror that he would not be able to go on living if that were to happen.

Lately he had not been content to owe the sight and proximity of the beautiful boy merely⟩ to daily routine and chance: he had begun pursuing him, following him obtrusively. On Sunday, for example, the Poles never appeared on the beach; he rightly guessed that they were attending mass in San Marco, and hastened to the church himself. There, stepping from the fiery heat of the Piazza into the golden twilight of the sanctuary, he would find him whom he had missed, bowed over a prie-dieu and performing his devotions. Then he would stand in the background, on the cracked mosaic floor, amid a throng of people kneeling, murmuring and crossing themselves, and the massive magnificence of the oriental temple would weigh sumptuously on his senses. At the front, the ornately vested priest walked to and fro, doing his business and chanting. Incense billowed up, clouding the feeble flames of the altar candles, and with its heavy, sweet sacrificial odour another seemed to mingle: the smell of the sick city. But through the vaporous dimness and the flickering lights Aschenbach saw the boy, up there at the front, turn his head and seek him with his eyes until he found him.

Then, when the great doors were opened and the crowd streamed out into the shining Piazza swarming with pigeons, the beguiled lover would hide in the antebasilica, he would lurk and lie in wait. He would see the Poles leave the church, see the brother and sisters take ceremonious leave of their mother, who would then set off home, turning towards the Piazzetta; he would observe the boy, the cloistral sisters and the governess turn right and walk through the clock-tower gateway into the Merceria, and after letting them get a little way ahead he would follow them – follow them furtively on their walk through Venice. He had to stop when they lingered, had to take refuge in hot food stalls and courtyards to let them pass when they turned round; he would lose them, search for them frantically and exhaustingly, rushing over bridges and along filthy culs-de-sac, and would then have to endure minutes of mortal embarrassment when he suddenly saw them coming towards him in a narrow passageway where no escape was possible. And yet one cannot say that he suffered. His head and his heart were drunk, and his steps followed the dictates of that dark god whose pleasure it is to trample man's reason and dignity underfoot.

Presently, somewhere or other, Tadzio and his family would take a gondola, and while they were getting into it Aschenbach, hiding behind a fountain or the projecting part of a building, would wait till they were a little way from the shore and then do the same. Speaking hurriedly and in an undertone, he would instruct the oarsman, promising him a large tip, to follow that gondola ahead of them that was just turning the corner, to follow it at a discreet distance; and a shiver would run down his spine when the fellow, with the roguish compliance of a pander, would answer him in the same tone, assuring him that he was at his service, entirely at his service.

Thus he glided and swayed gently along, reclining on soft black cushions, shadowing that other black, beaked craft, chained to its pursuit by his infatuation. Sometimes he would lose sight of it and become distressed and anxious, but his steersman, who seemed to be well practised in commissions of this kind, would always know some cunning manoeuvre, some side-canal or short cut that would again bring Aschenbach in sight of what he craved. The air was stagnant and malodorous, the sun burned oppressively through the haze that had turned the sky to the colour of slate. Water lapped against wood and stone. The gondolier's call, half warning and half greeting, was answered from a distance out of the silent labyrinth, in accordance with some strange convention. Out of little overhead gardens umbelliferous blossoms spilled over and hung down the crumbling masonry, white and purple and almond-scented. Moorish windows were mirrored in the murky water. The marble steps of a church dipped below the surface; a beggar squatted on them, protesting his misery, holding out his hat and showing the whites of his eyes as if he were blind; an antique dealer beckoned to them with crawling obsequiousness as they passed his den, inviting them to stop and be swindled. This was Venice, the flattering and suspect beauty – this city, half fairy-tale and half tourist trap, in whose insalubrious air the arts once rankly and voluptuously blossomed, where composers have been inspired to lulling tones of somniferous eroticism. Gripped by his adventure, the traveller felt his eyes drinking in this sumptuousness, his ears wooed by these melodies; he remembered, too, that the city was stricken with sickness and concealing it for reasons of cupidity, and he peered around still more wildly in search of the gondola that hovered ahead.

So it was that in his state of distraction he could no longer think of anything or want anything except this ceaseless pursuit of the object that so inflamed him: nothing but to follow him, to dream of him when he was not there, and after the fashion of lovers to address tender words to his mere shadow. Solitariness, the foreign environment, and the joy of an intoxication of feeling that had come to him so late and affected him so profoundly – all this encouraged and persuaded him to indulge himself in the most astonishing ways: as when it had happened that late one evening, returning from Venice and reaching the first floor of the hotel, he had paused outside the boy's bedroom door, leaning his head against the door-frame in a complete drunken ecstasy, and had for a long time been unable to move from the spot, at the risk of being surprised and discovered in this insane situation.

Nevertheless, there were moments at which he paused and half came to his senses. Where is this leading me! he would reflect in consternation at such moments. Where was it leading him! Like any man whose natural merits move him to take an aristocratic interest in his origins, Aschenbach habitually let the achievements and successes of his life remind him of his ancestors, for in imagination he could then feel sure of their approval, of their satisfaction, of the respect they could not have withheld. And he thought of them even here and now, entangled as he was in so impermissible an experience, involved in such exotic extravagances of feeling; he thought, with a sad smile, of their dignified austerity, their decent manliness of character. What would they say? But for that matter, what would they have said about his entire life, a life that had deviated from theirs to the point of degeneracy, this life of his in the compulsive service of art, this life about which he himself, adopting the civic values of his forefathers, had once let fall such mocking observations – and which nevertheless had essentially been so much like theirs! He too had served, he too had been a soldier and a warrior, like many of them: for art was a war, an exhausting struggle, it was hard these days to remain fit for it for long. A life of self-conquest and defiant resolve, an astringent, steadfast and frugal life which he had turned into the symbol of that heroism for delicate constitutions, that heroism so much in keeping with the times – surely he might call this manly, might call it courageous? And it seemed to him that the kind of love that had taken possession of him did, in a certain way, suit and befit such a life. Had it not been highly honoured by the most valiant of peoples, indeed had he not read that in their cities it had flourished by inspiring valorous deeds? Numerous warrior-heroes of olden times had willingly borne its yoke, for there was no kind of abasement that could be reckoned as such if the god had imposed it; and actions that would have been castigated as signs of cowardice had their motives been different, such as falling to the ground in supplication, desperate pleas and slavish demeanour – these were accounted no disgrace to a lover, but rather won him still greater praise.

Such were the thoughts with which love beguiled him, and thus he sought to sustain himself, to preserve his dignity. But at the same time he kept turning his attention, inquisitively and persistently, to the disreputable events that were evolving in the depths of Venice, to that adventure of the outside world which darkly mingled with the adventure of his heart, and which nourished his passion with vague and lawless hopes. Obstinately determined to obtain new and reliable information about the status and progress of the malady, he would sit in the city's coffee-houses searching through the German newspapers, which several days ago had disappeared from the reading desk in the hotel foyer. They carried assertions and retractions by turns. The number of cases, the number of deaths, was said to be twenty, or forty, or a hundred and more, such reports being immediately followed by statements flatly denying the outbreak of an epidemic, or at least reducing it to a few quite isolated cases brought in from outside the city. Scattered here and there were warning admonitions, or protests against the dangerous policy being pursued by the Italian authorities. There was no certainty to be had.

The solitary traveller was nevertheless conscious of having a special claim to participation in this secret, and although excluded from it, he took a perverse pleasure in putting embarrassing questions to those in possession of the facts, and thus, since they were pledged to silence, forcing them to lie to him directly. One day, at luncheon in the main dining-room, he interrogated the hotel manager in this fashion, the soft-footed little man in the French frock coat who was moving around among the tables supervising the meal and greeting the clients, and who also stopped at Aschenbach's table for a few words of converstion. Why, in fact, asked his guest in a casual and nonchalant way, why on earth had they begun recently to disinfect Venice? – 'It is merely a police measure, sir,' answered the trickster, 'taken in good time, as a safeguard against various disagreeable public health problems that might otherwise arise from this sultry and exceptionally warm weather – a precautionary measure which it is their duty to take.' – 'Very praiseworthy of the police,' replied Aschenbach; and after exchanging a few meteorological observations with him the manager took his leave.

On the very same day, in the evening after dinner, it happened that a small group of street singers from the city gave a performance in the front garden of the hotel. They stood by one of the iron arc-lamp standards, two men and two women, their faces glinting white in the glare, looking up at the spacious terrace where the hotel guests sat over their coffee and cooling drinks, resigned to watching this exhibition of folk culture. The hotel staff, the lift-boys, waiters, office employees, had come out to listen in the hall doorways. The Russian family, eager to savour every pleasure, had had cane chairs put out for them down in the garden in order to be nearer the performers and were contentedly sitting there in a semicircle. Behind her master and mistress, in a turban-like head-cloth, stood their aged serf.

The beggar virtuosi were playing a mandolin, a guitar, a harmonica and a squeaking fiddle. Instrumental developments alternated with vocal numbers, as when the younger of the women, shrill and squawky of voice, joined the tenor with his sweet falsetto notes in an ardent love duet. But the real talent and leader of the ensemble was quite evidently the other man, the one who had the guitar and was a kind of buffo-baritone in character, with hardly any voice but with a mimic gift and remarkable comic verve. Often he would detach himself from the rest of the group and come forward, playing his large instrument and gesticulating, towards the terrace, where his pranks were rewarded with encouraging laughter. The Russians in their parterre seats took special delight in all this southern vivacity, and their plaudits and admiring shouts led him on to ever further and bolder extravagances.

Aschenbach sat by the balustrade, cooling his lips from time to time with the mixture of pomegranate juice and soda water that sparkled ruby-red in the glass before him. His nervous system greedily drank in the jangling tones, for passion paralyses discrimination and responds in all seriousness to stimuli which the sober senses would either treat with humorous tolerance or impatiently reject. The antics of the mountebank had distorted his features into a rictus-like smile which he was already finding painful. He sat on with a casual air, but inwardly he was utterly engrossed; for six paces from him Tadzio was leaning against the stone parapet.

There he stood, in the white, belted suit he occasionally put on for dinner, in a posture of innate and inevitable grace, his left forearm on the parapet, his feet crossed, his right hand on the supporting hip: and he looked down at the entertainers with an expression that was scarcely a smile, merely one of remote curiosity, a polite observation of the spectacle. Sometimes he straightened himself, stretching his chest, and with an elegant movement of both arms drew his white tunic down through his leather belt. But sometimes, too, and the older man noticed it with a mind-dizzying sense of triumph as well as with terror, he would turn his head hesitantly and cautiously, or even quickly and suddenly as if to gain the advantage of surprise, and look over his left shoulder to where his lover was sitting. Their eyes did not meet, for an ignominious apprehension was forcing the stricken man to keep his looks anxiously in check. Behind them on the terrace sat the women who watched over Tadzio, and at the point things had now reached, the enamoured Aschenbach had reason to fear that he had attracted attention and aroused suspicion. Indeed, he had several times, on the beach, in the hotel foyer and on the Piazza San Marco, been frozen with alarm to notice that Tadzio was being called away if he was near him, that they were taking care to keep them apart – and although his pride writhed in torments it had never known under the appalling insult that this implied, he could not in conscience deny its justice.

In the mean time the guitarist had begun a solo to his own accompaniment, a song in many stanzas which was then a popular hit all over Italy, and which he managed to perform in a graphic and dramatic manner, with the rest of his troupe joining regularly in the refrain. He was a lean fellow, thin and cadaverous in the face as well, standing there on the gravel detached from his companions, with a shabby felt hat on the back of his head and a quiff of his red hair bulging out under the brim, in a posture of insolent bravado; strumming and thrumming on his instrument, he tossed his pleasantries up to the terrace in a vivid *parlando*, enacting it all so strenuously that the veins swelled on his forehead. He was quite evidently not of Venetian origin, but rather of the Neapolitan comic type, half pimp, half actor, brutal and bold-faced, dangerous and entertaining. The actual words of his song were merely foolish, but in his presentation, with his grimaces and bodily movements, his way of winking suggestively and lasciviously licking the corner of his mouth, it had something indecent and vaguely offensive about it. Though otherwise dressed in urban fashion he wore a sports shirt, out of the soft collar of which his skinny neck projected, displaying a remarkably large and naked Adam's apple. His pallid snub-nosed face, the features of which gave little clue to his age, seemed to be lined with contortions and vice, and the grinning of his mobile mouth was rather strangely ill-matched to the two deep furrows that stood defiantly, imperiously, almost savagely, between his reddish brows. But what really fixed the solitary Aschenbach's deep attention on him was his observation that this suspect figure seemed to be carrying his own suspect atmosphere about with him as well. For every time the refrain was repeated the singer would perform, with much grimacing and wagging of his hand as if in greeting, a grotesque march round the scene, which brought him immediately below where Aschenbach sat; and every time this happened a stench of carbolic from his clothes or his body drifted up to the terrace.

Having completed his ballad he began to collect money. He started with the Russians, who were seen to give generously, and then came up the steps. Saucy as his performance had been, up here he was humility itself. Bowing and scraping, he crept from table to table, and a sly obsequious grin bared his prominent teeth, although the two furrows still stood threateningly between his red eyebrows. The spectacle of this alien being gathering in his livelihood was viewed with curiosity and not a little distaste; one threw coins with the tips of one's fingers into the hat, which one took care not to touch. Removal of the physical distance between the entertainer and decent folk always causes, however great one's pleasure has been, a certain embarrassment. He sensed this, and sought to make amends by cringing. He approached Aschenbach, and with him came the smell, which no one else in the company appeared to have noticed.

'Listen to me!' said the solitary traveller in an undertone and almost mechanically. 'Venice is being disinfected. Why?' – The comedian answered hoarsely: 'Because of the police! It's the regulations, signore, when it's so hot and when there's sirocco. The sirocco is oppressive. It's not good for the health . . .' He spoke in a tone of surprise that such a question could be asked, and demonstrated with his outspread hand how oppressive the sirocco was. – 'So there is no sickness in Venice?' asked Aschenbach very softly and between his teeth. – The clown's muscular features collapsed into a grimace of comic helplessness. 'A sickness? But what sickness? Is the sirocco a sickness? Is our police a sickness perhaps? The signore is having his little joke! A sickness! Certainly not, signore! A preventive measure, you must understand, a police precaution against the effects of the oppressive weather . . .' He gesticulated. 'Very well,' said Aschenbach briefly, still without raising his voice, and quickly dropped an unduly large coin into the fellow's hat. Then he motioned him with his eyes to clear off. The man obeyed, grinning and bowing low. But he had not even reached the steps when two hotel servants bore down on him, and with their faces close to his subjected him to a whispered cross-examination. He shrugged, gave assurances, swore that he had been discreet; it was obvious. Released, he returned to the garden, and after a brief consultation with his colleagues under the arc-lamp he came forward once more, to express his thanks in a parting number.

It was a song that Aschenbach could not remember ever having heard before; a bold hit in an unintelligible dialect, and having a laughing refrain in which the rest of the band regularly and loudly joined. At this point both the words and the instrumental accompaniment stopped, and nothing remained except a burst of laughter, to some extent rhythmically ordered but treated with a high degree of naturalism, the soloist in particular showing great talent in his life-like rendering of it. With artistic distance restored between himself and the spectators, he had recovered all his impudence, and the simulated laughter which he shamelessly directed at the terrace was a laughter of mockery. Even before the end of the articulated part of each stanza he would pretend to be struggling with an irresistible impulse of hilarity. He would sob, his voice would waver, he would press his hand against his mouth and hunch his shoulders, till at the proper moment the laughter would burst out of him, exploding in a wild howl, with such authenticity that it was infectious and communicated itself to the audience, so that a wave of objectless and merely self-propagating merriment swept over the terrace as well. And precisely this seemed to redouble the singer's exuberance. He bent his knees, slapped his thighs, held his sides, he nearly burst with what was now no longer laughing but shrieking; he pointed his finger up at the guests, as if that laughing company above him were itself the most comical thing in the world, and in the end they were all laughing, everyone in the garden and on the verandah, the waiters and the lift-boys and the house servants in the doorways.

Aschenbach reclined in his chair no longer, he was sitting bolt upright as if trying to fend off an attack or flee from it. But the laughter, the hospital smell drifting towards him, and the nearness of the beautiful boy, all mingled for him into an immobilizing nightmare, an unbreakable and inescapable spell that held his mind and senses captive. In the general commotion and distraction he ventured to steal a glance at Tadzio, and as he did so he became aware that the boy, returning his glance, had remained no less serious than himself, just as if he were regulating his attitude and expression by those of the older man, and as if the general mood had no power over him while Aschenbach kept aloof from it. There was something so disarming and overwhelmingly moving about this childlike submissiveness, so rich in meaning, that the grey-haired lover could only with difficulty restrain himself from burying his face in his hands. He had also had the impression that the way Tadzio from time to time drew himself up with an intake of breath was like a kind of sighing, as if from a constriction of the chest. 'He's sickly, he'll probably not live long,' he thought again, with that sober objectivity into which the drunken ecstasy of desire sometimes strangely escapes; and his heart was filled at one and the same time with pure concern on the boy's behalf and with a certain wild satisfaction.

In the mean time the troupe of Venetians had finished their performance and were leaving. Applause accompanied them, and their leader took care to embellish even his exit with comical pranks. His bowing and scraping and hand-kissing amused the company, and so he redoubled them. When his companions were already outside, he put on yet another act of running backwards and painfully colliding with a lamp-post, then hobbling to the gate apparently doubled up in agony. When he got there, however, he suddenly discarded the mask of comic underdog, uncoiled like a spring to his full height, insolently stuck out his tongue at the hotel guests on the terrace and slipped away into the darkness. The company was dispersing; Tadzio had left the balustrade some time ago. But the solitary Aschenbach, to the annoyance of the waiters, sat on and on at his little table over his unfinished pomegranate drink. The night was advancing, time was ebbing away. In his parents' house, many years ago, there had been an hourglass – he suddenly saw that fragile symbolic little instrument as clearly as if it were standing before him. Silently, subtly, the rust-red sand trickled through the narrow glass aperture, dwindling away out of the upper vessel, in which a little whirling vortex had formed.

On the very next day, in the afternoon, Aschenbach took a further step in his persistent probing of the outside world, and this time his success was complete. What he did was to enter the British travel agency just off the Piazza San Marco, and after changing some money at the cash desk, he put on the look of a suspicious foreigner and addressed his embarrassing question to the clerk who had served him. The clerk was a tweed-clad Englishman, still young, with his hair parted in the middle, his eyes close-set, and having that sober, honest demeanour which makes so unusual and striking an impression amid the glib knaveries of the south. 'No cause for concern, sir,' he began. 'An administrative measure, nothing serious. They often issue directives of this kind, as a precaution against the unhealthy effects of the heat and the sirocco . . .' But raising his blue eyes he met those of the stranger, which were looking wearily and rather sadly at his lips, with an expression of slight contempt. At this the Englishman coloured. 'That is,' he continued in an undertone and with some feeling, 'the official explanation, which the authorities here see fit to stick to. I can tell you that there is rather more to it than that.' And then, in his straightforward comfortable language, he told Aschenbach the truth.

For several years now, Asiatic cholera had been showing an increased tendency to spread and migrate. Originating in the sultry morasses of the Ganges delta, rising with the mephitic exhalations of that wilderness of rank useless luxuriance, that primitive island jungle shunned by man, where tigers crouch in the bamboo thickets, the pestilence had raged with unusual and prolonged virulence all over northern India; it had struck eastward into China, westward into Afghanistan and Persia, and following the main caravan routes it had borne its terrors to Astrakhan and even to Moscow. But while Europe trembled with apprehension that from there the spectre might advance and arrive by land, it had been brought by Syrian traders over the sea; it had appeared almost simultaneously in several Mediterranean ports, raising its head in Toulon and Malaga, showing its face repeatedly in Palermo and Naples, and taking a seemingly permanent hold all over Calabria and Apulia. The northern half of the peninsula had still been spared. But in the middle of May this year, in Venice, the dreadful comma bacilli had been found on one and the same day in the emaciated and blackened corpses of a ship's hand and of a woman who sold greengroceries. The two cases were hushed up. But a week later there were ten, there were twenty and then thirty, and they occurred in different quarters of the city. A man from a small provincial town in Austria who had been taking a few days' holiday in Venice died with unmistakable symptoms after returning home, and that was why the first rumours of a Venetian outbreak had appeared in German newspapers. The city authorities replied with a statement that the public health situation in Venice had never been better, and at the same time adopted the most necessary preventive measures. But the taint had probably now passed into foodstuffs, into vegetables or meat or milk; for despite every denial and concealment, the mortal sickness went on eating its way through the narrow little streets, and with the premature summer heat warming the water in the canals, conditions for the spread of infection were particularly favourable. It even seemed as if the pestilence had undergone a renewal of its energy, as if the tenacity and fertility of its pathogens had redoubled. Cases of recovery were rare; eighty per cent of the victims died, and they died in a horrible manner, for the sickness presented itself in an extremely acute form and was frequently of the so-called 'dry' type, which is the most dangerous of all. In this condition the body could not even evacuate the massive fluid lost from the blood-vessels. Within a few hours the patient would become dehydrated, his blood would thicken like pitch and he would suffocate with convulsions and hoarse cries. He was lucky if, as sometimes happened, the disease took the form of a slight malaise followed by a deep coma from which one never, or scarcely at all, regained consciousness. By the beginning of June the isolation wards in the Ospedale Civile were quietly filling, the two orphanages were running out of accommodation, and there was a gruesomely brisk traffic between the quayside of the Fondamente Nuove and the cemetery island of San Michele. But fear of general detriment to the city, concern for the recently opened art exhibition in the Public Gardens, consideration of the appalling losses which panic and disrepute would inflict on the hotels, on the shops, on the whole nexus of the tourist trade, proved stronger in Venice than respect for the truth and for international agreements; it was for this reason that the city authorities obstinately adhered to their policy of concealment and denial. The city's chief medical officer, a man of high repute, had resigned from his post in indignation and had been quietly replaced by a more pliable personality. This had become public knowledge; and such corruption in high places, combined with the prevailing insecurity, the state of crisis into which the city had been plunged by the death that walked its streets, led at the lower social levels to a certain breakdown of moral standards, to an activation of the dark and antisocial forces, which manifested itself in intemperance, shameless licence and growing criminality. Drunkenness in the evenings became noticeably more frequent; thieves and ruffians, it was said, were making the streets unsafe at night; there were repeated robberies and even murders, for it had already twice come to light that persons alleged to have died of the plague had in fact been poisoned by their own relatives; and commercial vice was now taking obtrusive and extravagant forms hitherto unknown in this area and indigenous only to southern Italy or oriental countries.

The Englishman's narrative conveyed the substance of all this to Aschenbach. 'You would be well advised, sir,' he concluded, 'to leave today rather than tomorrow. The imposition of quarantine can be expected any day now.' – 'Thank you,' said Aschenbach, and left the office.

The Piazza was sunless and sultry. Unsuspecting foreigners were sitting at the cafés, or standing in front of the church with pigeons completely enveloping them, watching the birds swarm and beat their wings and push each other out of the way as they snatched with their beaks at the hollow hands offering them grains of maize. Feverish with excitement, triumphant in his possession of the truth, yet with a taste of disgust on his tongue and a fantastic horror in his heart, the solitary traveller paced up and down the flagstones of the magnificent precinct. He was considering a decent action which would cleanse his conscience. Tonight, after dinner, he might approach the lady in the pearls and address her with words which he now mentally rehearsed: 'Madam, allow me as a complete stranger to do you a service, to warn you of something which is being concealed from you for reasons of self-interest. Leave here at once with Tadzio and your daughters! Cholera has broken out in Venice.' He might then lay his hand in farewell on the head of a mocking deity's instrument, turn away and flee from this quagmire. But at the same time he sensed an infinite distance between himself and any serious resolve to take such a step. It would lead him back to where he had been, give him back to himself again; but to one who is beside himself, no prospect is so distasteful as that of self-recovery. He remembered a white building adorned with inscriptions that glinted in the evening light, suffused with mystic meaning in which his mind had wandered; remembered then that strange itinerant figure who had wakened in him, in his middle age, a young man's longing to rove to far-off and strange places; and the thought of returning home, of level-headedness and sobriety, of toil and mastery, filled him with such repugnance that his face twisted into an expression of physical nausea. 'They want it kept quiet!' he whispered vehemently. And: 'I shall say nothing!' The consciousness of his complicity in the secret, of his share in the guilt, intoxicated him as small quantities of wine intoxicate a weary brain. The image of the stricken and disordered city, hovering wildly before his mind's eye, inflamed him with hopes that were beyond comprehension, beyond reason and full of monstrous sweetness. What, compared with such expectations, was that tender happiness of which he had briefly dreamed a few moments ago? What could art and virtue mean to him now, when he might reap the advantages of chaos? He said nothing, and stayed on.

That night he had a terrible dream, if dream is the right word for a bodily and mental experience which did indeed overtake him during deepest sleep, in complete independence of his will and with complete sensuous vividness, but with no perception of himself as present and moving about in any space external to the events themselves; rather, the scene of the events was his own soul, and they irrupted into it from outside, violently defeating his resistance – a profound, intellectual resistance – as they passed through him, and leaving his whole being, the culture of a lifetime, devastated and destroyed.

It began with fear, fear and joy and a horrified curiosity about what was to come. It was night, and his senses were alert; for from far off a hubbub was approaching, an uproar, a compendium of noise, a clangour and blare and dull thundering, yells of exultation and a particular howl with a long-drawn-out *u* at the end – all of it permeated and dominated by a terrible sweet sound of flute music: by deep-warbling, infamously persistent, shamelessly clinging tones that bewitched the innermost heart. Yet he was aware of a word, an obscure word, but one that gave a name to what was coming: '*the stranger-god!*' There was a glow of smoky fire: in it he could see a mountain landscape, like the mountains round his summer home. And in fragmented light from wooded heights, between tree trunks and mossy boulders, it came tumbling and whirling down: a human and animal swarm, a raging rout, flooding the slope with bodies, with flames, with tumult and frenzied dancing. Women, stumbling on the hide garments that fell too far about them from the waist, held up tambourines and moaned as they shook them above their thrown-back heads; they swung blazing torches, scattering the sparks, and brandished naked daggers; they carried snakes with flickering tongues which they had seized in the middle of the body, or they bore up their own breasts in both hands, shrieking as they did so. Men with horns over their brows, hairy-skinned and girdled with pelts, bowed their necks and threw up their arms and thighs, clanging brazen cymbals and beating a furious tattoo on drums, while smooth-skinned boys prodded goats with leafy staves, clinging to their horns and yelling with delight as the leaping beasts dragged them along. And the god's enthusiasts howled out the cry with the soft consonants and long-drawn-out final *u*, sweet and wild both at once, like no cry that was ever heard: here it was raised, belled out into the air as by rutting stags, and there they threw it back with many voices, in ribald triumph, urging each other on with it to dancing and tossing of limbs, and never did it cease. But the deep, enticing flute music mingled irresistibly with everything. Was it not also enticing him, the dreamer who experienced all this while struggling not to, enticing him with shameless insistence to the feast and frenzy of the uttermost surrender? Great was his loathing, great his fear, honourable his effort of will to defend to the last what was his and protect it against the Stranger, against the enemy of the composed and dignified intellect. But the noise, the howling grew louder, with the echoing cliffs reiterating it: it increased beyond measure, swelled up to an enrapturing madness. Odours besieged the mind, the pungent reek of the goats, the scent of panting bodies and an exhalation as of staling waters, with another smell, too, that was familiar: that of wounds and wandering disease. His heart throbbed to the drumbeats, his brain whirled, a fury seized him, a blindness, a dizzying lust, and his soul craved to join the round-dance of the god. The obscene symbol, wooden and gigantic, was uncovered and raised aloft: and still more unbridled grew the howling of the rallying-cry. With foaming mouths they raged, they roused each other with lewd gestures and licentious hands, laughing and moaning they thrust the prods into each other's flesh and licked the blood from each other's limbs. But the dreamer now was with them and in them, he belonged to the stranger-god. Yes, they were himself as they flung themselves, tearing and slaying, on the animals and devoured steaming gobbets of flesh, they were himself as an orgy of limitless coupling, in homage to the god, began on the trampled, mossy ground. And his very soul savoured the lascivious delirium of annihilation.

Out of this dream the stricken man woke unnerved, shattered and powerlessly enslaved to the daemon-god. He no longer feared the observant eyes of other people; whether he was exposing himself to their suspicions he no longer cared. In any case they were running away, leaving Venice; many of the bathing cabins were empty now, there were great gaps in the clientele at dinner, and in the city one scarcely saw any foreigners. The truth seemed to have leaked out, and however tightly the interested parties closed ranks, panic could no longer be stemmed. But the lady in the pearls stayed on with her family, either because the rumours were not reaching her or because she was too proud and fearless to heed them. Tadzio stayed on; and to Aschenbach, in his beleaguered state, it sometimes seemed that all these unwanted people all round him might flee from the place or die, that every living being might disappear and leave him alone on this island with the beautiful boy – indeed, as he sat every morning by the sea with his gaze resting heavily, recklessly, incessantly on the object of his desire, or as he continued his undignified pursuit of him in the evenings along streets in which the disgusting mortal malady wound its underground way, then indeed monstrous things seemed full of promise to him, and the moral law no longer valid.

Like any other lover, he desired to please and bitterly dreaded that he might fail to do so. He added brightening and rejuvenating touches to his clothes, he wore jewellery and used scent, he devoted long sessions to his toilet several times a day, arriving at table elaborately attired and full of excited expectation. As he beheld the sweet youthful creature who had so entranced him he felt disgust at his own ageing body, the sight of his grey hair and sharp features filled him with a sense of shame and hopelessness. He felt a compulsive need to refresh and restore himself physically; he paid frequent visits to the hotel barber.

Cloaked in a hairdressing gown, leaning back in the chair as the chatterer's hands tended him, he stared in dismay at his reflection in the looking-glass.

'Grey,' he remarked with a wry grimace.

'A little,' the man replied. 'And the reason? A slight neglect, a slight lack of interest in outward appearances, very understandable in persons of distinction, but not altogether to be commended, especially as one would expect those very persons to be free from prejudice about such matters as the natural and the artificial. If certain people who profess moral disapproval of cosmetics were to be logical enough to extend such rigorous principles to their teeth, the result would be rather disgusting. After all, we are only as old as we feel in our minds and hearts, and sometimes grey hair is actually further from the truth than the despised corrective would be. In your case, signore, one has a right to the natural colour of one's hair. Will you permit me simply to give your colour back to you?'

'How so?' asked Aschenbach.

Whereupon the eloquent tempter washed his client's hair in two kinds of water, one clear and one dark; and his hair was as black as when he had been young. Then he folded it into soft waves with the curling-tongs, stepped back and surveyed his handiwork.

'Now the only other thing,' he said, 'would be just to freshen up the signore's complexion a little.'

And like a craftsman unable to finish, unable to satisfy himself, he passed busily and indefatigably from one procedure to another. Aschenbach, reclining comfortably, incapable of resistance, filled rather with exciting hopes by what was happening, gazed at the glass and saw his eyebrows arched more clearly and evenly, the shape of his eyes lengthened, their brightness enhanced by a slight underlining of the lids; saw below them a delicate carmine come to life as it was softly applied to skin that had been brown and leathery; saw his lips that had just been so pallid now burgeoning cherry-red; saw the furrows on his cheeks, round his mouth, the wrinkles by his eyes, all vanishing under face cream and an aura of youth – with beating heart he saw himself as a young man in earliest bloom. The cosmetician finally declared himself satisfied, with the grovelling politeness usual in such people, by profusely thanking the client he had served. 'An insignificant adjustment, signore,' he said as he gave a final helping hand to Aschenbach's outward appearance. 'Now the signore can fall in love as soon as he pleases.' And the spellbound lover departed, confused and timorous but happy as in a dream. His necktie was scarlet, his broad-brimmed straw hat encircled with a many-coloured ribbon.

A warm gale had blown up; it rained little and lightly, but the air was humid and thick and filled with smells of decay. The ear was beset with fluttering, flapping and whistling noises, and to the fevered devotee, sweating under his make-up, it seemed that a vile race of wind-demons was disporting itself in the sky, malignant sea-birds that churn up and gnaw and befoul a condemned man's food. For the sultry weather was taking away his appetite, and he could not put aside the thought that what he ate might be tainted with infection.

One afternoon, dogging Tadzio's footsteps, Aschenbach had plunged into the confused network of streets in the depths of the sick city. Quite losing his bearings in this labyrinth of alleys, narrow waterways, bridges and little squares that all looked so much like each other, not sure now even of the points of the compass, he was intent above all on not losing sight of the vision he so passionately pursued. Ignominious caution forced him to flatten himself against walls and hide behind the backs of people walking in front of him; and for a long time he was not conscious of the weariness, the exhaustion that emotion and constant tension had inflicted on his body and mind. Tadzio walked behind his family; he usually gave precedence in narrow passages to his attendant and his nun-like sisters, and as he strolled along by himself he sometimes turned his head and glanced over his shoulder with his strange twilight-grey eyes, to ascertain that his lover was still following him. He saw him, and did not give him away. Drunk with excitement as he realized this, lured onward by those eyes, helpless in the leading strings of his mad desire, the infatuated Aschenbach stole upon the trail of his unseemly hope – only to find it vanish from his sight in the end. The Poles had crossed a little humpback bridge; the height of the arch hid them from their pursuer, and when in his turn he reached the top of it, they were no longer to be seen. He looked frantically for them in three directions, straight ahead and to left and right along the narrow, dirty canalside, but in vain. Unnerved and weakened, he was compelled to abandon his search.

His head was burning, his body was covered with sticky sweat, his neck quivered, a no longer endurable thirst tormented him; he looked round for something, no matter what, that would instantly relieve it. At a little greengrocer's shop he bought some fruit, some overripe soft strawberries, and ate some of them as he walked. A little square, one that seemed to have been abandoned, to have been put under a spell, opened up in front of him: he recognized it, he had been here, it was where he had made that vain decision weeks ago to leave Venice. On the steps of the well in its centre he sank down and leaned his head against the stone rim. The place was silent, grass grew between the cobblestones, garbage was lying about. Among the dilapidated houses of uneven height all round him was one that looked like a *palazzo*, with Gothic windows that now had nothing behind them, and little lion balconies. On the ground floor of another was a chemist's shop. From time to time warm gusts of wind blew the stench of carbolic across to him.

There he sat, the master, the artist who had achieved dignity, the author of A *Study in Abjection*, he who in such paradigmatically pure form had repudiated intellectual vagrancy and the murky depths, who had proclaimed his renunciation of all sympathy with the abyss, who had weighed vileness in the balance and found it wanting; he who had risen so high, who had set his face against his own sophistication, grown out of all his irony, and taken on the commitments of one whom the public trusted; he, whose fame was official, whose name had been ennobled, and on whose style young boys were taught to model their own – there he sat, with his eyelids closed, with only an occasional mocking and rueful sideways glance from under them which he hid again at once; and his drooping, cosmetically brightened lips shaped an occasional word of the discourse his brain was delivering, his half-asleep brain with its tissue of strange dream-logic.

'For Beauty, Phaedrus, mark well! only Beauty is at one and the same time divine and visible, and so it is indeed the sensuous lover's path, little Phaedrus, it is the artist's path to the spirit. But do you believe, dear boy, that the man whose path to the spiritual passes through the senses can ever achieve wisdom and true manly dignity? Or do you think rather (I leave it to you to decide) that this is a path of dangerous charm, very much an errant and sinful path which must of necessity lead us astray? For I must tell you that we artists cannot tread the path of Beauty without

Eros keeping company with us and appointing himself as our guide; yes, though we may be heroes in our fashion and disciplined warriors, yet we are like women, for it is passion that exalts us, and the longing of our soul must remain the longing of a lover – that is our joy and our shame. Do you see now perhaps why we writers can be neither wise nor dignified? That we necessarily go astray, necessarily remain dissolute emotional adventurers? The magisterial poise of our style is a lie and a farce, our fame and social position are an absurdity, the public's faith in us is altogether ridiculous, the use of art to educate the nation and its youth is a reprehensible undertaking which should be forbidden by law. For how can one be fit to be an educator when one has been born with an incorrigible and natural tendency towards the abyss? We try to achieve dignity by repudiating that abyss, but whichever way we turn we are subject to its allurement. We renounce, let us say, the corrosive process of knowledge – for knowledge, Phaedrus, has neither dignity nor rigour: it is all insight and understanding and tolerance, uncontrolled and formless; it sympathizes with the abyss, it *is* the abyss. And so we reject it resolutely, and henceforth our pursuit is of Beauty alone, of Beauty which is simplicity, which is grandeur and a new kind of rigour and a second naïvety, of Beauty which is Form. But form and naïvety, Phaedrus, lead to intoxication and lust; they may lead a noble mind into terrible criminal emotions, which his own fine rigour condemns as infamous; they lead, they too lead, to the abyss. I tell you, that is where they lead us writers; for we are not capable of self-exaltation, we are merely capable of self-debauchery. And now I shall go, Phaedrus, and you shall stay here; and leave this place only when you no longer see me.'

A few days later Gustav von Aschenbach, who had been feeling unwell, left the Hotel des Bains at a later morning hour than usual. He was being attacked by waves of dizziness, only half physical, and with them went an increasing sense of dread, a feeling of hopelessness and pointlessness, though he could not decide whether this referred to the external world or to his personal existence. In the foyer he saw a large quantity of luggage standing ready for dispatch, asked one of the doormen which guests were leaving, and was given in reply the aristocratic Polish name which he had inwardly been expecting to hear. As he received the information there was no change in his ravaged features, only that slight lift of the head with which one casually notes something one did not need to know. He merely added the question: 'When?' and was told: 'After lunch.' He nodded and went down to the sea.

It was a bleak spectacle there. Tremors gusted outwards across the water between the beach and the first long sand-bar, wrinkling its wide flat surface. An autumnal, out-of-season air seemed to hang over the once so colourful and populous resort, now almost deserted, with litter left lying about on the sand. An apparently abandoned camera stood on its tripod at the edge of the sea, and the black cloth over it fluttered and flapped in the freshening breeze.

Tadzio, with the three or four playmates he still had, was walking about on the right in front of his family's bathing cabin; and reclining in his deck-chair with a rug over his knees, about midway between the sea and the row of cabins, Aschenbach once more sat watching him. The boys' play was unsupervised, as the women were probably busy with travel preparations; it seemed to be unruly and degenerating into roughness. The sturdy boy he had noticed before, the one in the belted suit and with glossy black hair whom they called 'Jasiu', had been angered and blinded by some sand thrown into his face: he forced Tadzio to a wrestling match, which soon ended in the downfall of the less muscular beauty. But as if in this hour of leave-taking the submissiveness of the lesser partner had been transformed into cruel brutality, as if he were now bent on revenge for his long servitude, the victor did not release his defeated friend even then, but knelt on his back and pressed his face into the sand so hard and so long that Tadzio, breathless from the fight in any case, seemed to be on the point of suffocation. His attempts to shake off the weight of his tormentor were convulsive; they stopped altogether for moments on end and became a mere repeated twitching. Appalled, Aschenbach was about to spring to the rescue when the bully finally released his victim. Tadzio, very pale, sat up and went on sitting motionless for some minutes, propped on one arm, his hair tousled and his eyes darkening. Then he stood right up and walked slowly away. His friends called to him, laughingly at first, then anxiously and pleadingly; he took no notice. The dark-haired boy, who had no doubt been seized at once by remorse at having gone so far, ran after him and tried to make up the quarrel. A jerk of Tadzio's shoulder rejected him. Tadzio walked on at an angle down to the water. He was barefooted and wearing his striped linen costume with the red bow.

At the edge of the sea he lingered, head bowed, drawing figures in the wet sand with the point of one foot, then walked into the shallow high water, which at its deepest point did not even wet his knees; he waded through it, advancing easily, and reached the sand-bar. There he stood for a moment looking out into the distance and then, moving left, began slowly to pace the length of this narrow strip of unsubmerged land. Divided from the shore by a width of water, divided from his companions by proud caprice, he walked, a quite isolated and unrelated apparition, walked with floating hair out there in the sea, in the wind, in front of the nebulous vastness. Once more he stopped to survey the scene. And suddenly, as if prompted by a memory, by an impulse, he turned at the waist, one hand on his hip, with an enchanting twist of the body, and looked back over his shoulder at the beach. There the watcher sat, as he had sat once before when those twilight-grey eyes, looking back at him then from that other threshold, had for the first time met his. Resting his head on the back of his chair, he had slowly turned it to follow the movements of the walking figure in the distance; now he lifted it towards this last look, then it sank down on his breast, so that his eyes stared up from below, while his face wore the inert, deep-sunken expression of profound slumber. But to him it was as if the pale and lovely soul-summoner out there were smiling to him, beckoning to him; as if he loosed his hand from his hip and pointed outwards, hovering ahead and onwards, into an immensity rich with unutterable expectation. And as so often, he set out to follow him.

Minutes passed, after he had collapsed sideways in his chair, before anyone hurried to his assistance. He was carried to his room. And later that same day the world was respectfully shocked to receive the news of his death.